Barnabas Tew and The Case of The Missing Scarab

Columbkill Noonan

CROOKED
CAT

Discover us online:
www.crookedcatbooks.com

Join us on facebook:
www.facebook.com/crookedcat

Tweet a photo of yourself holding
this book to **@crookedcatbooks**
and something nice will happen.

To Marc, mijn liefde,
who brings me
coffee every morning.

Acknowledgements

I'd like to thank my incredibly talented editor Maureen Vincent-Northam, who made the editing process not only easy but also quite fun as well. I'd also like to thank Laurence and Stephanie Patterson, who took a chance on my crazy story and helped me make it something amazing. And special thanks to Nicky Leavy, who believed in Barnabas even before anyone else ever met him.

About the Author

Columbkill Noonan has an M.S. in Biology (she has, in turn, been a field biologist, an environmental compliance inspector, and a lecturer of Anatomy and Physiology).

When she's not teaching or writing, she can usually be found riding her rescue horse, Mittens, practicing yoga (on the ground, in an aerial silk, on a SUP board, and sometimes even on Mittens), or spending far too much time at the local organic, vegan market.

To keep up with Columbkill, visit her blog at **www.Columbkill.weebly.com**, find her on Facebook at **www.facebook.com/ColumbkillNoonan**, or follow her on Twitter **@ColumbkillNoon1**.

Barnabas Tew and The Case of The Missing Scarab

Chapter One

Barnabas Tew sat bolt upright in the chair at his desk, nervously fidgeting with the accoutrements thereon. He made as if to stand up, but then changed his mind and sat hastily back down. He repeated this process a few times, until at last he settled on a posture somewhere in between the extremes of being either entirely up or entirely down. He blinked rapidly as he pondered the dilemma that now confronted him: should he or should he not answer the doorbell?

A ringing doorbell was not a common occurrence at the slightly shabby flat on the not-quite fashionable northeastern edge of Marylebone that served not only as Barnabas' home but also his office. Indeed, the doorbell of the squat little terrace on Carburton Street was rung so infrequently that the event was enough to cause no small amount of consternation and confusion on the part of its equally squat little occupant.

Barnabas Tew was a private detective, although by some accounts not an especially good one. Years ago, when he was still a young man studying at London University, a wonderful new book had been published. It was a collection of stories about the adventures of a clever and dashing detective, Sherlock Holmes, and his somewhat less clever and less dashing assistant, Dr. Watson. Barnabas was immediately enthralled.

He had loved everything about the stories: the astonishing feats of mental agility, the glamorous and daring acts of bravery in the interest of justice, and the loyal Dr. Watson whose less-than-stellar performances served as a perfect contrast to better display Holmes' glittering intellect. Barnabas fancied that, since he understood the deductions made in the story (after they were explained, of course, but

3

still!), perhaps he might one day be just like his newfound hero and have a loyal friend to assist him with all of his important and exciting capers.

And his capers would be terribly important, of that his young mind had been sure. He would be the most capable and clever detective in the entire country. Nay, the entire world! Scotland Yard would consult him whenever a case confounded the limited wits of their finest detectives, and members of the nobility would sneak to his door in the dead of night when they had problems that required the utmost delicacy and discretion. His offices would be in the finest part of Mayfield, perhaps in one of the grand old Georgian townhouses near Grosvenor Square (or overlooking Berkeley Square Gardens at the very least).

His assistant would be a perfect foil against which to showcase his amazing talents, of that he was also certain. His Watson would be only slightly less intelligent, less brave, and less handsome than himself, although even Barnabas had to admit that this might be a difficult feat since he was not terribly handsome. Indeed, he was quite short and very nearly as wide as he was tall, and so there was an overall effect of roundness to him. Nevertheless, the assistant would be his loyal sidekick, and Barnabas would always graciously thank him for his help, sincerely grateful for his invaluable services.

The dream of being a detective had stuck throughout his years at university, fueled by the release of subsequent adventures of Mr. Sherlock Holmes and Dr. Watson. And so it was that, after graduating, degree in hand and ambitious dreams dancing about in his head, Barnabas decided to get straight to it and open up shop for himself. Of course, he was not able to realize the dream of having a posh office in Mayfield, at least not right away, which he realized the moment the landlord of such a place informed him of the exorbitant monthly rate. He had a small portion from his late father, but it was not sufficient to get him started in quite so fancy an office.

Therefore, he had downsized his ambitions a bit, telling

himself it was only temporary, just until his reputation had a chance to take hold throughout all of London (and indeed the entire nation, nay, the entire continent!). He rented this small flat in this small house in Marylebone. That was ten years ago, but somehow his dream of solving crimes had never quite become manifest. Not only was he *not* a smashing success as a detective, it seemed that he was utterly confounded by most of the cases that he took on and solved only a precious few.

He was beginning to suspect that perhaps he was not as clever as he had hoped. He even feared that he might be better suited as someone else's pleasant-yet-perhaps-slightly-dim-witted assistant, whilst his own assistant, an eager fellow by the name of Wilfred Colby, might be better off as a chimney sweep or a government clerk, or really in any line of work that would at least make him a decent living. But still, Barnabas was loath to give up on himself, and he hoped for some miracle of miracles to unleash his dormant genius and thus lift him up to the success that he so dearly craved.

The doorbell rang yet again, rather insistently this time, and Barnabas fluttered his hands about his face, unsure of how to proceed. The conundrum was this: the person who was leaning on the doorbell so relentlessly might be a client, someone in need of Barnabas' aid and willing to pay for it. Conversely, it might be Mrs. Crowder, his landlady. Barnabas was two months behind on his rent and eager to avoid her.

To his consternation, he heard the rattle of keys outside of his door, and then he heard the voice of his assistant. "Well, hullo, Mrs. Crowder!" said Wilfred.

Barnabas, listening from upstairs, knew his safe refuge from the horrors of an angry, unpaid landlady was about to be exposed, and he put his head in his hands in defeat.

"Would you like to come in? Have some tea, perhaps?"

Damn Wilfred for his perfect manners, thought Barnabas sourly.

"Why yes," replied she. To Barnabas' great chagrin he could now hear footsteps upon the stairs and their voices were getting closer. He looked about his office, but there was neither means of escape nor a place to hide. Despite the clutter of papers, the furniture was sparse and not large enough to hide a stout man, even if he be on the short side. "I was only just looking for Barnabas, but he's not answering his bell so perhaps he's not... Oh!"

Mrs. Crowder broke off as she preceded Wilfred into Barnabas' office. His face was on the desk, his body slumped as low in the chair as he could go without his head slipping off the desk entirely. Whilst the two were making their way up the stairs, Barnabas had made the hasty decision to pretend to be sound asleep in order to explain his failure to answer the doorbell (although, truth be told, the effect was somewhat closer to someone either dead or in the process of dying rather than merely sleeping, as the muscles of his face were still tightened with consternation so that his visage was more that of someone in great pain rather than that of a peaceful sleeper).

However, Mrs. Crowder's astonishment was soothed when Barnabas lifted his head, blinking slowly and smacking his lips in an attempt to appear newly awakened. Mrs. Crowder gave him an odd look, but she either did not realize entirely that he was faking or was too polite to point it out.

"Mr. Tew," she said kindly (indeed she was not an angry, greedy sort at all, but rather, a kind old lady who tolerated a good deal of bad behaviour from her less-than-ideal tenant). "I've come to inquire as to your rent. You know I hate to be bothersome, but I do so need the money." She looked at Barnabas, who was still trying to appear sleepy and confused, and she felt a bit sorry for the poor man. "The stove doesn't heat itself, you know!" she said brightly, attempting to lighten the mood whilst still getting her point across. Mrs. Crowder hated confrontation of any kind, and she was loath to cause any further upset to Mr. Tew, who was looking quite red in the face. "Cost of wood and all!" she continued, politely trying to explain her request for the rent money so that she didn't seem quite so demanding. She did so dislike upsetting the poor man!

"Oh, yes, well, ahem," coughed Barnabas. He moved his

6

head to and fro, pretending to shake off sleep. "Of course, I'll have it shortly, I'm sure," he prevaricated. An idea came to him, and he perked up. "Late payment from a client, you see. I'm expecting it any day now, and then you'll have your rent money straightaway." This last came out sounding a bit petulant, even to his own ears, as though the rent money was an unreasonable demand and she ought not to be bothering him with it. But there was nothing for it. It couldn't be helped because Barnabas was in a petulant state of mind and Mrs. Crowder had come at the exact wrong time.

Not that there was ever a particularly good time for someone to come round asking for money, thought Barnabas wryly, but today just happened to be a particularly bad time. Just this morning Barnabas had lost a client. He did not lose said client to a competitor, which would have been a blow to his pride, to be sure, but a blow he was quite used to by now. Instead, Barnabas' client, Mr. Edmund Fothergill, had actually died. Worse, he died in no small part because Barnabas had failed to discover the truth behind the menacing letters the poor man had been receiving, which left him vulnerable to the plots of his malefactor, who had taken the opportunity to murder the bloke.

The news had come to Barnabas just that morning through the post, in a letter sent by Mr. Fothergill's son, Bennett. The letter not only informed Barnabas of Mr. Fothergill's demise but stated that no further payments would be made because Barnabas had failed so spectacularly in his duties.

It was not only the lost income (and, of course, the dead client) that had dampened Barnabas' mood. It was the tone of the letter. Bennett Fothergill had seemed so smug, so condescending, so high-and-mighty, so *pleased* with himself! As well he might, thought Barnabas now, as Wilfred and Mrs. Crowder stood there in his study looking at him. Mr. Fothergill the younger certainly had plenty of reason to be quite pleased with himself as he had just inherited a substantial fortune from his father. The only heir, the young man was certainly quite well off now. At least that should serve as a comfort to the boy…

Barnabas slapped himself on the brow as realization struck him. Of course! Obviously Bennett Fothergill had been his father's tormentor and murdered him for the money. How could he have missed so obvious a suspect? Ah well, thought Barnabas, there was nothing to be done now. It wasn't as if solving the case at this point in time would un-murder poor Edmund Fothergill, and there would certainly be no payment in it for Barnabas, anyway.

Which thought brought him back to the present circumstance of being in his office with Wilfred and Mrs. Crowder, who were still looking at him expectantly. Barnabas realized that one of them must have asked him something whilst he was wool-gathering and he hadn't the slightest idea what it was. He reddened a bit more, embarrassed, and hemmed and hawed to cover his confusion.

"Yes, well, the rent money," he guessed, for that was what they had been talking about before his thoughts meandered. "On its way, most certainly!"

"From Mr. Fothergill, yes?" prompted Wilfred gently. Due to the fact that his employer's mind often wandered, Wilfred had mastered the art of subtly bringing Barnabas back into the conversation.

"Oh yes, Mr. Fothergill!" Mrs. Crowder exclaimed. "What a dear, pleasant man that one is. Always had a kind word for me when he came to call. You have solved his problem for him? He is doing quite well, I hope?"

"Ah, yes," said Barnabas uncomfortably. Wilfred sent him a telling glance. "He's doing quite well. Smashing, really." This was not quite a lie, thought Barnabas, as the man was doing quite well at being dead (it was nearly impossible to imagine someone lying there dead incorrectly, after all!), and moreover, Barnabas assumed he had been quite smashed by the heavy cabinet that fell upon him, ending his life and transferring his fortune to his apparently murderous son.

"Oh, good!" said Mrs. Crowder warmly. "I do so like the fellow. Be sure to have him round for tea sometime, will

8

you?"

"Yes, yes," replied Barnabas. "Most certainly!" It was better to lie to Mrs. Crowder and hope she forgot about Mr. Fothergill and the entire affair than to upset the poor woman.

Satisfied, and glad that she hadn't seemed to upset Mr. Tew too much, Mrs. Crowder excused herself and bustled back to her rooms downstairs, leaving Barnabas and Wilfred alone.

"Mr. Fothergill is quite dead, then, is he?" said Wilfred, who had guessed this from Barnabas' agitated demeanour and the way he had gone all red in the face at the mention of the man. Wilfred had worked on the case tirelessly with Barnabas, but, knowing the threatening nature of the letters received by Mr. Fothergill in the past month, and considering the success rate (or lack thereof) of Barnabas' investigations, Wilfred had thought the man's death to be likely, if not inevitable.

"Oh Wilfred," wailed Barnabas. "I am a failure! I couldn't solve my way out of a wet paper bag, I'm sure."

"Now, now," soothed Wilfred. "That's not so! We have had many successes over the years."

"But many more failures than successes," bemoaned Barnabas. "Mr. Fothergill is not the first client we've lost to foul play. Remember Lady Rainford and her little dog Precious?" They both shuddered at the memory of the old dowager and her fluffy white poodle. The woman loved the dog immensely and was rarely seen without him sitting upon her lap or toted under her arm like a package. However, the woman was an absolute terror to her employees and her servants hated her with a passion. She had written to Barnabas that she was in fear for her life. She said she had overheard various clandestine conversations and therefore suspected that one of her servants might attempt to kill her. Upon receiving her letter, Barnabas and Wilfred took the next train to the country to interview all of the servants as well as those in the neighbouring manor houses. But neither Wilfred nor Barnabas suspected in the slightest what would happen next.

9

It seemed Lady Rainford was possessed of a terrific allergy to peanuts and swelled up with hives at the mere sight of them. They learned of this when Wilfred brought out a bag of the offending nuts with his lunch that first day. Lady Rainford had chastised him harshly and forbade him from ever bringing peanuts into the house again.

The case came to an abrupt end when Barnabas and Wilfred entered her parlour one morning to report on their continued lack of progress in discovering the identity of her would-be murderer. They found her stone-cold dead upon the floor, her face puffy and red. Precious lay by her side, licking himself furiously. The woman had apparently swollen up so badly she couldn't breathe and therefore asphyxiated.

Confounded as to what had happened, they noticed a strong smell of peanuts near the body. Closer investigation revealed that the dog was completely covered in peanut dust, which explained why he was cleaning his fur so vigorously. Someone had doused the dog with peanuts and sent him in to his mistress as an innocent, fluffy harbinger of death.

No one could say where the peanuts came from, exactly, for the dog to wallow in them, as there were no peanuts to be found in the house; but the local police had not cared enough to be bothered by the strangeness of the dog being peanut-dust covered. They deemed Lady Rainford's death an accident and closed the case (although Barnabas suspected that perhaps they too disliked the belligerent lady and thought her well rid of). Barnabas thought it likely that the maid who took in the dog after the murder was the perpetrator, but as it was impossible to prove, he and Wilfred had given up and gone home. The only witness was a poodle, after all, and so the truth of the matter would forever remain a mystery.

"And then there was poor Sophronia Slade, who lost her entire life's savings to that scoundrel. If only we had foreseen that he would…"

"Well, yes, I suppose there was that, too," interrupted Wilfred, determined to help his employer shake off his dismal mood. "But I say! Remember that case a few months

10

ago? The one we handled for the Egyptian fellow?"

"Ah yes," said Barnabas. "Mr. Kesim Kafele. We helped him find his missing amulet, or ankh, or whatever it was." Barnabas chuckled. "What nonsense that was! He seemed to think it had some sort of magical power. He was quite frantic about finding it, I recall."

Wilfred laughed too. "The poor fellow! He burst in here all in an uproar, with his face all red, huffing and puffing about how someone had stolen his ankh. A treasure more precious than could be imagined, he called it. I thought he was fit to burst from the anxiety of losing it!"

"What an odd character he was!" said Barnabas, for the moment caught up in the pleasant memory of a successfully solved case. But then his mood shifted again. "But the solution was so obvious. Lady Rainford's little dog could have solved it as easily as we did. That was no great success."

"Nay!" said Wilfred. "On the contrary! It was a stroke of genius to deduce that Mr. Kafele's cleaning lady was the culprit."

"Hmmph, well," said Barnabas. He was embarrassed and yet pleased by the compliment, and he was trying very hard to show neither.

"It was a job well done, I say!" said Wilfred. "Mr. Kafele was so terribly grateful and impressed. Surely he will refer our services to others in due time." He paused as they both considered the possibility that 'due time' might very well be far too long relative to the financial viability of their enterprise. Although it was doubtful that the kind Mrs. Crowder would ever evict them for failure to pay the rent, still a fellow needed to eat and buy clothes and the like. A paying client was sorely needed, and quickly.

"I know how to cheer our spirits!" Wilfred exclaimed. "It's no use sitting about being morose about the state of things. Let us go out and about and take our minds off of our troubles. There is an exhibit at the museum, of a mummy that they just found in a tomb in Egypt. It will be just the thing!"

"Why, my dear boy...," said Barnabas, his interest at

once piqued. There was something so very interesting, so very exotic, about the mummies the archaeologists were excavating from the ancient tombs of Egypt that Barnabas couldn't help but be fascinated by the prospect of viewing this new one. He thought this exhibit could indeed be a wonderful diversion and a perfect distraction from his current professional quandary. "I think you might be on to something. A mummy does sound quite interesting. And I fear I shall go quite mad if I continue to sit here for another moment, waiting for the bell to ring and yet fearing who it might be if it *were* to ring!"

"And the exhibit is free to the public, so it will be of no expense at all. Perhaps we may even find ourselves caught up in a caper whilst there!" said Wilfred, excited at the prospect of an outing.

"I wouldn't count on it," said Barnabas, laughing. "Such things only happen in stories. But we will make a pleasant day of it, nonetheless, adventure or no. And we do happen to be quite the experts on all things Egypt, don't we? Proper Egyptologists we are, I'd say!"

He rose and gathered up his hat and coat (which were, of course, a deerstalker cap and long trench coat so as to look the part of a proper detective, just like Mr. Holmes). Then he and Wilfred left the flat and hailed a cab, the both of them very jolly now, glad of a distraction from their woes and excited at the prospect of seeing a real Egyptian mummy. Thus, their steps were light and their conversation jovial as they made their way hence.

Chapter Two

The line to get into the museum was very long as the arrival of a real Egyptian mummy in London was thought to be very exciting in general, a spectacle not to be missed. Moreover, Barnabas and Wilfred had arrived rather late in the day and so were forced to wait at the end of the line. Consequently, it was very late indeed by the time they actually entered the museum. Indeed, it was close to evening, and the museum was quickly clearing out as people, satiated with the exotic sights of the exhibit headed home to their dinners and their warm fireplaces.

The exhibit was laid out in such a way that visitors were funnelled through a labyrinthine maze of convoluted corridors lined with assorted Egyptian relics before coming upon the main attraction; namely, the mummy. Most of the people had little interest in the ancient objects, having come merely for the thrill of the mummy, and so made their way quickly to that main exhibit.

Barnabas and Wilfred, however, were quite fascinated by the relics and lingered over them for some time. "Do you know," said Barnabas, who had taken a course in antiquities whilst at university and so fancied himself a bit of an expert on such things, "that they extracted the dead person's organs and put them in these jars for safekeeping until the poor fellow could get to the afterlife and reclaim them?" He gestured towards a set of four beautifully painted canopic jars.

"Interesting!" said Wilfred. "Which organ went in which jar, do you know?"

"Hmm, well, ah, not quite, I suppose," prevaricated Barnabas, embarrassed that his knowledge on the subject had run out so quickly. He paused, searching his brain for relevant information. Then he brightened. "But each jar is protected by a specific god. The four sons of, um, Horus, I believe. And Horus was the son of Osiris, who was very important indeed."

Wilfred smiled and nodded as they moved on past the jars. "Oh look!" exclaimed Wilfred. "A scarab!" He squinted as he pressed his nose into the glass to get a better view of the embossed enamel beetle that hung from a delicately wrought chain. "It looks similar in style to the ankh we found for Mr. Kesim Kefele. I wonder if this scarab is as magical as that ankh," he laughed.

"I'm sure they are all magical, to the minds of the ancients," replied Barnabas with a chuckle. He assumed the air of good-humoured smugness that people who fancied themselves modern intellectuals often affected when discussing the beliefs of other cultures. "What silliness! To think of believing in gods and magical scarabs and an afterlife where one's organs must be kept safe in a jar. Such poppycock!"

"But rather delightful poppycock, I must say," observed Wilfred, still looking at the beautiful scarab beetle. Barnabas smiled his agreement, for the relics were indeed a joy to behold. Indeed, Barnabas had most certainly found his antiquities class to be of the utmost interest. The complex relations of the gods and the intricacies of the rituals were terribly fascinating (although, of course, it had been terribly difficult to keep it all straight for the examinations). Still, Barnabas had enjoyed the subject immensely, and there was no denying the beauty of the objects on display here.

"The scarab had a special significance to the Egyptians, I believe," he said. He scratched his chin, trying to remember just what that significance might be. "Something to do with dung beetles. Yes, that's it! A scarab beetle is the same thing as a dung beetle. The Egyptians believed a god in the form of a scarab beetle rolled the sun across the sky every morning." He nodded sagely, pleased with himself for recollecting so much information.

"What was the god's name, do you know?" asked Wilfred, who was quite interested in all of this. He had very much enjoyed working on the case for Mr. Kesim Kafele (he too had taken a class on Egyptology at university), and enjoyed increasing his knowledge all he could about such things.

"Hmm, well. Hmmph," said Barnabas, embarrassed again, for he had no idea what the scarab god's name might be.

"Oh well," said Wilfred, who had moved on to a series of hieroglyphic paintings on plaster. "Perhaps we can get a book about it later. There is so much to know!"

"Yes, indeed," agreed Barnabas somewhat ruefully. "That is a splendid idea. It seems I could use a refresher on the subject, after all." Although easily embarrassed, Barnabas was, to his credit, also quick to admit to his own shortcomings. Indeed, he was ofttimes far too modest, and sometimes even prone to fits of extreme self-doubt.

They continued on in this way, lingering over everything in the exhibit and making comments here and there when they came across things of particular interest (gilded statues of cats particularly caught Barnabas' fancy, whilst Wilfred was captivated by a series of portraits depicting gods with animal heads that had been drawn on papyrus).

It took them so long to properly view everything that the entire queue quickly moved so that the people ahead of them were quite far ahead indeed; Barnabas and Wilfred only just caught sight of their backs as they rounded a corner and disappeared from view. Now Barnabas and Wilfred were entirely alone.

Barnabas checked his pocket watch. "Oh dear!" he exclaimed. "Look at the time! It's after five o'clock. Isn't the museum meant to close at five o'clock?"

"Yes, I think so," replied Wilfred. "Perhaps they only close the front doors but allow the people already inside to finish their viewing." He looked around doubtfully. "I don't see anyone else here, however," he said, and, in truth, it appeared that the lights had dimmed somewhat so that it was rather dark in the corridor. They must have been so engrossed in the ancient artifacts that they didn't notice the lights going down.

"Yes, we do seem to be the only people left here," agreed Barnabas. "But I'm certain that someone would tell us if they meant for us to leave immediately. Surely they wouldn't lock up the museum with us still inside!"

But even as he said this, he felt a bit nervous. Perhaps they had gotten so far behind the rest of the queue that the museum people had assumed that everyone was gone and closed up the museum with Barnabas and Wilfred left alone within. Barnabas greatly enjoyed looking at the artifacts, to be sure, but to be locked up with them all night was another thing entirely.

"I'm sure that is so. They must do a check to make sure everyone is out," said Wilfred. He laughed, then added, "Still, we should hurry so we can at least see the mummy for a few moments before we are thrown out of here on our coattails."

"Quite so, quite so," said Barnabas, anxious to get out of the museum before it closed but also curious about the mummy and loath to leave the museum without first having a proper look at it. To that end, he and Wilfred quickened their pace and reached the mummy display within just a few minutes.

Although they had hoped that there might still be a few stragglers milling about, lingering in front of the mummy, there was no one else there. Barnabas and Wilfred were alone (excepting, of course, for the mummy itself).

They knew they should hurry up, that there was a chance they might get locked inside the museum if it were to close before they exited the building. But they had been so pleased by the rest of the exhibit, and so excited at the thought of seeing a real mummy, that both found it difficult to pass by the mummy without giving it at least some small degree of their attention.

But both men thought it only a slight chance they would be locked in all night. There must be someone there after hours – a cleaning crew, security, administrative types – who could easily unlock the doors and let them out if need be.

So, they stopped in front of the mummy display, feeling like naughty schoolboys who had broken the rules. In fact, Barnabas discovered that he quite enjoyed this feeling; indeed he was quite exhilarated by it. He felt like a rebellious youth, a scoundrel, a man of adventure. And, of course, it was such a small infraction of the rules. Surely, any consequences would be quite minimal.

He glanced at Wilfred to see if he shared the same excitement, but the young man was regarding the mummy with an expression of skepticism on his face. Barnabas leaned closer to get a better look at the thing.

"Hmmm," he said. "Well." He found that he was at a loss for words.

He had been expecting to see a mummy like the ones depicted in newspaper articles, tidily wrapped in clean white linens and nicely propped up in beautiful sarcophagi.

But this one was just lying there on a raised platform behind a fence of red velvet rope. There were no pretty linens to hide the state of the decomposed body, nor was there even any skin left upon the thing. It was just exposed, preserved muscle, there for all to see. Little tufts of reddish hair puffed out from the top of its skull, and Barnabas saw from the placard that the sad, shriveled thing was called "Ginger" because of this.

"Ugh," agreed Wilfred. "I hate to say this, but it's really quite…well…"

"Disgusting?" supplied Barnabas. He wrinkled his nose. "I don't mean to disrespect the dead, but it's a bit gruesome, I think. You know, having all of one's under-bits just out there for all to see. Shouldn't they have wrapped it up or something?"

"Most definitely!" agreed Wilfred. "Perhaps it was wrapped before and the wrappings came off, and the archeologists didn't want to interfere with the historical nature of it, or some such?"

There was, in fact, a sarcophagus standing just behind the

mummy, and Barnabas wondered if perhaps the real mummy was inside of that. But the sarcophagus was standing well behind the rope enclosure, and was firmly closed. Barnabas may have been feeling a bit rebellious but not sufficiently so to cross over the ropes and into the restricted areas in order to pry open parts of the display. He shuddered at the prospect of the embarrassment he would feel if he were to be caught committing so egregious an act.

The two sat there and contemplated the skinless Ginger for a few moments, trying to see the educational value of merely placing a dead person on a platform with no skin on whatsoever. Neither man could, however, and feeling a bit queasy at the sight of it, they moved on, intending to leave rather quickly.

They had both been so caught up with the spectacle of poor Ginger that neither paid much attention to the sarcophagus behind the mummy. If they had, they might have noticed that, in the eyeholes of the sarcophagus, *actual* eyes moving about, and that those eyes were watching Barnabas with interest.

As Barnabas and Wilfred followed the corridor that they supposed led to the museum's exit, however, they grew a bit uneasy. There was no one in sight and, except for the sound of their own shoes clicking on the floor, the museum was quite dark and utterly silent.

There were several turns to be made, but none were marked. They quickened their pace, hoping that the exit would be just around each corner, but it never was. Soon enough they were miserably lost in a warren of corridors that all looked the same. They had evidently gone off the main path somewhere, and now they had no idea how to get back to the proper place.

"There!" exclaimed Wilfred, pointing ahead for he thought that he had seen a shadow moving in the hallway. "Pardon? Excuse me? Sir?" he called to the imaginary shadow, thinking that it must have belonged to a person. He hurried after it.

Barnabas was about to follow (although, in truth, he was

doubtful there was anyone there; still he had no wish to be left alone in this eerie place) when he heard a sound coming from behind him. He turned around and squinted into the shadows.

He heard the sound again, a bit closer this time, so that he was able to identify it as a voice. It wasn't his imagination after all! But there was something strange about the voice, a rhythmic sound to it as though someone were chanting. And underneath of that was a more subtle sound that he struggled to interpret. It sounded like something was being dragged across the floor.

Someone chanting oddly whilst dragging things along the floor made no sense to Barnabas, and he scratched his head as he thought about it. Should he be frightened? Was it a ne'er-do-well up to some cryptic or occult shenanigans in the bowels of the museum? Ought he to run after Wilfred and seek out the authorities?

Then it came to him. It must be a cleaning man singing as he pushed his mop to and fro. That would account for the chanting as well as the dragging. He laughed a bit at his own excitability. Clearly the mummy had spooked him more than he had thought.

"Hello?" he said, thinking smugly that perhaps he had found their deliverer whilst Wilfred was off chasing shadows. "Is someone there? We seem to be quite lost. If you could just point us in the right direction..."

But he broke off mid-sentence. It seemed that his first assessment of the situation had, in fact, been the correct one. The figure he saw rounding the corner behind him was most certainly a ne'er-do-well of the utmost kind, and what it was doing was the very description of occult shenanigans.

Incredibly, the thing (for surely this could not be described as a man!) that followed Barnabas looked something like a person but with the head of a jackal. This beast looked much like the pictures of the gods of the dead that he and Wilfred had so marveled over just minutes ago.

The creature was chanting in a deep, low voice and moving its hands strangely, almost like it was trying to

19

emulate an orchestra conductor even though there was no orchestra present. And then Barnabas saw what the movements and chants of the jackal-man were actually directing, and his feet froze to the spot in terror.

A terrible thing had emerged from behind the jackal-man and was now coming down the corridor at quite a pace. It had no skin! Indeed, it looked quite a lot like Ginger, the disappointing mummy. Such a thing surely couldn't be alive, much less running towards him and waving its arms in the most animated fashion. This was extremely impossible, thought Barnabas. This was unnatural. Nothing could run and flail about like that whilst it was so lacking in skin!

As it drew closer, Barnabas saw little tufts of reddish hair emerging from the thing's scalp, and he realized that it was indeed Ginger coming after him in this darkened hallway. And he realized that, if he didn't move quickly, the thing would be upon him shortly; and he was fairly certain it wasn't going to ask him to sit down to tea and scones.

This realization broke his paralysis and he opened his mouth to scream. "Aaaah!" he yelped as he turned to run. "Wilfred! Help! Help!"

His fancied he heard Wilfred's voice in the distance calling back to him, but alas, Barnabas' feet tangled up beneath him and he fell. He landed hard and the wind was knocked out of him.

As he struggled to catch his breath and rise to his feet, however, he heard the shuffling sounds of the mummy directly behind him. He turned about to face his attacker just in time to see the horrible skinless thing as it bore down on him, arms outstretched.

"Oooh!" he managed to peep one last time before the gruesome hands closed around his neck, preventing his breath from returning to him until a curtain of dark descended before his eyes.

Chapter Three

When Barnabas regained consciousness, he realized immediately that something was horribly wrong with him. To begin with, he felt quite light and airy, not like his usual self at all. Another problem was that he seemed to be lying on the floor of a dirty and decrepit boat made of moldy black wood.

He heard the sounds one would normally hear whilst aboard a boat: waves lapping against the sides, paddles slapping against the water, wood creaking as the boat moved up and down with the water. All of these were normal sounds with which he was quite familiar, as was the rocking motion of the boat, a movement that would have been very relaxing under other circumstances. It was not relaxing now for three very important reasons.

The first reason was that he had no idea how he might have got on a boat. The last thing he remembered was being attacked, remarkably, by an extremely ambulatory mummy that was (equally remarkably) seemingly directed by a man with an extraordinarily canine face. He supposed that he might have fallen, bumped his head, and experienced a very vivid dream; that theory, however, did not begin to explain his current provenance on this derelict boat.

The second factor that bothered him was the sky. Instead of being a nice, pretty blue, or the more usual grey of a London fog, it was, instead, a brownish-red. The sky was like a particularly ugly sunset that didn't darken into the black of night as sunsets normally did. Barnabas waited and waited for it to do so, but the hideous muddy smudge of a sky persisted.

But the most important thing that weighed on Barnabas' mind was a question: who was rowing this boat? That someone was doing so was not in doubt for, in addition to the sounds of the paddles moving in and out of the water, the boat hitched and lurched forward in a way that indicated the rhythmic strokes of a rower. Besides, Barnabas could hear the faint noises that one normally associated with the presence of another: a rustling of clothing as the person shifted, a soft whistling sound as he (or she) breathed in and out, the scratching of feet along the floorboards.

Still, he couldn't think of a logical reason someone would remove him from the museum. Surely, if he had fallen and hurt himself, a reasonable person would have taken him to see a doctor! A reasonable person would at least have helped Wilfred to get him bundled safely into his own bed in his own flat. Neither of these courses of action would require a ride in a dingy old boat.

And so, Barnabas reasoned, the person sitting in the back of the boat must not be a reasonable fellow (or lady) at all. Therefore, he was somewhat nervous about confronting the person to see what they were about with all of this nonsense.

But, Barnabas realized at last, he couldn't just lie there on the bottom of the boat refusing to look at his companion forever. There was nothing for it but to see who was there and ask whoever it might be *where*, exactly, they were and *why*, exactly, Barnabas was in this craft instead of in the museum where he belonged.

So, Barnabas sat up and turned to look towards the back of the boat. However, the moment he saw who was there with him (or, rather what, Barnabas thought with no small degree of consternation), he wished that he hadn't looked at all. It would have been better if he had just stayed still and feigned sleep, and if he had done so forever if that's how long it took for the thing that sat in the back of the boat to go away.

Barnabas blinked, thinking that perhaps his eyes were mistaken, that maybe some trick of the odd reddish light had deceived him. When that didn't work, he closed his eyes for a bit longer before opening them. But, to his chagrin, nothing had changed when he opened them again. Everything was just as it had been before.

The problem was that the person who sat on the bench, pushing the oars and looking entirely relaxed as though nothing at all was amiss, was not exactly a person at all.

The person, or rather the thing, in the boat with Barnabas put him in mind of the jackal-headed man from the museum, except this creature was possessed of a falcon's head rather than that of a jackal. His (its?) torso was (mostly) that of a man; although this creature had wings (which was a strange thing, thought Barnabas irrelevantly, because how on earth could one pull on an oar if one had only wings but no hands?), but the rest of him was entirely birdlike.

His smallish head was covered in dark brown feathers (which, if truth be told, looked a bit unkempt to Barnabas). A long orange beak extended from the man's snout and curved down to end in a jagged, cruelly sharp point. Small black eyes darted about quickly so that the falcon man looked incredibly alert.

The man (or falcon, Barnabas was not quite sure how to classify him just yet) somehow managed to ply the oars of the boat with his wings. The oars were jammed beneath them so that the ends disappeared from view into his armpit area. The falcon man rhythmically rolled his shoulders back and forth, which somehow, impossibly it seemed, moved the oars in a perfectly elliptical stroke. It was really quite impressive.

As for the fellow's feet… Well, they were most definitely bird feet, but the toes and talons were, for the most part, missing. It looked as if someone, or something, had lopped them off but made a shoddy job of it. Some of the stubs where toes had once been were longer than others. One of the smaller toes had escaped whatever misfortune had befallen the rest, however, and was possessed of a very long talon. From this single intact digit Barnabas could easily surmise how impressively large the rest of the talons must have been, and he shifted nervously on the boat's floor.

The falcon man cleared his throat, and Barnabas realized that he had been staring at those distressing feet for quite a long time. Embarrassed at his own rudeness, he flushed. He then pushed aside his consternation at his strange predicament and smiled politely at his companion.

He wondered if he ought to say something to begin a conversation. However, it seemed to him that the onus of social responsibility in this case must fall squarely upon the falcon man. After all, Barnabas was at quite the disadvantage: he had no idea where he was, how he had got here, or why he was here at all. Surely the falcon man owed him some sort of explanation!

But even as Barnabas determined that it was he who ought to be offended and not the other way around, his discomfiture at the uncomfortable silence began to overwhelm him. Soon he could take it no more, and he decided to take the high road and begin the conversation himself.

"Well," he said, "hello and good day to you, sir."

The falcon man merely nodded tersely in Barnabas' direction. So, thought Barnabas, somewhat affronted, this was a fine situation indeed! Not only was he in the midst of the strangest predicament of his life, but it seemed that his companion was determined to be quite surly.

"Well, then," he began again. "I'm Barnabas Tew of Marylebone. I was at the museum, and I seem to have got turned about somehow." He was trying to sound strident and forceful, but his voice quavered a bit. In addition, he had an unfortunate habit of raising his pitch at the end of his sentences. Both of these things conspired against him so that, instead of sounding confident, he came off as somewhat meek and apologetic.

Mr. Falcon-head simply continued to look at Barnabas.

"You can imagine my distress at finding myself in such an, um, unusual situation," Barnabas continued, a bit desperately. Why wouldn't the cursed fellow respond? His reticence was most impolite and was causing Barnabas no small amount of worry. The man's rudeness made the possibility of a reasonable resolution seem quite remote. In fact, Barnabas was beginning to feel as though he might be in some considerable danger after all.

An idea struck him, and he tried again. "I was with my

assistant, Wilfred. Surely Wilfred is looking for me and has of course roused the constabulary." Still his companion offered no response. "Where is this boat going?" Barnabas demanded, losing his patience. "I demand to be taken to Marylebone this instant!"

At last, the falcon-headed man responded, albeit in a less-than-pleasant way. He snickered (and it was quite a mean-sounding snicker, thought Barnabas). "Oh, calm yourself," said the creature. "You're quite beyond Marylebone. There's no going back there now, so don't worry on that account."

"Whatever do you mean?" asked Barnabas. "Beyond Marylebone? Where am I? And why am I here? Explain yourself, please!"

It seemed that the falcon-headed man's face softened somewhat. His next words were a bit less brusque, at least, and Barnabas thought that he detected a trace of pity in his tone. "Oh, you silly fellow," said the falcon man. "I am Anti, Ferryman across the River of the Dead." Anti paused, allowing the words to sink in to Barnabas' mind.

"River of the Dead?" repeated Barnabas slowly. "But that would mean… Surely you can't mean to imply…"

"That you are dead," Anti finished the sentence for him, although not unkindly.

"But," wailed Barnabas, "that cannot be! Surely I would remember, um, *becoming* dead!" But even as he said it, the uncomfortable memory of being attacked by the insane mummy presented itself. He quickly pushed the thought aside as a ridiculous impossibility. "It is quite impossible," he said.

"Well, it's not impossible because here you are," said Anti, somewhat defensively. "I didn't kill you, if that's what you mean to say next. I just ferry the dead across the river."

Barnabas realized that Anti must heartily tired of reluctant dead people taking their frustrations out on him, and he decided not to berate the poor chap any further. But still, he was quite upset at the news that he was dead and having a hard time believing it to be true.

25

"Perhaps there's been a mistake," he said. "Maybe I'm not really dead. Is there someone I could talk to? Someone who could straighten out this mess?"

"Sorry," said Anti. "But this is how it is. You wouldn't be here if you weren't dead."

"I just would have thought that dying would be, well, more noticeable," said Barnabas sadly.

"So does everyone," said Anti. "Almost no one really believes they are dead at first. And it must be especially hard for you, to have gone in such a, well, an unexpected way."

"So you know about the mummy?" asked Barnabas. Anti nodded. "Yes, well, I had quite hoped that I had gone mad and imagined that whole thing," said Barnabas tersely.

Anti laughed for the first time, a real laugh that made him seem a somewhat more pleasant fellow. "I've seen some strange things in my time," he said. "People die from all sorts of odd happenings. But yours most definitely is in the top ten of strange deaths that I've ever seen."

Barnabas, oddly, felt proud at this, as though this statement validated his sufferings somehow. He nodded and sat up straighter, attempting to appear noble and proud in the face of his remarkable travails.

"So," he said, after a long silence. "Where do I go from here?"

"I'm taking you to the Land of the Dead," said Anti, "where you will be judged. Your heart will be weighed against a feather. If it's lighter than the feather, you'll be ushered into the Land of the Dead, where you can live happily ever after."

"Hmm," said Barnabas doubtfully. He didn't think it physically possible for a heart to weigh less than a feather, and so he was worried anew about what might befall him next. "And who will be doing this judging?" he asked.

"Anubis, King of the Dead," replied Anti tersely.

At the mention of Anubis' name, Barnabas thought he perceived a sneer twitch on Anti's face. (It wasn't much of a sneer, merely a small twitch of the upper beak, but Barnabas imagined that even that had to be quite difficult to manage when one's upper lip was so rigid; indeed, it was quite impressive that Anti had been able to even give the *impression* of a sneer with that big beak of his).

He wondered what it was about Anubis that had reawakened the irritable side of Anti's personality. He noticed that, at the mention of the name, the boatman had begun to curl and uncurl the stumps of the talons on his feet.

Barnabas wondered again what had happened there, but it would be incredibly rude to just come out and ask. So, instead, he directed his thoughts towards his predicament and what he might do to get out of it.

"But wait!" cried Barnabas, remembering now what he knew about Egyptian mythology. "Anubis is the one with the jackal head. He was there in the museum. It was he who made the mummy attack me!"

"Ah," said Anti, "now you are beginning to understand."

"Um, yes," agreed Barnabas, who did not understand at all what Anti was getting at. "Except that, well, perhaps you could explain it to me? Just to see if we have come to the same conclusions, is what I mean."

Anti laughed and rested his wingtip upon Barnabas' shoulder for a moment. "Don't you see, my dear, innocent fellow? Anubis wants you for something."

"Wants me? What could an Egyptian god of the dead possibly want of a modest detective?" Barnabas was more perplexed than ever.

"The ways of the gods are inscrutable," replied Anti cryptically. "But be aware. Keep your eyes and ears open. If Anubis wants you, then you're going to have an adventure, that much is certain. And just pray that said adventure is not too bad."

Barnabas was alarmed at these last words, and he begged Anti to explain further, but the falcon-headed boatman either would not or could not. And so Barnabas arrived in the Land of the Dead under a cloud of anxious thoughts and was deposited there, alone on the black rocky shore, by Anti, who wished him well and then paddled off on business of his own.

Chapter Four

Barnabas, confused, stood on the beach where Anti had left him. Although the boatman did not look back, Barnabas waved at the retreating figure as he paddled away. After all, Anti was the only person to whom he had spoken since being dead, and therefore Barnabas considered him as his only friend in this horrible place.

He wondered why the boatman was so grumpy. Why he didn't give Barnabas the common courtesy of a farewell wave? He hoped that he hadn't said anything to offend Anti. Perhaps it was the business with the feet. Barnabas wished that he hadn't stared at the fellow quite so rudely, but really, was he to be blamed for that? It wasn't as if one woke up every day to find oneself in a boat with a falcon man. Anyone at all would have been quite shocked at such a thing, and Barnabas thought that he had comported himself quite handsomely. Indeed, he thought that he had been remarkably calm, considering the circumstances.

Besides, Barnabas did not have the time to worry about whether or not he had ruffled Anti's feathers. (He smiled to himself at the slightly snarky little joke and told himself that he must remember to tell it to Wilfred when he next saw him.) Right now, his most pressing problem was to figure out where he was and how he might get back to London.

The black rocks of the beach were extremely jagged and sharp. Indeed, they were quite uncomfortable to stand on. Barnabas looked about. It seemed that the rocks smoothed out somewhat about a hundred yards from the shore.

Barnabas glanced back at the water, thinking that perhaps he should stay there, find another boat, and thus go back the way he had come. But something about the water unnerved him. It was very dark, for one thing, so that one couldn't see beneath the surface in the slightest. It was also tinged with red and seemed to be very viscous, so that it looked a great deal like semi-dried blood. The waves didn't *splash* against the rocks so much as they *slurped*, so that each goopy heave of the stuff oozed up the rocks slowly before retreating again, leaving a slimy stain of deepest red on the sharp black rocks.

No, Barnabas did not think that he'd like to stay near this water at all. Besides, he could still see the water (and therefore any boats upon it) from the edge of the beach just as well as he could whilst standing here directly beside the river. If a boat came by he would have plenty of time to run across the beach to intercept it.

Thus decided, he tiptoed carefully across the strand until he got to the smoother part, then carefully sat down to think, heedless of the gravel that dirtied the back of his pants.

Anti had said that Anubis, the Egyptian god of the dead, wanted him for something; but the thought that an ancient, foreign, *made up* god could be behind his abduction was absolutely absurd. But then, equally absurd was the idea that an actual *falcon-person* had ferried him across a river into the Land of the Dead.

As Barnabas thought it through, it became more and more clear to him: Anti had obviously not been a real falcon at all but merely a real man dressed as one. It followed then that he was not dead after all but had merely been knocked senseless so that he might be abducted and henceforth led to believe the bizarre charade that his malefactors had so adroitly performed for him.

So who, then, was this Anubis character who had gone to such lengths to create the terrifying scene with the mummy in the museum, knocking out Barnabas and allowing the man in the falcon costume to kidnap him?

He must, thought Barnabas, be a scoundrel, a scallywag, an *outlaw* of some unknown sort. No one else would resort to such chicanery to apprehend a law-abiding detective who, whilst maybe not the most successful of his kind, was still an upstanding, perfectly respectable citizen.

29

Or, he thought, perhaps a Member of Parliament had instigated this nefarious plan! Perhaps, unknowingly, he had stumbled onto a plot of some kind, a sordid, top-secret government affair, and now the conspirator (*conspirators, even!*) was going to great lengths to throw him off the trail.

He swallowed hard with a mixture of fear and pride at the thought of it. He drew himself up, blinking rapidly, to sit stiffly upright so that he looked a figure of regal, stoic heroism (or thought he looked, rather. In reality, he looked a bit more like an alarmed meerkat, eyes darting back and forth whilst sitting up stiffly to attention).

Well, he thought dramatically, these government ruffians would find it not so easy to rid themselves of the attention of Barnabas Tew. He would sniff out their trail like a bloodhound after a fox. He would uncover their secrets like a badger digging out the tunnel of a rodent. He would...

"Aaah!" he yelped, startled out of his daydreams of grandeur by the sight of four tiny figures running straight towards him. His hands flew up to flutter in a great furor about his head, but he was far too frightened to leap to his feet.

The four figures racing towards him were about the size of children, but they, like Anti the grumpy boatman, were not entirely human. They each had the head of a different animal. One looked like a lion, another a hyena, yet another a tiger, and the last looked like a canary. (A *canary*? thought Barnabas. The other creatures looked ferocious and fearsome, but the canary was not that scary at all. Indeed, it was quite adorable, really.)

Still, Barnabas did not find it at all adorable when the four of them reached out, dragged him to his feet, and began to bear him away quite roughly.

"Unhand me!" he shouted, affronted and afraid. "You scoundrels! I'll have the bobbies on you before you... Ow!" he squealed as the canary delivered a mighty peck to his hand.

He looked at these new, tiny malefactors in shock. He happened to catch the eye of the hyena-child, who snarled at him. Thick saliva dripped from viciously sharp fangs, and Barnabas decided that discretion was most definitely the better part of valor. He stopped struggling and yelling (he most definitely did not want to be pecked by that awful little canary again) and decided to see where they would take him instead.

Perhaps they were taking him to meet with the rogue Parliament members right now! If so, Barnabas was confident in his ability to talk his way out of this mess. Surely even a law-breaking Parliament member must still be civilized enough to listen to reason. Barnabas would convince them that this was all a big mistake, a colossal misunderstanding, and they would let him go. Perhaps they would even lend him a carriage to take him back to Marylebone, which would be nice indeed, since Barnabas was quite exhausted from the adventures of the day.

However, such was not to be, for it was not to a Parliament member that the hostile animal-headed children delivered him. Instead, they dropped him rudely at the feet of a man who wore the head of a jackal.

"You!" cried Barnabas from where he lay in the black dirt. (He wondered briefly why all the ground here was so black, not a speck of grass to be seen anywhere. It was most unpleasant, thought Barnabas.) "It was you in the museum! You made the mummy attack me! That *thing* knocked me unconscious. I'll have quite the headache tomorrow from all of this, I'm quite sure!"

The jackal-headed man laughed. "Oh, I think not," he said, his tone quite amiable despite all that he had put Barnabas through. "You are quite beyond headaches now, I think." He smiled knowingly at the attendant standing beside him (who had the head, thankfully, of a normal person).

Barnabas, despite his fear, was quite put out with being spoken to in such a cryptic, condescending fashion. First, Anti had spoken to him thus, and now this jackal person. How dare they subject him to such things and then speak to him as though they enjoyed the idea that they knew things that he did not. It was really beyond tolerable, he thought.

Quite insufferable!

He put on the crispest, most politely aggrieved tone that he could manage. "Whatever do you mean by that? Such a statement! Beyond headaches? Why, it makes no sense, no sense at all. Kindly explain yourself, sir!"

The jackal-headed man made a placating gesture with his hands. (Or were they paws? Barnabas couldn't quite tell.) "Calm down, please," said the jackal. "No need to get all excited."

"Ah!" exclaimed Barnabas indignantly. "You want me to calm down, you say? You whisk me off to this terrible place and have these…these…" He gestured towards his four little abductors, searching for the proper term for them. "*Monsters*! Yes, you have these *monsters* snatch me from the beach and then ask me to calm down!"

The canary took great offense at being called a monster, it seemed, and made as though to peck Barnabas once more. "Oh!" squealed Barnabas as the fluffy yellow agitator nearly took him on the arm with its beak. Barnabas pulled his arm back just in time to avoid the blow.

Despite his terrible predicament (or, perhaps, because of it), Barnabas laughed. The sight of the adorable little canary, eyes blazing, feathers ruffled up, struck him as intolerably funny. Politely, he tried to hold back the laughter, but the giggles erupted from him uncontrollably. Soon they grew into great, heaving guffaws that shook his entire body.

In truth, there was a bit of hysteria in Barnabas' laugh, which made him seem a bit crazy. Anubis looked sidelong at the attendant beside him, raising his eyebrows and pursing his lips. The attendant shrugged and looked away uncomfortably.

Barnabas' laughter only enraged the canary further. It cheeped and puffed out its chest whilst scratching its little feet on the ground like an angry chicken (trying, it seemed to Barnabas, to seem threatening but only managing to look more than a little ridiculous). The lion, however, held the canary back so it could not assault Barnabas. The canary flapped its wings and squawked as it tried to lunge at the laughing detective. This, of course, made the situation even more absurd than it had already been, and Barnabas laughed all the harder.

"Enough!" boomed Anubis, whose voice was powerful enough to make the very rocks tremble beneath Barnabas' feet. Immediately, Barnabas and the canary desisted and, like naughty children, hung their heads sheepishly, and shuffled their feet.

Barnabas couldn't help but think that it was outrageous for this jackal-headed fellow to treat him, a respectable detective, as though he were a child to be chastised (and he was more than a little annoyed with himself for his own subservient response). However, Anubis' voice was simply so powerful, so absolutely commanding, that Barnabas felt quite intimidated.

He stole a sidelong look towards the canary and saw that the little bird was doing the same to him. The miscreant's face was scrunched up and his beak clamped tightly shut as though he were struggling to keep his mouth closed. This annoyed Barnabas, and so he pulled a face of his own, which he had to admit was quite childish but also extremely satisfying.

Anubis heaved a heavy sigh of exasperation, which made everyone immediately face forward again. "There," said Anubis. "That is better." He looked to his four animal-headed minions and gestured for them to leave. "Go. You have done quite enough. I have important business with the detective."

As the four creatures left, Barnabas couldn't help but look triumphantly at the canary. The canary, however, had apparently decided to take the high road and didn't even deign to glance at Barnabas, but instead walked with his back straight as a ramrod and his head held high. He looked out into the distance beyond Barnabas with a snooty air as though he had much more important things to attend to.

Barnabas, of course, felt immensely silly, shooting dirty looks at a canary who was in the process of ignoring him. He harrumphed grumpily.

"Are you quite done?" asked Anubis, a long-suffering

expression on his face.

"I'm quite sure I don't know what you mean," answered Barnabas primly.

Anubis sighed again. "Alright. Superb. Shall we get on with our business then?"

"Yes, indeed!" said Barnabas. "I should very much like to know why I am here!"

"You are acquainted, I presume, with a certain Egyptian fellow, a man by the name of Kesim?" asked Anubis.

"Mr. Kafele?" replied Barnabas. "Why, yes, I did quite good work for him not long ago. I helped him find his necklace that was stolen, as I recall."

"Yes, well, that *necklace* was an ankh, an object of great power. Mr. Kafele was not quite ready to wield that power and so it killed him."

"Oh dear!" exclaimed Barnabas, shocked and saddened that the one recent case that he had thought a success had actually turned out to be a failure after all. It was difficult to build a decent reputation for oneself, and to have repeat business or references, if most of one's cases resulted in the death of the client. "But that is terrible! The necklace killed him? What a tragedy!"

"Yes, yes, well, no time for sadness. Kesim Kafele is dead, and that's that," said Anubis briskly. Barnabas wondered for a moment if perhaps he ought not to have been so chagrined at the idea of *deadness* since, after all, Anubis was the god of the dead. (Barnabas had, by now, quite given up on the idea that this matter had anything whatsoever to do with Parliament. Now he was beginning to suspect that this Anubis fellow was precisely who he claimed to be.)

"Anyway," continued Anubis, "since Mr. Kafele is dead, he came here, of course. And that is how I learned of you."

"Mr. Kafele spoke of me? To you? He is angry then. He must wish to get revenge upon me for failing him," Barnabas said sadly, and with more than a touch of melancholic flourish.

"Revenge?" Anubis laughed. "On the contrary! He recommended you to me."

34

"Recommended?" asked Barnabas, confused. "For what?" His mind raced, trying to figure out the implications. Then his face dropped, aghast.

There was only one possible explanation for all of this. It was quite simple, when one thought it through. Anubis was the god of the dead. The work that Barnabas had done for Mr. Kafele had resulted in the man's own death. When added together, there was only one possible sum. "You want me to kill someone for you!" he exclaimed. "Well, I will not, I say. Barnabas Tew does not kill people."

Anubis shifted on his seat, looking a bit uncomfortable at this proclamation. "Yes, well," he said. "In fairness, Mr. Kafele might say differently."

"Oh, well, I suppose, but..." began Barnabas.

"And there was, of course, Mr. Fothergill..."

"Of course, but now, that was different."

"And poor Lady Rainford and the unfortunate business with the peanuts. One might say that you do, in fact, kill people. Somewhat regularly, it seems."

"Well, humph!" said Barnabas. "Yes, yes, all of that is true, but you see, all of those are *accidental* instances. I don't kill people *on purpose*."

"Alright, alright," said Anubis, impatient now. "You don't kill people on purpose. That is beside the point, however. You see, I don't want you to kill anyone. I'm not even sure why we are discussing it."

"Because you said that Mr. Kafele recommended me and that I had killed him," Barnabas supplied helpfully.

Beside him, Anubis' attendant appeared to be trying to hold in a laugh.

Anubis put his head down to cradle his forehead in his hands for a moment in exasperation. He muttered something under his breath. (Barnabas thought he said "Oh sweet baby Horus, why me?" but couldn't be quite sure.) Then he lifted his gaze to peek up at Barnabas through splayed fingers.

"Okay," he said with an exaggerated tone of patience. "Let's start from the beginning. Mr. Kafele had only very good things to say about you. He told me you found a certain object of great significance for him."

"That I did!" interjected Barnabas. "Can I help it if he killed himself with it? How was I to know that the ankh would make him dead?"

Anubis inhaled noisily through his nose and looked so put out by Barnabas' interruption that Barnabas apologized and put on what he thought was his most polite listening expression.

"Right," said Anubis. "So, I too have lost something of great value, and since you helped Mr. Kafele find his lost item, I thought that you could also find what I have lost."

"Ah, well, then," said Barnabas. "I suppose that I could do that." A thought occurred to him suddenly (and a dreadful one, at that). "It's not another death-ankh, is it? Because I certainly don't want to make a career of finding things of such ill repute."

"No!" boomed Anubis, losing his patience somewhat. "It is not a death-ankh." He breathed in again deeply. "Please try to follow what I am saying, and don't interrupt any more. Understood?"

Barnabas nodded sheepishly.

"Good. Listen carefully, then. You see, it is not a *thing* at all that is missing but a *who*. Do you know much about the Egyptian afterlife?"

"Well, yes. No. A little, I suppose," replied Barnabas.

"No matter. I can tell you what you need to know, and I suppose it won't be too difficult for you to figure out what you need to know to not get killed again." Barnabas would have stopped him here to ask how one might get killed again if one were already dead (if, that is, he were to accept that he was actually quite dead himself and this entire experience wasn't some bizarre scheme of sorts), but Anubis, alarmingly, continued at a rapid pace.

"You see," said Anubis, "Khepre has gone missing. Are you familiar with Khepre?"

Barnabas shook his head.

"Khepre is our scarab beetle. He is responsible for rolling Ra across the sky every morning and then down beneath the earth every night. Without Khepre the sun cannot move. The sun will no longer rise and set as it should."

"That is why it is so hot in here?" ventured Barnabas, proud of his deductive skills. He had noticed almost immediately how very bright the light was in this place and that the air was intolerably stuffy.

"Exactly," said Anubis. "And if this continues for much longer, the heat and the constant daylight will spill out onto the mortal world. There will be famine and death and chaos. You can see that this must not happen."

"Of course," agreed Barnabas. "That sounds perfectly dreadful."

"Dreadful, indeed," said Anubis. "That is the task that I have for you. You must find Khepre for us. The fate of the world depends upon it."

Barnabas felt a rush of pride at being not only recommended but also chosen to perform this task. To think that he, a small-time detective (who had only this morning thought himself an abysmal failure) would be personally selected to rescue the world from a dreadful end was an incredible honor.

He drew himself up, attempting, and nearly succeeding, in affecting an air of regal solemnity. "Fear not, Mr. Anubis," he proclaimed. "Barnabas Tew is at your service." He gave a stiff little bow to formalize his words. Anubis hid a smile behind a small cough.

"Very good," said he. "I am much pleased."

Anubis' assistant interjected, "It was Set that took him. Everyone knows it." He said this in a surprisingly petulant tone. Combined with the rather aggrieved look that Anubis shot him, it was clear that they'd had this discussion before.

"It may well be," began Anubis.

"Who, exactly, is Set?" asked Barnabas.

"The god of chaos and darkness," replied the assistant with the air of superiority that people get when they are enjoying the fact they know something they believe obvious whilst others do not. "In my opinion, he's the only one capable of such an outrageous thing."

"Again, I say, it may well be, but…" Anubis tried again.

"It *has* to be Set!" interrupted the assistant. "I mean, remember that time he chopped up Osiris? He's a terrible troublemaker and something should have been done about him long ago, if you ask me."

Anubis sighed heavily. He held up a hand and shot a warning snarl at his assistant. "I say!" he said. "It may well be Set, but there are others to consider. Things are not as black and white here as Peter may make it seem."

Barnabas wondered for a moment how an assistant to the Egyptian god of the dead came to be called Peter, but then he remembered that he himself, very much an Englishman, was in the Egyptian underworld as well. Clearly Anubis felt no compunction about harvesting British people when he needed them.

The assistant (Peter, Barnabas repeated his name, in case the fellow were to be revealed to be important later in his investigation) huffed. "Got to be Set," he muttered under his breath. He shuffled his feet so that he seemed like a small child who felt himself unfairly chastised. "I'll *bet* that it's Set, and I don't need to hire a detective to figure *that* out."

A sly expression crept over Anubis' face. "A bet, you say? Very well. If it does turn out to be Set who kidnapped Khepre, then you win. I'll make you into a minor god." He thought for a moment. "The god of investigation! There. If Set is the perpetrator, you will become my official investigator. You'll be the Chief Investigator of the Underworld!"

Peter nodded, clearly relishing the idea of himself as a god. Barnabas, ridiculously, felt a wave of jealousy as though the title of Chief Investigator of the Underworld (a title that Anubis had obviously just thought up on the spot) ought to have been his.

"But," continued Anubis with a mischievous glint in his eye, "if it is *not* Set who did this, then, well, what shall your punishment be?" He templed his fingertips and tapped them together lightly whilst he thought. "I know! If Set didn't do the deed, then I will make you into a bunny rabbit." He

38

clapped his hands together and laughed, delighted at the prospect.

Barnabas saw Peter blanch. It was clear that the assistant did not enjoy the idea of himself as a bunny rabbit nearly so much as his master did. There was a look of utter horror on his face as he contemplated the idea. But in the end, Peter's pride won out over his fear. "Fine," he muttered.

"Very good!" said Anubis. His tone was deceptively light, but Barnabas saw a clever intelligence writ upon the god's face as well as a hint of slightly malicious pleasure at his assistant's discomfiture.

Barnabas suspected that this bet had not been made on a whim, but rather, the entire situation had been quite manipulated by Anubis. He told himself that this god would bear watching, and that he had best be most careful in his dealings with him.

"So," said Anubis, turning those penetrating eyes upon Barnabas. "I suppose you'd best begin?" he suggested.

Barnabas looked about, wondering where to start. The task set before him was so important, so improbably immense, that he wasn't quite sure how to approach it. Besides, having seen two examples of Anubis clever deviousness already, cleverly trapping Peter into a silly bet in addition to cavalierly killing Barnabas with a mummy (a *mummy*!), Barnabas felt himself quite intimidated.

He thought of Wilfred and of how helpful the young man was to him. Barnabas knew that he was more than capable of making deductions on his own, of course, but having Wilfred to speak to as he worked out his thoughts certainly helped the process along.

He sighed, then muttered under his breath, "Oh, how I wish Wilfred were here."

Anubis looked at him for a moment, then turned to whisper behind his hand to his assistant. The man promptly bowed and hurried away. Barnabas wondered if this had something to do with him, but he immediately dismissed the thought. Surely Anubis had many tasks to perform that had nothing at all to do with Barnabas.

Anubis looked back at Barnabas and cocked his head impatiently.

"Well, then," Anubis suggested. "If you have no further questions, perhaps it's time to get started?"

"Oh!" said Barnabas. "Yes, of course. I was merely thinking of my strategy." This was a bit of a lie, because Barnabas had been thinking nothing of the sort. He had been thinking that, when his head was turned in that way, Anubis looked a bit like a dog waiting for a stick to be thrown. Barnabas was much too polite to say as much, however.

"Very good," said Anubis. "I trust you'll have Khepre found in no time at all, then." Anubis waved his hand, and thus was Barnabas dismissed.

Barnabas turned to leave. But as he did so, he took in the strange scenery: the black, jagged rocks, the dark sky with the reddish glow, the complete lack of wind…not to mention the strange fellow with the jackal's head who presided over all! He was reminded that not all was well. He turned back around to face Anubis.

"Am I…" he began.

Anubis sighed. "Yes?" he said. "Are you what?"

"Am I really quite dead, then?"

"Oh, well, that," replied Anubis. "Yes, I am afraid you are. It was necessary that you be dead in order to come here."

"Oh dear," said Barnabas, who was just now realizing that he ought to be very sad at leaving his life behind instead of excited about a new case, however exciting that case might be. It hadn't been the most *illustrious* life, to be sure, but it was *his* life, and he was certain that he would miss it. "Oh dear!" he repeated as the thought of *deadness* sunk in.

Anubis looked a bit uncomfortable. (As well he should, thought Barnabas indignantly. He had, after all, had him killed, and quite recently at that!) "Sorry about that, old chap," offered the god. "It had to be done, though. We can't have the living running around here in the underworld, you know. It just isn't done." Anubis looked over Barnabas' shoulder and his face brightened. "Here we are now!" he said happily. "Surely this will cheer you up!" He pointed, and

40

Barnabas turned about to look.

Coming from the same direction from which Barnabas himself had arrived were the same four scallywags who had born Barnabas hence. This time, however, the four little monsters were carrying Wilfred.

Chapter Five

"I say!" yelped Wilfred, sounding much aggrieved. "What are you about, you ruffians? I demand that you unhand me this instant!"

"Wilfred, I say!" cried Barnabas. "Oh, my dear boy, whatever are you doing here?"

"There has been an accident," replied Wilfred. "I think I might be quite dead, to tell you the truth."

"How? What has happened to you?"

"I ran out of the museum after we were separated. I thought that perhaps you had come out as well, and so I looked for you. I was just crossing the street so that I might get a better view of things when, as if out of nowhere, a carriage came along…"

"Oh my!" exclaimed Barnabas. "Are you alright?"

Wilfred shot Barnabas a sarcastic look. "I suppose I'm alright," he answered diplomatically, "for being dead and such." Wilfred looked around, taking in the strangeness of the place. "The odd thing is the driver of the carriage looked to me to be a…"

"Yes?" prompted Barnabas.

"Well, I think… I mean, that is to say…"

Barnabas waited patiently.

"I'm almost certain that it was a mummy driving the carriage. A *mummy*!" Wilfred shook his head to and fro in confusion. "But that cannot be. This…" He gestured to the black rocks, dark sky, and four animal-headed kidnappers. "*This* cannot be. I must be seeing things. I'm sure that I must have bumped my head."

"A mummy, you say?" asked Barnabas.

"Yes, a mummy. It was quite terrifying, really," replied

Wilfred. "I'm glad that it was just a hallucination brought on by my head injury."

Barnabas looked from Wilfred, who was struggling with the four little man-handlers, to Anubis. An awful realization came over Barnabas. Not only was *this*, as Wilfred had declared their now shared dilemma, entirely real but the cause of it all was sitting behind him, trying to appear quite busy.

"You!" he accused Anubis. "You killed Wilfred, too? How? Why?"

Anubis looked uncomfortable and pretended as though he hadn't heard Barnabas. He suddenly took a great interest in his fingernails, studying them carefully whilst whistling a happy tune and sneaking little glances at Barnabas and Wilfred.

"Oh!" said Barnabas, irritated that the god refused to meet his gaze. What sort of merciless person ran about having people killed by mummies willy-nilly? He reminded himself that Anubis was most dangerous indeed.

However, he was also very annoyed with Anubis for murdering first Barnabas himself and now Wilfred. "Anubis!" he yelled so that the god, reluctantly, was forced to acknowledge him. "Why did you kill Wilfred?" he demanded. "And don't try to say you didn't. People aren't typically run over by mummies every day in London, you know."

Anubis affected an innocent expression. "You said that you wished Wilfred were here," he replied in a tone that suggested he couldn't understand what all of this fuss was about. "And so," he said, opening his arms and holding his hands palms up beneficently, "here he is!" He widened his eyes and blinked like an amiable puppy, but Barnabas wasn't fooled.

"Ah!" he cried. "You... You can't keep killing people!" Anubis smiled, still blinking with his puppy eyes.

"Oh!" said Barnabas. "You are simply incorrigible! But if I am going to work for you, there must be no more killing people with mummies." Anubis hesitated. "You must agree or

43

find yourself another detective," Barnabas said with no small measure of righteous indignation.

"Very well," sighed Anubis. "No more mummies." He appeared to be contrite, but Barnabas saw that mischievous glint in his eye again and suspected that he might just have been tricked, just as Peter had been. He thought back over what was said but failed to see a loophole in the agreement that Anubis might exploit.

"Well, alright then," he said doubtfully. He turned to Wilfred and sighed. "I suppose we are both here now, so we may as well get on with it then," he said. He began to walk (he wasn't quite sure exactly *where* he was heading, but he felt a strong urge to get *away* from Anubis and his awful minions), and Wilfred, now free of the four minions of Anubis, fell into step beside him. "We have a case, you see."

"A case?" asked Wilfred. "What sort of case?"

"Anubis wants us to find Khepre. It seems he has gone missing."

"And who is Khepre?"

"Hmm," said Barnabas a bit smugly, as he was enjoying the feeling of knowing something that Wilfred did not and wanted to prolong the moment. It did not bother him in the slightest that he himself had only just found out about Khepre only minutes before. "Khepre," he continued, making a slight flourish with his hand for dramatic effect, "is the scarab beetle god of the Egyptian pantheon…"

"Oh!" interrupted Wilfred eagerly. "The one who rolls the sun about like a ball of dung?"

"Harumph!" said Wilfred, a bit petulantly. Really, he thought, Wilfred could be quite the know-it-all at times. It was a most annoying habit. "Yes, that's the fellow. However did you know that?"

Wilfred sensed his employer's displeasure and blushed. He quickly tried to soothe Barnabas' bruised pride. "I'm sure I only knew it from working on Mr. Kesim Kafele's case with you. That and the Egyptian Studies course at university…" His voice trailed off.

"Yes, well, that's the fellow. He rolls the sun around the

horizon, and without him to do so the sun will not move. It will be stuck up there…" He gestured towards the bright sun frozen at the high noon position. "Forever."

Wilfred shuddered at the thought. "Why, it will overheat everything. Crops will burn. Rivers will dry up. It will be terrible!"

"Indeed!" agreed Barnabas. "That is why Anubis himself has chosen me…I mean *us* to find Khepre and set things back to normal again. Oh, Mr. Kesim Kafele is dead, by the by."

"Oh dear! Really? Mr. Kafele? Dead?"

Barnabas nodded.

Wilfred paused to consider. "Was it something … Was it *our fault*?" He uttered those last words in a loud stage whisper, looking around to make certain that no one else could hear.

Barnabas shrugged and raised his hands as though to say, "Well, what can you do?" Wilfred cringed.

"Oh no," said Wilfred. "I do hope that he's not too put out with us about it."

"On the contrary!" said Barnabas. "He recommended us to Anubis for the good work that we did. We couldn't help it if his ankh killed him, after all. Which reminds me. We have a scarab beetle to find!"

Wilfred looked around at the bleak landscape of the Egyptian underworld. "Well," he said doubtfully, "where shall we start?"

"The locals around here seem to suspect Set," said Barnabas.

"I know who that is!" exclaimed Wilfred. He searched his memory for anything he may have learned about Set in his Egyptian Studies class. "Let's see. Set is related to Anubis and Isis and Osiris somehow. I can't remember exactly how…" His voice trailed off for a moment. "But no matter. I remember that he once chopped up Osiris into little bits and Isis had to run about the underworld finding his parts in order to reconstruct him."

"Yes, well, that story sounds *quite* familiar," said Barnabas (although, in truth, it did not sound familiar to him

45

at all). "But I think we should explore other suspects first. You see, the solution to a case is never the most obvious, or logical, one. The solution is usually quite convoluted and difficult to reason out."

Wilfred nodded agreement, although secretly he was quite sure that it was the other way around. However, it was not his place to correct his employer whilst he thought a case through, and so he kept his silence.

"So," said Barnabas. "It was the maid who stole Mr. Kafele's ankh, was it not? It stands to reason, then, that perhaps Khepre's maid stole Khepre himself!" He paused, overcome with his own genius.

Wilfred nodded again. He was quite certain that the god's maid probably hadn't kidnapped him (did Egyptian gods even *have* maids?), but he did think that it was a good idea to investigate Khepre's abode. They could interview the members of his household and perhaps glean some information from them. "Very well, then!" he said brightly. He hailed a man with a sheep's head who happened to be passing by them just at that moment. "I say, good sir, do you know the way to Khepre's residence?"

The sheep-man turned and pointed in the direction of a large, craggy mountain on the other side of a very wide river. It looked to be quite far away, and Barnabas and Wilfred groaned in unison at the prospect of walking such a distance. However, there seemed to be no other choice at the moment (there were no hansoms for hire in the underworld, it seemed, or at least not in this particular part of it), and so they set off without further complaint.

As they walked, Barnabas glanced at Wilfred. "Did you happen to come here by boat?" he asked.

"Why, yes. You?"

"Indeed. I suppose that must be the standard way one gets here," said Barnabas.

"Quite so. The ferryman to the Land of the Dead and what not," agreed Wilfred.

"And what did you think of the ferryman?" asked Barnabas.

"He seemed an amiable enough fellow," said Wilfred.

"Yes, of course," said Barnabas. He thought for a moment. "But did you find him a bit, er, *disconcerting* at first?"

"You mean because of the falcon-ness of him, the missing toes, and such?" said Wilfred.

"Precisely!" said Barnabas. "I fear that I may have been quite rude, but I was a bit taken aback, I must admit."

"Perfectly understandable," said Wilfred. "It's not every day one finds oneself in the company of a giant falcon man, after all. I'm sure he must understand, if not expect, a bit of a reaction to his unusual presentation."

"He must, indeed!" said Barnabas, feeling relieved. His less-than-polite initial reaction to the boatman had been bothering him, and he was pleased to be reassured that he hadn't behaved *too* improperly.

They walked for a very long time in the direction of the mountain. Wilfred looked about doubtfully as the place seemed quite deserted. It had been a long time since they had seen any other people about (the afterlife was not nearly as populous as one might assume, he thought) whilst Barnabas chatted single-mindedly on the subject of Khepre's hypothetically evil maid and her alleged crimes.

Wilfred paid little heed to Barnabas' ramblings; he was too concerned with where they were, where they were going, and whether or not either place was entirely safe. And moreover, he knew his employer well and therefore surmised that Barnabas would soon be distracted by something else and forget all about his fixation upon the poor maid, who may or may not even exist.

At last they came to the river that they had seen before setting out. Now that they had come to it, however, it seemed a great deal more impassable than they had thought. For one thing, the water flowed rather swiftly, so swiftly that they thought it might not merely buffet them about but knock them off their feet entirely. For another, the river was also very wide, and therefore it was impossible to tell from where they now stood how deep it might be in the middle. Neither

47

was very keen on getting wet up to their necks, or their chins, or their eyebrows.

But the worst aspect of the whole thing was the hippos. There, in the middle of the slimmest and shallowest-looking spot they could see, wallowed a great lot of the beasts. They were huge creatures, and whilst hippos seemed to be quite adorable, lazy creatures when seen from afar in a proper zoo, here in the wild they seemed a fair bit more daunting. The beasts had enormous sharp-looking teeth that were used quite liberally upon each other; indeed, the things went after each other mercilessly whenever one happened to bump into another, or indeed to encroach upon another's space by just floating by a little too closely.

Barnabas and Wilfred shared a trepidatious glance as they shared the same thought. Those teeth looked wickedly sharp and the jaws snapped to with tremendous force. Neither relished the idea of one of the giant beasts running after him with a wide open mouth and murderous intent in its eyes. Since the hippos all seemed to be somewhat cranky and very free with their teeth, such an occurrence seemed not only possible but quite probable. Even now, some of the hippos on the edge were eyeing them with nasty looking expressions, as though daring them to come any closer.

Still, their destination lay just on the other side of the river, and there were only two choices: cross the river somehow or give up their quest entirely. So they stood on the bank, scratching their heads and thinking about how they might get across the river unmolested by angry hippos whilst also not getting too terribly wet.

"I wonder if the hippos might not just up and leave at some point," ventured Barnabas at last. "Surely they must *go* places sometimes."

Wilfred frowned as he considered the hippos that barred their way. "They seem to be quite settled in at the moment," he said doubtfully. "Look. That one is having a proper nap."

Barnabas noticed that not just one but several of the hippos had closed their eyes and looked to be settling in for a good long sleep.

"I'm certain they'd wake up quick enough if we were to try to pass them by," he said somewhat resentfully, as though the hippos had placed themselves in the way solely to thwart himself and Wilfred.

"We could try walking upstream a bit," suggested Wilfred. "See if it gets any narrower or less, well, filled with hippos."

Barnabas looked upstream. "A good plan. But look, there," he said, gesturing. "That's a good sized cliff. We'd have to either climb it or go entirely around, and who knows how long that would take or how far we would have to stray from our path to that mountain?"

"Hmm," said Wilfred. "Perhaps downstream?"

"It only gets wider, it seems." Barnabas thought for a moment. "Perhaps we could throw things in the river and startle the hippos away."

Wilfred frowned. "It might just make them angry with us. I don't know how fast they can move on land, but I certainly don't want to find out."

Altogether it seemed that, for all of their ideas, they were making very little progress on their problem, and at last they gave up and simply stood there. They were growing more and more disheartened, feeling as though they had failed before they had even properly begun, when the monkey-things came.

Barnabas and Wilfred heard them before they saw them. A low whine thrummed through the air. It had, in truth, been audible for some time, but their attention had been so fully focused on the hippos and the problem of crossing the river that neither had paid it any mind.

However, the sound had steadily grown louder until it was so intrusive that it at last caught their attention.

"Whatever is that terrible racket?" griped Barnabas.

"I don't know," replied Wilfred. "But does it seem to be getter louder to you?"

The sound was, in fact, increasing quite quickly in volume now, as though whatever was making the noise had changed course and was making its way swiftly towards them.

"It sounds like bees," observed Barnabas, frowning. He was listening to the droning part of the noise, the part that sounded like the rapid flutter of insectile wings. Barnabas, who was afraid of bees and any other flying thing that stung, did not much relish the thought of a swarm of bees, particularly Egyptian underworld-type bees.

"Or a great lot of dogs barking," suggested Wilfred, who was now noticing the more vocal part of the noise, which sounded like an incessant chattering. It sounded like the sort of noise a great mob of people make when they are being rowdy but much more animalistic. He was not keen to find out what sort of a mob this might be that seemed to be approaching with such speed.

By this time the noise had grown so loud that the din made it difficult to think. Barnabas and Wilfred looked about, searching for the source of the noise. Neither, however, thought to look *up*, to look into the sky until it was too late.

A flicker of movement from the air at last caught Wilfred's eye. "Ahhh!" he screamed.

Barnabas, following his gaze, screamed as well. "Monkey-demons!" he squealed. (This statement would have seemed nonsensical to anyone who wasn't there or who hadn't experienced the Egyptian underworld first-hand. Unfortunately for Wilfred, though, the statement made perfect sense.)

The thing that had been making all the racket had come upon them at last, and it was far more terrible than either of them could have imagined: a great swarm of flying creatures about the size of cats. Since they were now quite close, Barnabas and Wilfred could see them individually, and neither much liked what he saw.

The creatures, though small, were quite terrifying. They looked like little gorillas, with high brow ridges and bushy eyebrows. Their eyes were red and mere slits, and their mouths were too small so that their long, yellow teeth, which looked horribly pointy, stuck out akimbo from between their lips.

The things shrieked and snarled and spit as they came close, so that the overall effect was one of extreme unfriendliness. In response, Barnabas and Wilfred gave in to panic and began to run about in circles. They flailed their arms in terror as the things descended upon them.

"Oh! Oh!" yelped Barnabas as a monkey-demon dipped down and swiped at his head with its claws. Only his hat saved him from suffering a cruel scratch to the scalp. The creature tried to fly away with the hat, but Barnabas held on to it tightly with one hand whilst swatting ineffectually at the loathsome creature with his other. "My hat!" he yelled. "Stop it, stop it, stop it!" Together, he and the flying monkey pulled back and forth determinedly at the hat in an absurd tug-of-war.

Two of the other monkeys grasped Wilfred by the arms of his coat jacket and seemed intent on carrying him away entirely. They were far too small to do so, of course, but as a third and then a fourth descended upon him, he saw that, if enough of the nasty little fellows worked together, they might just succeed. "Help!" he cried, waving his arms in a vain attempt to cast off his attackers.

In his struggles, he fell to the ground. Immediately, more of the things fell upon him. At last there were enough of them, and he felt himself being lifted off the ground. He turned his head, looking for help, and saw that Barnabas was suffering the same treatment.

Terrified, both men struggled madly to throw off their attackers, but it was no use. There were too many of them; each time one was kicked or swatted away, two more swooped in to take its place. It seemed that Barnabas and Wilfred had lost this battle and were to be carried away to whatever foul purpose the monkey-demons intended for them.

Suddenly, a greater, louder sound than that the monkey-things had made boomed across the land. It was so loud that the very air vibrated from it. The monkeys all stopped their chatter and froze in midflight so that there was a moment of complete and intense stillness.

The eyes of the little monkeys were no longer narrow slits, but round and wide with fear. Barnabas and Wilfred exchanged a glance from where they hovered in mid-air, still in the grip of their captors.

Barnabas and Wilfred were thinking the same thing: if they were afraid of the monkey-things and the monkey-things were afraid of whatever it was that had made this new, horrible sound, then it stood to reason that Barnabas and Wilfred wouldn't much like it either.

The booming sound happened again, and, at once, the monkey-demons sprang back to life. Hastily, they dropped their prisoners (who were, in truth, only a few inches from the ground, but nevertheless found the experience of falling most frightening and undignified). Then, making as much noise leaving as they had in coming, the monkey-demons flew swiftly away.

Wilfred looked to Barnabas, hoping that his employer would have some strategy for escaping whatever new menace now came towards them. Barnabas, however, merely squinched his eyes shut and pretended to be either dead or sound asleep. Wilfred, with no other better idea, did the same.

They heard footsteps approaching and soon felt a shadow fall over them.

"You can open your eyes, you know," said a voice.

Neither complied.

The voice sighed. "I know you're pretending," it said. "I'm not stupid." The toe of a boot prodded each one in whichever body part was nearest to the owner of the voice: the thigh for Barnabas and the ribs for Wilfred. At this, they decided there was nothing for it but to obey, and so they both reluctantly opened their eyes to see the figure that stood above them.

Chapter Six

Standing before them, blocking the sun from their view, was a large, barrel-chested man. Both were relieved to see an actual human rather than the strange hybrid creatures that were so prevalent here. He smiled a bit as he looked down at them, trying to hide a laugh at their absurd attempts to feign unconsciousness.

"Well, hello," said Barnabas, recovering his manners as best he might under the circumstances. "Who might you be?"

"I am Bes," said the man, "the god of sweet dreams."

"Sweet dreams?" asked Wilfred. "As in cakes and things?"

"I wouldn't mind a nice pastry," agreed Barnabas.

Bes blinked, taken aback by the silliness of the two people he had just saved. He wasn't quite sure how to answer, and he contemplated just leaving the two of them lying there. However, they looked so afraid, and yet so hopeful at the mere thought of pastry, that he found he didn't want to simply abandon them. In light of the fright that the two had just taken, he decided to take the way of patience.

"No," he said slowly. "As in the opposite of bad dreams. I chase away nightmares and other scary things."

"Oh," said Barnabas, clearly disappointed that there were to be no cakes or pastries.

"I believe that I've heard of you," said Wilfred. "You are one of the protector gods, yes?"

"Indeed I am," agreed Bes, thinking now that perhaps the two of them had a set of wits, between them at least.

"Ah, how exciting!" exclaimed Wilfred. "Barnabas, we have been rescued by one of the oldest gods in the Egyptian pantheon!"

"Well," said Barnabas. "Thank you very much." He rose and dusted himself off as best he could. Wilfred did the same beside him. "Those horrible monkey-things meant us no good, I am sure," continued Barnabas.

"No, they did not," agreed Bes. "Terrible creatures. They like to carry their prey alive to their dens and then…" He broke off upon seeing the looks of horror on Barnabas' and Wilfred's faces.

"Are they… Are they quite gone?" ventured Barnabas after a slight pause.

"Certainly," said Bes. "But I must ask: what brings you to this deserted place? It isn't safe to just wander about the underworld, you know."

"We are on a job," proclaimed Barnabas. He stood up tall and tried to look dignified. The effect was marred somewhat by the splotch of flying monkey feces that had landed upon his coat lapel, but he was blissfully unaware of that as yet. "We have been commissioned by Anubis himself."

"Ah, yes!" said Bes, tactfully ignoring the mess. "You must be the detectives Anubis hired to find Khepre."

"We are!" exclaimed Barnabas proudly.

"How did you know that?" asked Wilfred suspiciously at the same time.

"Oh, everyone knows everything around here," said Bes (sounding rather self-important, Barnabas thought). "It's a small place, you know."

Wilfred looked around the vast, empty place doubtfully. "Well," he said politely, "alright. I suppose so."

An idea struck Barnabas. "Well then!" he cried. "If everyone knows everything, then you must know the whereabouts of Khepre!" He smiled, pleased at the thought that he had solved the case so easily.

"Oh, well, no, not exactly," said Bes.

"But I thought you said…"

"Yes," said Bes peremptorily. He waved his hand airily. "A figure of speech is all. Of course I don't know where Khepre is or who might have taken him. But," he continued, pausing for dramatic effect, "I do have a clue for you."

Barnabas (who had pursed his lips and squinted his eyes in disapproval of Bes' dismissive tone) couldn't help but be excited anew at the prospect of a clue. His lips un-pursed and his eyes un-squinted as he leaned forward eagerly. Still Bes' dramatic pause continued on. It seemed the god was in no hurry to divulge his information. "A clue?" Barnabas prompted at last when he grew tired of waiting.

"Yes, indeed! Here it is," said Bes. He rummaged about in, first, one pocket and then the other. "Wait a moment. I had it just a minute ago." Bes searched his pockets for an aggravatingly long time whilst Barnabas and Wilfred waited impatiently. It seemed that Bes never looked quite all the way to the bottom of any of the pockets, merely patting about at the top, so that each pocket had to be investigated multiple times.

The process went on for so long (how many pockets did the fellow have, thought Barnabas, and why couldn't he look through any of them properly the first time?) that Barnabas was barely able to suppress a sigh of exasperation. But at last, Bes pulled something that looked like a stick triumphantly out of the very first pocket he had searched and thrust it proudly into Barnabas' face.

"Oh, yes, well, quite informative, that," said Barnabas politely, although he had no idea what the thing was.

But it seemed that Wilfred did have an idea. "Oh no!" he exclaimed when he saw it.

"Yes," said Bes gravely.

"Where did you find it?" asked Wilfred sombrely.

"Over there," said Bes, pointing towards the north towards the giant cliff that Barnabas had mentioned earlier and had been loath to go around. "In the desert. Near Set's abode," he added meaningfully.

"Ah, Set," said Wilfred thoughtfully. "So, it's just like before, then, you think?"

"Perhaps," said Bes. "It certainly doesn't look good."

"No," said Wilfred. "Not good at all."

"Yes, terrible," agreed Barnabas, not wanting to seem slow-witted, although he couldn't have said why the two of them were getting so worked up over a stick. Still, he was annoyed at being left out of the conversation and felt that he ought to contribute somehow.

"Well, that would certainly explain all of these hippos," said Wilfred.

"Indeed it would," agreed Bes.

"Mmmm," said Barnabas, attempting to appear to be carefully thinking over the matter of the stick whilst wondering what the hippos had to do with it.

"So," said Wilfred, "have any other of his, uh, well…" He paused delicately. "Have any of his other parts been found?"

"No," said Bes. "Just this…"

At that moment Barnabas realized that the thing that Bes was holding was no stick. Indeed, it was the leg of a giant bug. Probably, more precisely the leg of an enormous scarab beetle god named Khepre. "Ewww!" he squealed, horrified.

Wilfred and Bes looked at him quizzically, so that Barnabas flushed in embarrassment. "Sorry," he said. He tried to think of a way to cover his late arrival to the conclusion that Wilfred had reached so quickly. "Just a bit of hippo dung is all." He brushed at his shoe, pretending an interest in the imaginary excrement.

"Well, alright then!" said Bes, feeling that he had done his duty by these two odd little detectives and could now, in good conscience, leave them to their own devices. "Do be careful. And good luck!" he said by way of taking his leave. He turned to go, then looked down at Khepre's leg, which he still held in his hand. "Oh, here you go," he said, proffering the leg to Barnabas, who took it reluctantly and politely thanked him.

"One last question," said Barnabas. "If you don't mind, that is?"

"Of course," replied Bes graciously (masking his impatience to be off and away quite well, he thought. He had already spent more time than he had thought to spend with Barnabas and Wilfred, and he still had a lot of work to do today. After all, demons and nightmares were rampant across

56

the underworld, and, as the official god in charge of chasing away such things, he was kept quite busy.)

"Does... Did... Ahem, that is to say... *Is* there a maid employed at Khepre's estate?" asked Barnabas.

Bes thought for a moment. "Yes, I'm certain that Khepre must have had quite a few servants. Although I don't know what will become of them now that he is missing. Perhaps they have sought out work elsewhere by now."

Barnabas, feeling vindicated and clever once again, shot a significant glance at Wilfred, who suppressed an amused smile. Bes turned to leave again and waved his hand in farewell. "Good day to you both," he called over his shoulder, and he hurried off to be about his business.

Barnabas and Wilfred waved goodbye to their erstwhile rescuer and watched as Bes strode jauntily off. His bandy little legs moved with surprising speed under his stout body, he was soon gone from view.

"So," said Barnabas, turning to Wilfred. "Interesting bit about the hippos, isn't it?" He was anxious to know what Wilfred and Bes had been talking about, but he didn't want to seem as though he didn't know already.

"Yes indeed!" said Wilfred. "Quite coincidental, don't you think?"

"Obviously!" said Barnabas. He paused, trying to think of a way to get more information out of Wilfred without coming straight out and asking for it. At last, he had an idea. "What then," he tried, "do you find to be the most interesting connection with the hippos?"

"Well," said Wilfred, "we know that Set has already chopped up one god in the past. So we know he is quite capable of such a thing."

"Yes, yes," agreed Barnabas. He remembered that Wilfred had said something earlier about Set hacking somebody up and scattering him piecemeal throughout the underworld. He looked at the leg in his hand and thought he saw where Wilfred was going with this. He held up the leg and nodded sagely.

"So," continued Wilfred, "if he could do it to Osiris

himself…" (ah, yes! thought Barnabas, *that* was who had been chopped up. And, he remembered, Isis herself had gone about, collecting his parts and putting him back together), then he could easily do the same to Khepre."

"Indeed he could!" agreed Barnabas. A thought occurred to him. "But *would* he is the question! It seems so obvious that everyone would immediately think of Set as soon as they heard someone had been cut to pieces. Just as we did," he concluded, ignoring the fact that he himself hadn't jumped to that conclusion quite as quickly as he assumed everyone else would have.

"You have a point," conceded Wilfred, thinking it over.

"And," pointed out Barnabas, "one would expect a god to be a good deal more clever than to commit the same crime twice."

"Indeed," agreed Wilfred. "One would expect."

"So it must needs be someone else and they are framing Set," said Barnabas.

"And the coincidence of Set having a hippo head and all of these hippos, well, that could easily be part of a set-up as well."

"I'm sure that is what it is!" said Barnabas, glad to have the mystery of the hippo coincidence cleared up. "A set-up! A frame! Or," he conjectured, "perhaps that is what Set *wants* us to think. Perhaps he really *is* the perpetrator and made the crime point so obviously to himself that no one would think he could have possibly done it!"

The two of them thought this convoluted logic over for a few moments. However, no matter how hard they thought about the circumstances, they were unable to come to a satisfactory conclusion. They simply didn't have enough information. And the only evidence they had was the beetle leg in Barnabas' hand.

"I suppose," sighed Barnabas, "there's nothing for it but for us to go to Set." He eyed the huge cliff around which they must travel doubtfully. "Although I do wish that we didn't have to walk around that enormous thing," he said sadly.

"If only there was a way to cross the river," said Wilfred.

"The going looks far easier on that side."

Now, it seemed, they were back to the same problem they were grappling with when they were so shockingly interrupted by the monkey-things: how they might cross the river in light of the depth and the current and the hippos. Once more, the problem seemed entirely insurmountable as neither could think of a satisfactory solution.

"I know!" exclaimed Barnabas after quite a bit of time had passed. "We can wear disguises!"

"Pardon?" asked Wilfred, not seeing how wearing a disguise would help with the problem at hand.

"We can disguise ourselves so Set doesn't know who we are. If he doesn't know who we are, then he will have no need to chop us into little bits and scatter us about the place." In truth, Barnabas had thought so long and so hard on the issue of crossing the river that he had grown bored and his mind drifted to their next difficulty: namely, Set's penchant for separating people from their component parts.

"Oh!" said Wilfred. "Yes, quite so." He, too, thought about it for a few minutes. "But what shall we disguise ourselves as?" he asked at last.

Barnabas looked about for ideas. A field mouse rustled about in the grasses nearby, and a family of larks sang from the reeds that lined the riverbank. And, of course, the hippos were still there, lounging in the river. "Hmmm," said Barnabas, considering all of these things. "Little animals, perhaps? Set wouldn't feel threatened by two little mice poking about."

"No, he wouldn't," agreed Wilfred. "But how would we make such a disguise? It's not as if we have cloth or a needle and thread, or anything at all really."

"I suppose we don't." Barnabas sighed. "We'll just have to make do with what is available." He reached down, pulled up a handful of dried grass, and considered it for a moment. "This might do as fur," he thought aloud. "But how would we affix it to ourselves?"

Wilfred darted to the river bank (or as close as he dared, considering the ever-present hippos), and squatted to press his fingers into the mud. "This is quite thick," he said. "Perhaps we could use it as a glue of sorts."

"Smashing idea!" exclaimed Barnabas, excited now that one of their problems, at least, was being solved. "And we can rip off little bits of those reeds for whiskers!"

Immediately the two began to rush about gathering materials for their disguises. When they had enough, they approached the river bank, giving the hippos a wide berth, of course.

"Well," said Barnabas, looking doubtfully down at the thick, oozing mud. It stuck to the bottoms of their shoes and made slurpy suctioning sounds when they picked their feet up. There was also a ripe, earthy smell to it that wasn't altogether pleasant.

He didn't much like the idea of slathering the stuff all over himself, but he liked the idea of being disassembled by Set even less and they needed the mud to get the grasses and reeds to stick to them so that he might not recognize them. "I suppose there's nothing for it but to just get it over with," he said, and he promptly plopped himself into the mud. He rolled about so that soon he was entirely covered in the stuff.

Laughing, Wilfred followed suit, and once they were both properly encased in mud they sat up and began sticking their collections of assorted vegetation on atop it. The mud dried quickly in the hot, perpetually noontime sun, and so it took very little time for them to complete their costumes.

They stood up and surveyed each other's disguises. Of course, neither looked anything like a field mouse, or like any other kind of animal at all. Instead, they merely looked like people who had rolled about in some mud and stuck grasses all over themselves.

Each privately thought to himself that his own disguise must look a good deal better than his companion's, but both were far too polite to say so.

"You look...," began Wilfred, "great."

"As do you," agreed Barnabas.

They stood there for a moment, feeling quite pleased with themselves, and then Wilfred turned to regard the river and the hippos once more.

"So," he said, "what shall we do about crossing the river?"

Of course, Barnabas had no answer to this, and they were right back where they had begun. The only difference was that now they were covered in warm, dried mud that creaked and groaned when they walked and made even their light jackets feel quite stifling.

"I think that we ought to just walk in and see how deep it is," said Barnabas at last. "If it gets too deep, we can always just turn around."

"And the hippos?" asked Wilfred.

"They probably won't even notice us, now that we are disguised." He eyed Wilfred's get-up doubtfully. "Although it wouldn't hurt to get as far upstream from them as we possibly can."

Wilfred reluctantly agreed that this was the only course of action open to them. They walked up the river bank as far as they could before the cliff impeded their progress. When they could go no further, they shared a glance, steeled themselves, and stepped into the cool knee-deep water.

"Well, this is not so bad," said Barnabas. Emboldened, he waded out even farther, followed by Wilfred.

The hippos, for their part, were not fooled by the disguises, but neither did they have much interest in the two creatures who had bedecked themselves outlandishly and then splashed about so clumsily in the river. A few of the hippos exchanged disparaging looks, then continued about their business of lounging and bickering amongst themselves in the refreshing water.

As Barnabas and Wilfred reached the center of the stream, the water deepened a bit, but it went no higher than their waists. The current, too, was cooperative. It pushed gently at them so that they had to angle their bodies a bit to make sure that they maintained a straight line across and didn't drift downwards towards the hippos (who were most certainly feigning indifference, Barnabas and Wilfred were sure), but it never caused them to lose their balance or topple

61

over.

Of course, the water wetted the dried mud so that it washed off entirely from their waists down, taking the stuck grasses with it. This was how Anti, the falcon-headed boatman, found them: waist deep in the middle of the river with a great lot of vegetation bristling out from their heads and coats.

Chapter Seven

Barnabas and Wilfred were both glad to see Anti again and greeted him warmly.

"Hullo!" called Barnabas, waving to him. Curious, Anti rowed his boat to where the two stood, the river swirling about their legs.

"What are the two of you doing?" asked Anti.

"We are crossing the river," said Barnabas, "and then we must head upstream."

Anti sighed. He himself was heading upstream, and so there was no real reason he shouldn't offer the two of them a ride. "And you are going...where?" he asked.

"To Set's house," replied Barnabas.

"That is quite a distance," said Anti.

"Oh dear," said Barnabas.

"Oh no," agreed Wilfred, thinking about the uncomfortable prospect of walking a great distance in sodden shoes and eyeing Anti's boat wistfully.

Anti sighed again. "Hop in," he said, somewhat regretfully. He didn't much relish spending such a long time with the two silly detectives, but he felt sorry for them, and besides, it wasn't as if it would take him out of his way.

As Barnabas and Wilfred clambered aboard, they looked quite ridiculous with their upper parts entirely covered in mud and grass and their lower parts soaking wet and completely devoid of such accoutrements. Anti covered a snicker with his wing and gestured for them to sit on the bench in the prow.

"Where are you two fine fellows off to, besides Set's, that is?" he asked politely after they had offered him profuse thanks. He eyed their torsos with the grasses and reeds sticking out in all directions. "Is that some sort of British outfit?" he asked doubtfully.

"No, it is our disguise," said Wilfred.

"A disguise for what?" asked Anti.

"We have been hired by Anubis himself to investigate a kidnapping; indeed, it is a kidnapping that now seems to have become a case of murder most foul." He had always wanted to say that bit about "murder most foul" and was quite pleased that at last an opportunity had come for him to bring it into conversation in a natural sort of way.

"And so we are on our way to see Set," added Wilfred helpfully.

"Ah," said Anti, frowning, still not quite certain why a visit to the god of chaos and darkness might involve plastering oneself with riparian vegetation. "I...see?"

Seeing that Anti was still confused, Barnabas added, "As you no doubt know, Set is prone to chopping people up. Hence," he waved his hands to indicate his clothes, "the disguises." His tone was that of a man explaining the most obvious thing in the world.

Anti, of course, was no more enlightened as to the reason for the disguises now than he had been before the conversation began. However, he quickly lost interest in the topic as soon as Barnabas brought up the matter about Set's penchant for dismembering people. His ears pricked up and he leaned forward intently.

"And you are the official detectives on the case?" asked Anti. "Hired by Anubis himself?"

"Yes, we are indeed," said Barnabas proudly. "He sent for us specifically. Although," he frowned, "of course, the way in which he got us here was most undignified and quite frightening. Completely unnecessary, don't you think, to involve mummies?"

"Yes, yes," said Anti impatiently. He knew nothing about the mummies nor the manner in which Anubis had brought these two hence, nor did he wish to hear Barnabas expound upon such things. He fluttered his wings as though to hurry the conversation along. "But he brought you here, specifically, to investigate this kidnapping, this murder?"

"Quite so!" said Barnabas. "Hence the need to interview Set in all haste, and also, well, this." He gestured towards the bizarre disguises again, but Anti was quick to interrupt before he could go off on that particular tangent once more.

"So you think Set has something to do with, ah, this murder that you are investigating?" he asked.

"Why, of course," Barnabas said. He lifted Khepre's leg to show it to the boatman. "Who else would do something such as this!"

"I see," said Anti, a glint of something (malice? bitterness? spite? or perhaps it was merely the excitement of someone finding pleasure in the anticipation of something bad happening to someone else; a deplorable character trait to be sure, but yet, sadly, all too common) in his eyes. Wilfred saw the look, but he couldn't quite put his finger on what it was. He did know, however, that it made him feel a bit uneasy. "You found Khepre's leg?" asked the falcon man eagerly.

"Yes! It was given to us not an hour ago by..." Barnabas broke off, blinking rapidly, then drew back in suspicion. "Wait a moment! How did you know that this was Khepre's leg that I hold?" he demanded.

Anti sat back. "Oh," he said nonchalantly, waving a wing dismissively, "*everyone* knows that it's Khepre that has gone missing."

"But I don't think that *everyone* knows he was dismembered. We only just found out about that bit ourselves," replied Barnabas doubtfully.

"Well," sniffed Anti, putting on an air of injured sensibility, "it is quite obvious that it is an insect leg that you have in your hand. And since it is Khepre that has gone missing, and he is, indeed, an insect, and thus possessed of insect *legs*, plus the fact that you are going to visit Set, and Set likes to chop people up, well, it is easy enough to conclude that this must, then, be Khepre's leg."

"Oh dear," said Barnabas. He saw the sense in what Anti had said, and now he felt guilty for having offended the person who had just lifted them out of the water and was even now giving them a ride. "I'm terribly sorry," he said. "It's just been quite a trying day. I certainly hope that I didn't offend you horribly."

"No matter," said Anti in an aggrieved tone.

"Really, I meant nothing by it. I'm a detective, you know, and it's my job to question everyone and everything. Just being thorough, is all," concluded Barnabas lamely.

Anti sighed as he looked out over the water with a melancholic air, the very picture of falsely accused innocence. An awkward silence descended upon the boat, and they rowed in utter quiet for some minutes.

"Do you know much about Set?" asked Wilfred at last in an attempt to lighten the mood.

Anti let out a harsh laugh tinged more than a little by bitterness. "Do I know much about Set?" he asked wryly. "Oh yes, I could tell you some things about Set."

Barnabas and Wilfred waited expectantly, but it seemed that Anti wanted them to draw the information out of him piece by piece. Really, thought Barnabas, the manners of these underworld people were sorely lacking.

"Perhaps, then," he prompted, trying to keep the impatience from his voice, "you might tell us these things?"

"Well, what exactly would you like to know?" demanded Anti.

"Hmmm," thought Barnabas. "I suppose I'd like to know anything that you happen to know about him," he said.

"I know quite a bit, so that doesn't really narrow it down at all," replied Anti.

Wilfred, seeing that this conversation was swiftly going nowhere, decided to try to steer it towards a more productive course. "Have you yourself had any dealings with Set?" he asked Anti. "Anything that might cause you to think that he had some particular proclivity, some inclination, towards violence of this sort?"

"Other than chopping up Osiris, you mean?" barked Anti in what Barnabas and Wilfred took to be a laugh. "Oh yes, that god certainly has some violent *proclivities*, as you say."

He said this last sarcastically, and Barnabas and Wilfred exchanged a quizzical look.

"So," tried Wilfred again, patiently, "what have you, personally, seen him do?"

Anti laughed his harsh, squawking laugh again, although the sound was utterly humorless. "I've *personally* seen him chop off my toes, is what I've seen him do," he said bitterly. He wiggled the stubs of his missing toes at the two detectives, and the men cringed uncomfortably.

Barnabas, who had already gone through the process of becoming accustomed to the horribly mangled feet during his initial boat ride into the underworld, recovered himself first. "You are saying then that Set had something to do with, uh, well, your, um, misfortune there?"

"Yes, of course he did!" exclaimed Set, his exasperation obvious. "He chopped them right off. It was a punishment, he said."

"Oh my!" exclaimed Barnabas, shocked. "That seems quite a stringent punishment! Whatever transgression could have warranted such a thing?"

"It was no transgression," answered Anti. "It was a mistake, pure and simple."

"Well," prompted Wilfred again, "what was the mistake, then?"

"Hah!" cried Anti. "Set was all about having a secret meeting with a bunch of other gods. They all wanted to take over the underworld from Osiris and Anubis. Surely you've heard that story?" he asked, looking at Barnabas and Wilfred.

Barnabas looked at Wilfred and shrugged, having no idea what the ferryman was talking about, and Wilfred did the same. Then they both looked to Anti, waiting for him to explain. They all looked back and forth at each other until at last Anti sighed in an exaggeratedly beleaguered fashion.

"Fine, fine," he huffed. "I'll tell the story, although I hate thinking about it."

"Oh, no," said Barnabas politely, "don't distress yourself. It's quite alright if you don't feel up to telling us."

Anti waved his wing dramatically. "No, no, it's fine," he

said. "So, Set is having this secret meeting on an island, and I'm to ferry everyone over to it. But Isis, who is married to Osiris, was not supposed to come because she would certainly spoil their plot if she found out about it. Isis, now, is a very clever lady, and she dressed up as an old beggar woman. Her disguise was very clever. She looked nothing at all like herself, and she gave me a nice gold ring to take her over to the island so that she could beg from the gods there. It seemed innocent enough, and so I ferried her right over. How was I to know it was Isis herself I brought there?"

"Quite so!" agreed Barnabas. "Although, if she were a beggar, you might have found it strange that she offered you a gold ring," he suggested helpfully. "If she had a gold ring, she most certainly had no need to go begging, one would think."

Anti, of course, did not find this statement helpful at all. Indeed, it seemed to make him quite angry. "It was a clever trick, I tell you!" He scowled. "No one can be blamed for being fooled by Isis herself! It was not my fault, not in the slightest. Because she snuck into the meeting and ruined all of their grand plans, Set blamed me and took off my toes in sheer malice."

The poor falcon-headed boatman was getting quite worked up talking about it, so that Wilfred and Barnabas could see his face was flushing red under his feathers.

Wilfred attempted to soothe him. "Perhaps he is sorry about that," he offered. "Have you talked to him since?"

"Talked to him since?" sputtered Anti. "Of course not. I steer well away from Set. The god is a psychopath, I tell you."

Barnabas and Wilfred both wondered how an Egyptian god had managed to learn modern psychiatric jargon, but there was no time to ask for they had reached their destination. A large, black castle loomed on the east side of the riverbank. There was a dark wooden pier, followed by a black gravel path that led up to the castle.

Anti steered the boat expertly to the pier and held the boat steady so that his passengers could disembark. "Be careful," he warned ominously, once Barnabas and Wilfred stood on the creaking, rotting wood of the pier. "I'm quite certain that Set is your villain. He's the killer, mark my words. And I've taken a liking to you both and so I would hate to see anything *horrific* happen to you," he said, significantly looking at his missing toes. With that, he rowed away without even a glance back at his erstwhile passengers.

Barnabas, who had been waving farewell to him (just as he had done the last time Anti let him off his boat and then unceremoniously rowed away), lowered his hand awkwardly.

"Hmmph," he said, feeling a bit put out.

"Did you notice," whispered Wilfred, once Anti had paddled away far enough to be out of ear shot, "how strange his manner was, especially when we first asked him about Set? It seemed almost as if he wanted to tell us the information but didn't want to *seem* eager to be telling us."

"Perhaps he didn't want to be a tattle-tale?" suggested Barnabas. "Or perhaps he is afraid of Set. The fellow did chop off his toes, after all. One can see how someone might be loath to give testimony against such a ruffian as that."

"I suppose that could be so," agreed Wilfred. Indeed, Barnabas' theory on the matter made quite a good bit of sense, and was the easiest and most logical conclusion. Something, however, about the falcon-headed boatman seemed a bit off to Wilfred. Still, he supposed that he felt that way about this entire place, strange as it was. So he shrugged and disregarded his misgivings on the subject of Anti as due merely to the utterly foreign nature of this place and its inhabitants. After all, Anti had proved most helpful by delivering them as close as he dared to Set's estate.

"And," continued Barnabas, "his evidence was most compelling." He shuddered at the idea of having one's toes removed by an angry god of chaos. "And I am now doubly grateful for our disguises. At least we won't have that sort of thing to worry about now."

"Indeed," agreed Wilfred.

"Although," mused Barnabas, "I did forget to ask Anti about the maid." Wilfred sighed as Barnabas looked towards the retreating boatman, waving in a vain attempt to call Anti back, presumably to ask him about the poor maligned (and, Wilfred presumed, altogether imaginary) maid. "Ah well," Barnabas concluded sadly. "I suppose he's too far away to ask now. I suppose there's nothing for it but to go up to that castle and see what we can find out."

Together they climbed up the steep stone steps that led to Set's abode, Barnabas leading the way and Wilfred following along behind. The structure was immense, a giant, gleaming black castle set high upon a precipice that overlooked the river. Tall turrets and spires pointed sharply towards the sky, which was tinged a dull, ugly red and punctuated with black clouds that sparkled with angry red lightning. The massive edifice of the castle spoke of power, and might, and secrecy, as the walls were thick and seemingly entirely impenetrable. The whole effect was one of foreboding and of evil, and Barnabas and Wilfred's hearts were filled with trepidation.

Their nervousness was such that their steps slowed more and more the closer they got to the castle, until at last Wilfred reached out a hand to stay his employer.

"Wait a moment," he said. "How are we to get in?"

"Well," said Barnabas, considering. He turned to look up the last few steps. From the top of the stone staircase it was a matter of a short walk down a path of dark brick around the side of the castle to the front. There, they could easily see a wider causeway that presumably led to the castle gates. Barnabas pointed at that pathway, saying, "There's the front door. I'm supposing that we ought to go through it."

"But," said Wilfred, who was holding on to Barnabas' sleeve and refusing to let go, even as Barnabas turned to continue walking towards the main entrance, "I really think we should think this through a bit more." In truth, he was very frightened, and, now that it had come to it, had no wish to simply walk right up to the castle and demand admittance.

"We must talk to Set," pointed out Barnabas. "And we came all this way to do so, and now here we are. We really have no other choice but to go in."

"But it might be quite dangerous in there," said Wilfred,

eyeing the castle. "It doesn't seem entirely *friendly*, when you look at it."

Barnabas looked up to the terrible castle and felt his stomach churn with anxiety. Still, they had a job to do, a job of the utmost importance. It simply would not do for them to go back to Anubis and announce that they hadn't interviewed the prime suspect because they were spooked by his castle, however daunting that castle might be.

Also, it seemed that Wilfred's fear made Barnabas feel a bit more brave, and he was very proud to be taking on the role of the courageous detective who could approach any place, interrogate any suspect, and still make it home by tea time. Indeed, he thought, even Sherlock Holmes could scarcely show more bravery than this.

Thinking thus, he puffed up his chest and held his head high, assuming what he hoped was an imperialistic air of authority. "In we must go," he proclaimed, "and so go in we will!" With that, he turned and began to climb the last few steps (in a way he thought projected supreme confidence, but that really ended up looking a bit like a little boy pretending to march like a soldier). However, any effect he may have hoped for was quite ruined, as he was immediately yanked back by Wilfred's hand, which still clutched his sleeve unrelentingly.

"Really! I say!" exclaimed Barnabas, a bit annoyed at Wilfred's behavior. He pulled at his arm, attempting to free himself. Wilfred, however, pulled back to restrain him so that they ended up having a bit of a tug-of-war over Barnabas' sleeve for quite a few moments. At last Barnabas gave up. "What are you about, Wilfred? What has gotten into you?" he demanded.

"Quite sorry, really, I am," said Wilfred, embarrassed. "But it's just that we went to all the trouble to make these disguises, and it seems that all of that was for naught if we simply waltz up to the front door and announce ourselves."

"Oh," said Barnabas. He could see the sense of Wilfred's argument, and it gave him pause. "Quite right, I suppose," he admitted grudgingly. "So, then, how do you suggest we get into the castle?"

"Hmmm," said Wilfred, considering. "We could creep up to the doors, quiet as mice, so that no one sees us. Perhaps once we have a look we could devise a way to sneak in without attracting the attention of the guards. Then we can move about the castle and spy on Set, with him never the wiser to our presence."

Barnabas, whose ego had been much bolstered by the idea of himself as a heroic confident detective, was a bit deflated by the idea of creeping about Set's castle like a mouse. Still, he had to admit that the idea was a good one, and a good deal less likely to get them killed. Again, as it were.

He wondered if they even *could* be killed, since they were already dead. Then he wondered, if indeed they couldn't be killed yet again, and if that fact in itself might open up other possibilities, an outcome altogether worse than merely being killed. If that were the case, then surely Set, the god of chaos and evil, would have any number of horrible things at the ready for anyone who offended him. Barnabas shuddered, and then, at last, nodded his agreement to Wilfred.

"Alright," he said. "We shall sneak in." Once more he turned to continue up the stairs. "My arm, please," he said, pursing his lips.

"Oh yes, quite," said Wilfred, flustered. He let go of his employer's sleeve. "Terribly sorry," he muttered.

With Wilfred's hands safely tucked into his pockets and Barnabas' arm safely returned to his own possession, they continued up the stairs. Moving more stealthily now, they reached the top and quickly ducked behind a large boulder.

They could easily see the gates of the castle, huge wooden doors reinforced by massive crisscrossed bars of black metal and flanked by guards with large hippo heads. The guards interviewed every person who passed by (of which there were many; the place was far busier than Barnabas would have guessed).

Barnabas could see that, although most of the people

coming in pushed carts full of goods before them (probably for trade in the castle, he supposed), many were quite ragged and their carts not quite full. Still, the guards carefully inspected each cart that arrived and gruffly asked questions of the owners. Sad little apples and wilted sheaves of grain jostled about in the bottoms of near-empty carts as their owners formed a dejected-looking queue, awaiting their turn to be subjected to the hippo-headed guards' brisk scrutiny.

"Hippos," huffed Barnabas, rolling his eyes as if hippos were a problem that they faced with regularity.

"Ugh," agreed Wilfred, shaking his head as if in wonderment at the audacity of the hippos to be seemingly forever in their way.

"How ever will we sneak through?" asked Barnabas, frowning.

"Perhaps we could hide at the bottom of one of those carts?" suggested Wilfred. "Cover ourselves with apples and what not?"

Barnabas thought about the idea for a moment. "That could work," he began, then winced as one of the guards plunged a spear into a bag of rice, causing the contents to spill out at the feet of the protesting man to whom it belonged. "Or perhaps we'd best not," said Barnabas.

"Most definitely not," agreed Wilfred.

They continued to watch, hoping that some way of getting into the castle unnoticed would come to their attention.

"I know!" said Wilfred at last. "We could buy a cart from one of the peasants and then act as though we ourselves are delivering goods to the castle."

"And with our disguises, they will never suspect that we are detectives from England," said Barnabas. "They will think we are some sort of animals from the desert, or some such."

Wilfred looked doubtfully at his employer, taking in the assortment of reeds and grasses that still stuck out from Barnabas' upper half like bristles on a brush. "Or perhaps they will think we are some sort of plant-people," he suggested.

"Quite so." Barnabas sighed. "I suppose we must look a bit more, well, *vegetative* than mammalian.

"How shall we pay for the cart?" asked Wilfred. "Do you suppose they'd take British pounds sterling here?"

"Huh," said Barnabas, considering. "I don't see why not. It's good currency and recognized everywhere else in the world. I can't see why it wouldn't be the same here."

"What shall we do in case they don't?"

Barnabas thought for a moment. "Well," he said at last matter-of-factly, "I suppose there will be nothing for it but for us to knock the owner quite unconscious and take the cart by force, if it comes to that."

"Mr. Tew!" gasped Wilfred, shocked into formality. "You can't mean that!"

"We'll only just bonk them over the head and make them a *little* bit unconscious," said Barnabas defensively. "They'll wake up soon enough. Really, the fate of the world is in our hands. With great responsibility comes great, um... With great power comes great, uh..." He broke off, unable to remember the saying.

Wilfred took his meaning, however, and could see that they would indeed have little choice in the matter. "Still," he said, "let's hope that it doesn't come to that."

"Of course," sniffed Barnabas, still somewhat ruffled by his assistant's censure. "I don't much relish the idea of bonking people over the head either, but I'll do what I must."

Thus decided, they made ready to approach one of the incoming farmers. "Best we pick one of the smaller ones," pointed out Barnabas. "Maybe one of the ones with the mouse heads. In case we have to, well, *you* know."

Wilfred nodded, and together they crept out from behind the shelter of the boulder. No sooner had they emerged, however, than they were scooped up unceremoniously from behind. One very large hippo-headed guard held them both up by the necks of their coats so that their feet dangled ridiculously above the ground.

"What is this?" exclaimed Barnabas in surprise, kicking

his feet uselessly. "I say, put us down this instant!"

"Oh!" cried Wilfred, as the guard gave them both a small shake.

"You are sneaking about the castle of the great god of chaos," said the guard, his tone sounding quite reasonable. "You must be taken to Lord Set so he might ask of you what it is you are about."

"We have done nothing wrong!" yelped Wilfred.

"That's for Lord Set to decide," said the guard implacably. Embarrassingly, he carried them right up to the front gate, past the inquisitive eyes of all of the guards and the people who were lined up before them.

Barnabas and Wilfred ceased their struggles, trying to maintain as much dignity as was possible under the circumstances. "Would it be possible for you to put us down?" asked Wilfred politely. "We shall accompany you quietly, I assure you."

The guard merely laughed and continued to carry them into the castle. They passed through the gates and headed down a long corridor only dimly lit by torches in sconces on the walls.

"Really, this is most uncomfortable!" gasped Barnabas, who was turning quite red in the face. Indeed, his face was so red, and his expression so like that of a fish pulled from the water, that Wilfred feared that he might be asphyxiating.

Thankfully, they had, at that moment, reached the throne room of Set. The great hippo-headed god of chaos sat upon a huge golden throne at the front of the room. The guard stepped forward, still dangling his prisoners, and deposited them (none too gently) on the floor in front of the throne.

Chapter Eight

Set glowered down upon the two unfortunate detectives as they clambered carefully to their feet. "And who," asked the dreaded god of chaos, "are you?"

Terrified, Barnabas blurted out the first thing that came to mind, which just happened to be an amalgamation of all of the ideas for subterfuge that he and Wilfred had discussed just before being accosted by the giant guard. "We are farming plant-people from the desert!" he yelped. "We are cactus. Cacti! Cactuseses..." Unable to think of the correct plural form for cactus, his voice trailed off.

"Cactuses?" said Set, a quizzical look taking over his face.

"Yes, indeed!" cried Barnabas. "See?" He gestured to his vegetation-covered coat. Wilfred, beside him, remained silent and tried to appear as unobtrusive as was possible when one has been thrown upon the floor wearing a ridiculous outfit, and smelling quite a bit like hippo dung, in front of the throne of the god of all evil of the Egyptian underworld.

"Ah, yes," said Set. He glanced about the room, making eye contact with all those in attendance. Clearly, he was trying very hard not to laugh, and his mouth tightened against the smile that fought to come to the surface. "A farming, talking, cactus-person covered with reeds and hippo excrement—and with a British accent, no less."

Encouraged, Barnabas nodded wildly. "Yes, yes, exactly!" he exclaimed.

"And so," continued Set, who was very much enjoying playing with the oblivious detective, "where, precisely, are you from? I haven't heard of a place populated with cactus-covered farmers."

"Marylebone," answered Barnabas promptly, before realizing how very British that sounded. He immediately tried to convert it into a name that sounded more Egyptian. "Marylebonopatra," he said.

"Marylebonopatra?" said Set, having more and more difficulty hiding his mirth. "And where, exactly, is that?"

"Um," said Barnabas. "Well, that is... I suppose, it is close to... Uh, you know. Over there," he concluded lamely, pointing in first one direction and then another.

At this Set could hold in his amusement no more and let out a great guffaw. The rest of those in the room laughed along with him. Barnabas had no idea what was so funny, but he felt certain that having the god of chaos laughing was probably a great deal better than having him glower at you, and so he laughed as well. Wilfred, who had an idea that he and Barnabas were the butt of this particular joke, nonetheless smiled politely so as not to appear left out of the merriment.

At last the laughter died down and Set addressed Barnabas and Wilfred once more. He composed his face into a serious expression. "Are you certain," asked the god, now affecting an ominous glare, "that you are not, in reality, the detectives that Anubis hired to find Khepre?"

Barnabas and Wilfred cast alarmed glances at each other. Surely, if the god knew who they were and what they were about, they were doomed. However, Set saw their discomfiture and softened his tone. "No need to worry," he said. "I do not make a habit of harming the employees of other gods. And besides, since I had nothing to do with the kidnapping, I have no reason to feel insulted by your presence, do I?"

"No, no, of course not," agreed Barnabas. "We, of course, never suspected you!"

"No, not even for a moment," agreed Wilfred, thinking it prudent to speak before Barnabas could blurt out something that might prove harmful to their cause. He tried to think of a plausible reason as to why they would be sneaking around Set's castle in disguise. "We thought that, maybe, one of the many people coming into the castle might know something. Or, perhaps, you might have heard something or might give us some direction?"

"Hmm," said Set. "So why the disguises? Why the sneaking?"

"Well," said Wilfred, thinking quickly. "That was in case the real perpetrator discovered we were here. We didn't want to cause him to, well, *interfere* with you at all."

"I see," said Set, smiling at Wilfred's ridiculous excuses. It was obvious that the two little detectives were terrified of him, and he was quite enjoying it.

"And, you know, there's that business about Osiris and the chopping him up and all," muttered Barnabas.

"What?" asked Set sharply. "What's that got to do with it?"

"It's just, that, you know, Khepre was chopped up," said Barnabas, regretting at once his careless statement but feeling the need to explain himself nonetheless. "And since you... Well, there was the episode when you..."

"Yes, yes, I know," snapped Set irritably. "Geesh! You dismember one person and you hear about it for a thousand years." He sighed, collecting himself. "Anyway, I'm sorry that has happened to Khepre. And don't you think it would be a bit stupid for me to do something like that again? A bit too *obvious*, really?"

"Of course," agreed Barnabas politely.

"I'm sorry to say that I really don't know anything about it," said Set. "But I don't like it much, not at all. With the sun being up for so long, the crops are drying up and the people are starving."

Confused, Barnabas asked, "But aren't you the god of chaos? Isn't such a thing, well, right up your alley, so to speak?"

Set huffed indignantly. His expression became troubled, almost petulant. "It most certainly is not!" he declared. "What fun is it to cause chaos if everyone is suffering so miserably already? No sport in it at all. If there's going to be chaos, it'll be of my making and it will be incredibly amusing, thank you very much!"

"Oh, yes, I see," said Barnabas. "Very sorry." He thought for a moment, chewing his lip, then added, "I'm sure that your chaos is the best sort of chaos, really."

Set waved away the apology with a careless hand. "No matter," he said. "Still, I think that if Khepre is truly dead, then you had best put your efforts into solving the problem of the drought instead."

"Indeed!" agreed Barnabas, seeing the sense of the suggestion. "That's exactly what I was thinking," he said, although he had been thinking no such thing until just that very moment. "But," he asked, "how might we do that?"

"Well," answered Set, "if it were me, since the problem is that the land is drying up, I might go see Khnum, who is in charge of flooding the river. He lives on Elephantine Isle. Perhaps he could be of assistance."

"Excellent idea," said Barnabas.

"Never fear, we shall treat this matter as our top priority," agreed Wilfred.

"Very well then," said Set by way of dismissal. Barnabas and Wilfred, however, were unsure of where, exactly, Elephantine Isle might be and how, exactly, they might *get* there. Therefore, they simply stood looking blankly back at Set.

"Off you go!" said Set, a bit of annoyance creeping into his voice. It seemed that the god of chaos, whilst quick to mirth and a great deal more pleasant than expected, was also a bit short of patience.

Barnabas swiveled as though to obey, but then he stopped and turned back. He performed this quick little half turn, back and forth, forward and back, first facing Set and then the door, several times before at last stopping to face somewhere midway. "Um," he said carefully. The change in Set's mood had made Barnabas nervous again, and he felt very uncertain of what to do.

"Um, what?" asked Set, his jaw working in irritation.

"Well, it's just, you see, we are from quite far away, so… Well, where, exactly, did you say Elephant Isle was?"

"Elephantine Isle..." Set sighed.

"Yes, yes, of course!" said Barnabas. "So, it's..." He looked about in every direction as though his gaze might chance upon the proper course and the testy god could simply point him in that way.

"Bah!" exhaled Set loudly, exasperated. "One of my servants will take you in a chariot. You'll get there much quicker that way." He waved them off violently this time, dismissing them with finality. He'd had his amusement and now wished for the interview to be over so that he might pursue other, more enjoyable, chaotic pastimes.

Barnabas and Wilfred bowed as they took their leave. Eager to be out of the presence of the moody god, they hurried back to the door through which they had entered. They were led now by an attendant (which was a merciful change from being carried in by the rough hippo-headed guards). At last they reached the door, and were about to pass through it (and therefore out of the throne room and into the relative safety of the castle proper, which at least put them out of Set's immediate eyesight), when they heard his voice once more.

"And please," called the god, "do take a bath first. That *smell* is abominable."

Barnabas, his nerves bow-string tight, jumped. Wilfred blushed in embarrassment, but he managed to turn and bow respectfully once more. Then they were through the doors and in the hallway, and being bustled along by various servants who fluttered around them, preparing them for their trip.

Their clothes were stripped unceremoniously from them, even as they protested. They themselves were then thrust into two large wooden barrels filled with heated water (which, they had to admit, felt quite good), before being dressed in long tan robes.

Their trousers and jackets were never seen by them again, which they much regretted, although both were far too intimidated to ask questions or make demands about the matter. And, in truth, they had to admit the new robes were quite comfortable and much more appropriate for the warm weather here than their heavy British suits.

Soon enough, Barnabas and Wilfred found themselves in a horse-drawn chariot, proceeding at a goodly pace down an extremely bumpy road, their robes billowing about them in the wind. As the nervousness of being in the castle wore off, both began to relax, and Barnabas secretly thought that he must indeed make quite a dashing figure as he raced about the countryside in a chariot, his robe blowing dramatically about his legs.

When at last Wilfred felt that they had got far enough away from the castle to risk conversation, he said, "So, Set was not at all what I expected."

"Shhh!" hissed Barnabas, casting a meaningful look at the chariot driver, who was blithely paying them no mind whatsoever (nor did he intend to, if truth be told).

Wilfred dropped his voice to a stage whisper. "What did you think about Set?" he asked.

Barnabas scratched his chin, thinking. "Well," he said, "he was not quite as, well, *evil* as I had thought he might be."

"Not at all," agreed Wilfred. "And he seemed to have quite a good sense of humor."

"Indeed! Quite a smashing fellow, really. Good of him to give us this chariot to speed us on our way."

Wilfred nodded. They both stood quietly for a moment, before Wilfred began again.

"Although," he said, "his mood did change quite quickly towards the end. Honestly, it made me extraordinarily nervous. I was becoming afraid that he might do something...*chaotic*."

"Quite so!" agreed Barnabas. "Until that point, things were going along so nicely that I had quite relaxed. But then he became irritable so that I was on edge all over again."

"Very moody, is Set," said Wilfred.

"Mercurial, even," said Barnabas, pronouncing the large word slowly and carefully so that its gravity wouldn't be impaired by a mispronunciation.

The driver stopped the chariot then (having neither heard

nor cared to hear anything whatsoever of their loudly whispered conversation). "Here we are," he said as he gestured for them to vacate the chariot. "Elephantine Isle. There's a bridge to cross the river just there, on the other side of that little village. Just be wary of crocodiles. This is Sobek's country as well as Khnum's, you know."

"Sobek?" asked Wilfred.

"Crocodiles?" gulped Barnabas.

The driver hid a smile. "Yes, Sobek, the god of the crocodiles. You are on the Nile River, so of course there will be a few about. Just keep out of the water and you'll be fine."

Barnabas and Wilfred exchanged a glance, quite certain that they were *not* exactly fine, not when they were in a place where crocodiles were likely to be about. Still, they thanked the driver politely, then made their way uncertainly towards the village at the edge of the water.

The village was quite small and the two detectives attracted quite a bit of attention. Because the village sat near the bridge that led to Khnum's island retreat, the villagers were not entirely unused to seeing strangers. Many people made pilgrimages to pray to the god of fertility and abundance. However, despite the robes that looked exactly like those that everyone else was wearing, there was something innately foreign, something so very *British*, about Barnabas and Wilfred that the people in the village all stopped what they were doing and stared as they walked past.

The attention was such that Barnabas began to feel quite the celebrity. Indeed, he felt so important he began looking regally from side to side at the onlookers, waving to them as though he were the queen of England herself. "I say, Wilfred," he said, nodding at a small child who had, whether by accident or design, dropped a flower onto the street in front of them. "I do believe they must have heard of us and our exploits. We are quite famous here, it would seem!"

"So it seems," agreed Wilfred, who was very much enjoying the feeling of being the center of attention as well.

"And I am *very* glad these people are, well, actually people," whispered Barnabas, leaning in towards Wilfred so he could speak without offending anyone. "You know, with normal heads and such rather than the business with the animal heads that seems so common here."

Wilfred, seeing a man with the head of a crocodile standing nearby, jabbed at his employer with his elbow. "Shhh!" he hissed, inclining his head suggestively towards the man.

"What's the matter? Huh? Oh!" said Barnabas, seeing the reptilian fellow at last. He shuddered as he took in the long snout and the wickedly cruel teeth that protruded from it. He did not like to think of offending someone such as this.

"Do you think he heard?" he whispered loudly to Wilfred.

Wilfred looked at the crocodile man, who was standing about ten feet away on the street ahead of them. He searched the man's face for any indication that he had heard, or for any other sign of offence (or aggression for that matter; Wilfred, too was quite unnerved by the nasty-looking teeth) but the creature's flat, glossy eyes were quite impossible to read. "I don't know," he whispered back. "I don't think so."

"Are you quite sure?" asked Barnabas nervously as they drew closer to the subject of their speculation.

"No, I'm not sure at all," said Wilfred. "But we'd best stop talking about it or he *will* hear us, for certain."

"Yes, yes, quite right," said Barnabas. "I don't much like the looks of... Oh!" He broke off, distracted by the sight of a woman carrying an enormous basket of what looked to be a very exotic, very spiny variety of fruit upon her head. "I wonder what those are. I think I could fancy a nice, juicy piece of fruit after all we've been through!"

The woman heard Barnabas' exclamation. She reached up a hand into her basket and extracted two fruits. With a warm smile, she handed a fruit to Barnabas and one to Wilfred. Both accepted gratefully. However, unfamiliar with the things, they were unsure of how, exactly, to eat it.

Barnabas turned his piece this way and that, staring at it doubtfully whilst Wilfred contemplated his own with a frown of consternation. Not wanting to be rude, Barnabas felt that, after a few moments of considering the thing with the friendly woman watching them to see how they liked her gift, he had better just take a bite of this fruit with no further delay. So thinking, he made as if to stick it directly into his mouth, spines and all.

The woman gasped and reached out to stay his hand, an amused smile on her face. Barnabas saw other people smiling and laughing at his faux pas as well, and he felt himself flushing in embarrassment.

"Oh no," she said. "Like this!" She reached up to her basket again and took out another fruit. Expertly, she pulled at one of the spines, which gave way; and grasping the loose piece between her fingers, she pulled it in a spiral motion around the fruit so that the skin came off entirely, spines and all. Beneath the skin glistened juicy red flesh shining with juice.

Smiling bashfully, Barnabas and Wilfred did the same to their own pieces, and soon they were enjoying the most succulent, refreshing piece of fruit either had ever eaten. They thanked the woman profusely.

"Truly," said Wilfred, "I think that I have never tasted anything so divine!"

"We are lucky to be blessed with bountiful crops of such delicious things," said the woman with a smile. But then she looked up at the glaring sun, held perpetually in the noon position, and her smile faded. "I think that we must enjoy it whilst we can," she said sadly.

"Fear not, my good lady!" proclaimed Barnabas gallantly. "For we are here to help you."

"Are you the detectives hired by Anubis, then?" asked the woman. "The ones who are going to find Khepre so that the sun can move again?" The people nearby cheered at her words, and those who were out of earshot cheered merely because they could hear the others cheering.

Really, thought Barnabas, shooting a glance at Wilfred, it was most astonishing how quickly news traveled in this place. He wondered how it was that, if everyone knew so much about everything, no one knew anything about what had happened to poor Khepre.

"Indeed, we are," he said, keeping his thoughts to himself.

"Have you found him yet?" asked a man, rather stupidly since the sun clearly had not moved an inch.

"Well, no…," began Barnabas.

"Where can he be?" asked one voice plaintively. "Why haven't you found him?" demanded another. "Is he dead?" wailed yet another. Suddenly the entire street was a cacophony of curious people, angry people, scared people, and people who continued to cheer because they hadn't yet caught up with the change in mood on the street.

Barnabas, who did not much like crowds much less angry, volatile ones, looked about in growing panic. Wilfred saw his employer's discomfort, and he knew by Barnabas' frightened glances and twitchy movements that he was about to bolt entirely. Therefore Wilfred took it upon himself to attempt to quell the situation.

"Quiet please," he asked politely as he stepped forward. When no one paid him any mind, he raised his voice to a level that was quite rude indeed. "I say, quiet please!" he yelled. The people hushed and looked at each other as though to imply that Wilfred was quite obnoxious for carrying on so, although only a moment ago they themselves had been shouting as well.

"Thank you!" said Wilfred testily. He was quite irritated at being looked at as though he were a naughty child creating a scene in public when these very people had forced him to raise his voice in the first place. He looked to Barnabas for assistance, but Barnabas' face had gone entirely white and his eyes still darted about wildly. Wilfred knew he was on his own.

"Quite sorry for yelling," he began, "but honestly! Sometimes one must yell if one wants to be heard over an incredible racket."

"Well," replied one onlooker, "say what you're going to say, then, since you're making such a big deal of it."

"Really!" said Wilfred, affronted. "Oh, never mind," he

continued, as he saw that the man was about to argue further. "I merely wanted to say that, whilst we have yet to find Khepre, we are here to petition Khnum in order to solve your problems with the drought and such. We were sent here by Set himself!" he concluded to give their presence the air of official business.

These words seemed to placate the mob, and the mood turned to one of welcoming joviality again. The people began to smile and to encourage them, and even to cheer again (indeed, some of the people farther away had missed the unpleasant detour the conversation had taken entirely, and had never stopped cheering happily at all).

Thus, the crowd parted and Barnabas, who had gained some of his color back, and Wilfred were hastened along to the bridge to Elephantine Isle amid smiles and pats upon the back of encouragement and approval.

"Well," said Barnabas, once they had walked a good way along the bridge and thus were out of earshot of the waving people on the shore, "that was extraordinarily unpleasant."

"Indeed it was," agreed Wilfred. "Quite frightening."

"I suppose they must be very irritable, what with it being daylight all of the time," said Barnabas. "Still, there was no need for them to carry on so, as if any of this situation were our fault whatsoever!"

"People always need someone to blame," said Wilfred. "I suppose it can't be helped."

"Still," said Barnabas, "those fruits were quite nice. So, not *everyone* in that village was unpleasant."

"Most definitely," agreed Wilfred.

With that, they stepped off the bridge onto Elephantine Isle. As the sounds of the cheering villagers wafted towards them from across the river, they approached a large, ornately carved white marble edifice. An open archway formed the door, and assuming that this must be the entrance to Khnum's abode, Barnabas and Wilfred, exchanging a glance for bravery (for who knew what might await them inside?), passed through.

Chapter Nine

They entered a vast antechamber, eyes blinking as they adjusted to the dimly lit interior from the bright sunlight outside. Their footsteps echoed on the marble floor, and they heard the soft sibilance of whispered conversations coming from the various nooks and crannies of the place.

Discrete wall sconces holding small torches provided a soft light. Looking around, they saw, all too quickly, what they presumed must be Khnum.

It must be the god, they thought, because the figure they beheld was quite tall (indeed, he must have stood a foot higher than anyone else present in the room). Additionally, he was possessed of a giant ram's head. He was seated upon a great throne at the head of the room and flanked by the ubiquitous attendants that seemed to surround every god in the underworld.

Barnabas and Wilfred approached the throne and bowed low.

"Rise!" said Khnum. "What is your business here?" The god spoke in a sonorous voice that seemed designed to cover a slightly sheep-like bleating quality of the vowels.

"We are detectives," said Barnabas, most unhelpfully.

"Hired by Anubis," added Wilfred.

"To find Khepre, you see," continued Barnabas.

"And you need me for…?" asked Khnum.

"Oh, well, the drought, you see," said Barnabas, who was discovering that he found these Egyptian gods quite intimidating. It seemed they made him quite nervous, so that he couldn't quite get his thoughts together. Indeed, he did not much like talking with them at all. The confused look on Khnum's face told him that the god did not, in fact, see what he was getting at, not at all. "Because of the sun," he concluded lamely.

"You know," said Khnum, "that I cannot move the sun. Only Khepre can do that."

"Yes, yes, of course," said Wilfred. "But perhaps you, being the god of floods and fertility and abundance and what not, might counteract the drying effects of the sun."

"Ah, yes!" bleated Khnum, clapping his hooves together and forgetting his serious voice in his excitement. "You wish for me to flood the river? Why didn't you just say so? I do so love to do that, you know."

"Splendid!" exclaimed Barnabas.

"Smashing!" said Wilfred.

"When would you like for me to do this?" said Khnum, pulling out what looked to be an appointment calendar.

"As soon as can be," said Barnabas. "The crops are failing and people are beginning to grow hungry. They need water."

"Well, then, how about right now?" asked Khnum.

"Oh, yes, that would be most excellent!" cried Barnabas. "See, Wilfred, we have solved an aspect of our case already! Anubis will be most pleased."

"I am pleased to be of service," said Khnum, tilting his head downwards in mock humility.

"May I ask a question before we begin with the flooding?" asked Barnabas hesitantly. "It's just, well, there was a fellow in the village who had a crocodile head. Not that there's anything odd about having an animal head," he added quickly. "It's just that this fellow seemed a good deal more, well, *menacing* than anyone else we've met. Is it quite safe to go out there with him?"

"Oh," said Khnum airily. "That is Sobek. Nothing to worry about. He was probably interested to see what you might get me to do. He does *so* love it whenever I flood the river."

"Goodness, but that's a relief," said Barnabas, glad that the crocodile man, at least, would be pleased with what they had accomplished today and therefore presumably would not

88

feel the need to eat them.

"And I have a question for you," said the god. "How high, exactly, would you like for the waters to rise?"

Despite the god's downturned face, Wilfred thought he saw a glint of mischievous cunning in his eyes. He tried to shoot Barnabas a warning glance, but Barnabas was far too excited to pay him any heed.

"As high as you can!" declared Barnabas. "They need water, and so the more the better, I say. Right, Wilfred?"

"Uh, well, actually, perhaps we had best consider the repercussions...," began Wilfred cautiously.

"Nonsense!" cried Barnabas. He was quite overcome with excitement and therefore not thinking altogether clearly. "This good fellow has agreed to help, and we shall let him help as best he can!"

"It's just, well, maybe only a little bit of flooding might be better," said Wilfred. "Perhaps a great lot of flooding might cause some other problems."

"Oh," said Barnabas, deflating a little. "I suppose I hadn't thought of that." He turned to Khnum. "I think that perhaps we ought to start out with just a minor flood, after all."

Khnum, however, only laughed and waved a hoof dismissively. "Too late!" he cried, a slightly wicked smile playing on his snout. "You asked for the big one, and it has already started." The god of floods bounced up off of his throne and pranced across the marble floor in delight. "Come see! Come see!" he called back to the detectives. Uneasy and far from happy now, Barnabas and Wilfred obeyed.

The scene that greeted them as they emerged from the shelter of Khnum's sanctuary was even worse than they could have expected. The waters of the river were rising rapidly and alarmingly. The force of the current was such that it threatened to swallow not only the bridge that led to Elephantine Isle but also the entire village on the other side as well.

The villagers, seeing the danger, began to scream and run about in frantic circles, wanting to get away but not knowing where to go. Khnum pranced and danced joyfully beside Barnabas and Wilfred as they stood next to him, watching the tragedy unfold.

"Look!" cried Wilfred, clutching Barnabas' arm and pointing towards the center of the now-turbulent river. "It is the scary man from the village, the one with the crocodile head!"

Barnabas looked to where Wilfred was pointing, and he saw not just the one man with a crocodile head but several more as well. It seemed that the man had been joined by his fellows. They cavorted and splashed in the water, thoroughly enjoying themselves. It would have been a relief to see that some people, at least, would benefit from the flood, if it hadn't have been for the watchful look in their eyes and the way that they gnashed their teeth at the people running about on the shore. Indeed, Barnabas thought, the crocodile-folk looked quite predatory, and he feared for the villagers.

"Ahoy, Sobek!" called Khnum happily. "Isn't this delightful?" The crocodile man (the first one, the one who had given Barnabas and Wilfred a turn in the village) waved a clawed hand as his snout contorted into an altogether gruesome smile. Khnum then turned to Barnabas and Wilfred. "Well, how do you like your flood? Isn't it wonderful?" he demanded.

Wilfred managed to mumble a noncommittal reply. Barnabas merely stood there looking a bit sickly.

Even as they watched, an unlucky person, too slow to get out of the way of the swirling waters, was plucked off the bank and into the crocodile-infested maelstrom. Immediately, one of the crocodiles separated from the group and swam off to intercept him.

"Heavens!" exclaimed Wilfred.

"Oh dear," said Barnabas sadly.

"Well," said Wilfred. "Perhaps the crocodile is merely going to help the man."

"Hmmm," said Barnabas doubtfully. "Perhaps, but I have a terrible feeling that he intends to eat him, at that." Even as he spoke, several more people were washed away by the terrible current and several more crocodiles peeled off to follow them. "Oh! It is too horrible!" cried Barnabas, turning to Khnum. "Can't you make it stop?"

"Stop? Stop!? Why should we stop? Oh, no, we are just getting started!" Khnum exclaimed, twirling around like an ungainly ballerina. Wilfred and Barnabas exchanged looks. This god was obviously quite mad, and now it seemed there was nothing for them to do but to watch the grim spectacle unfold.

Wilfred pulled Barnabas a few steps away. "What can we do?" he hissed frantically.

"I've no idea," said Barnabas, wincing as yet another person was swept away by the flood. "I really do wish that someone would have warned us that Khnum was so tricksy," he added petulantly.

"Indeed!" said Wilfred. "Actually, I wonder if Set didn't expect for this to happen all along. Why else would he send us here and not tell us what to expect?"

"Aha! I think you must be right," said Barnabas. "I *knew* that he was not to be trusted. Being the god of chaos, and all."

"Quite," said Wilfred. He gestured at the terrible scene before them: raging waters tumbling over their banks; people being caught up in the flood, screaming frantically as they tried to keep their heads above water; grinning crocodiles cutting swiftly through the current towards the hapless swimmers. All in all it was a most awful sight. "And if this isn't chaos, I don't know what is," concluded Wilfred.

"Most definitely," agreed Barnabas, shifting his feet back and forth. His shoes had begun to make a small, squishy sound, and he kicked at the ground absentmindedly.

Wilfred looked down to see what was making the sound. "Oh no," he said.

"Horrible," agreed Barnabas, still watching the destruction of the village. "And to think of how friendly those people were to us," he mused melodramatically, forgetting the way that the villagers' attitude towards them had shifted towards petulance and then turned back once

91

again to amiability. He dashed at a single tear that trailed slowly down his cheek. "It is so sad that they would come to this."

"Yes, that, of course," said Wilfred. "But we seem to be experiencing another difficulty."

"Meaning?" asked Barnabas, displeased at the interruption to his melancholic reflections.

"Meaning that the water has risen quite above our ankles," replied Wilfred.

"What? Oh!" cried Barnabas, as he realized that the squishy sound was due to the rising river making a mud puddle at his feet. He backed away in an attempt to find high ground, but the island was quite small and quite flat, so that there was no place that was much safer than any other.

"What shall we do?" cried out Wilfred.

"I've no idea!" exclaimed Barnabas. The water rose even higher and now swirled about their knees. Barnabas began to run in circles, flailing his arms above his head as though reaching for an unseen life preserver above him. "Help!" he yelled, to no one in particular. "Oh, do help!"

Wilfred too began to panic and run about whilst Khnum danced and twirled and chortled with glee. "Help, help!" cried the two detectives. "Swim! Oh swim!" laughed Khnum. And, within moments, that is exactly what Barnabas and Wilfred were doing as the river picked them up and carried them away.

Barnabas quickly found a floating log (or, in truth, the *log* found *him*; as it was bounced about by the swirling current, it whacked him on the head and nearly knocked him unconscious, which would have been the end of him. Luckily, however, he was not knocked out cold and was able to grab onto the log instead). Wilfred managed to grab onto a large wooden door that had presumably been torn away from a house in the village, and he was able to float quite easily upon it.

Barnabas spied Wilfred and called out to him. "Wilfred! Are you quite alright?"

"Perfectly fine," said Wilfred, gasping and coughing out

a mouthful of dirty river water. "And you?"

"Quite well," said Barnabas, rubbing at the sore spot on his head. It was rapidly beginning to swell and throbbed most annoyingly. He glared resentfully at the log that had thwacked him so rudely upon his noggin. "Although," he continued as a thought rose in his mind, "I do think we should try to get out of this river. Since there are crocodiles and heaven knows what else in here, besides."

"Yes, yes, most certainly," agreed Wilfred. They kicked their feet, struggling to push their makeshift floatation devices against the current so that they might come closer to the river bank, but the flow of the water was too strong and neither was able to make any progress whatsoever. At last they gave up trying entirely, and they submitted resignedly to whatever fate the river would bring them.

As they were carried downriver, Barnabas saw the woman who had offered them the fruit. She had a piece of the spiny produce in her hand and was battering a crocodile about the head with it. "Good luck to you!" called Barnabas politely by way of encouragement. The woman scowled back at him. "Keep it up!" said Barnabas, deciding that her frown was clearly due to the crocodile and had nothing to do with Barnabas himself. "You've almost got him, I say!" And with that, he was swept around a corner and saw nothing more of what happened between the woman and the crocodile.

Luckily, no crocodile threatened Barnabas or Wilfred, and as the flood waters calmed farther downstream, the two were at last deposited on a sandy bank. They were sodden and bruised and quite exhausted but otherwise unharmed.

They lay there for a few moments catching their breath and being thankful that they had somehow survived their ordeal. At last they struggled to their feet so that they might get themselves entirely out of the river and begin to dry off. No sooner had they risen, however, than they were accosted by four tiny ruffians.

Barnabas took in the little figures (one with a tiger's head, the next with a lion's head, then the fellow with the hyena's head, and finally, of course, the nasty little canary) and cursed. "Oh, dear God!" he gasped as the canary and the hyena grabbed his arm roughly. "Will the indignities never end?"

Wilfred was similarly apprehended by the lion and the tiger, and together the two men were dragged across the sandy strand to a chariot that waited nearby. Roughly, they were thrown into the chariot. Their kidnappers jumped in beside them, and they were off.

"Ow!" yelped Barnabas as the canary took advantage of the close quarters and a bump in the road to thrust his pointy beak into Barnabas' shoulder. "You did that on purpose!"

The canary opened his eyes wide in an expression of innocence, but Barnabas saw the slight taunting smirk that twitched at the fellow's beak. "Why you monster!" he cried, kicking at the canary's legs.

The smirk fell from the canary's face, as did the expression of wide-eyed innocence, as he responded to Barnabas' attack with a vigorous kick of his own. Barnabas kicked back, and soon the two were in an outright scuffle in the close confines of the chariot. Feet and claws struck out and hands and wings flapped and slapped so that none in the chariot were safe from the altercation.

"Take that!" yelled Barnabas, landing a blow.

"Oof," yelped Wilfred, who had been the unintended recipient of the blow.

"Cheep!" squeaked the canary, gleefully trying to peck at Barnabas' eyes.

"STOP THIS NONSENSE!" bellowed Anubis. Everyone had been so engrossed in the fight that no one noticed they had arrived at their destination (which was Anubis' throne room), and that the chariot had come to a complete stop in front of it, and that Anubis himself had been standing there for some time, watching in disbelief as his very own minion and the detective he had hired slapped at each other like children in a schoolyard fight.

Chapter Ten

At the sound of Anubis' voice, everyone froze and turned wide, startled eyes in the direction of the angry god. Anubis would have laughed at the absurdity of the spectacle (and, later, when his temper had cooled and the detectives and minions were well on their way, he probably would have a good laugh, together with his assistant, about this sight) if he didn't have quite so much to be angry about just now.

Barnabas was the first to recover his wits. He untangled his hand from where it had got caught up in the canary's wing and straightened his coat. "Well, hullo!" he said, his voice tinged with indignation. "Honestly! Those little ruffians of yours have the most abominable manners!" He was so outraged that he had forgotten that he was, in fact, quite intimidated by Anubis (and, indeed, it is only prudent to speak respectfully to the god of the dead, particularly when that god had already had one killed once, besides).

"Bah!" exclaimed Anubis, clearly furious. "You dare to speak to me of manners? Was it good manners for you to flood the entire Nile?" Barnabas and Wilfred looked down and shuffled their feet sheepishly. "Do you think the people in the village that you destroyed will talk about what good *manners* you had?" continued Anubis, warming up to his subject. "Will they speak of how very *pleasant* you were as you marched off to ask Khnum to raise the waters higher than they've been in a thousand years? A thousand!"

"I say!" said Barnabas, who was quite through with being abused both physically and verbally. He was still highly annoyed at the rough treatment he had received at the hands (wings?) of the canary. Besides, his guilt over what had happened at the village made him feel defensive. "The

95

flood was not entirely our fault! Khnum tricked us! He is really quite mad. An awful fellow, really. Do you know he danced whilst the village was swept away? Danced and laughed, too!"

"Of course he would!" yelled Anubis, taken quite a bit aback by this display of sass from the meek and self-effacing detective. "He's the god of floods! Meaning, that he really, *really* enjoys floods. It's in his name, you see," he pointed out condescendingly.

"Oh, well, yes, but," grumbled Barnabas, "we only went there because Set told us to."

"And you listened to Set? The god of chaos?" asked Anubis, his voice a drawl of exaggerated patience as he tried very hard not to lose his temper entirely.

Barnabas flushed. "Well, he seemed quite nice," he said lamely.

"Yes, very nice indeed," said Wilfred in an attempt to help his employer. "A most helpful fellow, really."

Anubis scoffed and looked up at the sky for a long time. He was thinking of how best to impress upon Barnabas and Wilfred the magnitude of their mistake, but he could also see that their hearts were good and they had not intended any harm. And besides, they were not the first persons to be fooled by the wily Set and the equally tricky Khnum.

Still, he was very upset by the disaster they had caused. Therefore, he decided to play upon their guilt a bit more, so that they might learn to become more wary, more careful, before allowing them to continue on with their quest.

"So," said Anubis at last. "You wanted to talk about manners. You wanted to talk about crazy old Khnum. Let's talk, instead, about, oh, I don't know, people being eaten by crocodiles?"

"Oh dear," said Wilfred.

"Don't let's," said Barnabas miserably, as if not speaking of it might make the whole thing not real. He had quite hoped that no one had *actually* been eaten and the crocodiles were merely having a bit of fun, but Anubis' words seemed to give the lie to that idea.

"Oh yes," said Anubis. "Six people were eaten by crocodiles because of your little flood. And you are complaining about being pecked by a tiny canary?"

"Terribly sorry," said Barnabas. "Really I am." And, in truth, he was filled with immense remorse about the whole affair.

"And the mold," sighed Anubis. "The goddess of mold is having a smashing time, what with all the damp and what not."

"Heavens," said Barnabas sadly. He didn't care much about mold, though, not when he was still thinking about people being eaten by crocodiles. "But will the people who were eaten... I mean, that is to say..."

"What?" snapped Anubis. "You mean to say what? Out with it!"

"Since this is the underworld," managed Barnabas, at last speaking the thought that had worried him since his arrival, "and everyone is already quite dead... Well, can they become, um, *more* dead? Dead again? Twice dead? Thrice?"

"Oh yes," said Anubis. "People can die here, especially if they are eaten by crocodiles. And once they die here, they are simply..." He waved his hand in the air. "Poof! Gone!"

"Oh, no," said Barnabas unhappily. He was saddened at the thought of having had something to do with the deaths of those villagers (and such a gruesome death it must have been!). He also, ungallantly, felt his fears for the safety of his own person much renewed, and therefore he was exceedingly uncomfortable.

Anubis saw Barnabas' misery and decided that he had punished the detectives enough. "So then," he said briskly, "let's get on with it, shall we? Perhaps you should try investigating someone less *dire* than the god of chaos himself, at least initially."

"Yes, of course," agreed Barnabas, glad to change the subject. "But who might that be?"

"There are lesser gods of chaos," replied Anubis. "They could definitely be good suspects, and I imagine that they might be more your speed, so to speak. At least until you've had some practice dealing with evil gods and what not."

"Quite," said Barnabas, not liking the sound of yet more gods of chaos but feeling slightly relieved at the "lesser" amendment to their name. "But why would they be suspects?" he asked.

"Every night when the sun goes below ground, the sun god, Ra, battles and defeats the lesser chaos gods."

"I imagine that must grow quite tiresome for them, being defeated nightly like that," pointed out Barnabas.

"Ah!" said Wilfred. "So, perhaps, if the sun was left in the sky forever, never to go underground, then the lesser chaos gods would not have to be defeated!"

"Exactly!" said Anubis, regaining a bit of faith in his hapless detectives.

"Off we go then! We will accost these lesser chaos gods and find the truth of the matter in no time!" said Barnabas, feeling his enthusiasm for the job returning now that they had a direct course of action before them.

"Where are they? Who are they?" asked Wilfred, ever the practical detective-assistant.

Anubis sighed again. "Try Apep first," he said. "He lives under the mountain called Bakhu. Over there." He pointed at a dark peak far off on the horizon. "Good luck, and do try not to kill anyone else." With that, he dismissed them and Barnabas and Wilfred were on their way once more.

They walked quietly for some time, immersed in their own thoughts. At last Wilfred broke the silence. "Bad luck, that. About the crocodiles, you know."

"It is the worst of luck," wailed Barnabas. To Wilfred's great consternation, he saw that his employer was beginning to cry. "It seems that we have lost innocent clients once again."

"No, no," said Wilfred, patting Barnabas' shoulder to console him. "What could we have done about it?"

"But we have doubled the number of people we have killed, even if we killed them indirectly," said Barnabas. "No, tripled! Doubled? How many is it now?" Barnabas tried to count on his fingers, but the arithmetic eluded him.

"Don't even think it!" said Wilfred. "Those deaths are most assuredly Set's fault, and Khnum's. Not ours."

"Do you really think so?" sniffed Barnabas, wanting to believe Wilfred's words but still feeling as though it was his own actions that had doomed all of those poor villagers.

"Most definitely!" said Wilfred. "All we did was try to get a little bit of water for their crops. Who could have guessed that it would turn out the way it did?"

"Indeed!" agreed Barnabas. "And Khnum was horrible, the way he delighted in all the destruction. "No decent, sane person could ever have predicted that anyone would behave in such a way! How *could* we have known?"

"Exactly!" said Wilfred. "So you see? Our conscience is clear." He thought for a moment. "Although," he said at last, "it wouldn't hurt for us to be a bit more careful who we trust, as Anubis said."

"Quite so, quite so," said Barnabas. He leaned closer to Wilfred in order to whisper, even though there was no one around whatsoever to overhear what he said. "Don't you think that Anubis was quite a bit, well, *judgmental* about the whole business? Especially for someone who goes about killing people with mummies all the time?"

"Indeed!" said Wilfred. "He killed us both, directly, didn't he? And then we are merely involved with a bit of an accident, in the most peripheral of ways, and he behaves as if we were the most reprehensible people in the world."

"Most unfair," sniffed Barnabas. "When it comes down to it, we were only very slightly involved, really, in the flood. As you said before, it was entirely not our fault at all."

"Terribly unfair," agreed Wilfred.

The two walked in silence for a while longer (both were privately enjoying their sense of righteous indignation, and were quite pleasantly thinking about all of the indignities that had been foisted upon them in this place, and how outraged they were, and about how brave anyone hearing the tale would think them).

At last, they came upon a building that looked like an inn of sorts. It was a two-story affair, made of what looked to be some sort of brown stucco (or perhaps it was mud) with a steeply pitched thatched roof. The strange thing about it, though, was that the building was entirely cylindrical in shape so that the tall peak of the roof sloped down to form a cone shape that sat atop the curved walls like a silly hat.

A sign in front of the door (that was also round) labeled the place as the Grey Mouse. Delicious smells wafted from the open windows (which were, of course, round) as well as a soft tinkle of high pitched laughter.

"Oh!" exclaimed Barnabas. "How delightful! We simply must go in." He paused to rub his belly over his voluminous robe. "Really, I believe we haven't eaten anything since that wonderful piece of fruit from…" He broke off awkwardly. "Well, you know."

Wilfred grimaced at the memory of the ill-fated village, but then hunger and exhaustion overcame guilt. "We may as well eat something whilst we are here," he said, "and perhaps take a bit of a rest, too. I am quite overcome from so much exertion."

"Quite so. And a well-rested detective is a good detective, is what I always say," said Barnabas, who had never said any such thing (until just this very moment, that is).

Pleased with their decision, they pushed their way through the little round door (indeed, it was so small that they both had to duck so as not to bump their heads on the low frame) and entered the Grey Mouse. They found themselves in the main dining room. Everything here, too, was cut to a small scale: child-sized tables and chairs, a bar at the far end that came up only to about mid-thigh of an average-sized person, and ceilings that were so low that Barnabas and Wilfred were forced into an uncomfortable slouch.

The reason for all of this smallness was also readily apparent, and was the source of the high-pitched laughter that they had heard from outside. Seated at the little tables, eating off of little plates with little utensils, were groups of very little people. Each of these people had the head of a mouse. Whiskers twitched and snouts quivered as they ate and talked and laughed amongst each other.

"Oh, my," said Barnabas, finding the entire atmosphere of the place quite adorable. "It is quite like walking into a primary school classroom, isn't it? That is, if little mouse people went to primary school instead of ordinary children."

Wilfred nodded his assent as he looked about in wonderment at the strange, tiny place with its funny little patrons. He too was charmed by the mouse people and was entirely delighted with the place.

A mouse person (presumably a hostess of some sort, since she was wearing an apron over her long skirt) approached them and chirped something at them that was entirely unintelligible. However, she waved a beckoning paw as she moved towards an unoccupied table so that her meaning was quite clear, and Barnabas and Wilfred followed her.

They sat at the indicated table, the short chairs scrunching their legs up so high that their knees pressed into their chests as they perused the menus the hostess set in front of them. Luckily, the menu was comprised entirely of pictures of the available dishes, so that they could read it quite easily. The selection was very limited, catering, as the place did, to such a unique clientele, but Barnabas and Wilfred quickly settled quite happily upon a cheese and cracker platter.

When the hostess came back with their food, they made ready to dig in. However, the hostess chirped something at them that sounded, by the slight lilt towards the end, like a question. Barnabas, thinking that she must, of course, be asking where they were headed (which was a logical assumption, based on normal, polite conversation at an inn located, as the Grey Mouse was, directly on a roadway), replied, "We are going to Bakhu, to see Apep."

The hostess raised her eyebrows and immediately began chattering quickly at them. Soon, other diners seated nearby and overhearing the conversation, such as it was, joined in. It was not long before the entire company was chittering and chirping and squeaking. Whiskers twitched and paws flailed about as the mouse people gesticulated wildly.

Unable to understand a word of what anyone was saying, Barnabas and Wilfred could only nod and smile politely. "It seems," whispered Barnabas to Wilfred from the corner of his mouth, "that these fellows are quite excited by Apep or Bakhu or both. I wonder why?"

"I've no idea," said Wilfred. "I can't understand them in the slightest, can you?"

"Not one word," said Barnabas. "Still, they are quite animated on the subject. I would dare say that they must be quite enamored of Apep, as they seem very excited at the thought of him."

"Hmmm," said Wilfred, not at all sure their excitement was the positive thing Barnabas was taking it to be. Indeed, Wilfred thought that the reaction of the mouse people might instead be interpreted as one of extreme alarm, what with all the twitching and flapping about and wide mousy eyes bugging out over quivering mousy snouts.

Still, he kept his doubts to himself. Barnabas seemed so pleased with his own deductive skills that it seemed a shame to puncture his pride, and besides, Wilfred didn't know for *certain* that the mice were alarmed by the mention of Apep. And really, why should they be? He was merely a minor god of chaos and not nearly as terrifying as the actual god of chaos that they had already faced. Wilfred couldn't remember ever hearing anything about Apep (and he was certain that if the god had done anything *too* terrible, he most likely would have learned about it in his Egyptian Studies class). He looked about the room, and seeing all of the upset mice, frowned a bit despite himself.

Barnabas, although sometimes a bit of a naïve person, was still a detective, after all, and therefore not entirely obtuse, saw Wilfred's expression and instantly knew what his assistant was thinking. "What are you worried about now?" he asked, a bit cross at this example of what he considered to be Wilfred's slightly excessive (and, in truth, a bit tedious) cautiousness.

"It's just that they seem a bit *agitated*," pointed out

Wilfred.

"Agitated, excited, what's the difference?" asked Barnabas.

"Well, said Wilfred, "it just seems to me that maybe the mention of Apep made them quite nervous, is all."

"Bah!" said Barnabas dismissively. "They are happy!" He gestured towards the company. "Look at them waving their paws; listen to their squeaking!" He paused for a moment, thinking. "And, even if they *were* scared, what of it? They are mice. They would be afraid of a cat. Are *you* afraid of a cat?" With that, Barnabas sat back with the expression of a man who had just scored a 29 hand in cribbage.

Wilfred sighed. Perhaps Barnabas was right, and after all, it certainly never hurt to keep an optimistic outlook about things anyway. So thinking, he smiled kindly at Barnabas and nodded. "Very true," he said, acquiescing. "Quite so."

They both yawned then and agreed it was time to turn in for the evening. Barnabas hailed the hostess and dramatically mimed a man sleeping (although she had had no apparent difficulties in understanding their speech whatsoever; so far, indeed, the communication breakdown had occurred entirely the other way around).

Together, the two tired detectives followed the hostess up the short, narrow stairs to the second floor, where they were ushered into a room that boasted extraordinarily small round beds (that, in truth, looked a great deal more like nests than beds), and fell instantly asleep.

Chapter Eleven

The next morning they awoke early, even though they had both thought to sleep in (it seemed that mice tended to be early risers, and Barnabas had found it difficult to merely lie in bed whilst there was so much scurrying and scuffling going on in the rooms around them. Barnabas had tried to ignore the sounds for a while, but he had at last become quite unnerved by something that sounded like scratching on the other side of the thin wall and had jumped up, flustered, thereby waking Wilfred as well.)

Still, once they were both fully awake and had grown a bit more accustomed to the sounds of the busy mice all about them, they realized that their sleep, abruptly shortened as it was, had a restorative effect on their spirits. Barnabas felt positively buoyant, and he was excited to interview Apep and thus solve the case, and Wilfred too found that the new day had brought a greatly improved mood, so that he, too, was optimistic about their chances of success on the mountain Bakhu.

They went down to the restaurant area and breakfasted on an unsurprising yet satisfying meal of cheese and fruit, then made ready to leave.

"Well, good day, and thank you very much," said Barnabas to the hostess (the same one as the night before). He deposited a small pile of pounds sterling on the table, hoping that the British currency would be accepted in this place. She scooped it up efficiently off of the table with scarcely a glance, and Barnabas let out a short breath of relief. Too tired to think about the issue last night, he had worried a bit this morning about what might happen were the Grey Mouse to demand payment of a more local kind.

The waitress twittered something pleasant towards them, and they made their way to the door. Whilst they walked across the room, it seemed that all eyes were upon them (as well they might, as folk such as Barnabas and Wilfred, with their human heads, were quite rare in these parts). "Very well, then," said Barnabas, feeling as though something were expected of him, though he knew not what. "Regards to you all! We are off to see Apep."

At once the company broke into a furor just as they had the night before. Barnabas beamed. "See how they cheer for us?" he said to Wilfred with a broad smile.

Wilfred, though still far from entirely certain that the mice weren't dancing about and yelling in terror rather than acclaim, was at least also not entirely certain that they *were* terrified and not merely excited. "Hmmm," he said, prevaricating, as he saw that Barnabas was looking at him expectantly. He saw Barnabas' smile start to slip a bit, and so he quickly added, "They certainly do make quite a ruckus!" Barnabas took this for agreement, and the two detectives left the Grey Mouse, waving regally to the extremely excited (or, depending on one's interpretation, the completely terrified) group of little mouse people within.

They set out walking once more towards the great mountain that rose darkly from the horizon. As they drew closer, the mountain loomed ever larger and seemed ever more ominous. A great opening gaped across the front at the bottom, which they took to be the entrance into Apep's lair. The place was far from welcoming, and Barnabas felt the ebullience that the happiness of the mouse people had awakened within him fade away. His footsteps slowed and then stopped entirely. Wilfred paused beside him.

"Oh dear," Barnabas said, looking up at the intimidating edifice.

"Dear, indeed," agreed Wilfred, looking up at the mountain as well.

Barnabas lifted his eyebrows and exhaled noisily through pursed lips. "Well," he said, "I suppose it really would be better if we rang first. It's quite rude to just drop in on a fellow. We can send a note, pay a messenger... Maybe there are telegrams..." His voice trailed off nonsensically as he spun on his heels and made as if to walk back to the Grey Mouse. Indeed, he moved so quickly now that Wilfred had to trot to catch him up.

"Wait! Hold on!" he said as he drew up beside Barnabas. He reached out to hold Barnabas' elbow. Barnabas, wide-eyed, looked at the hand under his elbow, wriggled himself away with an unexpected, undulating movement of his arm, and quickened his steps even more.

Wilfred hurried along beside him, making snatching motions every few steps in a vain attempt to recapture Barnabas' arm. "A moment, please!" called Wilfred. "If we could just discuss..." Barnabas merely broke into a flat-out run in response.

Not much of an athlete, Barnabas looked quite a bit like a frightened chicken scurrying this way and that; little legs kicking out to the sides, arms circling and fluttering about. Wilfred found himself running double-time in order to intercept his employer's zigzag path.

At last exhaustion caught up to Barnabas where Wilfred could not. (Barnabas had only been in full flight for about a minute, but he was certainly not in peak condition. Wilfred was in slightly better shape, though he, too, was winded by the brief flurry of exercise.) They stood together, panting, for a long moment. Barnabas hunched over his bent knees with his hands on his thighs; Wilfred performed a slight backbend to open his lungs, hands to the back of his head.

"You were right," said Barnabas mournfully, once he had caught enough breath to speak. "We should not have come here."

"Well," said Wilfred, glad to have his opinion on the matter noted at last, "I didn't mean that we mustn't come here at all. I only meant that we should be *careful* about it, is all."

"Careful, like we were with Set?" asked Barnabas morosely. He sat, defeated, cross-legged upon the ground. "Or, perhaps, as careful as we were with Khnum? Or in the museum? Or with Mrs...."

"Yes, yes, but perhaps even more careful," interrupted Wilfred quickly, before his employer's mood could sink even farther into despair. It would not do to have Barnabas feeling so sorry for himself that he became immobilized on the road directly in front of Apep's mountain. "We can learn from what went wrong in those places and make a better job of it here."

"But how?" asked Barnabas, his voice muffled. His head was now in his hands and bowed so low that he spoke almost directly into his own lap.

"Well," said Wilfred, thinking aloud, "we have hitherto tried to employ subterfuge, yes?"

"Yes," said Barnabas (or, at least, that's what Wilfred *thought* that he said, as his voice was now so soft that it was nearly impossible to hear him).

"So, we could try a direct approach this time. Just come right out and say who we are and what we are doing. We can walk through those doors," he gestured grandly to the big, black opening in the mountain, though Barnabas was not looking at him at all but instead seemed to be intently contemplating the ground between his bent legs, "as calmly as you please!"

"Huh?" said Barnabas, lifting his head a bit.

"I mean, really," said Wilfred, trying a different tack. "It's not as if any of those things were our fault, remember?"

"You don't think?" asked Barnabas, lifting his head a bit more.

"Of course not!"

"And you think we will achieve something better here, with Apep, than we did there, with all of them?"

"Most definitely!" said Wilfred heartily.

Barnabas sighed. "But don't you think that Apep might be, well, *offended* if we just outright ask him where Khepre is?"

"We could just ask if he knows anything?" suggested Wilfred. "We could act as though we were interviewing him, not as a suspect, exactly, but more as a material witness or what have you."

"I suppose that could work," acceded Barnabas grudgingly. He sighed. "I suppose you think me quite foolish for rushing out here, acting for all the world as if we were simply going out for a Sunday stroll, only to fly into an utter panic."

"No, no, of course not," said Wilfred, attempting to mollify Barnabas.

"And with you urging caution all the while, whilst I behave as though we are doing nothing more consequential, nothing more dangerous, than a drive through the park!"

"Oh no, it's quite alright. Nothing really," said Wilfred.

"Still," said Barnabas, refusing to be completely soothed. "It was stupid of me to think that we could just waltz in without a care in the world, just accuse Apep. Stupid, stupid, stupid!"

"No, no!" said Wilfred, placatingly. "Not stupid at all! Indeed, you were quite brave to come here with no fear whatsoever. I was perhaps too cautious."

"Which turned out to be the correct way to proceed, in this case," said Barnabas.

Wilfred merely shrugged and looked aside, affecting what he hoped was an expression of humble acceptance of Barnabas' admission that he had, in fact, been right all along.

"No need to look so smug about it all, though," Barnabas pointed out.

"I'm sure I don't look at all smug!" protested Wilfred, quickly wiping the slightly smug smile from his face.

"Yes, well, you quite do," said Barnabas, reaching out a hand so that Wilfred could help him to stand upright. Once he was straightened out, they turned back around and began to walk, more carefully this time, towards the mountain Bakhu once more.

As they approached, they saw that the light of the perpetual-noon sun couldn't penetrate through the shadows cast by the enormous thing, so that the roots of the mountain appeared to be cloaked in evening darkness whilst the rest of the world was suffering through the glare of a too-bright sun.

Now that they were closer, they could easily see the great black gates that guarded the entrance to the home of their suspect. They viewed the gates with no meager amount of trepidation; neither really wanted to go in there.

There was a menacing air about the place that seemed to creep out of the shadows that shrouded it and diluted the yellow light of the sun. There was no question that the god who lived here relished chaos; disruption and discord and dissonance emanated from every pore of the mountain. The atmosphere was really quite oppressive as they stood there on the edge of the shadow of Bakhu, and Barnabas and Wilfred felt the small remnants of their courage draining away rapidly.

One might have expected Apep's home to be similar to Set's, perhaps on a smaller scale but at least with the same *theme*: that of organized, mischievous chaos. But it was not so. Indeed, this place felt, to Barnabas and Wilfred, far worse than Set's castle.

It was darker, more gloomy, more *secretive* somehow. The worst part, though, was that there were no people about.

"I wonder why there are no people about," said Barnabas, who had noticed this fact almost immediately and was now intensely wondering why.

"It does seem odd at that," agreed Wilfred.

"I wonder… I mean, why *wouldn't* there be people here? Oughtn't there be workers, or servants, or tradesmen, or *someone*, at least?"

"So one would think," said Wilfred.

"And yet there is no one," stated Barnabas again. If he was hoping for a word of reassurance from Wilfred, he was left disappointed. Wilfred merely nodded. It was obvious that they were the only people present, at least that they could see, and the only reasons that Wilfred could think of to explain such a thing were not pleasant ones. Therefore, Wilfred had no intention of speaking them aloud.

"Well then," said Barnabas at last. He squared his shoulders, attempting to regain, or at least to feign, some of the courage and positivity with which he had awakened in such abundance just this morning, but which seemed to have completely deserted him at the moment. "I suppose there's nothing for it. Onward we go!" With that he pointed his arm towards the gate in imitation of a general ordering the charge, and strode (with steps that, to his credit, faltered just a little) towards the ominous opening. Wilfred hurried along at his heels.

The gates, however, remained firmly shut when they came up to them, so that they were forced to stand uncertainly on the doorstep for some moments. At last Barnabas shrugged and rapped his knuckles upon the hard wood.

At once the gates swung open and Barnabas and Wilfred were faced with two startlingly reptilian guards. The guards' appearance was such that the two detectives were taken quite aback. Indeed, at the sight of the long snouts and the equally long teeth that extended from those snouts, both Barnabas and Wilfred involuntarily began to slowly back up.

Barnabas even began to think of ways that they might extricate themselves from the situation, but the excuses that came to mind (things such as, "We seem to have come to the wrong house," or "Oh dear, it's tea time," seemed far too feeble and perhaps might even be taken as rude by the reptilian guards. Therefore, when the guards asked their business, Barnabas could only murmur miserably, "We are here to see Apep. If it's not a good time we could most certainly come back later…"

The guards, however, ushered them in with utmost politeness, so that Barnabas felt a good deal more at ease. They were led down a long, dark hallway until they at last came to a pair of great gilded doors. "You see, Wilfred?" whispered Barnabas as the guards rapped to announce their presence and the doors began to swing open. "It's all about projecting confidence… Aaahhh!"

Barnabas broke off his pedantry because, between the time he began his sentence and the time that it was completed, the doors had come all the way open to reveal a large chamber. The chamber could not properly be called a throne room because there was no throne. There was no throne because the fellow who had come into view with the opening of the doors, and who lounged languidly on the floor of the place, could not comfortably have fit himself onto a throne. He could not fit onto a throne because he was, in fact, a giant snake.

"Oh my!" exclaimed Barnabas, backing up. He looked from one guard to the other. "I do think that maybe we've come to the wrong place, or at the wrong time, or something. It's tea time, I believe, or is it supper, or bedtime? Yes, that's it; it's bedtime. So kind of you. We'll just be off now…"

Barnabas' blabbering was cut short by a bellow from the snake in the audience chamber. "Bring them in! If they're going to disturb me, they'd best tell me what they are about." The tone was peevish and the voice a bit too loud for the space so that it quite assaulted the ears. There was, however, surprisingly little evidence of the sibilance that one would expect from a large snake-man (although, thought Wilfred, the words seemed to be spoken with a great deal of concentration, as though Apep, as that is surely who this must be, were taking great care not to sound *too* snakelike).

At the god's command, Barnabas and Wilfred had no choice but to move reluctantly forward. All too soon, they stood directly in front of Apep.

"Well?" demanded the god. "What do you want?"

Barnabas took a deep breath for courage. He thought it best to hide any trace of fear, so he squared his shoulders and tried to project his voice as confidently as possible. However, his heart yammered in his chest so violently that he found it quite difficult to get enough breath, and his words came out as little more than a whisper.

"We are here at Anubis' request," he said.

"What?" boomed Apep. "Speak up! I can't hear you. You sound like a little mouse."

"Anubis sent us," said Wilfred, managing a tone only slightly louder than Barnabas'. "To ask if you have any information that might help us to find Khepre."

"Why would I help you? Hah! Don't you know I'm a god

of chaos? And a god of chaos doesn't like to be helpful, now, does he?" Apep laughed at his own wit.

"Well," mumbled Barnabas, a bit annoyed at the god's mocking tone, despite his fear, "a *minor* god of chaos, really." In truth, he had said this in a voice that was a good deal quieter than the one he had used before, thinking that Apep would most certainly not hear him. It seemed, however, that he was wrong, and Apep's hearing was a good deal better than he had let on.

"What did you say?" screeched the god. "Well, I never! Have you ever heard such a thing?" he asked his guards. When they shook their heads, that no, they really had never, Apep laughed. The sound was somewhat maniacal, and Barnabas and Wilfred thought it entirely possible that this minor god of chaos was quite entirely insane. Even more so, perhaps, than the dreadful Khnum had been.

Apep turned his gaze back to the two detectives, who now stood frozen in fear. "If you're going to be rude to me, and in my own mountain, and cheeping like little mice, I suppose then you'll just have to *BE* mice!"

The great snake's gaze hardened, transfixing Barnabas and Wilfred with its malevolent power. Suddenly, they felt the world go topsy-turvy. It felt as if they were falling, but their feet never left the floor. Their bodies felt strange, as though they were being turned inside out, and everything in the room suddenly seemed a good deal bigger.

When the sensation passed, Barnabas looked at Wilfred and Wilfred looked at Barnabas. Mirrored in the other's eyes, each saw the same horror that he himself felt; and from this he knew that what had happened to his comrade had happened to himself as well. It seemed that they had been turned entirely into mice, and indeed shrunk to the size of the little mouse people from the Grey Mouse.

They looked up at the guards and saw matching strands of drool oozing from their mouths as the guards looked back at them, licking their lips. Apep continued to laugh maniacally, and the sound seemed even more obnoxious, more terrifying, when heard with their sensitive mouse ears.

Barnabas and Wilfred stared at each other with wide frightened eyes.

"Cheep," said Barnabas.

"Peep," agreed Wilfred.

And without further ado, they turned and ran.

Chapter Twelve

Barnabas and Wilfred ran as fast as their little mouse legs could carry them, the reptilian guards in close pursuit. Certain that they would be devoured if only the guards could catch them, their steps were made as fleet as could be by their fear. With smallness of size came adroitness of foot, and they soon managed to evade their pursuers by ducking through areas too small for the lizard guards to fit into.

Soon enough they found their way between the walls. They could hear the guards on the other side of the wall. From the sound of it, the original two had been joined by a great many others; or, perhaps, it was simply a matter of their overly sensitive mouse ears that made the voices of the guards sound like such a ruckus. For the time being it seemed that their pursuers had no idea where they had gone or how to find them. They had got away.

They bumbled about within the walls for a while, knowing they would not feel entirely safe until they had removed themselves completely from Bakhu and its environs. Luckily, their newly acute sense of olfaction allowed them to smell a hint of fresh air emanating from a narrow corridor, which was no more than a crack in the walls, really. The passage led to a small grating that opened onto the outer wall of the mountain. With a bit of wriggling, they were able to slip through the metal bars and thus made good their escape from Bakhu and the nasty god within.

Without pausing to think about which way they were headed, they simply scurried off in the direction they happened to be facing, running until they fell upon the ground from exhaustion. Their chests heaved as they caught their breath.

When at last Barnabas sat up and looked around, he could see they had come far enough that Bakhu was out of sight; and there was no sign of pursuit behind them (of course, had they thought about it, they would have realized no one would ever have gone to all the trouble of organizing a search party solely for the purpose of recapturing two little mice; indeed, they would have been no more than a tasty snack for Apep and his guards, and if the process of obtaining that snack proved to be more difficult than it was worth, well, that was what pantries were for).

"Squeak. Cheep. Ahem!" said Barnabas impatiently, trying to maneuver his lips around his newly elongated snout so that he might speak. He tried speaking very slowly and carefully.

"Wilfred," he began.

Wilfred, following Barnabas' example, moved his lips with care. "Yes?" he replied.

"Do you, peep, recall the mouse people?" asked Barnabas slowly.

"Yes," answered Wilfred.

"Well, um, do you... That is, are you aware...cheep cheep!" Barnabas flailed his arms above his head in frustration. He was finding it easier to keep the cheeps and peeps out of his speech when he remained calm, and conversely, the mousey sounds became more pronounced when he became excited. The trouble was, it was very difficult to remain calm under such extraordinary circumstances.

"Yes?" replied Wilfred helpfully. Wilfred didn't seem to be having the same trouble speaking as Barnabas, and once he had begun, he spoke with apparent ease. "At the Grey Mouse?"

Barnabas took a deep breath to calm himself, then stood up. Wilfred followed suit. "Yes, at the Grey Mouse. Do you know, peep, ah! That is, are you aware that you seem to actually *be* a mouse yourself?" He had decided that there was no way to state such a thing diplomatically and so it was best to just come out with it.

Wilfred put his hands to his face. He patted at the fur that now covered it, the whiskers that bristled from his nose, and the tiny pointed teeth that stuck out comically over his upper lip. He sighed. "I suspected that was the case," he said. "And you? You know that you... Well, you're...*you* know."

Barnabas pursed his lips together tightly and narrowed his eyes. "I. Have. Had. It. Up. To Here. With. This. Place," he said tightly. He could feel his temper rising, but as it seemed to be making it easier to speak rather than more difficult, he made no attempt to contain himself. "This is ridiculous. I have had enough. We are going to find this stupid scarab beetle fellow, restore this damnably hot sun, and punish the ne'er-do-wells who caused all of this trouble!" With that he strode off determinedly in no particular direction.

Wilfred hurried to catch up to Barnabas. "Where are we going?" he asked.

"What?" replied Barnabas testily. "We are going this way."

"Yes, but to *where* shall we go?"

"Oh, I don't know yet!" snapped Barnabas. "Do stop pestering me and let me think things through a bit, will you?" He paused, immediately regretting his harsh words. "Terribly sorry, Wilfred," he said. "It's just that I'm quite overcome..." He gestured towards his new mouse body with his right front mouse paw. "With all of this and what not."

"Me too," agreed Wilfred. "Me too."

"And how are we to know where to go in this accursed place?" exclaimed Barnabas, kicking at a stone. The stone went flying and bounced off of a small sign that stood at the beginnings of a narrow lane. "And as mice. Mice!" Barnabas continued.

"Um, Barnabas?" began Wilfred, pointing at the sign.

Barnabas ignored Wilfred and continued to kick at the dirt and gravel around him. "And for no reason whatsoever! I mean, I suppose I did point out that he was only a minor god, but he really wasn't supposed to hear that. And isn't it a terrible overreaction to turn people into animals simply

116

because of a harmless comment?"

"Barnabas, the sign there…"

"And to have those guards nearly eat us? Why, how we'll ever sleep again at night, with the memory of those horrible teeth slavering over us as though we were pieces of cheese or something?"

"Barnabas!" shouted Wilfred.

"What?" asked Barnabas, looking confused. "There's no need to shout. What are you going on about?"

"The sign," said Wilfred patiently. "Look at it."

Barnabas did so. "Thoth," he read. "God of Knowledge and Wisdom." An arrow on the sign pointed down the lane. Barnabas thought for a moment, his hand under his chin and his furry eyebrows furrowed over his beady eyes. "Hmmm," he said. "I'm not sure I follow… Oh! As in, this fellow might know things! Things that could help us!"

"Exactly!" said Wilfred. "And really, he couldn't help but be more agreeable than the gods we've already met."

"Quite so!" agreed Barnabas. "One would expect a god of wisdom to be civilized, at the very least."

"And perhaps he can help us find Khepre," said Wilfred.

"Or at least get us out of these ridiculous mouse bodies," said Barnabas, looking down ruefully at himself.

And so, with hope newly ignited in their hearts, the two detectives turned down the lane towards the home of Thoth. Barnabas walked in silence, but the set of his pursed lips and the brisk efficiency with which he moved gave Wilfred to know that he was still in a bit of a temper. Indeed, Wilfred had never seen Barnabas in such a state of annoyance, and he wasn't quite sure what to make of it. He tried to smooth his employer's ruffled fur, so to speak, by attempting pleasantries.

"Quite a lovely garden," he observed, as he peered at the flowering shrubs lining the lane. The bushes were mostly untrimmed and allowed to grow where they would, and the flowers were so profuse as to be nearly unruly, but Wilfred found that he quite enjoyed the effect. It was a bit wild, exotic, almost *Italian*, even, and so quite the opposite of the

117

English aesthetic.

"I suppose," said Barnabas tightly. "If you like things all out of order and askew and in a hodgepodge, then yes, I suppose it could be considered exceedingly lovely." He raised his eyebrows and looked about prissily, so that it was clear that he much preferred neatly trimmed hedges and flowers that stayed in their place.

Wilfred said no more, and they walked on for a few more minutes, until they came to an opening in the shrubbery. Looking in, they could see a bountiful rose garden lined with benches and punctuated by marble fountains here and there. Inside the bower worked a very gnarled, very wrinkled old man dressed in robes of a light, shimmery pink. His robes also happened to be quite dirty, the reason for which was readily apparent as the man was currently crawling on all fours in an attempt to reach a particularly reclusive low-lying branch with his hedge clippers.

"Hullo," said Wilfred after he had determined that Barnabas was petulantly refusing to hail the man. The man jumped, startled, then stood up and smoothed his robes, flicking clumps of dirt and leaves and assorted rose detritus on the ground.

He smiled at Barnabas and Wilfred and said in a soft, friendly voice, "Hello there!"

"Are you Thoth?" asked Wilfred. "Or, if not, would you perhaps know where we might find him? We have come to find Thoth because we are in need of some wisdom and such, you see."

"I am Thoth," said the old man. "And who might you be, you two who are in need of my wisdom?" Wilfred thought that there was perhaps a bit of amusement in the old man's kind blue eyes.

Barnabas stepped forward boldly, and if Wilfred could see a hint of his habitual nervousness written upon his face, so too could he see an alarming degree of defiance there as well. It was obvious that Barnabas had been pushed quite beyond his limits and was in the midst of a fit of indignant outrage.

118

"We," Barnabas said shortly, gesturing towards himself and Wilfred, "are detectives. Important ones, too. We have been brought here all the way from Marylebone to work for Anubis himself, retained to find the missing god Khepre, and yet we have been treated in the most outrageous fashion since our arrival."

"Oh?" asked Thoth politely. "How so?"

"Well!" said Barnabas. "Firstly, I have been killed by a mummy."

"Me too," said Wilfred. "And then dragged about by children with animal heads…"

Barnabas shot Wilfred an annoyed glance, and Wilfred coughed and stopped speaking.

"Yes, as I was saying, we were killed by a mummy, probably the same one, although who's to say? Perhaps it was two separate mummies, although I can't see how *that* would matter terribly…"

"Yes, yes, attacked by mummies and animal-headed children," said Thoth, rolling his hand in a hurry up gesture to get Barnabas back on track.

"Pecked by a horrible canary!" exclaimed Barnabas, his affront reddening his face and making his voice louder than it strictly needed to be in this quiet, peaceful garden. Wilfred cringed a bit at Barnabas' uncharacteristic rudeness, although he assumed that, under the circumstances, it was probably entirely understandable.

"Oh, well, that must have been quite frightening," said Thoth kindly.

"Indeed it was!" said Barnabas. "Then, oh… What else?" He began to list the unpleasant things that had happened to them during their short sojourn in the Egyptian underworld, counting them off on his fingers as he went. "So there was the mummy, the canary, then came the flying monkey monsters, and then there was Set. Although, I, at least, found Set to be quite delightful, not at all what you'd expect from the god of chaos and such. Although of course he did trick us, in a way…"

He broke off for a second, both because he needed to

119

take a breath and because he saw Thoth's eyes begin to drift longingly back to his rose bushes. "Ahem!" he said loudly, and then Barnabas commenced listing his grievances again once Thoth reluctantly returned his gaze to him. "There was Khnum, who tricked us into flooding the Nile and destroying everything and getting people eaten by crocodiles, and then another incident with the stupid canary, and then, lastly, a most outrageous interview with Apep. That fellow is simply the most abominable, most barbarous creature I have ever had the misfortune to meet!"

"All of that sounds very terrible," said Thoth. "You must feel very put out by it all."

"Oh yes, we are extraordinarily put out!" agreed Barnabas. Now that he had got it all out, his voice was beginning to return to its normal polite timbre. Wilfred sighed in relief. Barnabas' excitement was a bit trying on his nerves. "Oh, and also, it seems that we are mice," Barnabas added.

"I can see that," said Thoth. "Were you not, um... How do I say this? Are you not *normally* mice, then?"

"No, we are not normally mice!" yelped Barnabas, his voice rising in pitch again so that Wilfred flinched uncomfortably. "We are people, of course. Human beings! And it is unacceptable that we should be walking about as... as...rodents!" He was so excited that he was quite red in the face now (beneath his fur, that is), so that it appeared that he might suffer from an apoplexy at any moment.

"Yes, yes, of course," said Thoth softly, holding up a placating hand. "But what is it that you wish of me? I will be glad to help you in whatever way I can, you know."

"Well, the first order of business would be to turn us back into people," said Barnabas peremptorily.

Thoth thought for a moment, a frown deepening the creases on his kindly old face. At last he spoke. "I'm terribly sorry," he said. "But I'm sure that I can't do that."

"What!" exclaimed Barnabas. Then, overcome by outraged disappointment, he did the unthinkable: he hopped forward and nipped Thoth on the hand with his sharp mousey teeth.

Wilfred gasped in shock. Thoth yelped in surprise and pain. Barnabas looked back at Wilfred with Thoth's hand still in his mouth and his eyes as wide as he could get them, as though he were as confused as everybody else by what had just happened. Almost immediately, however, he realized what it was that he had done and was mortified at his own rudeness.

"Oh dear!" he cried, slowly dropping Thoth's hand. Awkwardly, he gave it a small pat as though to soothe any pain he might have inflicted. "I am so terribly sorry. I don't know what came over me. I've just been so upset and I'm a mouse and seem to have lost control of my own faculties..."

"Hush," said Thoth, his tone still polite but with a firmness to it now that brooked no disobedience. "It is quite all right, understandable even, under the circumstances. It must be that your mouse instincts kicked in."

"Still," said Barnabas, hanging his head miserably, "I am quite sorry. I shall never forgive myself."

"No need for all that," said Thoth, a bit wearily. "If you had waited for just a moment, you would have heard the rest of what I had to say."

Barnabas said nothing, but shuffled his feet and looked at the ground, abashed. Wilfred, shocked and embarrassed, also said nothing but attempted to plaster a polite smile on his face (the sort of smile that one puts on at an excruciatingly uncomfortable formal tea, but which seemed utterly ridiculous under the circumstances).

"So," continued Thoth, "what I was *about* to say was that, whilst I cannot change you back entirely, I can at least give you back your human bodies. It will be important for you to be of your regular size if you are to go to the house of Bastet. Unfortunately, you will have to keep your mouse heads for the time being."

Barnabas and Wilfred felt quite overwhelmed by Thoth's statement, and neither knew what, exactly, to say, or what questions to ask, or whether they ought to simply remain quiet and wait for Thoth to clarify. So, they both simply began to blurt out all of the thoughts that were now clamoring about in their minds.

"Oh thank you! How soon can we be people-sized again?" asked Barnabas.

"When are we going to Bastet's house? Where is Bastet's house? *Why* are we going to Bastet's house?" asked Wilfred.

"Can't we have our own heads back too? Is there a reason we must have mouse heads? Is there anyone who can restore our heads?" asked Barnabas.

"Wait, isn't Bastet the goddess of cats?" asked Wilfred.

"Hold on! Hold on!" said Thoth, laughing. "Slow down! I will answer all of your questions if you just listen for a moment." Barnabas and Wilfred dutifully shut their mouths.

"You will have your size restored immediately, that much I can do," said Thoth. Barnabas opened his mouth again, ready to offer profuse thanks once more, but Thoth raised a pointed finger for silence and Barnabas obeyed. "It is beyond my power, however, to change your heads back. I cannot undo all that another god has done. Only Anubis has that power. So, perhaps, he will restore you entirely. Once you have completed your task, that is."

Barnabas sighed with regret at that. The way things had gone thus far did not bode well for the successful completion of their task, and thus their odds of getting their own heads back.

"As for Bastet," continued Thoth, nodding towards Wilfred, "you should go to her because she, along with her army of cats, once defeated Apep. If you ask it of her, she may do so again as she bears no love for chaos of any kind. She especially hates Apep, a serpent and thus the natural enemy of the cat. When she defeats him again, he will be forced to tell you all he knows about Khepre's disappearance."

"So, she *is* a cat," said Wilfred ruefully.

"Yes, I am afraid so, which is why it is important that you regain your proper size straightaway. It is unfortunate that you'll still have your mouse heads, what with all the cats that will be about, but oh well, it can't be helped."

Thoth flung up his hands and smiled as though this were a matter of little consequence. Barnabas and Wilfred, not at all sure that this was such a good idea, shared a concerned glance. However, neither wanted to seem ungrateful to Thoth for his help (and Barnabas most certainly felt that he had insulted the friendly god quite enough already with his boorish behavior and unseemly outburst of violence) and so they simply nodded and thanked him.

"Wonderful!" exclaimed Thoth. "Then it is all settled. I will change you back." He waved his hands about airily in their direction, and immediately they felt their bodies shooting up towards a regular height once more; indeed, the effect was extremely disconcerting, almost as though they were falling *up* instead of down.

"Very good," said Thoth as he looked appraisingly at his handiwork. "I'm sure you'll be quite safe from the cats, now. You are far too big to be mistaken for prey, I would think. I would *hope*. Oh well. No matter. It's time to be on your way. I'll call for my chariot and you'll be there in no time."

And so, within minutes, Barnabas and Wilfred found themselves ushered into a chariot (somewhat reluctantly, if truth be told), and they were soon bouncing along the road on their way to the goddess of cats, their mouse whiskers and mouse tails twitching in trepidation.

Chapter Thirteen

And so it was that, restored to their normal sizes but still possessed of mouse heads, Barnabas and Wilfred arrived in short order at the temple of Bastet, Goddess of Cats. Both had, by now, gained control over their new features, and were able to speak quite easily, with nary a peep or a cheep erupting unbidden. (Barnabas, though, would admit later that he still felt a bit *mouse-ish*; indeed, he would say, he felt altogether snippy, as though he wanted to nibble on things, or, shockingly, nip at people. Wilfred, of course, was none too surprised to hear this, as he had seen the way Barnabas' snout quivered, and how he nibbled at his lower lip from time to time.)

All in all, the two detectives were feeling a bit better about things: they had their size back, if not their proper heads; they had found a reasonable person in Thoth, which was reassuring after all of the utterly *unreasonable* creatures they had met thus far; and they had a plan of sorts.

Neither, however, was entirely certain this plan was a good idea, considering the amount of cats likely to inhabit the place and the fact that cats typically considered mice to be dinner. Still, Thoth-the-wise had said that they should come here, and so, with no better idea between them, here they were.

They disembarked from the chariot, thanked the driver, and walked up the stone pathway towards the temple, which was quite beautiful. Made of white marble, it gleamed softly in the sunlight, and the curved staircase that led up to the polished maple doors seemed very inviting. The grounds were fastidiously kept, with neat orderly rows of trimmed hedges and well-mannered rose bushes.

"Well this certainly looks pleasant enough," said Barnabas, looking about the tidy place with approval. "This garden is much more to my liking than that, well, *wildness* at Thoth's house."

"Yes," said Wilfred agreeably. "The gardens are very lovely."

"You know you're in a civilized place when the gardens are well-kept," said Barnabas a bit pedantically. "A person who keeps the verge perfectly trimmed is a person of good manners and breeding, is what I always say."

Wilfred, who had never heard Barnabas say that, nevertheless nodded affably.

"And," continued Barnabas, "the very order of it is, in itself, making a stand against chaos. So we know that nothing untoward could possibly happen in a place like… Oh!"

A pretty calico cat had chosen that very moment to leap out from behind one of the orderly rose bushes and hiss at them in a very untoward sort of way. Barnabas, startled, leapt aside. In doing so, he collided with Wilfred, knocking him off his balance. The force of the impact was such that Wilfred was unable to keep his balance and began to fall. Barnabas' legs had somehow managed to become entangled with Wilfred's so that the two of them toppled down to the ground together in an inglorious heap.

"Oh my!" said Wilfred in surprise.

"Terribly sorry!" said Barnabas.

"Meow!" hissed the cat, now walking slowly towards them with bent legs and a twitching tail so that it appeared to be stalking them.

"Is he…she…it…licking its lips at us?" asked Wilfred.

"Why, yes, I do believe so," replied Barnabas.

"It looks like it might pounce upon us!" said Wilfred.

"Yes, it does certainly look that way. See how its front legs have become all, well, *bunchy*?"

"Indeed I do see that," said Wilfred. He regarded the approaching feline dubiously for a moment. "Although, we are quite a bit bigger than it is, and so I'm sure it couldn't possibly be hunting us. Could it?"

"Well, we are indeed too big for it to eat us, I'm sure," said Barnabas. "But it might give us a nasty scratch, at that. And we do still have these unfortunate rodent heads, you know, so the cat might very well *try* to eat us."

"Quite so," said Wilfred. "Perhaps we'd best stand up, then."

"Agreed," said Barnabas. They quickly disentangled themselves and stood.

"Nice kitty," said Barnabas in what he hoped was the soothing, sing-song voice that people used when speaking to children and pets. He leaned forward with his hand extended as though to pat it on its head.

"Hisssss!" spat the cat, baring its sharp little teeth.

"Uhhh," said Barnabas, cringing and stepping away from the ferocious little beast. He looked across the orderly yard and saw several more cats approaching, attracted, no doubt, by the commotion and the hisses of their fellow. "What do you say we go inside straightaway," he suggested, inching away from the cats.

"Most certainly," agreed Wilfred, who had also noticed the new arrivals.

Not wishing to make any sudden moves that might provoke the cats to pounce, the two sidled slowly sideways up the walk to the steps. When they reached them, they backed up the stairs slowly. Only when they reached the doors did they whirl about quickly. They fumbled a bit at the door handles, as both reached for the same one at the same time, so that they had a bit of a to-do in getting the door open. But at last they succeeded and scurried as fast as they could into the interior, shutting the door behind them.

They were greeted immediately by a cacophony of feline voices. Inquisitive meows, irritated yowls, and outright hostile hisses echoed in a terrible chorus throughout the interior of the marble chamber in which they found themselves.

The place was dimly lit, so it took their eyes a moment to adjust from the brightness of the sun outside; but as soon as they could see, they almost wished they could not. The place was filled entirely with cats, hundreds perhaps, and it seemed that each one had its eye on the two detectives.

"Oh dear," said Barnabas.

"Oh dear indeed," agreed Wilfred.

"Do you think they mean to eat us?" asked Barnabas.

"It certainly *feels* as if they might," said Wilfred. "Perhaps we should go back outside?"

"Well, yes, I would say so, if it weren't for *that*," replied Barnabas, gesturing to the small windows that flanked the door. Small, furry faces with slanted, curious eyes were pressed up against the glass, their noses leaving smudge marks and their breath leaving a fog upon the glass. It seemed their entourage of feline admirers outside had been quite a bit larger than those they had seen.

"Oh dear," repeated Wilfred.

"This really is most distressing," said Barnabas.

"Nonsense!" said a woman whom neither of them had seen in the shadowy room. They turned at the sound of her voice. Still, they only spied her once she stood up and stretched. She had been curled up on a cushion that was propped up high on a pedestal in the far corner of the room (not at all where you might expect a human person to be sitting, which was why they hadn't noticed her before; that, and the distraction of all of the hungry-looking cats.)

The woman leapt down from her perch with feline grace. As she walked across the room towards them, they saw that she pranced forward standing entirely on her tip-toes like a cat. This was less surprising than it might have been, since her face was that of a cat, as well.

"Hullo," said Barnabas, recollecting his manners quickly in the presence of a lady. He sketched a small, nervous bow. "You are Miss Bastet, I presume?"

The woman laughed, a sound that echoed the meowing voices of her multitude of companions (attendants? pets?) and waved her hand dismissively.

"Just Bastet will do. We are not much for such formality here," she said. "And what brings two Englishmen to my doorstep?" Her manner was teasing, almost flirtatious, as she looked sidelong at them through eyes that were mere slits and nearly purred as she spoke. "And however did you get such delicious, I mean, *adorable* heads?" She licked her lips suggestively and ran her fingers lightly up and down Barnabas' arm.

"I say!" exclaimed Barnabas, quite unsure how to respond to such coquettish behavior, having never really been the recipient of such. Indeed, her manner made him feel somewhat uncomfortable for he wondered if he and Wilfred were being toyed with. In any event, he did not much like being spoken to with such forwardness. "We are in no way adorable; in fact, we are detectives, important detectives sent by Anubis himself. And I would suggest, in light of our official status, that we conduct this interview with all due decorum."

Bastet laughed again at Barnabas' affront, but she pulled her hand back from his sleeve. "Very well, then," she said. "I am sorry if I have offended you, but we so rarely have visitors of any kind here, particularly of the handsome male variety. You must forgive me my little amusements." Her words were conciliatory, but a mischievous glint remained in her eye that alarmed Barnabas.

"Yes, yes, of course, Miss Bastet," he said. "One simply must remember that there is a certain professionalism expected during the investigative process. Moreover, I am not a man who goes in for shenanigans of any kind, nor is my esteemed assistant." He nodded towards Wilfred, who blushed furiously as Barnabas' gesture drew the lady's eye upon himself.

"Well," sighed Bastet, "I suppose we should get on with it, then."

"Yes, we should," agreed Barnabas, relieved to be on familiar ground at last.

Bastet raised her eyebrows expectantly, but neither Barnabas nor Wilfred spoke further. Both were looking nervously at the cats that had drawn perilously close. One was sniffing at Barnabas' shoe, and yet another was rubbing itself against Wilfred's leg, tangling his robes in a most alarming fashion.

"Don't mind my babies," she said. "They are merely curious. They won't hurt you."

"Of course," said Barnabas, still looking doubtful as one of his unwanted feline admirers shifted her attention from sniffing his shoe to stretching her claws out to hook upon his robe. "It's just, that, well, you know…" He pointed up to indicate his mousy features.

"Oh, you mean because of your adorable heads?"

"I say! Really!" huffed Barnabas, affronted.

Bastet laughed. "Sorry, sorry," she said. "Really, it won't happen again." Barnabas, of course, not being entirely naïve, did not believe her. In fact, he was entirely certain that this Bastet woman would take any opportunity to say and do things of the greatest impropriety. He heaved a beleaguered sigh and wondered if there was any end to the insults to be offered him in this Egyptian afterlife, and he wondered if he and Wilfred would ever be free of the place.

"So," continued Bastet, "pay no mind to my little friends. After all, you are certainly a great deal larger than they are. How about if you tell me who you are and what brings you here on such *important* business?"

Barnabas ignored the gently mocking tone in her voice and replied, "I am Mr. Barnabas Tew, and this is my assistant, Mr. Wilfred Colby."

"How impressive sounding," purred Bastet.

Barnabas flushed but continued bravely on. "We have been retained, by none other than Anubis, to find Khepre, who, as you may already know, has been kidnapped. Or worse, I suppose."

"Yes, of course," said Bastet, her tone turning peevish. "That is why the sun has been stuck in this interminable noontime. Cats hate that. We much prefer the nighttime."

Barnabas, who had no wish to find out why, exactly, cats preferred the nighttime, hurriedly resumed speaking. "During the course of our investigation, we interviewed Apep, who lives in the mountain Bakhu."

Bastet let out an annoyed hiss, which Barnabas ignored.

"During this interview," he said, speaking a bit louder to assert himself, "Apep took it upon himself to give us these unfortunate heads."

"And then he tried to eat us," added Wilfred. "Don't let's forget about that."

"Indeed he did," said Barnabas, shuddering. "He is an utterly appalling fellow, at that."

"I agree completely," said Bastet. "I have no liking for him either. I suppose you know that I once marched right into Bakhu with my cats?"

"And defeated him soundly," finished Wilfred.

"Exactly," said Barnabas. "Which is, presumably, why Thoth suggested we apply for your assistance in this matter."

"And what, exactly, would you ask me to do?" asked Bastet.

"March against Apep once more," urged Barnabas. "Arrest him so that we might see if he holds Khepre prisoner in that foul mountain of his. Or at least find out if he knows anything about where Khepre might be."

"I should be happy to help you," said Bastet, much to Barnabas' and Wilfred's delight. "I will relish a chance to humiliate Apep once more. If it helps us to have night back again, so much the better. And, besides, my kitties need to play once in a while, don't you, my dears?" She bent down to pick up one of the many cats that surrounded them, petted it and crooned in its ear. "Would you like some lizards to play with?" she asked in a silly high-pitched voice. Barnabas and Wilfred shared an amused yet condescending look. "Would you like to pull some little legs off of some very naughty little lizards? Yes, you would, wouldn't you?"

"Ahem," interrupted Barnabas, alarmed at the violent turn the conversation had suddenly taken. "No need for leg removal. Indeed, we should keep Apep intact so that we might question him."

"Oh, all right," pouted Bastet. "I suppose that is fine." She set the cat down, and it joined its fellows with a yowl. It seemed the cats could sense that something was afoot, and brimming with feline excitement, they now teemed about the chamber. They meowed and yowled and prowled about with agitation, even more so than before.

"When can you be ready?" asked Barnabas, eager to be out of this room with the seemingly hundreds of extraordinarily tense cats. Despite Bastet's assurances and the size advantage that he and Wilfred held, still he was exceedingly conscious of their rodent-like appearance.

"No time like the present!" said Bastet. She gestured towards the door, and Barnabas and Wilfred began to walk towards it. As they did so, she sidled up to Wilfred, hoping to find a more amusing playmate in him than in Barnabas. She took his arm and said, "We cats are not known for our patience. When we want something, we want it *now*."

She laughed at the terrified expression on Wilfred's face and at the sight of Barnabas' lips pinched tight in disapproval. She pulled away from Wilfred and put up her hands in a conciliatory gesture. "Sorry! I can see that you don't like my games," she said, smiling. Her smile faded and her lips pulled back in a fierce sneer. "Perhaps you will find my wrathful side more pleasing," she said, then laughed again when Barnabas and Wilfred's eyes went wide with fright. "Oh no!" she cried, clapping her hands in delight. "Not towards you, of course. Towards Apep."

"Yes, of course. I had assumed that was what you had meant," said Barnabas, although, for a moment he had been quite certain that she had suddenly decided to eat them, or perhaps pull *their* legs off, after all.

They passed through the doors and back into the bright light outside. Bastet danced ahead. "Come, my darlings!" she called, and cats emerged from trees, from behind bushes, through windows; really cats came from every imaginable place until there were thousands of them gathered. "Come, my dears!" sang Bastet. "We ride! We ride to conquer Apep! Let him suffer the wrath of Bastet once again!"

"Is it me," whispered Barnabas to Wilfred, "or is everyone here quite mad?"

"Completely mental," agreed Wilfred. "Even the nice ones are mad as hatters, it seems."

Barnabas sighed. "I do so miss Marylebone. Before the mummies came, that is."

As Bastet gathered her troops, so to speak, a number of human servants quietly appeared and readied a series of chariots. The cats piled into the chariots one after another until at last all were ready to go. Bastet turned to Barnabas and Wilfred as she stepped into the first and finest of the chariots. "You shall ride with me as guests of honor," she said. "You will have your vengeance upon the snake who made you into mice."

Barnabas and Wilfred shared one last questioning glance. Seeing no other choice, they shrugged and joined her in the chariot. Immediately, they were off and headed back to Bakhu.

They reached the ominous mountain all too soon for Barnabas and Wilfred, who looked up at the place with trepidation, but they were quickly comforted by Bastet. "You have nothing to fear," she said kindly, although the predatory glint in her eyes said that someone, at least, had something to fear. "Apep cannot harm you whilst you are with me and my army."

Mustering their courage, Barnabas and Wilfred followed their hostess and her cats as they piled out of the chariots and gathered together in front of the doors to Bakhu. Bastet had just opened her mouth to call out a challenge to Apep when something suddenly nipped Barnabas on the ankle.

"Ow!" he yelped, whirling around to see what had bitten him. He looked suspiciously at the yellow cat that stood nearby, but the cat looked back at him with wide, innocent eyes. Another nip at his other ankle drew his attention back to himself. "Oh, ouch!" he cried, jumping up in the air to get away from whatever it was that accosted him so.

To his horror, he saw his malefactor scuttling away (or, perhaps more precisely, *slithering* away, since it was a snake that had bitten him).

"Oh heavens!" he cried. "I have been bitten by a snake! Twice!"

"Are you quite alright?" asked Wilfred, alarmed.

"I most certainly am not alright!" exclaimed Barnabas as he danced from one foot to another in agitation. "Did you hear me? I was bitten by a snake, and not once but twice!"

"Oh, how horrible," said Wilfred. He looked down at Barnabas' ankles where four little trails of blood issued from four tiny puncture marks, two on each ankle. "I say, I'm sure I could staunch the bleeding if perhaps you'd only stay still for a moment."

Barnabas suddenly stopped moving and stood entirely motionless. "Wasn't Cleopatra bitten by a snake?" he demanded.

"Well, yes, but…"

"And didn't she die from said snake bite?"

"Well, I'm certain that is not the case here…" began Wilfred.

"Didn't she?" said Barnabas again.

"Yes, but…"

"Ahhh!" screeched Barnabas, now running about in a panic. With no particular destination in mind, his trajectory consisted of random circles around the field, scattering annoyed and yowling cats in his wake. "I'm bit just like Cleopatra! I'm Cleopatra!"

"Barnabas, I'm sure that you are not at all Cleopatra," said Wilfred.

Meanwhile, Bastet had captured the offending snake and held it up, regarding it with sardonic amusement. "It's just a garden snake," she said. "And a small one at that."

"Oh the tragedy," yelped Barnabas, ignoring them both. "To die like Cleopatra but no Marc Anthony in sight. Oh, the unfairness of it all!" He had gone quite pale by now, from his exertions and his upset, so that it appeared that he might actually faint at any moment.

"Really," said Bastet, trying not to laugh but failing. "There's no poison at all in this little fellow. You'll be quite alright."

Barnabas stopped running abruptly and dropped to the ground. "I feel so sick!" he said weakly. "How long till I die?"

"Probably quite a while," said Bastet.

"Cleopatra died immediately, did she not?" asked Barnabas, his voice quavering a bit.

"Yes, I do believe so," said Wilfred. "But…"

Barnabas cut him off. "So why haven't I died yet?"

"Because it was just a garden snake and not poisonous at all," suggested Bastet reasonably.

Wilfred, who knew his employer well, tried a different tack. "Probably because you are made of much tougher stuff than Cleopatra," he said. "I'm sure it would take much more than just two snake bites to fell someone like yourself."

"Well," said Barnabas, "I do feel a bit better already." He patted himself all over as though to make certain of this, and then he sat up. "I may be a little dizzy, but you might be right. The poison must be fading away already."

"Your body must have fought it off with remarkable speed then," said Wilfred. He offered Barnabas a hand so that he might have an easier time standing up. Once upright, Barnabas dusted himself off.

"Well," he said, "I guess I do seem to be quite alright after all."

"Indeed," agreed Wilfred, "and your color is coming back nicely."

"Had I gone terribly pale, then?" asked Barnabas, putting his hands to his face and patting as if he might ascertain the blood flow in that way.

"A bit," said Wilfred. "But you look very well now."

"Well, I suppose I shall be fine then," said Barnabas. "Really I am feeling almost as though nothing had happened at all. It is quite remarkable."

"Incredibly remarkable," agreed Wilfred.

"It's like I always say, exercise and proper diet are the most important things. One must keep up one's strength, you know. I suppose Cleopatra must not have eaten very well."

"Probably not," said Wilfred.

Bastet, who had been listening to this exchange with no small degree of disbelief and looking from one mouse-headed man to the other in amused astonishment, interjected

134

at last. "So, might we begin our attack on Apep now?" she asked.

"Quite so," said Barnabas. "Do carry on."

Bastet shook her head, unsure what to make of the strange little duo, and closed her eyes in exasperation. "Alright then," she said briskly, opening her eyes and raising a hand to rally her troops (which had scattered during the commotion and were now dashing about to and fro, chasing butterflies, bees, and each other).

When at last the cats were called to order once more, Bastet reached for a horn that one of her human servants carried and sounded the attack. The cats prowled forward, a vast swarm of feline fury intent upon tearing down the door of Apep's mountain. The attack on Bakhu had begun.

Chapter Fourteen

Barnabas and Wilfred watched from a safe distance as the cats used their claws, with terrible efficacy, to quickly tear the doors to Bakhu asunder. A terrible noise ensued as the reptilian folk within came out to defend their lord and their home against the onslaught of ferocious feline fury. Barnabas and Wilfred shuddered at the dreadful din.

"Should we, uh, help, or something?" suggested Wilfred.

"Hmmm," said Barnabas. "It does feel a bit *useless* to just stand here and do nothing." He glanced down and considered the two small pricks in his ankle where the little garden snake had bitten him. "Still, I don't think that Thoth meant for us to actually *engage* in this sort of thing. I think we have done more than enough just getting it all started."

"Quite so," said Wilfred, relieved. He had not much relished the idea of getting in the midst of the fray. "And I'm sure Anubis would be most displeased if we, the detectives that he went to so much trouble to bring here, were to be wounded by foolishly jumping into a battle of this sort."

"Indeed!" said Barnabas. "I am quite certain he would be most unhappy with us. We are far too valuable, and our safety is necessary for the success of this case. And there does seem to be a lot of teeth and claws and, well, *violence* going on in there. Not at all the sort of thing for us, I'd say."

"No, it is not in the slightest the sort of thing for us. We are meant to work with our brains, not our brawn," said Wilfred.

"Exactly!" said Barnabas, pleased. "And so we shall stay here and trust that these cats take care of their business as well as we have acquitted ourselves with ours."

And so the two stayed back and waited. The sounds of

the battle ebbed and flowed, getting softer at times as the fighting moved deeper into the mountain, or getting louder as it pushed back towards the entrance.

Each time Barnabas and Wilfred heard a particularly loud noise (the angry hissing of an enraged cat; the screeches of a stricken lizard; the crash and tumble of things being knocked over in the kerfuffle) they jumped and took a few steps backwards; so that by the time Bastet at last emerged from the mountain, they were quite a distance away.

Bastet stepped through the doorway and looked at the place where they had originally been standing. Not seeing them, she was puzzled and glanced about the plain. At last her sharp eyes found them several hundred yards from where they had begun. She shook her head and frowned, crooking a sharp claw at them in a beckoning gesture.

Seeing her displeasure, Barnabas and Wilfred felt quite embarrassed and hurried over to her, faces red with shame.

"We only just thought that perhaps we should stand quite out of the way so as not to interfere with your battle tactics," said Barnabas.

Bastet raised her eyebrows. "I'm sure," she said sardonically. Gone was her flirtatious manner, and in its place was a certain brisk aggressiveness; and a bloodlust that was frightening in its intensity shone in her eyes.

"I presume that you have won?" asked Barnabas, since it was she who had come out from the mountain rather than a group of marauding reptiles.

"Of course we won!" snapped Bastet. She sniffed. "A few paltry lizards against my cats? It was too easy. My kitties are just rounding up the stragglers now and deciding what to do with the prisoners."

"Any sign of Khepre?" asked Barnabas eagerly, hoping that the poor scarab beetle god would be found and the case solved. Of course there was the matter of the beetle legs that Bes had shown them, but perhaps that was the only damage the kidnapped god incurred. Barnabas supposed that a beetle could live well enough with a few legs missing, since they had so many to start with, after all.

"No," said Bastet, crushing his hopes. "It was not Apep who kidnapped Khepre. Or, if he did have anything to do with it, he most definitely did not keep Khepre here. We have searched the place. There is no sign of Khepre whatsoever."

"Bah!" exclaimed Barnabas in frustration. He turned to Wilfred. "Every clue we have turns to naught! Where shall we look now? We are out of leads," he concluded sadly.

Wilfred shrugged. "I have no idea," he said. "But I'm sure we'll think of something…"

"Yes, yes." sighed Barnabas, who was hoping Wilfred would have some sort of idea and therefore found his answer most disappointingly unhelpful. "I hope we will, at that. I suppose we may as well start by interviewing Apep to see what he knows." He turned again to Bastet. "So, is Apep, well, is he quite, um, secure? I mean, is it safe for us to go to him now?"

"Apep? Hmmm? What?" asked Bastet, suddenly studying her claws with focused intensity. The ferociousness of her manner had dropped away as quickly as it had come, and now she looked like nothing more than a naughty kitten who had just knocked over a teapot. Barnabas and Wilfred, perplexed, exchanged a glance.

"Yes, Apep. Where is he? I must speak with him."

"Um, yes, well, I don't know. I'm sure someone saw him somewhere, or something…" said Bastet vaguely. She began to nibble at a chip in her claw, refusing to meet Barnabas' eye.

"I say!" cried Barnabas impatiently. "Where is the fellow? I absolutely must see him this instant. And it is quite obvious that you are hiding something from us!"

"Me? No, of course not," said Bastet, at last looking up at the two detectives. Her eyes were wide, giving her face an expression of adorable innocence. "It's just that, well, you won't really be able to talk to Apep right now."

"And why ever not?" demanded Barnabas. "And just *when* might I speak with him, then?"

"Well, you see, it might be a while," said Bastet in a high, sweet voice.

"How long?" said Barnabas. "Speak! What is the reason for this?"

"Well, probably never, is the thing. I don't think he will be able to answer your questions very well, you see."

"What!" sputtered Barnabas. "Why not? What is the matter with him that he can't speak to me?"

"It's just that I ate him, you see," said Bastet, blinking her long lashes at Barnabas.

"You *ate* him?" exclaimed Barnabas.

"Yes," said Bastet.

"As in, you ate him…entirely? He is, um, no more?"

"Yes," said Bastet. "Should I not have done that?"

"Should you not have done that?" yelled Barnabas. "Of course you should not have done that! How on earth are we to find out what he knows if you have eaten him?"

"Huh," said Bastet, a grumpy tone entering her voice. "Really there's no need to shout so. I stormed the mountain for you, after all. And now you say that I didn't deserve a little treat for my efforts." She put on a pouty face. "Most ungrateful you are. And I do find snake meat so very delicious, too." She licked her lips as though to savor whatever might be left of Apep upon them.

"Ugh," said Barnabas, turning away in disgust. He exhaled heavily. "Very well then," he said to Bastet, his voice stiff with politeness. "I thank you for your help in the matter, and I suppose we'll just be on our way now. Good day."

He turned on his heel and strode off in a huff. Wilfred flushed and sketched the lady a quick bow. Her eyes twinkled with their habitual mischievousness as she waggled her claws in farewell and turned to rejoin her army in Bakhu, her tail describing an undulating *S* as she sauntered jauntily back to the doors of the mountain.

Wilfred shook his head, amazed at the capriciousness of the goddess of cats, then hurried to catch up to his employer.

"Quite a puzzle, that one," he observed. "Her moods change faster than a politician's viewpoints, don't they?"

"Insufferable!" said Barnabas, still highly annoyed. "She *ate* the only suspect we have, Wilfred. Ate him!"

"It was most...unexpected," said Wilfred.

"Indeed! It is incredibly absurd. What on earth, or *wherever* we are now, I suppose, are we to do? Go back to Anubis and say, 'Oh, we had a lead, but then our witness, sadly, got eaten?' He will be furious."

"Well," said Wilfred, "I'm sure he will understand."

"He will most certainly not understand," said Barnabas morosely. "Especially since we haven't made any progress at all in solving the case. Perhaps if we had something to go on, some new bit of evidence to bring him, or a decent plan, or what not. But we have nothing. Nothing, I say."

Wilfred sighed, wracking his brain to come up with something, anything that might help. Then an idea struck him. "Hullo!" he cried. "What if this whole thing is not about chaos at all? What if it's simply part of some sort of, I don't know, political maneuvering of some sort and Khepre is just a pawn in the matter?"

"My goodness, Wilfred, you are a genius!" said Barnabas. "That is a splendid idea! It might just be the thing!"

"Oh, well, thank you," said Wilfred, pleased and embarrassed at the praise. "It just came to me. It might not be right, even."

"Nonsense!" said Barnabas. Now that he had an idea to work with, his manner was entirely changed. Where he had been despondent, now he was quite happy; and Wilfred was very pleased to see the improvement in his mood. "But what sort of political thing might this be?" continued Barnabas. "A play for power? Vengeance? And if so, upon whom?"

"It could be anything," said Wilfred. "There are so many possibilities..."

"Then is it nearly impossible to know where to start," concluded Barnabas. He thought for a moment. "I have it!" he exclaimed at last. "We could go see Bes again to see what he has to say. Since he scares away all of the evil spirits, then it follows that he would know quite a good deal about them, too."

"And he would know who held a grudge against whom,"

finished Wilfred.

"Exactly," said Barnabas.

"So, off to Bes!" said Wilfred.

"Onward!" said Barnabas, raising his arm like a general signaling the charge.

Pleased with their keen insights into the matter, Barnabas and Wilfred walked with lighter hearts and a bounce in their steps as they headed in the direction they thought they remembered having seen Bes previously. Still, it was quite a good distance away, and having had yet another long day, they began to grow tired quickly.

"I suppose we'd best just go back to that inn and get some rest first," said Barnabas.

"Great idea," agreed Wilfred. "Perhaps we can hire a cab in the morning as well."

"Indeed, we most definitely should. And I suppose we will fit in quite well at the inn now, considering," said Barnabas as he gestured at their heads.

"Oh!" said Wilfred. "I'm sure. And maybe we will be able to understand what they say, now that we are, well, a bit more like them."

"In all likelihood, I'm certain that we shall. So, it's decided: off to the Grey Mouse!" said Barnabas. "To bed!"

"And a nice, hot meal," said Wilfred. "All of this excitement has put me in the mood for that delightful cheese platter they serve."

"Oh yes, with those fabulous crackers with the little seeds on them. That would certainly hit the spot right about now. Fighting a battle is hungry work, is what I always say," said Barnabas.

Wilfred diplomatically didn't mention the fact that since Barnabas had never actually been in a battle before (and, if one were being entirely accurate, he had not actually participated in one today, either), it was highly unlikely that he had ever said such a thing. And so after a bit of discussion as to which was the proper way to go, they headed off in a new direction, making their way, once more, to the Grey Mouse.

Chapter Fifteen

Because neither was entirely certain of which way to go, it took them quite some time to actually find the place. However, they eventually crossed paths with a mouse dressed in a tunic and loose fitting pants and pushing a wheelbarrow full to the brim with large wheels of cheese. They hailed him and asked if he might show them the way. Since they could now differentiate among the series of squeaks and peeps that made up the mice's language (being partially mice themselves now), things went a great deal more easily than they had the last time they tried to communicate with a mouse person.

They discovered that his name was Babak, the cheese delivery man (mouse?) for the Grey Mouse Inn. Indeed, that was where he was headed now.

"Oh, happy coincidence!" said Barnabas. "Would you mind terribly if we joined you? We are exceedingly famished and have been wandering around for hours."

"Of course," said Babak, amiably enough. He looked in the direction from which they had come, and from where one could just see the tip of Bakhu rising up from the horizon. "I don't suppose you got caught up in all the terribleness over by that mountain over there? I reckon that would put you right out of your way, it would."

"Caught up in?" exclaimed Barnabas. "My heavens, we were the primary players in the terribleness!"

"For real?" said Babak, impressed. "You were in the battle? The one that saved us all from Apep and his awful lizards?"

"Indeed, we were," said Barnabas proudly. "We had gone to interview Apep, you see, for Anubis…"

"Anubis himself sent you? My goodness, but you must be important folk," said Babak.

"Yes, yes, well, I don't like to brag but Anubis did collect us specifically all the way from London to make use of our expertise," said Barnabas, puffing out his chest a bit under all of this unprecedented admiration.

"I never did hear of London. I reckon it must be a good ways away," said Babak.

"Terribly far," said Barnabas.

"In every way," said Wilfred wryly. Barnabas shot him a glance, a bit irritated at being interrupted whilst he was enjoying Babak's attention so much.

"Yes, well, that's beside the point," he said quickly. "Anyway, we interviewed Apep..."

"You never did!" exclaimed Babak. "Nobody goes into Bakhu on purpose. Probably because nobody gets out of Bakhu without, well, without..." He gestured towards his own mousiness, and then towards that of Barnabas and Wilfred.

"We had a job to do, and valor is the better part of discretion, my boy," said Barnabas.

Babak squinched his face up quizzically as he tried to work this out. "Are you sure that's the way it goes? Seems to me it might be a bit backwards-like, or something..."

"Anyway, in we went, right into the very heart of the mountain," continued Barnabas, "and talked directly to Apep. A most unpleasant fellow, to be sure. We didn't like his answers..."

"He was terribly unhelpful," supplied Wilfred helpfully.

Barnabas glared at Wilfred, who quickly closed his mouth. "*So*," said Barnabas, "we went straightaway to Bastet..."

"Well, first Apep turned us into mice," interrupted Wilfred.

"Yes, yes, of course, but then off we went..."

"To Thoth first, remember?" interrupted Wilfred helpfully. "And then he told us to try Bastet."

"The *point* is," said Barnabas pointedly (as Babak, trying

to follow the rapid-fire story, swiveled his head comically from one to the other), "we went to Bastet and enlisted her army of cats in order to defeat Apep."

"So you were in the battle?" asked Babak, his eyes wide with awe.

"Yes indeed," said Barnabas.

"Well, sort of off to the side," said Wilfred at the same time.

"So," said Babak, confused, "you were in a battle that was off to the side?"

"Something like that," said Barnabas with a testy glance at Wilfred. "But, as I was saying, the point is, the battle wouldn't have happened without us and now Apep is quite entirely gone."

"So I've heard," said Babak. "And you have no idea how happy everyone is. Just wait until we get to the Grey Mouse. Folks will be most excited to see you, I know it. Why, you'll be famous in these parts!"

"Oh, well, I'm sure we only did what anyone would do," said Barnabas, reddening a bit and affecting an air of faux modesty.

"Now don't be silly," said Babak. "You did a right good thing there for us all. Folks weren't safe, not with all those lizards being about and us being mice and all, but now we can just go about our business with hardly a care in the world."

Barnabas, of course, immediately took in the small size of their new friend and thought about Anti and all the other birds of prey that seemed to inhabit this place. He was certain that falcons and hawks and eagles, and possibly even ravens, would find Babak a tasty little morsel. Of course, he didn't say anything about this, but merely pursed his lips tightly to keep quiet. A glance at Wilfred confirmed that his assistant's thoughts ran much along the same lines as his own.

"So," he began, to break the awkward silence. "Shall we?"

"Of course, of course, where are my manners, just standing here like this!" said Babak. "You must be famished!

You just follow me and we'll be at the Grey Mouse in no time. And dinner's on me!"

They did as Babak suggested and soon found themselves pushing through the doors of the Grey Mouse. The day was quite spent (although, thought Barnabas, one would never know it from the infernally hot blaze of the interminably noontime sun), so that the inn was very crowded with those enjoying a nice cool drink or two after dinner.

As soon as they entered the place, Babak called out for everyone's attention.

"Look who we have here!" he said. "It's none other than…" He paused and looked at Barnabas and Wilfred. "What are your names again?" he whispered loudly. Wilfred quickly told him. "Lord Barnabas and Sir Wilfred!" announced Babak dramatically.

"Well," corrected Wilfred, "we aren't really lords of the realm or anything, just detectives…"

"Who are the great heroes of the Battle of Bakhu!" continued Babak, ignoring him.

It seemed that the story of the battle had preceded them, and they were given a hero's welcome. "Hurrah!" shouted the mouse people, raising their glasses to them and applauding with their tiny mouse hands.

Barnabas stood tall and proud and looked as though he might be entirely overcome with emotion, and even Wilfred felt himself beaming under the praise.

The same hostess as before hurried over to them, shushing the crowd as she moved across the room. "Hush now," she scolded amiably. "Let them have their peace. They must be famished after their adventure, and much too tired to deal with the silliness of all you people to boot."

The patrons obediently quieted immediately (although as soon as her back was turned a few raised their paws in a celebratory fashion and mouthed things like: 'well done, brilliant, and Osiris bless you, at them). Still, the general din was much reduced as she ushered them to their table, and they were left to enjoy their heaping cheese platter (on the house, of course, rather than paid for by the gracious Babak)

145

in relative quiet.

The hostess (whose name was Bindi, as they found out after Barnabas shyly asked her) was very attentive, and made sure they had all they needed in order to feel comfortable. Wilfred noted with some surprise, however, that Barnabas seemed to become more and more flustered each time she appeared with a refreshment of their crackers or a new bottle of wine. Indeed, as the evening wore on, Barnabas' face was flushed so deeply (as was evidenced really only by the inside of his ears, where the fur was sparse) and stammered over his words so badly that Wilfred began to wonder if perhaps his employer was quite drunk.

Bindi came to their table once more and asked if all was well.

"Very much, no. Cheese, quite a lot of it, too!' said Barnabas somewhat nonsensically, patting his belly.

"So, you want more cheese?" asked Bindi, confused.

"Heavens no," said Barnabas, flushing even more. "Good cheese is all I meant. No more though. Wilfred?" He looked to his assistant as though pleading for help.

"We are very well, thank you very much," said Wilfred smoothly. "We are quite full and very happy, is what Barnabas here means to say."

Bindi, as though she understood entirely, smiled and nodded politely. "Very good then," she said. "Your room is ready whenever you are. You can collect the key from the boy over there." She indicated a young boy who stood near the stairs, listlessly pushing a mop to and fro across the floor. "He'll show you to your room. Sleep well!"

She walked away, and Barnabas watched her as she went. Wilfred stared at him in some consternation. "Is all well with you?" he asked at last. "Are you feeling all right?"

"What?" asked Barnabas, startled out of his reverie. He sighed. "She's quite a nice lady, don't you think?" he asked after a moment's pause. To Wilfred's relief he now seemed able to enunciate perfectly well, and the flush seemed to be receding from his ears.

"Who? The hostess?" asked Wilfred.

"Yes, Bindi," replied Barnabas. "Don't you find her to be very pleasant and personable?"

"I suppose so, yes," said Wilfred. "I think she puts me in mind a bit of Mrs. Crowder. Seems very motherly in her approach to people. Oh how I do miss dear Mrs. Crowder!"

"Yes, yes, of course," said Barnabas. "A fine woman, most definitely."

"Mrs. Crowder, you mean?" asked Wilfred.

"No, Bindi," replied Barnabas. "Not that Mrs. Crowder is not a fine lady as well," he corrected himself hurriedly. "Only I just meant to say that I think that Bindi is also quite a nice lady, too."

"Heavens, Barnabas, do you fancy Bindi?" gasped Wilfred, astonished. His suspicion was immediately confirmed when Barnabas' ears began to redden once more.

"Of course not," lied Barnabas quite obviously. "You know I'm not one for that sort of silly thing. "But if I were to be," he added, "I suppose that one could do far worse than such as her. Just hypothetically, of course."

"Of course," said Wilfred, hiding his smile. "Excepting for the fact that she is a mouse and you are not. Well, I suppose that you *are*, in fact, a mouse at this very moment, but that is temporary, I am sure."

"Well, yes, of course, which is exactly why it's a hopeless fancy. I mean, assuming, hypothetically, that one were to have such a fancy, which I most certainly do not. Since, as I said, I don't go in for that sort of thing, you know. Love and romance are not for one such as myself."

"Of course not," agreed Wilfred. "You are far too sensible."

"I err on the side of sensibility so much as to nearly be insensible," said Barnabas.

"Indeed," said Wilfred.

"A true paragon of sensibility could hardly be more sensible than I," said Barnabas.

"Hardly," said Wilfred.

"Still," said Barnabas, sighing a little once more as they rose and prepared to find their rooms and their beds for the night, "one could certainly do much worse than one such as Bindi, if one were to be of the romantic sort. Which I most certainly am not," he added emphatically.

"Not in the slightest," agreed Wilfred. And with that, they headed off to bed and slept the deep sleep that is only possible when one is utterly exhausted and completely stuffed full of wine and cheese.

They awoke early the next morning. Barnabas opened his eyes first and, seeing the sun high in the sky, presumed that they had slept till noon; forgetting, of course, that the sun was perpetually in the noon position, which was why they were there in the first place. He leapt up in a panic, also forgetting that they were no longer in London (indeed, they were no longer in the land of the living at all), and therefore no longer restrained by the rules of scheduling and time management that prevailed there.

"Wake up, Wilfred!" he yelped. He hopped about the room, clumsily trying to put his robes on whilst bouncing about in search of his socks. "Goodness, but we've slept past noon! Oh, do wake up!" He found his sock, balled it up, and threw it at the unresponsive Wilfred's head.

"Huh? What? What's happened?" cried Wilfred as he opened his eyes to see his employer running frantically about their shared room.

"It is noon, is what's happened," said Barnabas. "We've wasted the entire morning."

Wilfred sat up and looked at the clock that hung on the wall.

"It's quite all right," he said, pointing towards the clock. "It's only just half past seven."

"What?" said Barnabas, looking in some confusion from the clock to the window through which the sun shone from high in the sky. "But the sun… Oh, right." Realizing his error, he was silent for a moment. "But still," he said at last. "We've got work to do. And seeing as we are both awake anyway, we may as well get on with it."

Wilfred obligingly rose and dressed, and in no time at all the two were seated in the dining room downstairs to break their fast. The waitress on duty (who, whilst pleasant enough, was not Bindi, and therefore fell far short in her waitressing duties in Barnabas' eyes; her manner was not as amiable, the service not as prompt, even the table itself was not nearly so good as the one that Bindi had brought them to the previous evening) quickly brought them another heaping board full of cheese and crackers. This too proved to be quite a bit less appetising than the night before. Great amounts of cheese taste much better when one is famished and not already stuffed to the brim with the same from the night before.

Barnabas looked about eagerly for Bindi, but she was nowhere to be seen. He didn't think it seemly to ask about her whereabouts, and so he satisfied himself with stealing quick glances every time the door to the kitchen opened, disappointed each time because Bindi did not come out.

At last, Barnabas could no longer delay their departure by feigning interest in their unappreciated cheese platter. He pushed back his chair and sighed. "All right, then," he said. "I suppose we'd best be off."

"Certainly," said Wilfred. "To see Bes?"

"I think that the most strategic course of action, don't you?"

"Most definitely," agreed Wilfred. He thought for a moment. "How shall we get there?"

"Well, we could, um… That is, hmmph," said Barnabas. "I suppose I hadn't thought that through. How does one get around in this place?"

"We could walk," suggested Wilfred.

"We could," agreed Barnabas. "So, we'd head…" He turned about in his chair. "That way," he said, pointing towards the east at the exact moment Wilfred said the same and pointed towards the west.

"Huh, well," said Barnabas. "It looks as though we've got somewhat turned around, what with all the adventures we've had."

"Quite," said Wilfred. "And we came some of the way by chariot, took a few detours to see Set, and then the uh, *episode* on Elephantine Island…" They both shuddered at the

149

memory of the insane Khnum, the flooding, and the fearsome crocodiles.

"Dreadful thing that," said Barnabas.

"And aside from that," said Wilfred, changing the subject, "then we came all the way out here to see Apep, and then Thoth and Bastet, and then Apep's mountain again..."

"So it's really no wonder that we have no idea which way to go," said Barnabas. "Indeed, I don't suppose anyone could keep their bearings in this place."

"'Scuse me, Lord Barnabas. Sir Wilfred," interrupted Babak, who had come up behind them some time before and, not wanting to interrupt, was patiently waiting for a break in their conversation. "But if you're looking to find Bes, my cousin Babook is heading that way right now and I'm sure he wouldn't mind taking you along."

"Oh!" said Barnabas, jumping with startlement. "Must you sneak up on one so?"

"No offence," said Babak apologetically. "I only didn't want to break into your conversation and all, but it's just you seem to be having some difficulties getting to Bes. So I thought I could be of help. But if you don't want to go with Babook..."

"No, no," said Barnabas quickly, hoping that his hastily spoken words hadn't offended the kind fellow. "I'm certain that we do. You just gave me a fright, is all. Sorry about that. A battle with giant lizard people makes one a bit jumpy, you know."

"And I should have cleared my throat or something, so as you'd know I was there," said Babak.

"Well, in any case, your help is much appreciated," said Barnabas. "I'm sure we would love to travel with your cousin. Is he leaving soon?"

"In about five minutes," said Babak. "I can carry your things out for you, if you'd like, and you can ride in his cart. Won't be any trouble at all. He'll be glad of the company, too, I'm sure."

"Five minutes, you say? Splendid," said Barnabas, although he couldn't help but look about the room, as though searching for something. "How can we thank you?"

"Aww, well, it's the least I could do, seeing as how you got rid of Apep and his minions for us."

"Perhaps a bit of cheese?" said Barnabas, indicating the cheese platter that lay nearly untouched on the table. Since a mouse never refuses cheese, Babak gladly began to dig in. "And, of course, your cousin is welcome to have some as well."

"He will be glad to," said Babak, going outside to collect Babook. Barnabas and Wilfred watched as the two nibbled voraciously at the cheese, and Wilfred wondered why Barnabas seemed to have abandoned his hurry and seemed now to be delaying their moment of departure instead.

The reason for his prevarication became clear the very next moment, when Bindi at last appeared in the room. Barnabas stood up tall and smoothed the fur on top of his head.

Bindi smiled and made her way over to them. "I suppose you'll be off now?" she asked.

"Yes," stammered Barnabas, looking down at the floor.

"We are off to see Bes," said Wilfred. "I don't suppose we will be back this way for some time, if at all, but we'd like to thank you for your hospitality."

"And thank you for your heroism," she said, placing a small paw on Barnabas' arm. "Apep's lizards were a terrible scourge, and you saved us from them."

"Er, yes, lizards. Well, a bad lot they are," said Barnabas.

Wilfred looked at Barnabas in some consternation, wondering what was the matter with him. Barnabas simply continued to stare at the floor and his whiskers began to twitch furiously.

"Well, then, are we ready?" asked Babook, wiping the last of the cheese from his mouth.

"Quite so," said Wilfred, turning to follow Babook out of the inn. "Barnabas?" he asked when he saw that his employer was still standing there, rooted to the same spot in front of Bindi.

"Yes, well, here I come. Good day then," he said,

nodding briskly towards Bindi. With visible effort, he spun on his heels and strode out the door. Wilfred, bemused, followed him.

Babook helped them into the back of his cart, climbed up onto the driver's bench, and snapped the reins (which were attached to two sheep-like creatures that apparently served mouse people in the same way that horses did normal people). Barnabas remained pensively quiet for some time, and Wilfred knew better than to try to engage him whilst he was thus preoccupied with his thoughts. And so it was that they were off to see Bes, with Babook humming merrily in the front of the cart, Wilfred enjoying the scenery from the back, and Barnabas pondering the cruel twist of fate that had led him, an avowed bachelor who had no time for silly emotions, to fancy a mouse woman who lived in the farthest reaches of the Egyptian underworld.

Chapter Sixteen

Barnabas' depressed, reflective mood passed after about an hour on the road. He was, after all, a naturally happy, if also somewhat nervous, sort of fellow; and he was also a very responsible man. He knew that, right now, he had a job to do, one of incredible importance, and it simply wouldn't do for him to indulge himself in a sea of lovelorn melancholy.

Therefore, he decided to pick himself up by his bootstraps and mentally brush himself off, so to speak. "Sorry I've been so quiet, Wilfred my boy," he said, trying to inject a bit of hearty joviality into his voice. "Just a bit tired out, I suppose."

Wilfred, who understood very well that it was not tiredness at all that had so dampened his mood, nodded and smiled. "Yes," he said, "we certainly have had an adventuresome few days. I'm quite knackered myself."

"Understandably so," said Barnabas, nodding. "Anyone would be after all we've been through." He paused, thinking, as they bounced along the bumpy road, listening to the creak of the wheels and the quiet hum of Babook's singing. "Do you suppose Bes will be able to help us out at all?" he asked at last.

"I'm sure," said Wilfred. "Indeed, I wish we had asked him a bit more when we had the chance."

"Yes, well, we were so very focused on going to Set..." said Barnabas.

"Which didn't turn out to be very helpful in the end, I suppose," said Wilfred.

"Not very helpful at all," said Barnabas. "Really, it turned out quite horribly, not just for us but also for that poor village..." They both pulled faces of remorse and horror at the memory of the villagers and the flood and the crocodiles.

"Which," resumed Barnabas after a moment of silence, "was really the fault of Khnum, whom we went to see on the advice of Set."

"As Anubis had told us to do," added Wilfred.

"Quite so!" said Barnabas. He scratched his chin and frowned. "And remember that Anubis told us to interview Apep as well."

Wilfred caught his breath as Barnabas' point struck him. "And that didn't turn out very well, either, did it?"

"Not very well at all," said Barnabas. "I think there's a lesson to be learned there."

Wilfred waited a moment for Barnabas to state the lesson that they were supposed to have just learned. When no explanation was forthcoming, he prompted, "That perhaps it is better *not* to follow Anubis' advice?"

"Precisely!" said Barnabas, triumphantly raising a finger in the air. "I was just about to say *precisely* that!"

"Of course," said Wilfred. "I could see where you were going with your line of thought."

"And so," continued Barnabas, "if we oughtn't to listen to Anubis, well then…" He paused, thinking.

"We should follow our own intuition?" supplied Wilfred.

"Precisely!" said Barnabas again, once more proffering a single finger to the air. "After all, going to Thoth was an idea entirely our own."

"It was indeed!" said Wilfred. "And of all the things that we have done thus far, that was the most productive by far."

"By far," agreed Barnabas. "And so I am certain that we are on the right track by going to interview Bes more thoroughly."

"Surely he will know something. He will have heard a rumor of some sort or perhaps have a theory of his own to espouse," said Wilfred.

"And perhaps he knows a bit more about Khepre's servants. I did, after all, put the idea in his head when I asked about the maid. Or was it Anti that I asked about the maid? Oh dear, I'm sure that I can't remember."

"Yes, the maid, of course," said Wilfred doubtfully.

"It's always the maid," said Barnabas sagely, shaking his head.

Engrossed in their conversation, neither noticed that Babook had stopped humming some time ago and was now clearing his throat noisily in an effort to get their attention. Frustrated in his vain attempts, the delivery man at last turned around entirely, leaving the two sheep-things that pulled the cart to steer for themselves.

"Sorry to interrupt...," he began, looking from Barnabas to Wilfred and back again.

"Hmmm, what?" said Barnabas, startled. In truth, he had quite forgotten all about Babook, but he managed to mostly suppress the little jump of surprise that the cart driver's interjection had given him.

"Well, I don't like to interrupt and all, but it's just I couldn't help but hear what you'uns were sayin' about Khepre's servants and all."

"Yes?" said Barnabas. "Do you have something to say on the matter?"

"Well," said Babook modestly, "I'll bet you already know lots more than what I could say, but, well, bein' a delivery mouse and all, well, you see things sometimes."

"Such as?" said Barnabas, drawing his words out with exaggerated slowness. Wilfred thought that the air of patient condescension that his employer was trying to effect was made implausible (ridiculous even) by the fact that he was still possessed of a mouse's head. His little eyebrows drawn up in the middle of the furry forehead, his sardonically twitching whiskers and tiny nose wrinkled up: all conspired to make Barnabas look slightly adorable rather than intimidatingly intellectual (as he so clearly wished to be seen).

Wilfred giggled a bit at the sight of Barnabas attempting to appear stern with a mouse face. Barnabas shot him an annoyed glance, and Wilfred quickly hid his mirth behind a feigned sneeze.

"Pardon," he said. "Something in the air."

"Humph," said Barnabas, looking at Wilfred suspiciously. "I'm sure." He pursed his lips disapprovingly and turned back to question Babook further.

For his part, Babook didn't know quite what to make of the two strange detectives riding in the back of his cart. His cousin Babak had said that they were great heroes of some kind, and Babook was sure that, if Babak said it, then it must be so, but still…he couldn't quite picture these two behaving in an *heroic* sort of way. He sighed and put the matter from his mind. He didn't know much about heroes, had never met one before, and so, he thought, probably couldn't tell the difference between a hero and any other sort of person. Perhaps heroes only seemed to act silly to people such as Babook only because people such as himself weren't smart enough to understand what it was, exactly, that they were saying. Anyway, he thought, it didn't matter: Babak had given him a job to do, and therefore he would take these two where they needed to go and tell them what they needed to know.

"So," Barnabas was saying impatiently, "you know something about Khepre's servants?"

"It probably ain't much," said Babook.

"I'm sure that it will be quite helpful," said Barnabas whilst shooting Wilfred a glance that said that he was sure it would be anything *but* helpful.

"All right, well, it's just that I heard that a bunch of folks who used to work for Khepre were taken in by Anti and Montu. You know, Anti, that falcon man who runs the ferry and Montu, the old warrior god that nobody thinks much on anymore."

"Yes, yes," said Barnabas impatiently. "I *know* who Anti is. So you say that Khepre's servants went to work for Anti and, um, the other one…"

"Montu," said Babook. "Which I wouldn'ta paid much attention to exceptin' to think that it was mighty nice of those two to take 'em in, considering."

"Considering what?" asked Barnabas, his interest piqued now. He wasn't sure how, but he felt certain that this was

156

important information that might prove immensely helpful, if only they could puzzle out the meaning of it all. But to do that he must first extract every piece of knowledge that he could from Babook, who was proving to be a maddeningly slow storyteller.

"Well, considering the council and all," said Babook.

"*What* council?" asked Barnabas, having a difficult time hiding his impatience.

"You know, the council where the old gods were put off and a bunch of new gods took their place."

Barnabas sighed. "I'm really not sure what all of that has to do with Anti and Khepre and Mundo," he said.

"Montu," corrected Babook.

"That's what I said," said Barnabas. He waited for Babook to explain further, but Babook remained silent. "So," said Barnabas slowly, "will you tell us *what* that council has to do with Anti and…well, everything else?"

"It's just that Khepre was *part* of the council," said Babook. Seeing that Barnabas and Wilfred still didn't understand, he sighed and wondered at the lack of historical knowledge possessed by these particular heroes. "And Anti and Montu were two of the gods set down."

"Anti was once a major god?" interjected Wilfred. "As in, Anti the boatman?"

"One and the same," said Babook, feeling important that he had been the deliverer of information that was clearly new to them and of increasingly apparent interest. "Anti was one of the great warrior gods from before. Montu too. But then the new gods come in and take over, and that was that for the likes of Anti and Montu and such. The old gods got pretty salty about it, too, from what I hear."

"So it is quite surprising indeed that either of them would hire servants who worked in the household of someone who was an integral part of their deposement," observed Wilfred.

"Uh, yeah, I guess," said Babook, who was not at all sure what Wilfred had just said, but who also didn't want to admit that.

"Do you know which servants went to whom?" asked

Barnabas.

"Well, all that I don't know. But I think that there was a maid who went to work for Anti not a day after Khepre disappeared. I thought it sort of ungrateful-like to just up and go without even waiting a couple days at least…"

"Aha!" exclaimed Barnabas, cutting off Babook mid-thought. Wilfred and Babook looked at him expectantly, so that he flushed with embarrassment. "It's just I did say, you know, that it is always the maid. So when Babook said that bit about the maid, I got a bit carried away, I suppose."

"Quite so," said Wilfred. "And I must admit that it all does seem a bit extraordinary. But what, exactly, should we make of it?"

Barnabas opened his mouth to answer, then closed it again. His first instinct upon hearing about Khepre's maid going to work for Anti (and in such a precipitous manner, too!) had been to feel vindicated in his original suspicion. However, upon further reflection, he was not quite sure at all what this information actually meant. He was certain that the information was important, but he didn't know exactly *how* it was important or *which* part of it was important or *what* they ought to do about it.

Wilfred was still looking at him, waiting for an answer. He sighed and admitted, "I suppose I don't entirely know. We should think about it, and hopefully an answer will come to us soon."

"Shall we still go talk to Bes, then?" asked Wilfred.

"I don't see why not," said Barnabas. "After all, we've come all this way and may as well see if he has anything to suggest."

"Well, you'uns are in luck, then," said Babook. "'Cause if it's Bes you're wantin' to see, that there is the road to his house, right up there. We'll be there in less than five minutes, I'm thinkin'.'"

"Very good, very good," said Barnabas distractedly. The problem of what to make of the information about Khepre's maid and Anti and Montu jigged about uncomfortably in his mind, and he was still thinking about it (with no progress towards satisfaction whatsoever) a few minutes later when Babook's cart pulled up in front of the large structure that served as Bes' home.

Barnabas' thoughts were pulled from the problem by the spectacle of Bes' house, which was built entirely within the boughs of the tree, its boards nailed haphazardly together this way and that like a tree house built by child. Only this structure was much too enormous to have been constructed by childish hands.

Barnabas and Wilfred gazed up at it for a time. Wilfred found the place quirky and delightful in its eccentricity, but Barnabas was disturbed by the precarious way in which the great wooden boards, all of uneven size, leaned akimbo upon their neighbors so that none of the walls were entirely straight and none of the corners were even close to true.

"Shall we knock upon the door?" suggested Wilfred at last.

"If we can find the door," replied Barnabas, frowning up at the towering, disheveled structure with distaste.

Wilfred pointed to a crooked wooden ladder that led up through a small hole in the underside of the house. "I think it must be up there," he said.

"Hmm, well, yes," said Barnabas, frowning even harder. "I thought you might say that." He sighed, then laboriously (and, to both Wilfred's and Babook's eyes, a bit overdramatically) climbed out of Babook's cart. Wilfred followed suit (with a bit more ease, although it must be said in Barnabas' defense that Wilfred was Barnabas' junior by nearly a decade and it *had*, after all, been a long and bumpy cart ride, which could make anyone's joints stiffen up).

Once both of his passengers were removed from his cart and safely deposited on Bes' lawn (which was as overgrown with weeds and wildflowers as one might expect from someone who would live in a house such as this, thought Barnabas dourly), Babook nodded his head to them in farewell.

"G'day to ya both, then," he said. "I hope you'uns have very good luck."

"Luck is made by he who is prepared to make it, not bestowed upon those who merely await it," said Barnabas sagely.

Babook smiled politely back at him, thinking once more that he really did not know what to make of this funny little detective. "Well, then," he said, "I hope that you got yourself a whole lotta luck prepared, then." With that, he snapped the reins and was off.

"Strange little fellow," observed Barnabas as he watched Babook and his cart bounce off down the lane. "Don't you think?"

"Quite," agreed Wilfred. He gestured towards the ladder that almost certainly led to the entrance to Bes' home. "Shall we?"

Barnabas sighed. He found the whole place far too rickety and unkempt for his taste, and he was far from certain it was structurally sound. Indeed, he feared that to step a foot upon that ladder might very well bring the entire building toppling down upon their heads. Still, he had no wish to appear a coward in front of Wilfred (or even to himself; if truth be told, he much enjoyed the feeling of thinking of himself as the Great Hero of the Battle of Bakhu). Therefore, he couldn't very well balk at the prospect of climbing up a simple ladder, no matter how ill-constructed the thing might be. "Very well," he said at last, unable to keep the reluctance from his voice. "I suppose there's nothing for it." He took a few steps towards the ladder, then paused at the bottom of it. "After you," he said politely, gesturing for Wilfred to precede him.

Harboring far less compunction about the ladder than his employer (Wilfred had been quite an outdoorsman as a child, and had built his fair share of lopsided tree houses, all doomed to collapse), Wilfred readily grasped the rungs and began to climb. Barnabas waited until Wilfred was nearly all the way up before following him, which he did with a great deal less enthusiasm and a great deal more effort.

At last Wilfred reached the top and rapped his fist softly on the underside of the trap door that barred their path. After a moment's wait, the door lifted and Bes' wide, round face peered out. The god reached his great big hand down to help pull them up into his abode; first Wilfred, who stood beside him as they waited for his employer, and then Barnabas a few long moments later.

"Come in, come in!" said Bes jovially. "Good to see you again, my fine fellows! Barnabas and Wilfred, is it not?" Soon enough, they had both been hoisted up to stand in the entrance room of the tree house. Wilfred looked about delightedly, taking it all in. Barnabas, on the other hand, found himself terribly distracted by a disturbingly large gap between the boards beneath his feet, through which he could see the ground some thirty feet below. He tried to look away and pay attention to the business at hand, but his eyes disobeyed him and repeatedly returned to that spot until he felt nearly ill from vertigo. He was much relieved, therefore, when Bes suggested that they sit and ushered them towards a very large, very puffy sofa.

"Would you like something to drink? Tea, perhaps? Some ale?" asked their host.

"Oh yes, please," said Barnabas quickly. "Tea would be just the thing right now." He hoped that it would settle his stomach, which was churning alarmingly from the height and precariousness of the house. Wilfred also accepted the offer of a beverage and thanked Bes for offering.

Bes waddled off to fetch the tea, and Wilfred leaned in towards Barnabas. "How do you suppose he recognized us, what with these, you know, mouse heads and what not?" he whispered.

"What? Oh, yes, I had wondered that myself," said Barnabas, who had not wondered that at all until just now, when Wilfred brought it up. "I suppose that it's because we are quite famous, perhaps? Probably word has got back to him of our exploits, as well as..." He gestured from his own furry head to Wilfred's and back again. "Our travails."

"Huh," said Wilfred. "If everyone knows everything around here, then how come no one knows anything whatsoever about the one thing that we are trying to figure out?"

"A good question," replied Barnabas. "It would seem to point to a conspiracy, don't you think?"

"Indeed," said Wilfred. "And a right convoluted one, too."

"Quite so," said Barnabas. He paused for a moment, then craned his head to peer around the corner as best he might to be certain that Bes wasn't returning just yet to overhear what he wanted to say next. Satisfied that they were still alone, he dropped his voice even lower to whisper, "Did you see how his tongue just sort of, well, *lolls* out of his mouth?"

"I did! It is most curious! I wonder that I didn't notice it before. Did you notice it? Before today, I mean?"

"Not at all," said Barnabas. "And it is curious, because it is definitely the sort of thing that might grab one's attention, what with the tongue just sticking out and flapping about in every direction. But I suppose it *must* have been that way before?"

"I suppose, since people don't usually just start sticking out their tongues all the time suddenly and for no reason. As I said, it's a wonder that we didn't notice it before."

"Well, I suppose that we were a bit distracted by all the flying monkeys and what not," said Barnabas. He shut his lips together hurriedly as Bes returned carrying a large platter with overflowing teacups jiggling precariously atop it.

Fearing that Bes may have overheard them speaking about his unusual tongue (which was still sticking out and waggling from side to side as the god walked into the room) in such a disparaging sort of way, Barnabas sought to cover their gaff. "So!" he said, a bit too loudly, "as I was saying, the moors really *are* exceedingly unpleasant this time of year, is what I always say."

Bes, who had not heard the two detectives discussing his tongue (and who would not have been offended in the slightest if he had; he was well aware already of the whereabouts of his tongue) gave Barnabas a quizzical look. "You often talk about the unpleasantness of moors?" asked Bes, with a confused frown.

Barnabas saw the perplexed expression on Bes' face and took it to be one of ill humor. A terrible idea dawned upon him then, that perhaps Bes had thought that the moors to which he referred were the Moors of the Arab variety who had inhabited the southern areas of Spain, rather than the hilly, heath-covered moors that were merely a landscape variety common in rural England. He tried to work out whether or not an Egyptian god would have anything to do with the Moors, or at least to feel enough fellowship with them to be offended on their behalf if someone were to insult them, which he, Barnabas, may just have accidentally done.

He was unable to unravel the thread of logic that would have drawn him to a conclusion on the matter and therefore flew into a small panic. He flapped his arms about his face frantically.

"Oh!" he cried, greatly upset. "Not Moors, but moors! I talk all the time about moors, don't I, Wilfred? But of course not about Moors, because why on earth would I talk about Moors? Not that they aren't worthy of speaking about. Oh dear me, no, I didn't mean that. They must have been quite splendid with all the plumbing and the fancy architecture. I'm certain that I would have quite liked the Moors quite a bit more than the moors, which are ghastly hot in the summer and terrifically cold in the winter and so there is nothing much amenable about that sort of moor at all..."

He trailed off, terribly upset. His whiskers twitched furiously as Bes simply stood there gaping at him, not knowing what to make of Barnabas' strange little speech and oddly excitable manner. Bes now remembered that he had found the company of the two detectives quite trying the first time he met them, and that he had been very eager to be rid of them. He sighed, regretting, now, that he had offered them tea and would therefore be subjected to what promised to be no small amount of nonsensical ramblings.

However, here he was with a platter of teacups (and a great lot of assorted snack foods besides), and hospitality demanded that he serve his guests, no matter how annoying they might prove to be, and speak politely with them whilst

163

they consumed their repast.

"Yes, the moors, of course," said Bes, hoping to forestall any further exposition by Barnabas on the topic. "Very hot. And cold, too."

"Exactly!" said Barnabas, relieved that Bes had understood him. Bes sighed again and sat down on a giant wooden chair opposite his guests. He gestured that they might begin eating. Barnabas and Wilfred both thanked him as they accepted their cups of tea.

"So," he began, "you have mouse heads now."

"Hmm, well, yes. *Obviously*," said Barnabas, a bit annoyed at having that fact pointed out. He selected a dried fig from the platter and nibbled on it. "A most unfortunate encounter with Apep. But he certainly got his comeuppance, did Apep! Didn't he, Wilfred?"

"Indeed he did," said Wilfred, who was daintily nibbling on a sugared pastry. "I dare say he won't be troubling any of our kind, that is to say, people who happen to also be mice, however temporarily, again."

"Yes, I'm certain that Bindi is now quite safe, thanks to us," said Barnabas.

"Bindi?" asked Bes politely as Wilfred shot Barnabas a knowing, amused glance.

Barnabas reddened at the ears. "And Babak and Babook and everyone at the Grey Mouse," he said hurriedly. "I was about to say all of them, of course, until I was interrupted…"

"Of course," said Wilfred, trying to soothe his employer's discomfort. "Each of them, far too many to name, will be quite glad that Apep and his lizards are no longer about to harass them."

"Yes, yes," said Bes impatiently. "I heard all about that, of course. But I must ask: why have you come to me? I don't mean that rudely, of course. I am merely curious as to what your business is here."

Bes was trying, obviously, to prompt Barnabas and Wilfred to get down to the matter at hand (as in, the reason that they had come to trouble him, and at his home, no less!). He hoped they would be on their way all the more quickly if he gave them whatever information they had come for. To hurry the interview along even more, he stuffed a great fistful of candied dates into his mouth.

"We are here to ask... That is... Well, we were wondering...," said Barnabas, completely distracted by the spectacle of Bes' tongue. It still stuck out in an alarming fashion, even though the god's mouth was stuffed quite full of mushed-up dates. Barnabas couldn't stop staring and found his train of thought entirely disrupted. "Wilfred?" he said helplessly.

"We are here to ask for your assistance in finding Khepre," began Wilfred.

"I told you before," said Bes. "I haven't the slightest idea who took him."

"Yes, we know," said Wilfred, "but we thought perhaps you might have some valuable ideas."

"Since you know a great deal about all of the evil-doers in this place," offered Barnabas, collecting himself. "The obvious suspects have come to naught, but we thought that, perhaps, you might know something about Khepre's history, or who might have a grudge against him. For example, we found out that several of Khepre's servants have gone to work for Anti and Montu."

"Really?" said Bes, interested in this information despite himself. "That is most curious, considering..."

"That Khepre was part of the council that deposed both Anti and Montu," interrupted Barnabas.

Bes pressed his lips together and breathed deeply.

"Right," he said. "Still, I don't think that in itself means much. Servants change employers all the time."

"Of course." Barnabas sighed, disappointed.

"Well," said Wilfred helpfully, "can you think of any others who might hold a grudge against Khepre? Or perhaps someone who might simply enjoy causing trouble?"

"My, but there are plenty of gods who greatly enjoy causing trouble," said Bes. He thought for a moment. "Have you interviewed Hathor yet?" he asked.

"Hathor?" asked Barnabas. He looked to Wilfred, who

shrugged and shook his head indicating that he knew no more about Hathor than did Barnabas.

"Yes, Hathor," said Bes. "She is the goddess of sun and deserts, and so this constant noontime would be very much to her liking, you see."

"Is she quite villainous, then?" asked Barnabas nervously. Whilst he still felt quite brave after the battle at Bakhu, he had no wish to push their luck too far.

"No, not at all," said Bes. Barnabas let out his breath in relief. "Well," continued Bes, causing Barnabas to catch his breath once more in alarm, "not usually. There was this one time, though…"

"This one time *what*?" asked Barnabas, dreading the answer but nevertheless very anxious to find out the extent of the potential danger.

"It was the time Ra asked her to punish humans for some transgression or another," said Bes. "She went quite mad with it. She went about, well, *over-punishing* people I suppose you could say." Barnabas hung his head and put his hands over his face. "Ra had to sneak ale into her water to get her to fall asleep and stop killing people," continued Bes, either unaware or uncaring of his guest's discomfort at his story. "So you could say that she has a bit of a nasty side."

"To say the least!" said Wilfred.

"And how, exactly, did she kill everyone?" asked Barnabas, peeping from behind his fingers.

"Well, she's a cow-woman, you see," said Bes. "So, you know, with her horns." He made stabbing gestures with his hands held atop his head, causing his tongue to swing violently back and forth. "And of course there were her hooves." Now he balled up his fists and punched them in the air. Barnabas and Wilfred cringed in their seats. "So," said Bes brightly. "If you're ready, I'll take you to her right now!" Unceremoniously he rose and collected their cups, even pulling an unfinished sweetmeat from between Wilfred's fingers. "Shall we?" he said.

"Splendid," said Barnabas sadly, shaking his head, not pleased at all at the prospect of interviewing yet another bloodthirsty god. Still he could see no reasonable way to refuse to go, and so, sighing, he stood up and motioned for Wilfred to do the same. Together, they followed Bes out of the tree house so that they might be delivered to Hathor, the angry cow goddess of the desert.

Chapter Seventeen

Once outside, Bes reached out with his long arms and scooped up Barnabas and Wilfred so that they were lifted entirely off of the ground. "Oh my!" exclaimed Barnabas. His cry was cut off as Bes began to whirl in circles (quite sickeningly, thought Barnabas) and rose like a cyclone up into the air. A mighty noise sounded as Bes began to fly, creating a great vortex of air that sucked in leaves and insects and even a startled bird or two.

They flew in this fashion, spinning and twirling in Bes' arms, until at last they began to descend. They landed in the midst of a great desert that was covered almost entirely with yellow sand and punctuated here and there by prickly green cacti.

Bes deposited them carefully down upon the sands, where they, feeling very ill indeed, promptly fell upon their bums. "Well, here you are then," said Bes jovially. "I suppose I'll be off. Unless you'll be needing a ride back…"

"No, no, that's quite all right," Barnabas managed to squeak. He was finding it quite difficult to maintain control of his lurching stomach, and he had no wish whatsoever to repeat the experience. A quick glance towards Wilfred (who looked quite green about the gills, so to speak) confirmed that his assistant felt the same.

Barnabas tried to look around and take in their new surroundings. A great marble palace stood directly in front of them, rising majestically from the warm desert sands. Barnabas was certain it must look quite pretty if only the world would stop spinning around it.

He shook his head, closed his eyes, and then opened them again. Finding that the dizziness had yet to pass, he groaned and repeated the process until at last he began to feel himself steady a bit.

"Well," he said to Wilfred, "*that* was exceedingly dreadful."

"Quite," moaned Wilfred, whose voice was muffled due to the fact that he had somehow managed to bend himself almost entirely in two from the cross-legged position in which he sat so that his face was nearly buried in his lap.

"Are we agreed then," said Barnabas, "to politely decline if Bes is ever disposed to offer us a lift again?"

"Yes, please," said Wilfred, lifting his head and blinking rapidly.

Barnabas, feeling nearly recovered, drew his legs up beneath him. He carefully stood up, and slowly turned so he was pointed in the direction of the palace. Finding that he had regained his equilibrium, he proffered a hand to Wilfred. "Shall we?"

Wilfred nodded, grasped Barnabas' extended hand, and rose laboriously to his feet. He closed his eyes and swayed a little, arms out to his sides for balance. Barnabas waited patiently until Wilfred had steadied himself, then led the way to the great shining palace.

Copious amounts of sand fell from their robes as they climbed the hard, polished steps to the entrance. They had, after all, just been sitting in the sand, and once one gets sand in one's robes, it tends to take an absurdly long time for one to get it all out again. Therefore, the sand slid and bounced and clattered about their feet with each step they took up the stairs. The cow-headed guards, who had watched as they were rather ignominiously deposited upon the ground by Bes, snickered in amusement.

Reaching them, Barnabas held his head high and mustered all the dignity he could, considering the incredible amount of sand that still slid from his robe to puddle at his sandaled feet. "We are here to interview Hathor," he said with as much grandeur as was possible. "We are on official business. We were sent by Anubis and have been brought here by none other than Bes."

One of the guards managed a straight face, although the struggle not to laugh showed in his eyes. "We know," he said. "We saw you arrive." The corners of his mouth twitched.

"And just what, pray," said Barnabas tightly, "is so amusing?"

"Nothing, sir," said the first guard, staring carefully straight ahead, his face a mask of careful nonchalance.

The other guard, however, was not nearly as stoic as the other, and had a bit of a mischievous streak. "Yes, indeed we did," said he. "We saw you land just there." He pointed at the place where the sand bore two indentations roughly the size of Barnabas and Wilfred's hind ends.

Barnabas turned to look where the fellow had pointed. His motion caused a small whirlwind of sand to waft up around him. Two loud giggles escaped the guards.

"Oh yes," said Barnabas indignantly. "I suppose you two could have managed a better landing." He sniffed, offended.

"Very sorry, sir," said the first guard, not looking at all sorry, really.

"I should say so!" retorted Barnabas. "This is most unprofessional."

"Very sorry," repeated the guard, whilst the other continued to snicker uncontrollably. "Hathor is just inside. Please make yourself at home and she will be with you directly." He turned to open the door, and though Barnabas and Wilfred could see his shoulders shaking with scarcely controlled mirth, the guard managed to usher them into the palace with some degree of decorum. "Two visitors for Hathor," called the guard into the large antechamber in which they now found themselves. "Sent by Anubis and brought here directly by Bes."

That statement brought on a second fit of laughter from the second guard, so that the first one, finding his fellow's mirth contagious, had to shut the door hurriedly to avoid laughing directly in their faces.

"Well I never!" exclaimed Barnabas. "The rudeness! The affront!"

"I suppose we may have looked quite amusing, landing

the way we did," offered Wilfred, trying to smooth over the situation.

"And I suppose *they* would have managed a graceful landing, eh?" demanded Barnabas.

"I think that no one could," said Wilfred soothingly. "Still, they are just guards and beneath our notice. Let them laugh a bit."

"You are a more patient man than I, Wilfred," said Barnabas. "I simply cannot bear the course behavior of people such as that. It is shameful."

"Most shameful," agreed Wilfred.

"And to think that they are making fun of us when they themselves have the heads of cows instead of proper heads!"

Wilfred, finding it prudent to avoid pointing out the fact that Barnabas and Wilfred themselves were currently in possession of animal heads of their own, nodded.

"Being laughed at by *cows*, can you imagine?" continued Barnabas. He opened the door behind them a crack so that he might address the still-laughing guards outside. "Where are your bells, you silly cows?" he sniped. "Did you lose them whilst you were being milked, Bessie?"

A woman's voice interrupted Barnabas before he could give the guards what-for any further. "You find it amusing to make fun of cows?" she asked, her voice quiet but commanding.

Barnabas whirled, hurriedly letting go of the door so that it slammed shut behind him. A large woman, seven foot tall or more, was walking towards them slowly. She wore a shimmering robe of brown, white, and black, and atop her shoulders was the enormous head of a cow.

The regality of her bearing, the authority in her voice, and the soft glint of danger in her wide brown eyes led Barnabas to know that this woman could only be Hathor.

"Oh!" he gasped as she approached and stopped to stand only inches from him and Wilfred, her brindled robe swirling as she leaned in to look closely at him.

"Well, do you?" she demanded, her nose nearly touching Barnabas' own.

171

"Dear me, no," said Barnabas hurriedly, his whiskers twitching violently with nervousness. He had seen enough of angry gods in this place and had no wish to find out what this Hathor might do if he annoyed her enough. "It's just a turn of phrase, I suppose. Of friendship! Yes, it is a friendly phrase!"

Hathor frowned. "A phrase of friendship, you say?" She narrowed her eyes. "Do not think to toy with me or to deceive me," she warned.

"No, really, I meant it quite nicely!" insisted Barnabas. "As in, 'here, would you like a nice bell?' It's all meant in politeness, you see."

Wilfred, seeing Barnabas struggle and, further, seeing that Hathor was far from believing his rather flimsy subterfuge, stepped in. "Indeed, it is so," he said, bowing gallantly to their hostess whilst preparing to lie through his teeth. "In our country people commonly ask others if they'd like a bell. It's a greeting of sorts."

"Huh," said Hathor dubiously. "Seems a silly sort of thing to say." She sighed and pulled back a bit so that Barnabas let out a breath of relief. She turned to walk towards a chaise longue that stood at the far corner of the room, beckoning for Barnabas and Wilfred to follow. "Still, I suppose different peoples do have all sorts of odd customs, so I'll give you the benefit of the doubt." She whirled about dramatically, bristling her eyebrows up and down so that Barnabas quickly sucked back in the breath that he had just let out. "For now."

Seeing their nervousness, she laughed. Barnabas and Wilfred looked wide-eyed at each other, alarmed. Clearly this woman was enjoying toying with them, and they knew that they must be extremely vigilant in order to avoid offending her again. And they knew all too well by now how very difficult it was to avoid trespassing upon the unpredictable sensibilities of yet another capricious god.

"So," began Barnabas carefully once Hathor was seated comfortably upon her chaise, "Bes brought us here so that we might ask you, very respectfully of course, if you know anything about the disappearance of Khepre."

"You mean to accuse me of kidnapping Khepre?" Hathor demanded, her eyes narrowing once more.

"Oh no," said Barnabas quickly. "Never that, my fair lady!" He cleared his throat nervously. "I only meant… I mean, that is to say…Well…"

"Out with it!" demanded Hathor.

"Only that perhaps you might know something regarding persons of interest," squeaked Barnabas.

"And who, may I ask, are they?"

"A god named Montu," said Barnabas. "Probably you've never heard of him. He's not terribly important anymore from what I hear. Terribly sorry to have wasted your time. We'll just be seeing ourselves out…"

"Nonsense!" said Hathor. "Of course I know Montu. In fact, here he is right here. He was passing through on some business of his own and stopped in to pay his respects. You can speak to him yourselves." She snapped her fingers and waved to a man across the room, beckoning him. "Montu, dear," she said sweetly. "These two visitors would like to ask you some questions."

Barnabas and Wilfred's eyes widened in dismay as Montu walked towards them. Wilfred leaned in to Barnabas to whisper ironically, "How lovely. Another falcon. If only we had been turned into something, oh, I don't know…."

"A bit less dinner-like?" supplied Barnabas. Wilfred nodded.

Soon enough said falcon had joined them, and Barnabas swallowed noisily as he took in the predatory way that Montu looked from himself to Wilfred and back again. "Well?" squawked Montu. "What do they want with me?"

"Mind your manners," corrected Hathor in a tone one might use to reprimand an ill-behaved child. Barnabas saw Montu bristle at the insult and thought that he might argue with the formidable cow goddess, but the falcon-headed god merely pressed his beak shut and inclined his head in deference to Hathor.

Hathor motioned to Barnabas, inviting him to question Montu for himself. So Barnabas cleared his throat and put his

173

hands behind his back, affecting a posture that he thought must appear very official and lawyerly-like.

"We have reason to believe," he began, speaking in a stentorious voice as he paced back and forth sedately before Montu, "that you are harboring refugees from the household of none other than Khepre, someone with whom you have been known to be at odds in the past, and, moreover, someone who is now currently missing."

Barnabas paused, waiting for Montu to respond. Unfortunately, however, he had stopped at the apogee of the ellipse that he had been describing on the floor so that he was turned to face almost entirely away from everyone. Also, no one was quite certain if he had asked a question, exactly, and so no one spoke.

"Well, what say you?" demanded Barnabas, shooting a dramatic, penetrating glance over his shoulder at his falcon-headed quarry. He waggled his eyebrows up and down in a way such as he imagined Sherlock Holmes doing whilst confronting villains. The effect, however, was far from intimidating, considering Barnabas' current mousy appearance.

Wilfred saw Barnabas' efforts to appear authoritative and intimidating, and whilst he inwardly applauded any efforts that Barnabas made to behave with more confidence, he also saw the dismissive expression on Montu's face and wished heartily that his employer had been able to pull it off just a bit better.

Montu smirked and chuckled. "Well, what off it?" he asked, his tone somewhat belligerent.

"Aha!" exclaimed Barnabas. "So you admit to taking in some of Khepre's servants?" He tried to bristle his eyebrows even more dramatically, and Wilfred looked down at the floor to avoid seeing the spectacle.

"Well, why ever wouldn't I?" said Montu, shrugging.

"Because Khepre is your sworn enemy, that's why!" cried Barnabas.

"Sworn enemy might be overstating things a bit," said Montu. "I needed a servant. The woman came to me, and so I

174

hired her."

"But you don't deny that Khepre was instrumental in your deposition from the heights of the pantheon to your current, well, less lofty state?"

Montu bristled, clearly offended. "Now you listen here!" he snapped. "I'm still a god, and a falcon besides. What are you? A detective? And a mouse, no less. A quite tasty one, I'm sure."

"Now, now, Montu," interrupted Hathor. "That's quite enough. Apologize to our guest, who is merely doing his job."

"But I don't want to," said Montu petulantly.

"Do it anyway," commanded Hathor.

Montu looked down at his talons and mumbled under his breath.

"What?" said Hathor. "We can't hear you."

"I said I'm sorry," said Montu in a tone that suggested he was not in the least bit sorry at all.

"Hmmph," said Barnabas, unmollified.

Hathor sighed. "You can go now, Montu," she said, waving him off dismissively. "Ugh. What a trial these older gods can be. Ridiculous egos that must be placated every moment of the day." She rolled her eyes. Montu, who had not got very far, heard what she said and turned back to glare at Barnabas and Wilfred. He snapped his beak in the manner of a raptor snatching up a meal, then pointed a wing significantly at them before striding off.

Barnabas and Wilfred cringed at the obvious threat as Montu stomped off in a temper, his sharp talons slapping and scratching along the marble floor. Hathor, however, seemed oblivious to their discomfort.

"So, will that be all?" she asked, contemplating her hooves, obviously bored now and hoping to be rid of them.

"Well, ah, I suppose so," said Barnabas.

"Unless you have anything helpful to add?" asked Wilfred, without much optimism that she would.

"I'm sure that I don't," said Hathor. "You'll be on your way, then?"

"Of course," said Barnabas, bowing slightly to the lady and turning on his heels to stride off with as much dignity as he could muster. Wilfred followed, but he nearly collided with his employer's back as Barnabas stopped abruptly and turned back around.

"Yes?" said Hathor with another sigh.

"I don't want to presume on your hospitality," he said, "but we could certainly do with some assistance with transportation. I'm sure that Anubis would be most grateful for any help you might give us, to facilitate the completion of our work."

"And where will you be going?" asked Hathor. She still looked down at her hooves as though bored, but Wilfred thought that her disinterest suddenly seemed a bit feigned. He also saw a keen glint in her eye as though she were a good deal more interested in where they might go than she wanted them to know.

"Oh, I think that we will go back to Bes, to see if he has any other ideas," said Barnabas lightly.

"Very well," said Hathor. "See Faas outside. He will see to lending you a chariot." With that, she stood and walked off with no further ado. The interested light had gone from her eyes the moment Barnabas said they would go back to Bes, and Wilfred wondered what it all might be about.

Barnabas called out their thanks to the back of the retreating goddess, and then he and Wilfred let themselves out of the grand palace. Luckily Faas proved easy to find, as he was standing just outside and had a nametag on his robe. They told him their needs, and he summoned a chariot immediately.

They climbed into the chariot. "Where am I taking you?" asked the driver.

"To Bes' house," said Barnabas, nodding to Faas in thanks. The driver clicked the reins and they were off.

Wilfred, doubting if they would get any further information from Bes, at last ventured to say, "Are you quite certain we should go back to Bes? I feel as though he has told us everything he knows…"

176

Barnabas, however, had been looking back repeatedly towards the great marble palace of Hathor, and he now saw that they had passed from the sight of it. Ignoring Wilfred's question and smiling enigmatically at his assistant, he tapped the chariot driver on the shoulder.

"There is a change of plans. We won't be going to Bes's house after all. Instead, make all haste to the throne room of Anubis. From there, we shall go directly to Montu's abode."

"Yes, sir," said the chariot driver, turning at the last minute from one direction to another so that Barnabas and Wilfred were jostled quite alarmingly.

Once they had righted themselves and the chariot was rumbling smoothly along on its proper course, Wilfred looked questioningly at Barnabas. "To Anubis?" he asked. "Then Montu? Why?"

Barnabas smiled smugly, feeling quite clever and enjoying the apparent confusion on Wilfred's face. "Yes, my dear boy," he said. "We go to Montu to spy. There was something quite sneaky about him, and I'm sure that we shall find out a great deal by seeing what he is about in the privacy of his own home."

"Ah!" said Wilfred. "That is brilliant!"

"Yes, well," said Barnabas, secretly agreeing with Wilfred but still feeling a flush of modesty. "And, of course, we can't very well go with, well, *these*." He waved a hand in front of his mouse head. "Montu knows us with these mouse heads, and besides, I didn't care much for the way he looked at us."

"As though we were dinner?" asked Wilfred.

"Indeed," said Barnabas. "It was most alarming, really."

"Quite," agreed Wilfred. He thought for a moment. "But if Anubis restores us to our usual appearance, then, well... What about Bindi?"

Barnabas sniffed. "There is nothing for it. We must have our proper heads about us. And besides, I don't go in for that sort of romantic silliness. As I told you before."

However, the flush of red in Barnabas' ears and the sudden quietude into which he fell belied the nonchalance of his words, and Wilfred regretted bringing the matter up as they rode the rest of the way to Anubis' throne room in awkward silence.

Chapter Eighteen

Barnabas had regained his composure by the time they reached their destination (and, indeed, would have denied vigorously that anything had been wrong with him at all, if anyone would have asked) so that they dismounted from the chariot in relatively good spirits. This was in stark contrast to their mood at the start of the trip, and quite a good way into it, as well.

At the beginning of the journey Barnabas had been sunk in deep contemplation of the fruitlessness of his unfortunate affection for the mouse-headed hostess whilst Wilfred tormented himself with guilt over bringing up a subject that so clearly caused Barnabas distress. It seemed to him that apologizing would only exacerbate the situation, and so he had held his tongue.

Therefore, they bounced along in silence as the chariot flew along the rutted dirt road. At last, however, after the driver turned round and announced that the journey was nearly over, Barnabas spoke. "I do hope that Anubis proves to be more helpful this time than he has in the past," he said, a conciliatory smile on his face.

Relieved, Wilfred smiled back to show all was well. "As do I," he agreed. "He is a terribly cagey fellow, is he not?"

"Ha!" snorted Barnabas. "Cagey is putting it gently, my dear boy." Barnabas looked up towards the sky, thinking. "In fact, I wouldn't be at all surprised if he had something to do with this whole business," he mused.

"Really?" gasped Wilfred. "You think that Anubis... But then why go to all the trouble of bringing us here?"

Barnabas sighed. "No, no, I suppose that can't be it. Still, he has proven himself to be quite tricksy and not above a bit of moral turpitude when it suits him." He wagged his finger towards Wilfred pointedly. "He's not to be trusted, I say. We would do well to be exceedingly careful around him."

"Most definitely," said Wilfred. "You know, it really was quite genius to misdirect Hathor and Montu in that way." (He had put together all of the necessary pieces in his mind during the long and quiet ride, so that he completely understood Barnabas' strategy now.)

"Thank you very much." Barnabas beamed, pleased. "It was nothing, really. Just a bit of quick thinking to stay ahead of one's suspects, which is something all good detectives should do." He tapped the side of his forehead with his finger, feeling himself to be quite smart indeed.

"So," continued Wilfred, who had gone a bit farther during the time he had had to think. "Since we are staking out Montu, ought we not do the same to Anti?"

"Anti?" asked Barnabas, frowning. "But, why should we spy on Anti?"

"Well, for the same reasons we are spying on Montu. Namely, that he has suffered demotion due, in part, to Khepre and that he, too, has taken in some servants from Khepre's household."

"Huh," said Barnabas, frowning. "I suppose they do have that in common. But it was Montu who acted suspiciously and not Anti."

"True," said Wilfred, "but ought we not take a look at him just the same? After we're finished with Montu, of course."

"Well, we could, I suppose. Although I am quite certain that the case will be quite closed once we've seen what Montu is about. And I simply don't believe that Anti could have anything to do with it. He's been quite helpful, really, and he seems very harmless. Why, he doesn't even have all of his toes anymore! How could he grab onto a giant scarab beetle such as Khepre? I don't think Anti could snatch up a normally sized scarab beetle with those things."

"You must be correct, I'm sure," said Wilfred. "Although, you must admit Anti has been a bit, well, moody at times."

"Well, yes, to be sure," said Barnabas. "Perhaps his temper could use some improvement, but he certainly hasn't looked at us as though he might gobble us up at any moment as Montu has."

"Quite right," said Wilfred. "But then again he hasn't seen us with these yet." He pointed at their mouse heads. "He may behave differently once he has."

"Yes, well, I suppose that is possible," said Barnabas (a bit snippily, if truth be told). "But really we ought to focus on our current suspect."

"Quite right," capitulated Wilfred, sensing that his employer's good humor was beginning to evaporate.

"Who is currently Montu," added Barnabas firmly.

"Yes, of course. Montu is the most suspicious of them all. I was merely speculating aloud," said Wilfred placatingly.

"Yes, he *is* the most suspicious," reiterated Barnabas. "Don't you agree?"

"Completely," said Wilfred. "I am certain that we will find our stakeout of his home most enlightening."

"Yes, we shall," agreed Barnabas, now cheered. "Yes we most certainly shall. Oh! And here we are. Anubis' place!"

The chariot came to a stop and the driver came round to help Barnabas and Wilfred disembark. Barnabas bade the man to wait for them, and he and Wilfred walked along the riverside that served as Anubis' reception hall.

"Hullo?" said Barnabas, looking about the empty strand. "Sir Anubis?" He peeked around behind the empty throne, but no one was there. "Huh," he said again. "Where can he have got off to? Doesn't he have to greet the dead or something?"

"Indeed he does," said Wilfred, disturbed. "He greets them and leads them to Osiris to have their hearts judged."

"To have their hearts judged?" asked Barnabas. "And how, exactly, does one judge a heart?"

"Well," replied Wilfred, "if I remember correctly from my Egyptian Studies course, Osiris takes their heart and puts it on a scale. A feather is placed on the counterbalance. In

181

order to get into the afterlife, one's heart must prove to be lighter than the feather."

"But that is impossible!" exclaimed Barnabas. "And entirely preposterous. A heart simply cannot weigh less than a feather. Unless it were to be an extraordinarily heavy feather, I suppose…"

"Yes, well, that is what the Egyptians believed, nevertheless. I suppose one could take it as an allegory," Wilfred suggested.

"And how does he separate the heart from the body? I mean, one needs one's heart in order to live!"

"Yes, well, the Egyptians buried people with their various parts in jars that they could carry with them into the afterlife," said Wilfred.

Barnabas shuddered. "Barbarous!" he said. "Most unacceptable. Perhaps that is why everyone here seems to be in such a bad temper all of the time. I suppose one might be a bit put out if all of one's organs were in jars instead of inside of them where they belonged."

"Quite so," agreed Wilfred. "Still, it is an important job that Anubis does, escorting the newly dead to see Osiris. So his absence now may be cause for concern. Something must be terribly wrong."

"You could not be more right about that if you tried!" exclaimed a pot-bellied baboon-faced man who had snuck up unheard behind them, giving them both a terrific start.

"Oh my!" exclaimed Barnabas. Then, remembering his manners, he added, "Thank you?"

"You're welcome!" said the baboon man jovially. "Although for what I'm not sure!" He laughed at his own cleverness (a bit maniacally, thought Barnabas privately).

Barnabas and Wilfred waited patiently for the man to stop laughing and state what it was that he was about. Unfortunately, his mirth seemed inexhaustible, and after a decent interval had passed, Wilfred decided to prod things along a bit.

"I say, good man," he said politely, "you wouldn't happen to know where Anubis has got off to, would you?"

"Of course I do!" said the man. "I'm his cousin, after all... No, wait, nephew? Cousin-nephew once removed? Really, I'm not sure at all what you'd call it, but we're family, you see."

"Splendid," said Wilfred. "Now, about Anubis..."

"Oh look!" interrupted the baboon man, jumping up and down in excitement. "Speaking of family, here come my brothers! I was wondering where they were, they were right behind me just a moment ago, and then I saw you, and then I didn't see them anymore, so I wondered, but it's alright, because here they are now!"

So saying, he bounced over to greet the newcomers with a flurry of excited babbling.

"Oh dear," said Barnabas.

"Oh dear indeed," agreed Wilfred.

"I do hope that his brothers aren't all as, well, *excitable* as he is, whoever he is. The fellow is actually *capering*, I do believe."

"If that's not capering, I don't know what is," said Wilfred.

"And for no reason that I can see, either," said Barnabas. "Perhaps we should just move along before he notices us again..."

They had just begun to slink off quietly to the side when the baboon man whirled about to face the place they had been when he left them just moments ago. "Shall you come meet my brothers, then?" he called, talking to empty space. He looked about until he saw them standing sheepishly twenty feet away, half hidden by a large boulder. "Well what are you doing over there? Come back here and say hello. Don't be shy!"

"Lovely," muttered Barnabas under his breath, sighing. Grudgingly, he complied with the baboon man's request, followed by Wilfred.

"I see you've met my brother Hapi," said one of the newcomers, a fellow with (refreshingly, thought Barnabas and Wilfred) the face of a person. "I am Imsety, this is Duamutef," he continued, gesturing towards a man with a

183

jackal head, "and this is Qebehsenuet," gesturing to the last brother, who had the head of a falcon. "You must excuse Hapi. He is most," (here, he paused dramatically), "exuberant."

Barnabas was far too polite to agree out loud, but inwardly he was extremely thankful that one brother, at least, seemed to be level-headed.

"You must be the detectives Anubis hired," continued Imsety. "He asked us to keep an eye out for you in case you returned."

"I see," said Barnabas. "Because you are his cousin-nephews?"

Imsety rolled his eyes (quite rudely, Barnabas thought). "I suppose you could say that," he said. "We are Horus' sons, you see."

"Ahhh," said Wilfred, understanding at last who these fellows were.

"Ahhh," said Barnabas, still having no idea who they were but not wanting to seem left out.

Wilfred, of course, understood the ways of his employer all too well and diplomatically came to his rescue. "So you are the ones who manage the canopic jars, then?" he asked. "The jars where the lungs and livers and what not of the dead are placed for safekeeping before they enter the afterlife properly?"

"That is us, and none other!" cried Hapi happily. "I'm in charge of the lungs."

"Very good, Hapi," said Imsety dryly. "Thank you for enlightening us all."

"Well, this is all very well and good," interjected Barnabas, "but we really must find Anubis and be on our way. Do you know where he is or when he might return?"

"He will be gone for some time," said Imsety. "He has gone to fetch Ma'at."

"Ma'at?" asked Barnabas.

"The goddess of truth and justice," supplied Wilfred. "She carries the feather against which people's hearts are weighed. If their heart is lighter than the feather, they may

184

continue on into the afterlife."

"What happens if their heart is heavier than the feather?" asked Barnabas. "I suppose that must be quite common, considering that most things are heavier than a feather, really."

"I don't believe I know," said Wilfred.

"Well, they are eaten by Ammut, of course," said Qebehsenuet (with a bit too much enthusiasm, thought Barnabas).

"Is that so terrible, if they are already dead to begin with?" Barnabas asked.

"Well, yes," said Imsety. "It's bad enough to die once, but to die twice would obviously be twice as unpleasant, don't you think?"

"I suppose so, if you put it that way," said Barnabas.

"And Ammut is part crocodile, part lion, and part hippopotamus, so it really is quite grizzly," said Qebehsenuet. Duamutef barked a quick laugh at that.

"Uhhh," said Barnabas, unsure of what to say in reply.

"Perhaps you can help us?" asked Wilfred, attempting to change the subject.

"I suppose that depends on what you need done," replied Imsety.

"Of course we'd be thrilled to help!" cried Hapi, earning himself a harsh look from his more taciturn brother.

"Well," said Wilfred, "we need to go spy on…" A quick smack from Barnabas on his arm made him catch himself just in time before spilling the entirety of their plan. "We need to spy on someone, but we are concerned that we might not be entirely safe, what with these mouse heads and all."

"People do seem to want to eat us quite a bit, since we've obtained these," added Barnabas. "And there are a great lot of falcons about. It's enough to make one terribly nervous." He looked at the falcon-headed Qebehsenuet. "No offence meant, of course," he said hastily. Qebehsenuet merely looked back at him inscrutably, and Barnabas flushed and looked away.

"Hmmm, yes," said Imsety. "I see your predicament.

185

Sadly, however, we do not have the power to change your heads back to whatever they were before you became mice."

"Why, we were people, of course!" said Barnabas indignantly. He looked at Imsety, then at Hapi, Duamutef, and Qebehsenuet; three of whom were not entirely people. "No offence, again. I'm quite sorry. I didn't mean to imply that there's anything *wrong* with having a, well, *unique* head. It's just that, when you're used to having your head in a certain way and then all of a sudden it's a different way, well…"

"Yes, yes," interrupted Imsety, waving away Barnabas' apology impatiently. "But as I said, we simply don't have the power to do anything about that."

"We could add some things on," suggested Duamutef, "to make them look more fearsome. Perhaps some antlers. Then no one would know what they were, exactly, and maybe not want to eat them because of that."

"And do you have any antlers handy?" asked Imsety.

"Well, no," said Duamutef.

"So that's not terribly helpful, is it?" sniped Imsety. Duamutef curled his lip at his brother but said no more.

"We could peck their heads off right now," said Qebehsenuet, snapping his beak peckishly. "That way no one could peck them off later." Barnabas and Wilfred looked wide-eyed at each other, terribly alarmed.

Imsety sighed. "And how will they do their job if you've pecked their heads clean off?"

"Well, you never said anything about what they'd do after," said Qebehsenuet. "And you must admit, it would solve their problem of having mouse heads quite nicely. Because they wouldn't have mouse heads anymore, you see."

"No, no, that really won't do," said Imsety.

"We could put these baskets on their heads!" chirped Hapi, proffering two woven reed baskets. "They're just the right size, and I can cut little eyeholes out of them, and put a strap under the chin, and no one will have any idea what's under there!" So saying, he went to work, busily modifying the baskets in the ways he had indicated and then sticking

186

them unceremoniously atop Barnabas' and Wilfred's heads.

The effect was quite comical, really, and all of the brothers, including the humorless Imsety, enjoyed a good chuckle at the sight. And though they felt ridiculous, still Barnabas and Wilfred had to admit that the things were functional, at least. They could see easily through the eye holes, and their mouse heads were quite hidden from view.

"Well, there you have it," said Imsety. "Now you'd really best hurry. You can go on down to the ferry and Anti will take you where you need to go."

Dismissed, Barnabas and Wilfred trudged off towards the ferry, stumbling a bit as they strove to find their balance with the somewhat ungainly weight of the baskets upon their heads.

"Really," grumbled Barnabas, "this is most absurd. I'm sure Sherlock Holmes never had to go about with a basket on his pate."

"Sherlock Holmes never had a mouse head either," pointed out Wilfred reasonably.

"Well I cannot argue with that," said Barnabas, "and I admit that it is the only plan that made any sense at all, and so we may as well resign ourselves to it." He looked back to be certain that the brothers were out of earshot. "And what is it with all of these falcon-headed people trying to bite our heads clean off? It is incredibly rude!"

"The very height of rudeness," agreed Wilfred.

"I must say, I do not like these raptors whatsoever," continued Barnabas. He thought for a moment. "Well, except for Anti. I suppose that Anti is alright."

"I suppose," agreed Wilfred reluctantly. He was not at all certain that Anti was entirely above suspicion just yet.

He had no time to voice his concerns, however, because just then they came in sight of the river and Barnabas began to hail the boat that was moored in the center of it. "Yoo-hoo! Anti! It's Barnabas and Wilfred again," he called. "We'd like another ride, if you have the time for it, that is."

It was a matter of only moments for Anti to raise anchor and paddle over to the landing. The boatman tossed them a rope, which Wilfred caught and used to tie up the boat. Then Anti offered each of them a wing to help them climb aboard. As they found their seats, Anti unhooked the rope. They were off, and Wilfred's chance to discuss his concerns was gone.

Chapter Nineteen

"Where are you headed to now?" squawked Anti. His bored tone implied that he didn't really care at all where they were going and, in fact, was a tad put out that he was the one who must take him there; but his bright eyes that darted quickly from Barnabas to Wilfred and back again suggested at least a little interest.

Wilfred wondered why Anti might feel the need to conceal such a thing, then remembered that the fellow had behaved much the same way each time he had seen them. Perhaps this appearance of disingenuous boredom was merely a quirk of Anti's personality. Perhaps it had contributed to his lack of popularity amongst the other gods in the realm, which had got him demoted from powerful god to mere boatman so long ago. Wilfred found himself feeling sorry for the prickly falcon man.

"Hullo," Barnabas was saying, somewhat aggrieved that Anti either failed to recognize them through their disguises or simply didn't care who it was that sat in his boat. "It is Barnabas and Wilfred. Remember us? We've met before. On several occasions, actually."

"Yes, I know who you are," said Anti peevishly. "That's why I asked where you were going. I don't take just anyone anywhere, now, do I?"

"Hmmph," said Barnabas. "But however did you know it was us, what with these baskets on our heads?"

"I was moored just over there the whole time Horus' sons put the things on you, wasn't I?" said Anti. He grimaced as he said the words 'Horus' sons' as if speaking of something unimaginably foul.

"Oh," said Barnabas, slightly mollified. "But we look

different from the last time you saw us, what with our mouse heads and what not. How did you know it was us?"

"Who else would it be, prancing in to Anubis' place and being helped by those four idiots just as pretty-as-you-please?" snapped Anti, annoyed. Barnabas pressed his lips tightly together to keep from retorting and just sat there blinking. "So, if you don't mind," continued Anti, "you can tell me where you want to go. Or we can just sit right here all day. Up to you."

"Of course, that makes perfect sense," said Wilfred placatingly. "We'd like to go to Montu's please."

"Montu, eh?" said Anti, putting his oars in the water heavily so that Barnabas was doused by a great splash. "And what brings you there?"

"Our business is most secret, thank you very much for your interest," snipped Barnabas, affronted at the way Anti had spoken to him and very much put out by the fact that his basket was now dripping wet on one side.

"Now, now," said Anti, amused at Barnabas' temper. "No need to get all testy. Just making polite conversation."

He swung the boat around and plied the oars until they were coasting along at a good clip down the river.

"I suppose the detective work is going well?" asked Anti after they had gone on a bit.

"Yes, very well, thank you," said Wilfred. Barnabas sat stiffly, still a bit sullen (and sodden).

"Finding out lots of good thing? Maybe you're getting close to finding Khepre. It would be nice to have a break from this incessant noon. The hunting is terrible at this time of day…" He looked at Barnabas and Wilfred as he heard them both take in quick shocked gasps of air and realized that they wouldn't much care for talk of rodent hunting. "But that's neither here nor there," he continued. "So, Khepre?"

"Well," said Wilfred, "we have some leads and we've found out quite a bit of information, but I'm sorry to say that we haven't a definitive idea just yet as to where, exactly, Khepre might be."

"A shame, that," said Anti.

"Yes, well, we do have *some* ideas, and we are hoping to have some significant progress soon," said Barnabas.

"Great," said Anti politely. "Well I do hope so. Seems like you are becoming quite the detectives, eh?"

"Why, yes. I think so," beamed Wilfred, delighted at the compliment. "That is, we've found out quite a bit and haven't got anyone killed..."

"Except for all those people in the village because of the flood and the crocodiles and what not," interrupted Barnabas, stuck in his morose mood.

"Well, yes, I suppose, if you count *them* I guess that's so," said Wilfred. "But that wasn't really our fault, remember?"

"Right," said Barnabas. "The people just drowned and ate themselves."

"Well, no, of course not, but really it was Set and Khnum who were to blame."

"Hmmph," said Barnabas.

"So what do you want with Montu?" asked Anti. He looked disinterestedly around at the passing scenery as though the conversation was one of excruciating boredom for him. It was clear he found the two detectives more than a bit tiresome.

"Just to ask him a few questions about Hathor," said Barnabas.

Wilfred wondered at Barnabas' sudden caginess, but he said nothing. He knew that the mood would sort itself out in a few minutes, and so all three sat quietly for the rest of the trip. Anti didn't seem to mind the silence; indeed, he seemed to prefer it. Anti hummed discordantly to himself whilst Wilfred and Barnabas sat engrossed in their own thoughts until, at last, they reached the pier that served as the landing for Montu's waterside abode.

Anti expertly maneuvered the boat so that Wilfred could grab hold of one of the wooden pilings, and he held the craft steady whilst the two detectives awkwardly disembarked. Barnabas adjusted his basket, which had come askew during the journey, looked about at the surroundings, and snorted derisively.

The lawn, such as it was, was completely overgrown with unkempt palm trees and various other unruly types of tropical shrubbery. A rough sandy path snaked its way through this disheartening vegetation and ended in an even more disheartening door that led, apparently, into a giant gaping crevice in the rocky outcropping that dominated the landscape. Above the doorway stood a carelessly lettered sign indicating that this, indeed, was the dwelling of Montu.

Even as Barnabas and Wilfred stared with sinking hearts at the door (through which they knew they must go if they wished to spy on Montu), it opened wide. They caught a glimpse of what was behind it and their fears were confirmed: Montu's home was essentially a cave carved from the massive boulders that formed the outcrop.

"By all the saints, does anyone live in a nice, decent *house* in this place?" grumbled Barnabas.

"Well," said Wilfred, "Hathor's place was quite nice, and Thoth's…"

"Oh, do hush!" said Barnabas. Then, seeing the stricken look on Wilfred's face (who had only been trying to lift the mood, after all), he immediately repented his hasty words. "I'm just in a terrible state, it seems. And besides, look there!" He pointed down the path.

A man with the head of a dog (if it could truly be considered a proper dog, thought Barnabas unkindly; the fellow seemed to have more the aspect of a Japanese Pug than anything else) had emerged from the now-open doorway and was even now headed down the path towards the pier.

Barnabas and Wilfred looked quickly about for a place to hide; they were, after all, here to spy, and to be seen would be the ruination of their plan. Unfortunately, however, Anti saw the man and called out a loud greeting.

"Hullo, Muatep!" he yelled out, waving a wing wildly to get the man's attention. The man looked up and instantly called back, "Oh, hullo, Anti!" with a wave of his own.

"I've brought two visitors for your master," called Anti. Barnabas groaned and tried to surreptitiously hush Anti, but to no avail. "The two detectives that Anubis brought to find Khepre."

Barnabas raised his hands in the air in vexation, but the fellow Muatep was already upon them and therefore he had no chance to bemoan their sad luck to Wilfred. Indeed, they had no choice but to say hello and exchange polite pleasantries.

After a few moments of discussing the weather, and where they were all from, and the sad state of things (what with the never-ending noontime sun that beat down upon them most uncomfortably), Muatep asked if basket-headed people were common in England.

"Oh, no," said Barnabas. "Not at all. Indeed, I daresay we must be the only two Englishman ever to have been afflicted so."

"Oh?" said Muatep. "If you don't mind my asking, then, how did you come to have them yourselves?"

"It was Apep," said Barnabas. "He turned our heads into these... Well, you can see what he turned them into."

Realizing that Muatep most certainly could not see what their heads looked like, what with the baskets atop them, Barnabas reached up to remove his disguise. It was useless now, of course, since Anti had told the man who they were. Besides, the thing was terribly uncomfortable. It was, however, quite snugly affixed round his neck, and the strings and knots had become twisted so that it was impossible to loosen them enough to remove it. He struggled for a few moments, and then uttered a great "hmmph" of frustration.

"Anyway," he continued, "Apep turned our heads into mouse heads, you see, or at least you would see if I could get this damnable thing off of me, which, of course, I can't just now it seems..."

"Apep, eh?" asked Muatep, interrupting Barnabas' ramblings.

"Yes, yes, Apep, as I said. He did this to us. But we came back and defeated him most soundly in a great battle." His voice was filled with pride as he remembered the heroic nature of that day.

"So you've been to the Grey Mouse, I presume?" asked Muatep.

"Yes, indeed," said Barnabas. "A splendid place."

"With a most agreeable hostess, too," said Muatep. "Bindi, I think her name is. Quite a little vixen, that one. I should visit there more often, really. I certainly would like to get to know her a bit better, if you know what I mean." He waggled his eyebrows suggestively.

"Well I never!" cried Barnabas. "How dare you!"

Muatep put his hands up placatingly. "No harm meant, there, good fellow. I was just meaning that she's quite the looker. Just a bit of fun between us boys, you know."

"She is far above your loathsome speculations! I will not have you speak of her in such a way. I simply will not tolerate it!" Barnabas huffed. He was furious, and a mere verbal reprimand simply didn't seem enough in response to the great disrespect Muatep had just shown Bindi.

So, Barnabas tugged at his hands, looking for his gloves. Not finding them there, he patted down his robes in search of them before remembering that he had lost all of his proper clothes in the flood.

Still in the throes of an incredible temper, he stalked over to a nearby palm tree and ripped a long frond from it. Holding it in an outstretched hand, he marched over to Muatep. Then, to the stunned amazement of everyone, he swung his arm so that the frond slapped Muatep across the face.

"I challenge you to a duel in defense of Bindi's honor!" cried Barnabas.

Wilfred gasped, aghast. He grasped at Barnabas' arm and whispered harshly in his ear (or, more precisely, the area of the basket just over where one might expect an ear to be). "What are you about? You must take it back!" He glanced at Muatep, whose shocked expression was quickly turning to one of extreme annoyance. He had no doubt that, for all his silly appearance, Muatep could prove most deadly in a duel. "Immediately, I should think."

"I will not!" said Barnabas self-righteously. "He insulted

194

Bindi, and I cannot allow that to stand."

"I'm sure that he didn't mean it, exactly," said Wilfred, attempting to defuse the situation. He turned to Muatep. "We have different strictures of behavior in England," he said, hoping to mollify the insulted pug-man. "You must forgive us if we are slow to learn the customs here."

"I *was* merely joking," said Muatep. "I had no idea that it would be taken so personally."

"Well, if you didn't mean the insult, I suppose…," said Barnabas grudgingly.

"So that's that," said Anti, brushing his wingtips together as though wiping them clean of the matter. "Muatep wanted to defile Bindi, but now he won't say things like that again. Even if he continues to think them."

"Anti!" cried Wilfred.

"Aha!" yelled Barnabas. "So you do harbor uncouth thoughts? If so I simply must reiterate my challenge."

"No, no," said Wilfred. "I'm certain that is not the case. It is merely a miscommunication. I'm sure that we can take Muatep at his word when he says he meant no harm."

"Really, I *was* just joking. This is all just a bit ridiculous," sniffed Muatep.

"Well, if you really think so," said Barnabas to Wilfred. His anger was beginning to cool, and he was in truth beginning to feel a bit nervous at the thought of participating in an actual duel.

"You have done all that is proper to defend Bindi's honor. I think the situation is resolved most acceptably," said Wilfred.

"I suppose," said Barnabas cautiously. "If he didn't mean it the way I thought, I suppose there's no need to take it any further."

"Exactly!" said Wilfred. Seeing Anti open his beak to speak again, he hurriedly added a bit too loudly, "It's settled, then. Now, if you'll excuse us, we really should be getting on with our business. Quite nice to meet you, Muatep; and thank you very much for the ride, Anti." So saying, he grabbed Barnabas' arm once more and hustled him forcibly down the

195

path towards Montu's cave.

Instead of going up to the door, however, he led Barnabas off to the side of the entrance. Quickly checking to make sure that Anti and Muatep weren't looking in their direction, he found a place where they could sit entirely hidden by the dense undergrowth yet still see and hear anything that might happen at the mouth of the cave.

Once they were settled, he released Barnabas from his grip and looked at him sternly. "I think it is time we talked about the elephant in the room," he said.

"Oh, good God, man!" said Barnabas, looking around nervously. "Is there one of *those* here now too?"

"No, well, not a literal elephant," said Wilfred, sighing. "I mean that I think we must discuss Bindi. Or, more precisely, whatever, um, well, *feeling* of affinity you may harbor towards her."

"I have told you," said Barnabas huffily, "I hold no special feeling towards her, or towards anyone else for that matter."

"Perhaps there is a bit of a feeling there that you may not have noticed?" prodded Wilfred. "I wouldn't press so except for the fact it seems to be affecting your mood a bit lately."

"It is this confounded heat that affects my mood," said Barnabas. "And the terrible manners of these people. Why, it just affronts me so."

Wilfred pressed no further, and they spent a few minutes quietly watching the cave entrance for any activity that might indicate the presence of a kidnapped dung beetle inside.

Soon enough Muatep returned up the path alone. He strode jauntily as though he hadn't a care in the world. Barnabas sniffed loudly so that Wilfred gestured frantically for him to be silent so their position would not be betrayed. Luckily, the sound was muffled by the basket over Barnabas' head, and so Muatep heard nothing and continued on his way.

Muatep passed into the cave and returned just a moment later, rolling a great big ball of what looked like dung. He pushed it along a path that led to the other side of the cave and, judging from the great racket that suddenly came from that place, had a bit of trouble putting it into its final destination.

Muatep repeated this process several times. "Piles of dung, do you see?" Barnabas asked Wilfred.

"Indeed I do," replied the assistant.

"Such as what might be accumulated by a scarab beetle, perhaps?"

"And a very large one at that," added Wilfred.

"At least this would tend to indicate that Khepre still lives," said Barnabas. "But it seems as though we have our culprit. We must go back to Anubis and tell him immediately."

"Agreed," said Wilfred. "As soon as Muatep goes back inside for good, we should make all haste for Anubis."

"Most definitely," said Barnabas. He watched Muatep as he rolled yet another great pile of dung out of the cave. The fellow was being most careless with the things, so that he was quite covered in smears of dung himself. Barnabas curled his lip in disgust.

"And to think that someone such as he would think to have a chance with Bindi," he said. "It is most unconscionable."

Wilfred merely looked at Barnabas, trying to keep the sympathy for his employer's lovelorn state from showing in his eyes. If Barnabas could even see his eyes through the small eye holes through which he peeped, that is.

Barnabas sighed. "Perhaps you are right after all," he said sadly. "But there is nothing for it. It is impossible, and we must put our work before all else. No, my silly thoughts must stay my own and my own alone." He sighed again, heavily, and Wilfred put a comforting hand on his arm.

At that moment Muatep disappeared within the cave and they heard the heavy door slam shut. Barnabas stood up briskly, shaking his head as though to dispel his melancholia. "Shall we put this case to rest at last, then?" he said, offering a hand to help Wilfred up.

"Yes, let's," said Wilfred, and they were off to tell Anubis all that they had learned.

Chapter Twenty

They walked quickly back to the pier, anxious to be off before they were spied by Montu or any of his servants. Luckily, it took them very little time to see a passing boat plied by a man (or, at least, someone who passed for a man in these parts; neither Barnabas nor Wilfred was entirely certain what kind of animal the fellow was exactly). In any case, he was willing to take them back up the river for a small fee, and so they climbed aboard.

Once they had traveled a distance from Montu's cave, Barnabas began to fiddle once more with the strings that affixed the basket to his head. "There is, after all, no need for these confounded things anymore," he explained to Wilfred.

Wilfred quickly removed his basket whilst Barnabas continued to tug and pull at the hopelessly tightened knots of his own. Somehow, though, he merely managed to make everything tighter, so much tighter that, after a few minutes, he could scarcely breathe.

Without so much as a word let alone a question about his passengers' strange choice of headgear, the boat operator reached beneath his seat, pulled out a small knife, and handed it to Barnabas.

Wilfred carefully removed it from Barnabas' hands, which were beginning to flail about in a panic as the too-tight basket began to induce a state of claustrophobia, and quickly sawed through the strings. As soon as it was loosened enough, Barnabas tore the thing from his head, flung it so that it went entirely out of the boat and into the river, and hunched stiffly over, trying to catch his breath.

"Oughtn't throw things in the river," chided the man who owned the boat. "Just think what it would be like if everyone did that. A terrible mess it would be, wouldn't it?"

"Huh," grunted Barnabas. Wilfred noticed that his eyes were bugged out and his tongue lolled alarmingly out of his mouth as he panted heavily.

"Very sorry, sir," said Wilfred to the man. "It shan't happen again." He turned back to Barnabas. "I say, are you quite alright? You look a bit, well, *peaked*."

"Fine," croaked Barnabas, although he looked anything but. "Splendid."

"Of course," said Wilfred, looking skeptically at Barnabas. "It's just that your tongue seems a bit blue, and…"

"Well, look at that!" interrupted Barnabas briskly, pointing at the shore. "Here we are then. And in very good time, I might add."

Wilfred looked and, sure enough, there was Anubis' beach. The boatman pulled on the rudder and angled them towards it. Within minutes they had paid the fellow in pounds sterling (which the fellow scrutinized curiously but then accepted with a shrug) and were climbing from the boat onto the rocky shingle.

Wilfred cast a concerned glance towards Barnabas, still worried that he might be suffering adverse affects from being nearly garrotted by his basket. Barnabas, however, seemed to be quite recovered. The pink was steadily creeping back into his tongue and he was already setting off at a good clip across the beach, clearly excited to share their information with Anubis. Wilfred decided to leave well enough alone, and trotted to catch up to his employer.

"Come now! Do hurry!" called Barnabas over his shoulder. "Time is of the essence!" Suddenly he stopped dead in his tracks. Wilfred, all but running to catch up, nearly bowled him over.

"What's the matter?" asked Wilfred, grasping on to the back of Barnabas' robe to steady them both.

"Oh, be careful now, won't you?" said Barnabas irascibly. He sighed. "I just, well, I pray that Anubis is actually *here* to hear our news. And more than that, I hope that Horus' abominable sons aren't here instead."

"They weren't so bad," said Wilfred. "They did *try* to help, at least."

"They were idiots," said Barnabas simply, and Wilfred laughed.

"Yes, I suppose they were that indeed," he said. "But I'm sure that they meant well."

"Well-meaning idiots are idiots nonetheless," said Barnabas. "And their help nearly killed me."

"Well, we shall be more careful next time they try to help us," suggested Wilfred (who, to tell the truth, had not much cared for his own uncomfortable basket disguise either). "Still," he continued, "they are sons of a rather important god. We ought to be sure to be polite whilst carefully avoiding their help."

"Precisely what I was just about to say," said Barnabas. "It wouldn't do to have Horus angry with us, since he's related somehow to Anubis."

"Cousins, they are," supplied Wilfred.

"Yes, yes, exactly as I said," said Barnabas.

"Of course," said Wilfred patiently.

Barnabas sighed again. "Well, I suppose there's nothing for it but to go ahead and hope for the best," he said.

"Quite so," agreed Wilfred.

They began walking again, this time at a more sedate pace. Barnabas seemed to be very much torn between excitement at sharing their findings and receiving what he imagined would be extraordinarily effusive accolades, and trepidation at the chance of once more being the subject of Horus' sons' misguided altruism. Therefore, when they rounded the boulder that marked the edge of Anubis' throne room and saw the jackal-headed god himself sitting there, they were both much relieved.

Standing beside Anubis was a tall woman. She wore a great headdress made of what appeared to be the feathers of some enormous bird, and she held an even more enormous feather clasped in her hands in front of her.

Barnabas, in his excitement, somewhat rudely ignored the woman and nearly bounced straight up to Anubis, bursting with his news.

"We have found Khepre!" he announced grandly.

Anubis' eyes widened. "You have?" he asked, incredulous. He looked from Barnabas to Wilfred and then all around the beach. Seeing no one other than the two detectives, he craned his head in an attempt to peer around the boulder. "Well," he said at last, "where is he, then?"

"Oh!" said Barnabas. "Well, we don't *have* him, exactly. But we know who took him."

Anubis sighed and pressed a finger between his eyes, and shook his head. At last he looked up again. "So where, exactly, is he then?"

"Well, uh, he is… That is to say…," began Barnabas, beginning to feel as though he may not have delivered the information in quite the right way.

"We believe that Montu kidnapped him," said Wilfred helpfully.

"And why do you think that?" said Anubis. "Did you actually *see* Khepre or not?"

"Not exactly," said Wilfred. He hurriedly continued as he saw Anubis' eyes begin to roll. "But we saw his servant rolling great balls of dung out of his cave."

Anubis stopped mid-eye roll. "Dung balls, you say?"

"Giant ones!" said Barnabas, recovering himself. "And since Khepre was on the council that deposed Montu, I'd say we have not only circumstantial evidence, in the form of the dung balls, but also a clear motive."

"Indeed you do," said Anubis. "It is certainly worth looking into." He turned to the woman standing beside him. "Don't you think, Ma'at?"

Ma'at nodded. "I do," she said. "I'd like to see for myself, if you don't mind."

"Of course," replied Anubis. "I'd expect nothing less. This is your area of expertise, after all." He glanced at Barnabas and Wilfred. "If you don't know, Ma'at is the goddess of judgment and justice, and she'll deal with Montu if he is indeed guilty."

Ma'at set off immediately. Anubis called after her.

"Hurry back, please," he said. "There's going to be a terrific hailstorm in Cairo today and I expect we'll need your feather."

"Certainly," called Ma'at over her shoulder. "I'll only be a few minutes." With that, she stretched her arms over her head, heaved herself up in a mighty leap into the air, and was gone flying like a cannonball towards Montu and, presumably, Khepre. Barnabas and Wilfred stood there looking confused.

"You do know about Ma'at's feather, no?" asked Anubis when he saw them looking back and forth at each other.

"Of course we do," said Barnabas, although he had absolutely no idea who Ma'at was or why her feather might be so important.

"Well, I don't," admitted Wilfred. "Could someone explain it to me, please?"

"Detective?" said Anubis. "Would you like to do the honors?"

"Uh, well…," said Barnabas. He coughed several times. "I would, but I seem to have something in my throat."

Anubis pursed his lips in disapproval before turning to Wilfred. "Ma'at's feather," he said, "is the very feather used to judge the weight of a dead person's heart. If the heart weighs more than the feather, then they can't proceed into the afterlife."

"Ah, I see," said Wilfred. "We knew about the feather, of course, but not to whom it belonged."

"Oh!" exclaimed Barnabas, his cough entirely forgotten. "So the hailstorm…"

"Indeed!" said Anubis (a bit too happily, Barnabas thought). "Lots of new arrivals today!"

"Well, that's…nice?" said Barnabas.

"Yes, well, it won't be so nice if Ma'at isn't back in time," said Anubis. "Nothing worse than a backlog of dead people cluttering your beach, eh?"

"I'm sure," said Barnabas politely.

"Ah well, I'm sure there's nothing to worry about. Ma'at will make short work of Montu, if he does indeed have

Khepre held prisoner."

"I do hope so," said Barnabas, and Wilfred nodded his agreement.

"And once Ma'at has returned with Khepre safely in tow, then the two of you can be on your way," continued Anubis. "With your compensation for a job well done, of course."

"Splendid!" said Barnabas. "Will you be putting us back into the museum, then? Or perhaps you might deposit us at home straightaway instead. Oh yes, I do think that I would much prefer home to the museum, if you don't mind."

"Museum? Home?" asked Anubis frowning. "Why ever would you want to go to those places?"

"Well, as I said, I'd much prefer to go home. The museum has been a bit, well, spoiled for me in light of recent events."

"I'm sure," said Anubis. "I was wondering why you'd want to be all cooped up in a sarcophagus. Being a mummy isn't a great deal of fun, you see. Although I'm not certain that being a ghost would be much better."

"Quite so," said Barnabas. Then he saw the unhappy, slightly shocked expression on Wilfred's pale face and replayed Anubis' words in his mind. "Wait! What?" he said. "A mummy? A ghost? Why on earth would we want to be either of those?"

"Well, what else can you be when you're dead?" Anubis pointed out reasonably. "Those are the things that dead people are when they are in a museum or a home, respectively."

"But I don't want to be either of those!" cried Barnabas. "And I'm certain that Wilfred feels the same." Wilfred nodded vehemently in agreement.

"Then why did you ask to be in the museum or your house?" asked Anubis, perplexed.

"Because I want to go home, of course!" sputtered Barnabas, outraged.

"So you *do* want to be a mummy or a ghost?" said Anubis, confusion written on his face.

"No!" cried Barnabas. "I want to be a living person, of

course, as we were before you so rudely abducted us."

"Oh," said Anubis, looking a bit abashed now. "Well, you see, that's just not possible.

"What in heaven's name are you saying?" said Barnabas, flapping his hands in frustration. "You took us from there, so just put us *back* there."

"As I said, it is not possible," said Anubis. "You are dead, you see."

"Made so by you," said Barnabas.

"Of course," agreed Anubis. "Terribly sorry about that."

"So if you did it, then it follows that you can *un*do it," said Barnabas.

"Well," said Anubis, "it doesn't really work that way. Once you're dead, you're dead, and there's nothing that anyone can do about that."

"This is most egregious! Completely unacceptable!" yelled Barnabas, in a fine temper now.

"I'm sorry you feel that way," said Anubis diplomatically. "But you'll be well rewarded in the afterlife. That'll be nice, won't it?"

"It most certainly will not be!" said Barnabas.

"And you won't even have to stand in line with the others. I'll see that you pass right on in," said Anubis as though he and Barnabas were in accord on the matter.

"But I don't want to pass right on in," said Barnabas. "I want to go home."

"And I'll make sure that Ma'at weighs your hearts against a heavier feather," continued Anubis, winking. "Being friends with a god does have *some* benefits, you see."

"A heavier feather?" sniffed Barnabas, offended. "As though Wilfred or I have any need of that."

"Well, it never hurts to be on the safe side," said Anubis.

"Speaking of Ma'at, by the way," interjected Wilfred (being a practical man, he had resigned himself to the inevitability of remaining in the Egyptian afterlife forever a bit faster than Barnabas and had noticed that quite a bit of time seemed to have gone by. "Shouldn't she be back by now?"

Chapter Twenty-One

Barnabas and Wilfred stood alone, forgotten for a time, as Anubis called for his advisors and minions to attend him. Ma'at had indeed been gone for far too long and the entire place was in an uproar. Everyone ran about trying to figure out what could possibly be delaying her.

Suddenly, Anubis' four obnoxious minions came scurrying in (the very ones that had escorted Barnabas and Wilfred from the ferry upon their first arrival and then again after the unfortunate incident on Elephantine Isle). They dashed up to Anubis with utmost haste. The little tiger whispered urgently into Anubis' ear, whose face went rigid with shock and displeasure. Their business was apparently of the greatest importance; indeed, the canary spared only a moment for the smallest of snarls in Barnabas' direction before they all hurried off together in a tiny, agitated cluster.

"Stupid fluffy yellow meat-bagger," muttered Barnabas, almost inaudibly.

"Barnabas!" hissed a shocked Wilfred. "I say!"

"Well he is," grumbled Barnabas, shuffling his feet and scowling.

"Detectives!" yelled Anubis. Wilfred was startled, but he was also afraid the god may have heard his employer's provocative remark and been angered by it; Barnabas jumped guiltily for the same reason.

"Whatever is the matter with the two of you?" snapped Anubis, shaking his head at the sight of the slightly cringing detectives. "Get over here immediately. You are detectives, and we need you to, well, *detect* please."

"Of course, of course," said Barnabas. "At your service." He and Wilfred hurried back over to Anubis. "What then shall we detect exactly?"

"Why, Ma'at, of course. You sent Ma'at after Montu and now she's missing. Have you not been paying attention?"

"A detective *always* pays attention," sniffed Barnabas, somewhat miffed by the implication that he was not performing up to expectations. "And he waits to act until all of the information has come in."

"Well," said Anubis, "I can't imagine what more information might come in—unless the detectives I hired might see fit to go out and collect some, that is."

"Yes, that would be just the thing," said Barnabas.

Everyone looked at Barnabas, waiting for him to do as Anubis asked, but he just stood there looking about with a somewhat prim expression on his face.

"So go!" boomed Anubis. "Now! And don't come back until you find Ma'at!"

"Cheep!" chirped Barnabas, his mouse instincts taking over with the fright of being yelled at by the great jackal-headed god.

Wilfred took his arm and led him away, bowing first to Anubis and saying placatingly, "We shall do our utmost to bring her back safely."

"And be quick about it!" shouted Anubis after them, making Barnabas jump and cheep once more.

As soon as they were out of sight and earshot, Barnabas said huffily, "Well, he's certainly a fine fellow to speak to us so."

"Quite rude," agreed Wilfred.

"Most *incredibly* rude," asserted Barnabas.

"And terribly unfair, too," added Wilfred.

"Indeed!" said Barnabas. "It's not as if we insisted that Ma'at go off on her own, or as if we had any way of knowing that she'd not be coming back."

"We most definitely did not," said Wilfred.

"Still," sighed Barnabas, "I suppose we'd better do our best to find her. I don't relish the idea of provoking his temper again, as we are sure to do if we return without her."

"That is the best plan, I'm sure," said Wilfred. "Where

shall we begin?"

"Well," said Barnabas, thinking. Wilfred waited patiently, but the moments stretched on until he began to wonder if perhaps Barnabas hadn't forgotten entirely what they were about.

"If I may offer a suggestion?" Wilfred asked tentatively.

"Of course," said Barnabas quickly.

"Perhaps we ought to query the neighborhood. You know, ask folk if they've seen Ma'at in the vicinity of Montu's place. It would be awfully difficult to forget seeing such a tall lady with a great big feather on her head, I should think."

"Why, that's exactly what I was thinking to do," said Barnabas.

"Of course," said Wilfred.

"I would have said it, only I was just thinking through all of the possible permutations of the plan," insisted Barnabas.

"I'm sure," said Wilfred amicably. "Were any permutations deleterious?"

"No. Well, ah, that is to say… I suppose all permutations were quite *un*-deleterious," said Barnabas doubtfully.

"Splendid!" said Wilfred. "Then we have our course laid out for us."

"Indeed we do," said Barnabas. He pointed to a small cluster of buildings on the bank of the river, their sloped thatch roofs just visible in the distance. "Let's start there. I believe I remember seeing a small town whilst we were on Anti's ferry going to Montu's the first time, and I'm sure that must be it."

Wilfred agreed and so they set off walking towards the town. Barnabas, deep in thought, remained silent for a while, until Wilfred at last asked him if anything was amiss.

"No," said Barnabas slowly. He chewed his lip as he considered the little town that they were even now approaching. "It's just that…"

"Yes?" prompted Wilfred. "What is it?"

"Well, things aren't quite adding up is all," said Barnabas.

"How so?" asked Wilfred.

"Consider, for example, the motive. We've assumed that Montu wanted revenge and therefore kidnapped Khepre. But why, then, Ma'at?"

"Hmm," said Wilfred, thinking. "Perhaps she simply got in the way? Or to keep her from rescuing Khepre?"

"But to what end?" argued Barnabas, surprising Wilfred with the astuteness of his question. "What, exactly, does Montu have to gain from kidnapping Khepre, and then Ma'at as well, other than the enmity of Anubis? And, I'm sure, Osiris as well. And why, if he wanted vengeance, would he take it only on Khepre?"

"I'm not quite sure I follow," said Wilfred.

"Khepre wasn't the only, um, person on that council was he?" Barnabas pointed out (a bit pedantically, thought Wilfred). "And I'm sure that he wasn't the most important either."

"Ah," said Wilfred. "I see what you're saying, but if that's so, then we've been coming at this problem all wrong."

"Indeed we have, my boy. Indeed we have," said Barnabas.

"Have you any ideas as to what, then, might be going on?" asked Wilfred.

"I do," said Barnabas, and then paused for dramatic effect. Wilfred waited patiently for as long as one could be expected to (and then a bit longer as well) but when no answer was forthcoming he rolled his hand to hurry Barnabas along.

"I think," said Barnabas slowly, "that perhaps Khepre was not the target after all." He took in Wilfred's expression of shock triumphantly as the implications of his assertion struck his assistant.

"Ma'at, then?" gasped Wilfred.

"Of course. It's the only thing that makes sense," said Barnabas.

"But," said Wilfred, "if that is the case, how did Montu know that Ma'at would be the one to come to Khepre's rescue and not someone else?"

"Who else would be sent?" said Barnabas. "Ma'at is the goddess of justice, no? Of course she'd be the one to go."

"If what you say is correct, then this is an incredibly complex and sophisticated plot," said Wilfred. "Which means we have woefully underestimated our opponent."

"Indeed," said Barnabas. "I think that we have done exactly that."

"But to have deduced all of this," said Wilfred admiringly, "is most impressive."

Barnabas nodded graciously, but Wilfred saw that he stood up a bit straighter and puffed up his chest with pride. Barnabas' self-admiration was short-lived, however. A lingering doubt niggled at him and he visibly deflated.

"Is something the matter?" asked Wilfred with concern, detecting the quick change in his employer's mood.

Barnabas sighed. "It's nothing, I suppose," he said. "Only... Well, I'm still bothered by the question of Khepre's servants."

Wilfred forcibly restrained himself from rolling his eyes. "Oh, that," he said dismissively. "I'm sure that it's nothing. You've figured out the main problem, I'm sure."

"Have I?" said Barnabas, a melancholy air taking over his demeanor as though he were a heart-broken maid staring longingly across a misty moor. He sighed again. "Perhaps I have," he said. "Or perhaps I haven't."

"I really feel that the servants aren't that im..."

"I know, I know," interrupted Barnabas. "And mayhap you are correct. Nevertheless, the question shall bother me until we've figured it out entirely."

"Perhaps it will become clear once we've found Ma'at," suggested Wilfred.

"Perhaps," said Barnabas doubtfully.

"Shouldn't we go back to Anubis directly then?" said Wilfred. "With this new information?"

"Not just yet, I think," said Barnabas. "We still ought to ask about to see if anyone has actually seen Ma'at just to make sure. Besides, we've just about reached the town and I'm feeling a bit peckish to tell the truth."

They had, in fact, made it to the very edge of the town even as they concluded their conversation. Luckily, the first building they saw was an inn, and they entered it, eager for both food and news.

They were disappointed in neither; the moment they passed through the door they were greeted first by a host, who escorted them quickly to a table and promised to hurry back with a "feast fit for a pharaoh" and secondly by none other than Mr. Kesim Kafele.

"Why, Mr. Kafele!" exclaimed Barnabas with genuine pleasure. The three of them shook hands heartily, and after exchanging pleasantries, agreed to sit down and enjoy the coming repast together.

"How come you to be here?" asked Mr. Kafele. "Not to pry, of course, but the Egyptian afterlife seems an odd place to run into two London detectives!"

They quickly filled in their erstwhile client on their recent experiences as the host brought out the most delightful assortment of foods and placed it on the table in front of them. They immediately set to, talking as they ate.

After offering his apologies for recommending them to Anubis (which were politely waved away as being entirely unnecessary, although Barnabas privately thought that it was recommendation that he could have done very well without), Mr. Kafele became thoughtful.

"So, Montu kidnapped Khepre in order to trap Ma'at?" he said.

"That is what we think," said Barnabas. "Indeed, I think it must be the only answer that adequately fits the evidence."

"A dastardly plan indeed!" said Mr. Kafele.

"Diabolically ingenious, really," agreed Barnabas.

"And Khepre's servants are now working for Montu, you say?" wondered Mr. Kafele.

"Indeed they are," said Barnabas. "And for Anti as well."

"Anti, too?" asked Mr. Kafele, scratching his chin. "Odd, that."

Barnabas shot a triumphant look at Wilfred. "Exactly what I thought," he said.

Mr. Kafele thought for a moment, then shook his head. "Still," he said at last, "I can't think that the answer is anything other than what you've come up with. Although Anti *was* acting a bit strange just now."

"Anti was?" asked Barnabas, his ears pricking like a hound on a scent. "How so? When?"

"Why, just now, right before you arrived," said Mr. Kafele. "He docked his boat a few minutes ago, and was practically prancing about town, such a good mood he was in."

"Prancing?" asked Barnabas, trying to reconcile the idea of a happily prancing falcon with the taciturn ferryman with whom he was acquainted.

"Yes," said Mr. Kafele. "Prancing. Strutting about in the most grandiose fashion. He had even plucked one of his feathers and put it on his head, just so." Mr. Kafele had taken a stick of celery and placed it upright on his forehead.

"Oh dear!" cried Barnabas, leaping up and startling both Wilfred and Mr. Kafele. "Oh sweet mother of pearl, we have been blind, I say, blind!"

"Barnabas," said Wilfred, "whatever are you on about? Do calm down!"

"Nay!" said Barnabas. "The time for calm has passed. Now is the time for action. Come, Wilfred. Make haste!"

Wilfred complied after a rueful look at all of the food that was still uneaten, and Mr. Kafele looked at both of them with no small amount of confusion.

"Terribly sorry," called Barnabas to Mr. Kafele as he hustled Wilfred out of the inn. "But we really must be going. You've been most helpful!"

He rushed out of the inn with Wilfred close on his heels. He looked about, spied a dock with Anti's boat tied up to it, and pointed. "Aha!" he said. "He's still here. We're not too late."

Even as he spoke, Anti emerged from a building on the other side of the dock and began walking towards his boat. Indeed the falcon did have a jaunty bounce to his step that Barnabas was certain hadn't been there before, and he

211

whistled a happy tune as he swaggered towards the dock.

"Hurry now," urged Barnabas. "We must get on that boat!" He grabbed Wilfred by the hand and practically dragged him down the street. As they got closer, however, he stopped suddenly and leaned in to whisper in Wilfred's ear. "Try not to look excited," he warned, "or suspicious. We don't want to tip him off." Wilfred, who had no idea what was going on, thought the request supremely easy to comply with.

They slowed their pace so that they walked up to the pier rather sedately (Barnabas with studied nonchalance; Wilfred with confused hesitation). They reached Anti's ferryboat just as he was preparing to untie the ropes and cast off.

"I say, old friend," said Barnabas a bit too heartily. "Could you give us a ride back to Anubis' place?" He patted his belly. "We've had a bit too much to eat, and you know what they say about walking with a full belly."

"Uh, no, what do they say?" asked Anti.

"Well, um, that is, that you oughtn't do it?" said Barnabas, without being at all sure that anyone at all had ever said such a thing.

"Oh," said Anti. He shrugged. "All right, then, I suppose I could go out of my way for my two old friends. Hop on in!" he said with uncharacteristic cheerfulness.

Barnabas and Wilfred climbed aboard and took their customary seats in the front of the boat whilst Anti took the helm in the back.

"So," said Anti. "Any luck on the investigation?"

Barnabas shot a warning glance to silence Wilfred, who had opened his mouth to speak.

"Not much. Indeed, we've had quite a setback. It looks as if Montu has made off with Ma'at now in addition to Khepre," said Barnabas, feigning an air of dejection but peeping up slyly through downturned lashes to observe Anti's reaction. He was not disappointed. A smile pulled at the corners of the fellow's beak.

"Ah, that Montu!" chirped Anti happily. "You've got to watch out for the likes of him!"

"Indeed, he has quite foiled us at every turn," said Barnabas.

"No shame in that," said Anti. "You wouldn't be the first to be fooled by one of the old gods. People tend to underestimate us...uh, them, you know."

"Yes, I *do* know," said Barnabas. "I suppose the likes of Wilfred and I never really had a chance against such a wily mind as Montu's."

"Never in life!" agreed Anti.

"So," said Barnabas, "I wonder what will happen now that Ma'at is gone. What with the need for a feather to weigh against the hearts of the dead and all."

"Well," replied Anti, preening his own feathers a bit. "I suppose Anubis will be needing a new feather, won't he?"

Wilfred's eyes widened and he caught Barnabas's eye. Barnabas nodded and winked as he saw his assistant come to the same conclusion that he had whilst talking with Mr. Kafele.

"Yes," he said to Anti, feigning supreme naivety. "I suppose he will. I wonder where he will get one."

Anti pursed his beak primly and looked regally off into the distance. "I wonder," he said grandly. "Perhaps a falcon's feather might do just as well as an ostrich's. Just a thought, of course."

"Of course, and a splendid one at that," said Barnabas.

"Yes, it is!" agreed Anti. Done now with talking, the falcon turned his attention to the river and sang happily to himself in a raspy, terribly off-key voice.

Seeing their host distracted, Wilfred turned to Barnabas. "Can it be?" he hissed.

"I think very much so," whispered Barnabas. "Anti means to take Ma'at's place. He wants to bear the feather that judges the hearts of the dead. He wants to be the god of judgment and justice!"

"But it is incredible! Ma'at was the target all along!" said Wilfred.

"It certainly would seem so," agreed Barnabas. "But we mustn't let him know we know, because, if he knows we know, it may put Ma'at in even more danger than she is in now."

"And we still have to find out where, exactly, she is, so we can rescue her," said Wilfred, nodding at Barnabas' sagacity.

"Exactly," said Barnabas a bit testily, for he hadn't quite thought that far ahead just yet. "Anyway, we must be quiet, act normal, and not raise his suspicions in the slightest."

Soon enough they reached the landing by Anubis' throne room. "Thank you very much," said Barnabas, sticking out his hand. He was attempting nonchalance but ended up seeming quite stiff and awkward instead, since Anti had no hand to shake, only wings. So, Barnabas grasped the tip of a wing feather and shook it, instead.

"Goodbye!" said Wilfred heartily. "Good luck to you! See you soon, I'm sure!"

"Not too soon, though," said Barnabas. "I mean, we shall see you the next time we need a ride, I'm sure, but not before that because why else would we see you?"

"Unless we run into you in town, of course," supplied Wilfred. Both he and Barnabas were a bit flustered at being in the presence of an arch villain, and both were talking far too much to cover up their nervousness.

"Or wherever!" cheeped Barnabas. "Either way, good to see you, I'm sure!"

"Quite good," agreed Wilfred.

"All right, then," said Anti, looking now as though he were eager to be off and away from his annoying passengers. Barnabas and Wilfred, out of nonsensical things to say, closed their mouths and reached for the wooden pilings.

And so the two detectives climbed out of Anti's ferry and, trying very hard not to appear as though they were suspicious of Anti and rushing to tell Anubis about it, hurried off, anxious and agog to tell Anubis the news.

As they rounded the boulder and entered Anubis' throne room, however, they stopped short in their tracks, aghast.

"Mrs. Crowder!" gasped Barnabas. "Whatever are you doing here?"

Chapter Twenty-Two

Mrs. Crowder sat behind a long, low table in front of Anubis' throne. There was a long line of people in front of the table and a great lot of paperwork on top of it. Mrs. Crowder held a pen in one hand and what seemed to be a very lengthy list in the other.

The people who stood in the line seemed to be in varying stages of distress. Some were merely very old and frail, but others seemed to be a bit damaged or perhaps not entirely intact. These wore bruises or cuts or wounds of various severity, and quite a few of them appeared to be sopping wet.

"Oh dear," groaned Wilfred. "The hailstorm."

"Oh my," said Barnabas. "But how comes Mrs. Crowder to be here?" He considered her carefully. "She doesn't seem, well, *drowned* does she? Or hailed upon?"

Barnabas and Wilfred watched as their landlady briskly and efficiently greeted each person who approached the table in turn. She asked a few questions of each, consulted her list, and made quick notes upon the list with her pen.

At the sound of Barnabas' shocked exclamation, she paused in the middle of greeting a particularly damp and battered-looking individual and looked up, a happy smile of recognition on her face.

"Why, Barnabas! Wilfred!" she exclaimed. "How nice to see you! Anubis told me you've been quite busy." She beamed with pleasure.

"But Mrs. Crowder," said Barnabas. "What are you doing here?"

"Well that's a fine way to greet an old friend," chided Mrs. Crowder good-naturedly.

"My apologies," said Barnabas hastily. "Of course I'm

happy to see you. It's just, well, you know, um, that is, do you know…" He broke off and looked to Wilfred for help as he failed to come up with a polite way to ask Mrs. Crowder if she were aware of the implications of where she was. Wilfred, however, was as much at a loss as his employer and simply stood there with an overly wide smile on his face.

"Oh my," said Barnabas again.

"Whatever is the matter with you two?" asked Mrs. Crowder, chuckling a bit to herself as she saw that the two of them were quite unchanged since she had last seen them.

"Well," said Barnabas. "Um, well. Huh. You do know that everyone here is not quite, well, *alive*?"

"Well I should think that would be obvious," said Mrs. Crowder. "That is why I'm here, you see." She took in the blank look on Barnabas' face and the stiff smile on Wilfred's and sighed. "The dead people were piling up. So Anubis set me to cataloguing them and sorting them into groups until he's found a feather or some-such."

"Cataloguing?" asked Barnabas. "Groups?"

Mrs. Crowder leaned forward as if to whisper conspiratorially, though everyone in line could obviously hear her. "Yes, groups," she said. "I am to sort them out into those I think will pass the test and those I think will not." The people standing in line looked alarmed.

Mrs. Crowder made a mark on her list and smiled distractedly at the fellow who stood in front of her now before waving him on. Barnabas and Wilfred looked after him and saw that there were indeed two clusters of people, one quite large and one very small in comparison. Both were guarded by Anubis' attendants and kept entirely separate from each other.

"I wonder which group is which," whispered Wilfred to Barnabas.

"Ugh," said Barnabas. "Dreadful. I hate to even think of it." He shook his head. "But Mrs. Crowder," he continued, "you do realize that this means that you, too, are, well…"

"Dead?" she said, smiling kindly. "Yes, I know. A scorpion crawled into my bed last night just as pretty as you

216

please. And here I am." She spoke as though she were discussing morning tea or the state of a neighbor's garden.

Barnabas, however, was horrified at her words.

"A scorpion!" he exclaimed. "How very dreadful!" The implication of her words sunk in and he turned to Anubis. "You agreed that you wouldn't kill anyone else!" he said accusingly.

"No, I agreed not to kill anyone else with mummies. Which I didn't," said Anubis reasonably.

"I clearly remember that a condition of my continued employment with you was that you would refrain from killing anyone else in the future," protested Barnabas.

"I'm sorry but your memory is a bit faulty," said Anubis. "You said you wouldn't work for me if I persisted in killing people with mummies. And I have not killed anyone else with a mummy. Not even one." Anubis seemed proud of this, as though he were announcing that he had broken off of a bad habit.

"It's quite all right," said Mrs. Crowder. "There was no mummy involved, you see. Although that scorpion did give me quite a fright, and the stinger was a bit unpleasant..." Her voice trailed off. "But all that's neither here nor there," she continued, working as she spoke, sending the next person in line to the second, larger group. "I'm here now, and I am quite busy, as you can see."

"But I still think that this is not quite in the *spirit* of our agreement," insisted Barnabas.

"Nevertheless, there was no mummy, and so it's all on the up-and-up," said Anubis.

"He's right, you know," added Mrs. Crowder, looking up from processing an extremely bedraggled woman who had what appeared to be a baby crocodile gnawing on her arm. The comment earned her a scowl from Barnabas, though Mrs. Crowder was, of course, far too busy to notice it. The woman pulled distractedly at the hungry little reptile as she followed Mrs. Crowder's pointing finger and waddled over to join the rest of the people waiting in the smaller group.

Barnabas watched the woman and her new crocodilian

appendage with distaste, then turned back to Anubis.

"I still think you oughtn't to have killed Mrs. Crowder," he said petulantly.

"Well, what's done is done," said Anubis briskly. "And look what a good job she's doing! I really don't know how I ever managed without her."

Mrs. Crowder beamed happily under the praise as she continued to sort through the newly dead. Barnabas shook his head in befuddled bemusement at the spectacle.

"It's just, well, unconscionable," he said in a low tone.

"What?" said Anubis. "Oh well, never mind." He brushed his hands together briskly, signaling an end to the debate about the morality of murdering Mrs. Crowder with a scorpion. Clearly the god of the dead was now weary of placating the sensibilities of his easily offended little detective.

Wilfred, seeing that further protest would not only prove fruitless but might also serve to anger their client, decided to distract everyone with a far more productive line of conversation.

"Well, it *is* good to see you, Mrs. Crowder," he began. "I'm sure that we'll have time for some tea once this business is concluded." She nodded and smiled her agreement. "Good," continued Wilfred. "And we *do* have some good news. Don't we, Barnabas?"

"Good news?" asked Barnabas, looking skeptically down the seemingly endless line of dead people waiting to be sorted by Mrs. Crowder.

"You know, about the investigation." When Barnabas still looked blank, Wilfred added, "Anti? Ma'at?"

"Ah, yes!" exclaimed Barnabas. "How could I forget? That's why we are here in the first place. I was about to say it, only I was thrown off by the presence of Mrs. Crowder, you know."

"Say what?" asked Anubis, his patience wearing thin. "Have you found something out about Ma'at?"

"I do believe that we have," said Barnabas. His annoyance at finding Mrs. Crowder here in the Land of the

Dead quickly faded as the pleasure of presenting the fruits of his clever deductions asserted itself.

"So, where is she then?" asked Anubis.

"We are sure that Anti is the villain behind all of this," said Barnabas.

"Anti?" asked Anubis skeptically. "The raggedy ferryman?"

"One and the same!" proclaimed Barnabas.

"I seriously doubt that," said Anubis. "Anti couldn't form a plot to save his life."

"I assure you the evidence is incontrovertible," insisted Barnabas. His pleasure was quickly withering in the face of Anubis' disbelief.

"But to what end?" asked Anubis. "What could he possibly hope to gain?"

"He wants to take Ma'at's place," said Barnabas. "He wants his feather to be used to judge the hearts of the dead instead of Ma'at's."

"Pshaw!" said Anubis. "That is ridiculous. He must know that would never happen. Why, I'd get lice from handling the dirty thing."

"Lice?" said Barnabas. He and Wilfred shared a glance and then both surreptitiously scratched at their heads and arms, suddenly itchy. Barnabas shook his head. "Still, ridiculous or not, I assure you this is the truth of the matter."

"I think perhaps you've been in the sun too long," said Anubis. "Now I suggest you get back out there and find Ma'at. Mrs. Crowder is delightful, but we still need Ma'at's feather to get this lot of people properly into the afterlife, don't we?"

"Well, yes, I suppose, but oughtn't you to go after Anti?" said Barnabas.

"It's you who should be going after people, not me," said Anubis sternly. "That is what I hired you for. Now off with you!" He made a shooing gesture with his hand. "Go find Ma'at and bring her back."

Barnabas rolled his eyes but muttered his acquiescence. He and Wilfred grudgingly took their leave of Mrs. Crowder.

As they slunk away, feeling a bit defeated by Anubis' censure, the god of the dead called after them, "I suggest focusing your energies on Montu. Forget this nonsense about Anti!"

"Of all the un-amiable, ignorant jackal-heads in this place, I do swear that he is the worst!" exclaimed Barnabas once he and Wilfred were out of earshot. "He wouldn't know sense if it smacked him across his face."

"Quite so," agreed Wilfred. "He didn't even take a moment to entertain our theory!"

"Not one!" said Barnabas. "It is most dreadful to work for someone with such a lack of insight and such an egregious degree of moral turpitude."

"Most dreadful," said Wilfred, nodding. "So, do we go now to Montu's as he suggested?"

"As he *dictated*, more like," grumbled Barnabas. "But I think we shall ignore his commands for now. We shall hire a chariot, and then it is off to Anti's house!"

"Defy Anubis?" asked Wilfred excitedly.

"Yes indeed we shall!" said Barnabas bravely.

"Won't we be in terrible trouble if we're caught out?" asked Wilfred.

"Huh," said Barnabas. "Well, yes, I suppose." His brave front faltered for a moment, but then he marshaled his courage and stood up as straight as he could, even standing on his tippy toes a bit. "But valor is the better part of discretion, as they say!"

"Isn't it the other way around?" asked Wilfred.

"Of course not," said Barnabas, miffed at being questioned. "That would make no sense whatsoever, would it?"

"I think it might make *more* sense..."

"Poppycock!" said Barnabas. "Valor is better than discretion and that's that. Besides, there's nothing for it. We were told to get Ma'at and we know that Anti has her. So, to Anti's!"

He raised his arm to signal the charge, so to speak. Conveniently, this was also the signal used in these parts to

220

hail a chariot, and since one happened to be passing by just at that moment, it stopped beside them.

"Where to?" asked the driver.

Barnabas ducked his head a bit in embarrassment, but nonetheless managed a small show of bravado, swaggering a bit like a sheriff of the American West as he and Wilfred climbed into the back of the chariot. "To Anti's house, please," he said politely to the driver. "And, if you don't mind, take the back way if there's one."

Chapter Twenty-Three

They arrived at the back entrance to Anti's property within the hour. Looking about, they were astounded at the ramshackle quality of the place. The yard was overgrown with weeds, and the house itself seemed in a sad state of disrepair. Any paint that may have previously clung to the wooden boards had peeled almost entirely off, and many of the boards themselves seemed determined to follow that paint, as was evidenced by the great gaps in the walls and the slovenly piles of rotting wood that lay on the ground around the foundation.

Reminded of Anubis' comment about lice, Wilfred and Barnabas felt inexplicably itchy again as they climbed out of the chariot, paid the driver, and contemplated the run-down place.

"Well," remarked Barnabas. "One can tell that he's not the most *kempt* person, necessarily, but *this*… It is certainly eye-opening, to say the least." He made a broad gesture that encompassed the whole of the property.

"The place is most distasteful," agreed Wilfred, wrinkling his nose. "And the smell! What in good heavens is causing this horrendous stench?"

"Oh!" sniffed Barnabas. "I just caught a whiff myself." He gagged dramatically. "Oh dear, it is unbearable!" He began to scurry about in circles as though he might thusly outrun the smell.

He was just working himself up into a proper tizzy when Wilfred suddenly leapt through the air without a word and tackled him to the ground.

"I say!" cried Barnabas (although, in truth, it came out sounding quite muffled since Wilfred's hand was placed firmly over his snout). "What are you about?" Barnabas wriggled in a vain attempt to escape his assistant's grasp, but Wilfred proved most tenacious and refused to relinquish his hold.

"Shhh!" hissed Wilfred.

"I will not shhh," mumbled Barnabas around the fingers that held his lips shut. "*You* shhh."

"Anti and Montu are here!" whispered Wilfred urgently. "If I let you go, will you please be still?"

Barnabas' eyes widened in surprise, and though he was still quite a bit put out by Wilfred's impromptu initiation of a wrestling match, he quickly saw the sense of what his assistant said and nodded his assent.

Wilfred released his hold and rolled off of his employer. Barnabas huffed to catch his breath (which had been quite knocked out of him by the impact of Wilfred's flying body onto his own), then looked side-eyed at Wilfred.

"Was that entirely necessary?" he asked with no small degree of irritation in his voice.

"Quite sorry," said Wilfred. "I saw Anti and Montu coming up the walkway over there, and I also saw that you were in danger of being spied by them. I couldn't think what else to do, so…" His voice trailed off, a hint of apology in his tone.

"I think you broke my rib," said Barnabas, casting Wilfred a petulant glance whilst dramatically clutching his abdomen. Unfortunately, the place he happened to grab did not happen to be the location of any ribs whatsoever, whether in mouse or in man, and so Wilfred knew he was play-acting.

"Oh, don't look at me like that," snipped Barnabas. "You did land on me quite hard, and you certainly *could* have broken my rib. Just because it *didn't* break doesn't mean that it *couldn't* have, now, does it?"

"Well, I'm sorry that I *could* have broken your rib, even though I *didn't*," said Wilfred.

Barnabas blinked at the unprecedented sarcasm in his assistant's voice. "No need to get so defensive about it, I'd say," he said.

"It's just that I was trying to save you, and in fact *did* save you, and yet you chastise me nonetheless. Who knows what Anti and Montu might have done had they seen you." Wilfred, patient though he was, still sometimes felt a bit undervalued and put upon by his moody employer.

"I was just taken a bit aback, is all," said Barnabas, sorry to have offended his loyal assistant. "I didn't mean anything by it."

Wilfred sighed. "I know," he said. "I can see why you'd be surprised."

Barnabas laughed gently. "You really might consider a career in rugby football, with a tackle like that," he teased.

A chuckle escaped from Wilfred's lips at the thought. Barnabas, encouraged, laughed a little harder, until Wilfred, finding Barnabas' mirth contagious, followed suit. Though Barnabas could be prickly at times, it was not in Wilfred's nature to shun an olive branch no matter how subtle. Nor could he remain upset with anyone for long.

"So," said Barnabas, when they had stopped laughing. "You saw Anti and Montu, you say?"

"Oh!" said Wilfred. "Yes. Yes I did. Just over there." He pointed towards the far end of the weed-choked mess of brambles that passed for Anti's lawn. The place was completely empty. No one was visible at all and, save for the sounds of small animals scurrying about in the undergrowth, Barnabas and Wilfred seemed entirely alone.

"I don't see anyone," pointed out Barnabas.

"They were there," insisted Wilfred, "walking together just as thick as thieves. I'll bet they went into the house."

"Or snuck up behind us during all the commotion," said Barnabas, looking over his shoulder fearfully. "So as to whack us about the head, or some such."

"I'm sure we would have heard them," soothed Wilfred.

"One never knows," said Barnabas. "Criminals can be quite stealthy. And they both have big, nasty beaks…"

"Yes, but I'm sure they didn't see us," said Wilfred. "Which was why I tackled you in the first place."

"Oh, *that*," said Barnabas. "Well, if they aren't over

there…" He pointed across the lawn. "And they're not behind us, then where are they?"

"Probably in the house," said Wilfred again.

"Wouldn't you think we'd hear them if they were inside that rickety place?" said Barnabas doubtfully. "Or see them, with all those holes in the wall and… Oh look! There they are!"

Barnabas pointed and, sure enough, there were Anti and Montu emerging from the house. "They're coming out of the house just now," added Barnabas needlessly.

Wilfred pursed his lips but nodded pleasantly enough. "What is it they've got there?" he asked. Two large objects preceded Anti and Montu down the path, one in front of each of the falcons. The objects were round and dark and appeared to roll lightly as the villains pushed at them with their wingtips.

"Is is me or has the smell got worse?" said Barnabas.

Wilfred lifted his nose to the air and inhaled deeply, then stifled a gag. "Ew!" he whispered. "It has indeed!" He put a hand over his face to cover his nostrils. "Where is it coming from? Can you tell?"

"It must be whatever it is that Anti and Montu are rolling in front of them since the smell got worse the moment they appeared," said Barnabas. He squinted at Anti and Montu as they strolled down the path, talking and laughing as though they didn't have two enormous balls of stench before them.

Suddenly Barnabas clutched at Wilfred's sleeve with excitement. "Oh!" he exclaimed loudly, earning himself an admonition to lower his voice from Wilfred. They both ducked, trying to hide in case Barnabas' cry of excitement had been heard, but a quick peek through the weeds told them that Anti and Montu continued on their way, oblivious to the observers who lurked behind the detritus of Anti's lawn.

Wilfred heaved a sigh of relief, and Barnabas continued, albeit in a much lower tone of voice. "The balls!" he whispered. "They are great big dung beetle balls!"

Wilfred's eyes opened wide. "Truly?" he asked. "If that's

225

so, then we really have found Khepre!"

"And that's not all," added Barnabas, waggling his eyebrows as he savored the feeling of having juicy news to impart. "Stuck all about within the balls of dung are feathers." Seeing that Wilfred remained confused, he said, "Feathers, Wilfred! Think, man!"

Suddenly the import of what Barnabas was saying struck Wilfred. "Ostrich feathers?" he gasped.

"Most definitely!" said Barnabas with great satisfaction. "Brown and white and very, very large. What other bird could it be?"

"Why, we have our proof then!" said Wilfred.

"That we do," said Barnabas smugly. "We were right all along, weren't we?"

"Uh," said Wilfred noncommittally.

Together they watched as Anti and Montu pushed the dung balls over to the edge of a steep hill. One at a time they pushed the balls over the edge so that they were lost from sight, then returned up the path to the house.

Seeing the two villains strolling along as though they hadn't a care in the world infuriated Barnabas. He huffed indignantly. "They behave as if they haven't got a dung beetle and an ostrich lady falsely imprisoned in that…that *hovel*! Oh, what rapscallions are they!" he hissed.

"They are conscienceless, I'm sure," agreed Wilfred.

"Oh, but it is unbearable!" said Barnabas. "The way they lied to us! The way Anti pretended to be our friend! And playing us for fools all the while."

"Unforgivable," said Wilfred. "They will certainly pay the price for their crimes, I'm sure. Once we tell Anubis what we've seen…" He broke off as Barnabas suddenly made to rise, pointing an accusatory finger towards the two villainous falcons.

"*J'a…*" Barnabas began to yell, but he was cut short as Wilfred's hand slapped over his snout, pinching his lips shut. "Mmmm-mmm," mumbled Barnabas in irritation.

"Shhh!" hissed Wilfred. "They'll hear you!"

Barnabas squinched up his face in a temper, but Wilfred's

hand over his mouth was implacable, and at last he gave up struggling to speak.

"Do you promise not to yell, at least until we've discussed it?" asked Wilfred sternly. Barnabas grudgingly nodded his assent and Wilfred hesitantly released his hold. "Whatever was *that* about?" he asked, lowering his hand only after it became clear that his employer not only did not intend to shout again but appeared to be quietly pouting instead. Besides, a quick glance at the walkway leading up to the house showed that it was empty, which Wilfred assumed meant that Anti and Montu had gone inside, putting them, hopefully, out of earshot.

Barnabas looked away and grumbled unintelligibly under his breath.

"What?" asked Wilfred.

"I said I was going to yell '*J'accuse!*' like a proper detective," repeated Barnabas a bit more audibly. "Until you so rudely pinched my lips shut, that is."

"Anti and Montu would almost certainly have heard you," said Wilfred, defending himself.

"Which was exactly the point," said Barnabas. "But now they've gone and, with them, my chance to officially accuse them."

"Nay!" said Wilfred soothingly. "I'm sure you will have your chance. Only consider that they are falcons with great big beaks and nasty temperaments whilst we are mice. Perhaps we ought to have Anubis with us when you call them out?"

"Well," said Barnabas, "I suppose I can wait until Anubis is here. Since you're afraid, that is."

Wilfred ignored the dig and nodded. "Good," he said. "Off to Anubis, then? I'm sure he will be most interested in what we have to tell him."

"Indeed he will," said Barnabas, brightening a bit. "Do let's hurry then. I wouldn't want our quarry to slip away yet again."

So saying, they crept away, taking care to remain unseen by those inside the house. They intended to walk back, but as soon as they made it down to the river a great thunderstorm struck. The storm came on suddenly, with nary a warning. One moment the sky was clear and the next it was as though all the furies of heaven had been unleashed.

The sky turned black as a huge storm cloud raced overhead. Wind whipped their robes into a frenzy and the rain seemed to come at them from all directions: up, down, and side to side. Soon both Wilfred and Barnabas were entirely and miserably drenched.

"Oh dear!" cried Barnabas, trying and failing to shield his face from the dreadful downpour.

Even as he spoke a loud rumble came from the sky. They both jumped as a bolt of lightning struck a tree branch nearby with a terrific crack. Shards of bark flew in all directions and the branch fell to the ground, blocking the path that led along the river towards Anubis' throne room.

"What do we do?" yelled Wilfred over the din of the storm.

"I don't know," said Barnabas, turning round and round in a circle as though the solution to their problem might present itself at any moment from any direction and he simply had to be facing the right way in order to see it.

Unfortunately, what presented itself to him was not a solution at all, but was instead an exacerbation of their problems.

"Wilfred," said Barnabas, pointing at the river itself. "Look."

What Wilfred saw filled him with dismay. The water was rapidly rising. It rose so quickly that it would certainly overflow the banks and flood the very place they stood unless the rain stopped straightaway. The rain seemed to intensify, and small surges of river water began to lick at their feet.

"What shall we do?" cried Wilfred again, more insistently.

Barnabas looked at the rising river that threatened to overwhelm them at any moment. He looked at the felled tree branch that barred their path upriver. And he looked back up the hill, where Anti and Montu lurked in a shack with their prisoners.

"Up the hill!" shouted Barnabas. "We can shelter beside the house!" They had been sneaking about the place unseen only moments ago, and so it was entirely possible that they should succeed once more and continue to evade the notice of Anti and Montu whilst staying out of the rising flood.

Together they made to bolt back up the hill from which they had so recently descended. To their chagrin, however, the rain had made the thing into something of a mudslide, so that they could find purchase with neither hands nor feet. They tried repeatedly to scramble up only to slide immediately back down again.

"It's no use!" yelled Wilfred. "It's impossible!"

Barnabas looked up at the now insurmountable hill, then back to the maelstrom that the river had become. "Oh, Wilfred," he said sadly, "it seems as though there are no viable options available to us. I think we must certainly die." Streams of water fell down his face, but whether they were tears or rivulets of rain water (or a combination of both) was impossible to say.

"There must be something we can do!" cried Wilfred, although he, too, was at a loss for any particular ideas.

The water was up to their knees now, and it looked as though they would certainly be taken by the river at any moment. Once swept away, it was almost certain that they must drown.

"We should hold hands," said Barnabas solemnly, "hold fast to each other. Perhaps we shall stand more firm that way. Or, at least, die together."

"Or I could give you a ride," suggested a voice behind them.

Chapter Twenty-Four

"Ah!" yelped Barnabas and Wilfred in unison the moment they turned and saw the source of the unexpected third voice. It was none other than Sobek the crocodile god, who had slunk up quietly in the river just beside them so stealthily that neither had heard nor seen him.

In his fright, Barnabas jumped back and promptly got his foot tangled in a long vine that was being whipped about by the rising water. "He's got me!" he cried. "Run! Save yourself!" Wilfred, however, was too loyal to his employer to do so and instead took firm hold of Barnabas' hand.

"No need to run," said Sobek mildly.

In their panic, neither Wilfred nor Barnabas paid any heed to Sobek's words. Trying to pull Barnabas away from the terrible jaws and teeth of Sobek, Wilfred pulled on Barnabas' arm with all his might, which only served to pull the vine tighter about Barnabas' foot. Terrified, Barnabas thrashed and kicked about wildly and became even more entangled in the vine.

Too afraid to look, Barnabas assumed that the increasing pressure he felt upon his ankle was due to the closing jaws of the dreadful crocodile god. Thinking himself as good as dead, he ceased to struggle and began to cry.

"It's no use," he said mournfully. "I'm a goner."

"Don't give up!" said Wilfred. "If we can just get your foot free…"

"It's got my foot between its teeth," said Barnabas.

"I really don't," said Sobek.

"In fact I'm certain that it has probably eaten my foot entirely by now," said Barnabas, ignoring Sobek.

"You're terribly mistaken," said Sobek. "How could I

talk if I had your foot in my mouth? If you'd just calm down and think about it for a moment…"

"I've got you," said Wilfred. "Just give it a good kick and I'll pull you free."

"Really, it's just a vine. See there? It's wrapped around your foot," said Sobek.

"It's too late," said Barnabas. "It's eating me, I'm sure. You should run, uh, swim for it whilst it's still busy chewing." The water had risen to an alarming height so that it now swirled furiously about their thighs.

"I'll not leave you here alone with that…that…*thing*!" cried Wilfred. He sat down with a loud splashing plunk and buried his face in his knees.

"Well *that* was uncalled for," said Sobek. "I do have feelings, you know."

"No sense in us both being eaten," said Barnabas. "Oh, it's too cruel. First I'm killed by a mummy and now a crocodile! How embarrassing." He sighed. "Tell Bindi… Oh, never mind. I'm just glad that she's not here to see my ignominious end." With that he closed his eyes, laid his head in the crook of his elbow, and waited to be eaten up entirely.

"Sweet mother of Osiris," muttered Sobek to himself. "You eat one tiny little village and everybody gets all judgmental about it." He settled down into the water and watched quietly for a few minutes as the two hysterical detectives cried it out together.

After a while the sniffles and whimpers coming from Barnabas and Wilfred began to slow, and eventually their sniveling ceased entirely. Barnabas opened an eye and peered up at Wilfred.

"Wilfred?" he ventured.

"Yes?" replied Wilfred.

"Are you eaten yet?" asked Barnabas.

Wilfred patted himself all over. "I don't think so," he said. "You?"

Barnabas pulled himself into a sitting position, then carefully lifted first one leg and then the other out of the water (the ensnaring vine had unwrapped itself from

231

Barnabas' foot once he ceased tugging and pulling at it). "I seem to be intact," he said doubtfully. "Although perhaps we've been eaten and this is the *after*-afterlife?"

"I suppose it's possible," said Wilfred. "Although I would have assumed it would hurt a bit more to be eaten, wouldn't you have?"

"Yes, but having never been eaten by a crocodile before, I don't really have a frame of reference for the experience either," Barnabas pointed out.

"Will the two of you please pay attention to what I'm saying for just one minute?" said Sobek.

Barnabas noticed Sobek once more, but he was too exhausted to be properly alarmed again. "He's still here," he whispered loudly to Wilfred. "Can he eat us twice, do you think?"

"Who knows?" hissed Wilfred. "The rules in this place are unfathomable, really."

"I didn't eat you the first time," said Sobek.

"Do you think we should listen to what he has to say?" asked Barnabas.

"He does seem to be trying awfully hard to tell us something," said Wilfred. "Still, he *is* a crocodile, and we mustn't forget he ate up that village."

"And perhaps us as well," pointed out Barnabas.

"You know," said Sobek, "you are quite likely to drown whilst you sit there arguing about whether you ought to talk to me or not." Indeed, the water had risen quite a bit more, and was now up to their armpits.

"He does have a point," said Barnabas to Wilfred. He turned back to Sobek and addressed him for the first time. "Still, you can see why we might be reluctant to talk to you, I'm sure. Seeing as how you ate up that entire village and we two as well."

"I only ate a couple of people from that village," protested Sobek. "And I assure you I didn't eat you either. You are both entirely uneaten, as I'm sure you would see if you'd consider the facts for a moment."

"The facts?" asked Barnabas. "I saw you gnashing your

big teeth there in the water and felt a terrible pain in my foot immediately thereafter. What other explanation can there be?"

"Well, is your foot still there?" asked Sobek.

Barnabas pulled his feet up out of the water again. "Well, yes, but…"

"And are there any teeth marks or other sign of being gnawed upon by a crocodile?" interrupted Sobek.

"There is a scratch here, here, and also up here," said Barnabas, pointing out said scratches.

Sobek curled his lips back to show his teeth. "Don't you think these would cause much larger scratches than those?" he said.

Barnabas shuddered with distaste at the sight of the jagged yellow teeth. "I suppose so," he agreed reluctantly.

"Then I didn't eat you, did I?" Sobek said quite reasonably.

"I suppose not," said Barnabas. "But you might have, had you felt like it. After all, you *did* eat those people in the village."

"Only a couple," said Sobek.

"No, almost the entire village was eaten," insisted Barnabas, although he really couldn't remember how many, exactly, had perished.

"But not all by me," said Sobek. "There are other crocodiles in the river, you know."

"I suppose so," said Barnabas. "But you can hardly blame us for not really trusting you, nonetheless."

"Almost anyone would have thought you meant to eat us," added Wilfred. "It is a most reasonable assumption, considering."

"But I don't *always* eat people, is the point," said Sobek. "And if I wanted to eat you, I would have done so by now."

"Well, then, what do you want with us?" said Barnabas. "And you'd best hurry because the water is getting up to our necks and I'm sure we will float away soon."

"That's exactly what I wanted to talk to you about," said Sobek. "I was going to offer you a ride on my back."

"Why would we want a ride on your back?" asked Barnabas, confused. "Do people do that often here? Seems an odd hobby, to ride on a crocodile, don't you think Wilfred?"

Wilfred nodded. "I'm sure there are much safer ways of transportation," he agreed.

Sobek chuffed impatiently. "It's not for *fun*," he said. "I am offering you my help. To keep you from drowning, you see."

"But why ever would you want to help us?" said Barnabas.

"Can't a crocodile just be a good person and want to help others for no reason?" said Sobek, widening his eyes innocently. Of course, being a crocodile, the affect was not so much endearing as it was horribly unsettling, and Barnabas and Wilfred cringed at the sight. "Okay," said Sobek, allowing his face to go back to normal. "I have *reasons* for wanting you to succeed, is all."

"Such as?" asked Barnabas.

"It's this weather!" said Sobek. "The heat is fine, and so are the floods, but the constant sunshine is just awful. It's very hard to sneak up on people, um, that is to say, zebras, when it's broad daylight all the time."

Barnabas and Wilfred exchanged a look. "All right," said Barnabas. "So you want to help us. But how do we know you won't change your mind and eat us later?"

"Well, I suppose you'll have to either take that chance or drown here whilst you think about it," said Sobek.

Seeing the sense of this and, further, seeing no better alternative plan to get out of their current predicament, Barnabas and Wilfred nodded to each other. Standing up, they hesitantly waded over to the waiting crocodile and gingerly climbed onto his back, carefully keeping their eyes on his snout as they did so.

The moment they were securely mounted on his knobby back, Sobek began to swim rapidly away. Barnabas and Wilfred were relieved to be out of the rising flood, but both immediately noticed that they were heading away from Anubis' lair rather than towards it.

Wilfred raised his eyebrows and tilted his head pointedly in the opposite direction from the way they were currently heading. Barnabas cleared his throat loudly and shifted his weight around in an attempt to attract Sobek's attention, but to no avail.

"Ahem," said Barnabas at last. When Sobek made no reply, he tried a more direct approach. "I say, is it possible that we might be going in the wrong direction?" he asked politely.

"No," said Sobek. Barnabas and Wilfred shared a confused glance.

"Are you quite sure?" persisted Barnabas. "I believe that Anubis' place is the other way. In fact, I am nearly certain of it."

"Yes, that is correct," said Sobek. "But Hathor's place is this way."

"Hathor!" sputtered both Barnabas and Wilfred at once.

"Yes, of course," answered Sobek. "Did I not mention that was where we were going?"

"You most certainly did not!" said Barnabas. "Indeed, Hathor is the absolute last person we'd wish to see. Well, Montu and Anti would be the last, or should I say the first…"

"And second, since there are two of them," interjected Wilfred.

"Yes, exactly," said Barnabas. "So that would make Hathor the third last person we'd want to see."

"Although we mustn't forget Set," Wilfred pointed out. "I'm in no hurry to see him again."

"Oh, quite so!" agreed Barnabas. "Or Apep. Although I'm sure we couldn't see him anyway, seeing as how he was eaten and what not."

Wilfred shuddered. "A dreadful fellow!"

"Terribly dreadful," said Barnabas. Then, remembering that he was attempting to make a point, he addressed Sobek once more. "But that is beside the point. The point is that we mustn't go to Hathor."

"It is to Anubis that we must go so that he might rescue Ma'at and Khepre," added Wilfred.

"But...," began Sobek. Barnabas, however, cut him off.

"No, no, I must insist," he said. "To go there would be most unwise. She is working with Montu, you see."

Suddenly Wilfred gasped. He opened his mouth and closed it again as though he had something dreadful to say but was loath to utter it aloud.

"Whatever is the matter with you?" hissed Barnabas.

"It's just that, well, the thought just occurred to me..." His voice trailed off.

"What thought? Out with it!" demanded Barnabas impatiently.

"What if Sobek is working with Montu as well?" whispered Wilfred loudly. "What if he's taking us to Hathor so that she might deliver us to Montu and Anti?"

"You know I can hear you when you whisper like that," said Sobek mildly.

"Oh my," said Barnabas, ignoring the crocodile. "I hadn't thought of that."

"It fits the evidence at hand," said Wilfred. "And if we've learned one thing in this place, it's to be prudent in whom we place our trust."

"Should we jump off, then?" asked Barnabas, eying the choppy waves and erratic currents of the river warily. "Try to swim for it?"

"That would be most unwise," said Sobek. "There are other crocodiles in this water, and I cannot guarantee they wouldn't like a couple of tasty mouthfuls like yourselves."

"Hmmm," said Wilfred. "I'm not sure that I can swim with the waves so high. Plus, there may be other crocodiles in there."

"Quite right," agreed Barnabas.

"Just as I said," said Sobek.

"Plus *this* one," Barnabas said, wagging his head to indicate Sobek, "might gobble us up once we're off his back."

"How many times do I have to assure you that I'm not planning on eating you?" sighed Sobek.

"So it seems that our safest course is to stay precisely

where we are," said Wilfred.

"Exactly," said Barnabas. "Once we are on dry land we can make our escape."

"Or ask for Hathor's help," said Sobek.

"Hathor's help?" exclaimed Wilfred, acknowledging Sobek at last. "Why would we do that? Haven't you heard a word we've said?"

"You should really try to listen better," chided Barnabas.

Sobek chuffed in exasperation once more. "All right," he said with exaggerated patience. "If you'd just listen for a moment, I have something important to say."

"Huh," said Barnabas, offended by Sobek's condescending tone. "As if *we* were the ones who don't listen."

"Preposterous," agreed Wilfred.

"Are you finished? Can I talk now?" asked Sobek a bit more loudly.

"Very well then," said Barnabas. "If you'd just get on with it, then."

Sobek rolled his eyes and gnashed his teeth a bit in annoyance. Perhaps, he thought, it would be easier to just eat the two high-strung detectives, after all. He immediately thought better of it, though. They would probably give him heartburn and besides, as unlikely a set of heroes as they seemed, still he needed them in order to rescue Khepre and get the infernal sun moving again. Therefore, he mustered all the patience he could find and tried again.

"Hathor is *not* working with Montu," he said. "Indeed, she doesn't much like him at all."

"But, why then was he there with her when we saw her the first time?" asked Barnabas.

"Because she likes to keep an eye on those she mistrusts," said Sobek.

"Why does she mistrust Montu?" asked Barnabas.

"Well," said Sobek, "Hathor is a bit of a feminist, you see. And Montu behaves as if the female goddesses are beneath the male gods. To be honest, I think Hathor simply enjoys putting him in his place from time to time."

"She *did* seem a bit snippy with him," conceded Wilfred.

"That she did, as though she relished being able to command him," said Barnabas.

"And for his part, Montu seemed to resent her authority quite a bit," said Wilfred.

"And if Hathor, feminist that she is, were to hear that Montu and Anti had kidnapped Ma'at in addition to Khepre…," said Sobek.

"She would be quite angry about it!" said Wilfred excitedly.

"Exactly," said Sobek.

Barnabas thought for a moment. "Exactly," he said at last, slowly. "So why is that good for us, I wonder?"

"Why, because when Hathor gets angry, all hell breaks loose!" said Sobek.

"Remember the story of her being so enraged that she laid waste to all of Egypt?"added Wilfred. "The only way they could stop her was to trick her into drinking beer so that she fell asleep."

Sobek chuckled. "The only thing Hathor likes better than social justice for women is beer," he said.

"So we want Hathor to destroy Egypt?" asked Barnabas, still not understanding the point of all of this.

"Exactly," said Sobek. "With her rage directed at Montu and Anti, well, let's just say it'll be quite a show." He chuckled diabolically (which, in truth, is the only way that a crocodile can chuckle). Wilfred cast an alarmed glance at his employer, but Barnabas was far too excited to pay any heed.

"And whilst *they* are occupied with a furious and rampaging cow goddess, *we* can sneak in and rescue Ma'at and Khepre!" exclaimed Barnabas, as proudly as if he had come up with the entire plan himself.

"And we won't even have to seek Anubis' help," added Wilfred. "He will be very pleased with us, I'm sure."

"Quite so," said Barnabas. "Perhaps then we will be rewarded at last for all of our work." He paused, considering. "And besides, I'm not entirely certain that Anubis would be much help even if we *were* to ask him," he said, his voice hushed conspiratorially.

"No?" asked Wilfred.

"Not in the slightest, actually," replied Barnabas. "Think about it. How has he helped us thus far?"

Wilfred thought, and finally shrugged. "I'm sure I cannot think of one instance, really. Except maybe to hail a chariot for us," he suggested diplomatically.

"Huh," sniffed Barnabas. "I would posit that he has not helped us in any sort of material way even once. Indeed, I might even venture to say that the only thing he has really accomplished so far in this business is simply killing people to bring them here!"

"That is a bit harsh," chided Wilfred, "don't you think?"

"Nay!" said Barnabas. "On the contrary. It is a most fair assessment."

"Extremely fair," interjected Sobek. "Anubis *is* a bit of a cumberworld."

"Precisely," agreed Barnabas. "He is most ineffectual. Why, when we told him who had Khepre the only thing he accomplished was to send Ma'at to get kidnapped too!"

"I suppose you do have a point," conceded Wilfred. "Although I'm sure he's *trying*, at least."

"Well, *trying* isn't going to get the sun moving again, is what I always say," said Barnabas (for the first time, of course). "So it is time we take matters into our own hands."

"Now you see the way of it," said Sobek, chuckling again with delight. (This time Barnabas *did* notice the menace, the inherent *creepiness* of the sound, and realized it wouldn't do to forget that Sobek could be quite dangerous. He might be a crocodile who was currently in agreement with the detectives, but still, he was a crocodile nonetheless). Barnabas looked to Wilfred and raised an eyebrow in warning. Wilfred, for his part, silently resolved to keep a wary eye on Sobek, just in case he turned coat and decided to gobble them up after all.

"Hmm, yes, well," said Barnabas uncomfortably. "I think that we do, indeed." Again he shot a pointed glance towards Wilfred to be certain his assistant understood the double meaning behind his words. Wilfred nodded to indicate that he did.

It was with some relief, therefore, that they heard Sobek suddenly exclaim, "Look! Here we are already. May I present (again, I suppose), Hathor's palace!"

Chapter Twenty-Five

Lifting up their robes, which had nearly dried by now and neither detective particularly enjoyed the feeling of soggy clothing, to avoid wetting them, Barnabas and Wilfred hastily climbed off Sobek's back. Their feet splashed in the shallow water as they hurried to get to the relative safety of the shoreline. Neither entirely trusted Sobek even now, and they were acutely aware of the fact that there was a potentially hungry crocodile with a definitively treacherous personality directly behind them. Therefore, they ran through the water with their knees high, each feeling as if Sobek's gnashing jaws were mere inches from his ankles. But when they reached land and turned around, they saw that Sobek hadn't moved and was instead watching them with laughing eyes and a giant grin on his snout.

"Well," snorted Sobek, "*that* was amusing. I'd almost think that you don't trust me, even though I've told you quite a few times I have no interest in eating you."

"Heavens, no," said Barnabas, afraid that they had insulted Sobek with their obvious distrust, and might thereby invite him to reconsider his pledge to leave them undevoured. "The water was cold, is all. Most unpleasant on the feet, really."

"And the sand was squishy," added Wilfred. "Very disgusting." He proffered up a mud-encrusted foot as proof of the disgusting nature of the sand.

"*Extremely* disgusting," said Barnabas, regarding his own feet with some dismay. He hadn't noticed it before, but now that Wilfred mentioned it he found the feeling of wet sand stuck betwixt his toes most unpleasant.

"All right, then," said Sobek. "I'll be off now. Best of

luck with Hathor!" With that, the crocodile god submerged and was gone from sight. Only a few bubbles rising up from the depths betrayed the fact that he had been there at all.

"Thanks!" called out Barnabas, certain that Sobek couldn't possibly hear him, being underwater as he was, but still feeling compelled to observe whatever social niceties he could. Then he turned to regard the beautiful marble palace that served as Hathor's home. "So," he said to Wilfred. "Shall we?"

Wilfred followed Barnabas across the hot sand to the broad marble steps that led up to the palace. Flanking the wide doors at the top of the stairs were the same two bovine guards who had laughed at them the first time the detectives visited. From the looks on their faces, Wilfred surmised that they were about to do so again.

Barnabas either felt the same or else continued to hold a grudge against the two smiling guards because his tone was peremptory to the point of rudeness when he addressed them. "We are here," he said. "Let us in."

One of the guards bowed his head (whether in deference or to hide his mirth Wilfred could not tell) whilst the other looked them up and down most offensively before smirking and casually flinging open the door and waving them in. "As you wish," he said, sweeping his arm broadly to indicate that they might pass. His tone, whilst outwardly polite, managed to convey such a degree of derision that Barnabas' nostrils flared with outrage.

"What? Haven't you ever seen two men riding on a crocodile before?" he demanded. "I fail to see what is so amusing about that!"

"With all due respect," said the guard in a voice that was utterly devoid of respect, "I've seen *people* riding crocodiles but not *mice*. You must admit it is a bit out of the ordinary."

"Oh!" exclaimed Barnabas. Wilfred laid a restraining hand on his shoulder, but Barnabas would have none of it. "That's nice, coming from a...a rotten piece of *beef cheeks*!" he said, making Wilfred cringe and glance anxiously inside the doors to be sure that Hathor hadn't heard. "And besides,"

242

continued Barnabas, his cheeks puffing in and out with outrage, "we earned these mouse heads in honorable battle. What have you ever done to earn acclaim? As far as I can see you just stand there all day, don't you?"

"Well," huffed the guard, offended at the 'beef cheeks' comment. "I happen to be a member of Hathor's Royal Guard, a job which requires far more bravery than merely being carried about everywhere by various gods. And as far as I heard, those mouse heads were given you as a curse by Apep, not as a reward for any valor."

"Why, what a dreadful flibbertigibbet he is!" cried Barnabas to Wilfred. He drew himself up to stare haughtily down his nose at the guard. "And yes, we get carried around quite a bit by gods, which means that they are our allies. So you'd best hope that we don't call Sobek back here. He was quite hungry, if you catch my drift."

The guard's eyes widened and he opened his mouth as if to make a retort, but just then a low, silky voice emanated from the interior of the palace.

"Why, is that Barnabas Tew and Wilfred Colby?" asked Hathor. "Why in heavens name are you standing around out there? Come in, please." Her words were a polite invitation but there was no denying the command in her voice. Barnabas glanced at Wilfred meaningfully. Hathor was accustomed to getting her own way. All that was left for them to do was to get her to see that their plan was in her best interest as well.

"Coming, my lady," answered Barnabas. He swept past the guard, glaring triumphantly, whilst the guard, for his part, pretended not to notice him.

Hathor, seated upon her chaise longue, beckoned them over to her once they had entered the palace. "So," she said, once they had come closer. "To what do I owe the honour of a second visit from Anubis' esteemed detective and his venerable assistant?"

Barnabas and Wilfred bowed their heads in greeting and in acknowledgement of her gracious words. "My dear lady," said Barnabas, "I am terribly sorry to be the bearer of news most dire. Indeed, the news I have come to tell you is a blow against all Egypt and an affront to womankind especially."

"What news is this?" asked Hathor. She sat up straight now, her interest piqued. "What news could be so terrible to warrant this mysteriousness? It must be troublesome indeed, for though your words are gallant, I can see the consternation in your eyes."

"It truly *is* news of the most troublesome kind," said Barnabas.

"Well?" said Hathor impatiently as it became apparent that Barnabas was no closer to expounding any further. "If you've come to tell me, then perhaps you should, well, *tell* me." There was a slight edge of frustration to her voice now that made Wilfred nervous, but when he glanced at Barnabas his employer seemed completely unperturbed.

"I shall, of course, tell you," said Barnabas calmly, "but in good time. First, I must insist upon one thing."

"Which is?" asked Hathor, her temper visibly fraying. Her voice had dropped an entire octave, so that it sounded most dangerous to Wilfred.

"That you promise not to become too terribly angry," replied Barnabas. "We wouldn't want to do anything rash or...*ill-considered*." Wilfred looked once more to Barnabas, surprised. He had thought the entire point of their visit was to incite Hathor's anger so that she would fly into a rage and go after Anti and Montu. But Barnabas, seeing Wilfred's startled glance, merely winked slyly and so Wilfred had no choice but to trust that his employer knew what he was about.

"Out with it!" demanded Hathor, visibly agitated now. "Or I will behave in a most *ill-considered* fashion—towards *you*."

"Very well," said Barnabas deferentially. He took a deep breath as though to steel himself, although to Wilfred, who knew him so well, it seemed a bit theatrical as though Barnabas was pretending at something. Confused, Wilfred could only watch as the conversation unfolded.

Barnabas sighed. "It grieves me to tell you that you have been betrayed in a most grievous fashion by your erstwhile friend, Montu. Indeed, he has played you quite falsely."

"How so?" asked Hathor. "You'd best have some details behind such an allegation or…"

"Indeed we do," interrupted Barnabas before she could complete her threat. "You see, we have seen Montu, along with his co-villain, Anti. Together they have taken Khepre."

"Oh," said Hathor, deflating a bit. "Terrible, I'm sure, but it doesn't really have much to do with me, so…" She reclined once more and looked as if she were about to dismiss them.

"But," proclaimed Barnabas loudly, "that is not all. Not only have they kidnapped Khepre, but they have also taken Ma'at, and are holding her under most egregious conditions."

"Ma'at?" asked Hathor, sitting back up again. Her turquoise jewelry jingled discordantly with the violence of her motion."They've kidnapped *Ma'at?* Why would they do that?"

"I cannot speak to the motivations of men such as that," said Barnabas. "To hold a lady against her will and to keep her in such deplorable conditions… Why, it is unconscionable!"

"In what conditions exactly?" asked Hathor.

"Well," said Barnabas slowly as though he were reluctant to impart such repugnant news. "She is being held at Anti's house, which is a most dismal shack. And the place is rank with dung beetle balls."

"Ma'at, the goddess of justice, being held in a shack filled with dung beetle balls?" yelped Hathor loudly, outraged. "And by two *lesser* gods at that!"

"It would seem that neither of them have any respect for women whatsoever," added Barnabas, "to treat her so. And I know it must pain you to think that Montu attended you here in your court, and behaved so obsequiously towards you, whilst all the while he was tormenting a fellow goddess. The whole matter is so horribly insulting. I am truly sorry you have been so deceived."

Of course, Ma'at hadn't been kidnapped yet whilst Montu was still at Hathor's court, but Hathor was by now far too worked up to question the timeline of events, which suited Barnabas' purpose just fine.

"The chauvinistic scoundrel!" cried Hathor. "To think that his deference to me was merely facetious, and all the while he has been holding a goddess against her will!"

"It is most unforgivable," said Barnabas. "But still, you mustn't get too upset. The last thing we want is for anyone to behave rashly."

"Don't tell me how to behave!" boomed Hathor. She leapt to her feet. "A sister goddess is in trouble, and I *will* go to her aid. Montu and Anti will rue the day they disrespected a goddess!"

In her anger she charged across the floor and began to carom around the room, calling out instructions to her servants (to ready her chariot; fetch her spear; remember to water the plants whilst she was away). Indeed, her movements were so quick, her energy so explosive, that Barnabas and Wilfred merely stood there for a moment, dumbfounded.

"Why did you tell her not to behave rashly?" whispered Wilfred. "I thought the whole point was to incite her to anger."

"Exactly," said Barnabas, smiling shrewdly. "And do you see how angry she is?"

Wilfred looked just in time to see Hathor knock over a servant who wasn't quick enough to get out of her way and then simply trample the fellow as he lay sprawled on the ground, making him grunt with a great "oof!"

"Yes, she does seem extraordinarily angry," he agreed.

"Which she may not have done had it seemed as though I *meant* to enrage her."

"Ah," said Wilfred, understanding. "So by bidding her remain calm, you merely enflamed her even more?"

"Exactly!" repeated Barnabas.

At that moment Hathor, apparently finished with her preparations, turned back to them and barked, "Well? Are you coming?" Then she turned and swept out of the palace. Barnabas and Wilfred shared an excited look.

"And so it begins," said Barnabas. "The completion of

our mission is nigh!" So saying, he trotted off to follow Hathor with Wilfred close behind him. They clambered up into her chariot just as she snapped the reins. The chariot lurched into motion and soon they were flying at breakneck speed across the desert, on their way to Anti's house to rescue Khepre and Ma'at.

The wind whipped at Barnabas' and Wilfred's robes, so that the detectives clutched at them (with varying degrees of success) to keep them from billowing about their necks. The chariot lurched most alarmingly over bumps and dips in the sand, and at times it seemed as though they must overturn altogether. Still, the thrill of the chase was upon them (and besides, Hathor's somewhat maniacal outrage was strangely contagious) and so they found themselves grinning from ear to ear with excitement.

Soon enough, the chariot was bouncing up the rutted track that led to Anti's shack. The path ended a hundred yards or so from the ramshackle structure. They all alighted, and Barnabas and Wilfred dropped low in order to hide between two giant prickly weeds.

"If we stay low and remain quiet," whispered Barnabas, "we can crawl through the lawn and approach the house unseen. Stealth is of the utmost consequence."

"Agreed," said Wilfred.

"MONTU! ANTI!" boomed Hathor, stomping loudly through the tall weeds and grass. "GET OUT HERE NOW!"

Barnabas and Wilfred looked at each other with wide eyes.

"I don't think she places the same importance upon stealth that we do," supplied Wilfred unhelpfully.

Barnabas sniffed and rolled his eyes. "Well, I suppose there's nothing for it but to follow her," he said, rising from his crouch. As soon as he was upright, however, he was bowled over by a great heavy fluff of dirty brown feathers.

Chapter Twenty-Six

"Ooof!" said Barnabas as the blow knocked the wind from him and sent him tumbling heels over head. Wilfred, who had not yet stood up all the way, was merely pushed into taking an impromptu seat.

Wilfred's behind, however, had been unfortunately positioned directly above one of the prickly weeds so that he was jabbed most painfully by the sharp spikes and thorns as he fell. "Aaack!" he yelped, rolling onto his side and plucking at the thorns that dotted the back of his robe.

The brown poof of feathers (which, of course, was Anti) was upended by the collision with Barnabas and skidded face-first into the ground. Slowly and with a great deal of complaining and groaning, Anti pulled himself to his feet. Seeing the two detectives lying sprawled in front of him, his eyes narrowed.

"Ugh!" he said. "You two again. Can't you see I'm in a hurry?"

"What's the rush?" asked Barnabas innocently, hoping that Hathor would notice that one of her two birds had flown. He feared, though, that she was too intently focused on Montu (for whom her animus was somewhat personal) to pay much heed to Anti's whereabouts.

"Oh, nothing really," said Anti with faux casualness. "I just have an appointment, is all." He shook out his wings and plucked at his flight feathers, which had become quite bent in his fall.

"Here, let me help you," said Barnabas. Wilfred looked on with astonishment as his employer approached Anti and appeared to begin to help the villain smooth out his feathers.

"Thank you," said Anti. "Very helpful of you."

Barnabas, however, had no intention of being helpful. Indeed, his intention was entirely the opposite. Knowing that he and Wilfred could not apprehend the large falcon on their own, he had decided that the best he could do was delay Anti's flight for as long as possible and hope Hathor would come back in time. Wilfred quickly saw what Barnabas was about and rose to help him.

"Too kind, too kind," said Anti. "Wait, no, you're doing it all wrong. They're bent worse than before." He looked at the two detectives as they fussed at his wing feathers, spoiling them entirely (Barnabas had even managed to tie a few of them into a terrible knot). Further, he saw Hathor's chariot nearby and at last put two and two together. "Oh!" he cried angrily. "You're with *her*!"

He wrenched his wings away from Barnabas and Wilfred and tried to flee once more. He couldn't fly with his wing feathers tied up in knots, however, and so he was limited to a ridiculous hopping-flapping-run across the lawn.

Reduced though their suspect's speed might be, still Barnabas and Wilfred knew that they couldn't arrest him themselves. It was with great relief, therefore, that they heard Hathor's footsteps coming rapidly from the direction of the house.

The cow goddess easily overtook Anti and snatched him up by the neck. He kicked his skinny legs futilely for a few moments. Then, seeing that his struggles were useless, he gave up and just hung there looking miserable.

"Aha!" cried Barnabas, peeping out from behind Hathor. He pointed his finger at Anti, then waved it dramatically in the air. "*J'accuse!*" he yelled with great satisfaction. "Arrest that man, uh, bird… Well, bird-person-man, I suppose…"

Hathor, Anti, and Wilfred all sighed.

"Well, I've always wanted to say that," muttered Barnabas, too pleased with himself to be properly embarrassed.

"And you've earned the right to," said Wilfred supportively.

"Seriously?" said Anti, exasperated. "*This* is what caught

me out?" He flapped a wing to indicate Barnabas and Wilfred.

"Indeed!" said Barnabas. "You sorely underestimated us, and now your diabolical plot has come to naught!"

"It was *not* diabolical," protested Anti.

"Was so," said Barnabas childishly.

"The whole affair was simply to right a terrible wrong that has been done to me."

"Think of all the trouble you caused!" chided Barnabas. "The drought! The flooding! So many have perished because of you. And you say that your motives were honorable? I call foul play, sir!"

"You don't understand!" said Anti.

"So explain yourself then," suggested Barnabas.

"I used to be the greatest god of all. Me and Montu together were the bee's knees, if you will. Now I've been demoted to just a ridiculous ferryman."

"But why kidnap Khepre?" asked Barnabas. "Was it revenge because he was part of the council that deposed you?" He thought back on the case and remembered that, early on, Bes had shown them a very large dismembered insect leg. A leg that might, in all probability, belong to Khepre. "And is Khepre alive?" he asked. "Is he…intact?"

Anti flushed and kicked his feet. His head turned this way and that as he refused to make eye contact with Barnabas.

"Did you or did you not chop up Khepre?" demanded Barnabas. "Speak!"

"Well, just a little," mumbled Anti, looking down.

"What?" said Barnabas. "One is either chopped up all the way or not at all. I can't see how one could be chopped up *a little*." He looked to Wilfred, who shook his head.

"It was just his legs," said Anti.

"But that is terrible!" cried Barnabas. "Oh, the cruelty! You are more of a villain than I thought!"

"No, no, you don't understand," said Anti. "Dung beetle legs grow back, you see. Khepre is just fine, I can assure you." He turned his head away and whispered, "Now, anyway."

"Oh," said Barnabas (he hadn't heard the last part). "That's better, I suppose. But why chop him up at all? To what end?"

Anti heaved a great exhale. He looked about once more as though looking for help, then gave one last half-hearted struggle. Seeing that escape was all but impossible, he gave another big sigh and began his full confession.

"I was the greatest god in all the underworld, you see," he began.

"We know. You've already said that," pointed out Barnabas.

"Anyway," said Anti loudly, annoyed at being interrupted, "as I've said, I was the greatest. Then came the council that deposed me, and they put the usurpers, Osiris and Anubis, in my place. Yes, Khepre was part of the council, but it was Set who decided to lop off my toes for punishment. *He* is the one who likes to chop people up around here, you know."

"Ah," said Wilfred. "Like he did to Osiris when he scattered him all around the desert."

"Precisely," said Anti. "So my plan was two-fold. First, I'd kidnap Khepre, knowing that Anubis must needs send someone after him. Since Anubis doesn't do much for himself, it was easy to surmise that he would send Ma'at, her being the goddess of justice and what not. Then I could kidnap her, too."

"But why?" interrupted Barnabas.

"I'm getting to that, if you'd just stop interrupting," snapped Anti. Barnabas bowed his head in apology, and Anti continued. "So, without Ma'at's feather to judge the hearts of the dead, Anubis would find himself in a tight spot. Then I could offer my own feather up as a replacement, which would make me the god of justice and what not, which would be a nice step up from ferryman. Then I could promote Montu as sort of my assistant. Being a former god of war, he would make a nice enforcer of my judgments, I thought. And he was content with that. Of course, things got a bit more complicated when you two showed up. I didn't want *you* to show up to rescue Khepre rather than Ma'at, and so I had to throw you off somehow. *That's* why I scattered Khepre's legs around the desert. Since Set is notorious for doing things like that, I figured that finding Khepre's legs would put you on his trail instead of mine. Perhaps you might build a strong enough case against Set based on Khepre's legs and his own history of chopping people up, and therefore get *him* punished just as he had done to *me* before."

"So you used us to take out your enemy for you?" said Barnabas.

"Exactly," said Anti.

"But," persisted Barnabas, "if we were to come up against Set, wouldn't the odds be more in his favor than in ours?"

"Well, maybe. I mean, I suppose, if you want to look at it like that…" said Anti.

"So we were cannon fodder for you against Set?" demanded Barnabas, quite upset at the personal betrayal. He had, after all, considered Anti to be something of a friend at first.

"I really was rooting for you," said Anti. "And really it was Montu who came up with that part of the plan."

"Hmmph," said Barnabas, frowning.

"If you're all done yammering," said Hathor, "I'd like to finish rescuing our victims. If you don't mind," she added pointedly. "And besides, I have Montu tied up in the kitchen and I need to finish my, um, interrogation."

"Oh," said Barnabas, wondering what form, exactly, an interrogation by the angry Hathor might take. "Of course."

"I'll leave you two to guard Anti whilst I deal with Montu and set Khepre and Ma'at free," she said.

"But how will we hold him?" asked Barnabas, alarmed.

"I'll tie him to the chariot and you just make sure he doesn't escape," said Hathor.

"Well, all right," said Barnabas, doubting this was going to work out at all well.

"He really must not escape," said Hathor

252

condescendingly as she stared pointedly into Barnabas' eyes. "It is extremely important. Are you absolutely certain you can manage it? Or must I somehow not only apprehend but also guard not one but two prisoners whilst somehow managing to free the two victims, and do so all at once?"

"Of course not," said Barnabas.

"Of course not meaning you cannot manage to guard Anti, or of course not I don't have to do all this by myself?" Her voice was calm but the expression on her face was utterly terrifying. Her rage, though aimed for the present at Anti and Montu, seemed as though it could spill over quickly onto anything or anyone who happened to annoy her.

Barnabas found himself dreadfully flustered under the weight of her growing disapprobation. "Your command is our wish," he said.

"What?" said Hathor, scowling. "Do you mean my wish is your command?"

"Yes, as I said," said Barnabas.

"We will guard Anti most closely," added Wilfred, stepping in.

Hathor gave them both a searching glance before shaking her head in exasperation. "Very well then," she said. "I'll go get Khepre and Ma'at, and deal with Montu besides. Just don't, well... Don't do anything *stupid*."

So saying, she pulled a rope out of the back of the chariot and tied one end to the axle and wrapped the other around Anti several times until the falcon could scarcely wiggle his wings. Without another word she stomped off towards Anti's house, leaving Barnabas and Wilfred alone with Anti.

"It was Montu's idea, really," said Anti.

"What was?" asked Barnabas.

"I think it might be better if we don't converse with him," whispered Wilfred, fearing some unforeseen subterfuge on Anti's part.

"That we pit you against Set," said Anti. "I wanted no parts of it, but Montu insisted it was the only thing to do."

"You could have said no," said Barnabas petulantly. "I thought you were the leader of this affair, not Montu."

"Really, it's probably better not to speak," said Wilfred.

"Ha!" said Anti. "It is not easy to ignore Montu. He is very aggressive, you see, and a little scary."

"He's trying to manipulate your feelings," warned Wilfred.

"So you're saying that Montu is the one to blame for everything, and not you?" asked Barnabas.

Anti sighed and hung his head. Great tears of remorse welled in his dark eyes (crocodile tears, thought Wilfred) and he slumped his shoulders so that his head hung down. In truth, he made for a very contrite and most piteous sight.

"Oh no," Anti said sadly. "I'll take my responsibility. I should have known better than to work with someone like Montu. I should have known he would make me do things that were wrong. But I am truly sorry for what I've done. I see now the error of my ways."

"Well," said Barnabas. "I am glad to hear you say that."

"He's trying to manipulate your feelings," said Wilfred. "I don't believe a word of this."

"I really was hoping you'd come out on top. I even cheered when you bested Apep. You can ask anyone."

"Yes, well, most wouldn't have survived such an encounter," said Barnabas with false modesty.

"Probably no one but yourselves!" said Anti. "Such bravery! I knew then that you stood a better than fair chance to survive this place."

"Of course," said Barnabas. "I can see how you would think so."

"Barnabas, really," said Wilfred. "I'm quite certain that I don't trust him…"

Anti wriggled uncomfortably within the rope cocoon that Hathor had constructed around him. "My wings are falling asleep," he said.

"I'm sorry to hear that," said Barnabas politely.

"And I really was on your side the whole time," continued Anti. He shifted himself about again. "Hey, do you think you might loosen the rope just a bit? It really does hurt." His tone had become wheedling, making Wilfred's skin crawl with disgust at the obviousness of his ploy.

"Well…," began Barnabas, looking searchingly at Anti.

Wilfred, afraid that Barnabas might actually be falling prey to Anti's treachery, blinked rapidly in alarm. "Hathor said…" he began.

"I won't do anything," said Anti. "I'm not a monster, you know."

Barnabas took a couple of steps forward so that he stood nearly snout-to-beak with Anti.

"Barnabas, no!" cried Wilfred.

For a moment it seemed as though Barnabas would loosen Anti's bonds. The falcon's eyes sparkled with excitement, all trace of his feigned remorse gone as he readied himself to take advantage of the opportunity to gain his freedom. Barnabas raised his hand and extended it towards Anti.

Wilfred caught his breath, already thinking of how they might escape Hathor's ire when she returned to find her prisoner gone. But Barnabas reached his arm high about his head and brought it down sharply to deliver a mighty clout to the top of Anti's head.

"Not a monster?" said he. "Who but a monster would deliver up two innocent detectives, who have nothing to do with what happened to you, to certain doom? Set is the god of chaos, for heaven's sake, and we mere British citizens! And all the while you purported to be our friend." Barnabas shook his head in disgust.

"I really was your friend," protested Anti. "It's just…"

"Just that your own interests were of more importance to you than the fate of Wilfred and myself?" supplied Barnabas. "Yes, you are a villain, a rapscallion, a *devil* of the very worst kind."

"No, really…" began Anti.

"Yes, *really*," said Barnabas, sneering. "And the way you betray your accomplice and try to shift all the blame to him! What happened to 'honor among thieves'? I say, sir, that of honor, you have none. So this conversation is at an end, I say, and *good day*."

With that, Barnabas turned his back upon Anti and held his arms akimbo across his chest.

"But that isn't fair!" whined Anti. "I'm the victim here! I'm the one whose toes got lopped off and whose power was stripped. It is Anubis who is the villain, not me!"

"I said *good day*," snipped Barnabas peremptorily, then pressed his lips firmly shut.

"But…," said Anti, before Wilfred interrupted him.

"No use talking now," said Wilfred smugly. "Once he's said good day he'll never say another word to you."

Barnabas looked up at the sky and began to hum "Come into the Garden, Maud."

"Come now, it really wasn't…," tried Anti again, but Barnabas merely hummed louder until the falcon gave up at last and slumped against the chariot, defeated.

Just then Hathor emerged from the shack leading Ma'at and a very large dung beetle with exceedingly short and shiny legs that Wilfred supposed must be Khepre. Not wanting to be rude, he tried not to stare at the legs, which were out of proportion to the massive size of the rest of the god's body. It would, he supposed, take a while for the legs to grow back properly.

Hathor took in the scene; with Anti hunched over and grumbling in his bonds whilst Barnabas inexplicably belted out a jaunty tune it was a strange sight indeed. She shook her head and sighed.

"Lovely song," she remarked sarcastically. It seemed her temper hadn't much abated despite having rescued the victims and apprehended the villains. Barnabas flushed and stopped singing. "If you'd just help Ma'at and Khepre into the chariot," she ordered peremptorily, "I'll go back in and fetch Montu so we can be on our way."

Even as she spoke a loud crash sounded and one of the shack's few intact windows suddenly shattered. Shards of glass splattered outward to fall like hail upon the yard.

Ma'at had already begun to walk towards the chariot (indeed, from the furious look on her face Barnabas imagined she was about to impart some choice words to Anti) so she was out of range of the fallout. Khepre had been slower to move, but the shards merely bounced harmlessly off of his hard exoskeleton. Hathor, however, was not so lucky.

Having turned back towards the shack in order to fetch her prisoner, she took the brunt of the explosion full in the face. She squealed in surprise and pain and turned away, pawing at the sharp pieces that had lodged in her hide.

With Hathor thusly disoriented and distracted, Barnabas and Wilfred saw, to their horror, first one long, skinny bird leg stick out from the broken window and then another. Those legs, they knew, could only belong to Montu, who must have escaped from whatever bonds Hathor had placed upon him.

Even as they watched, the rest of Montu emerged from the window. The two detectives saw that he hadn't managed to free himself completely, as his wings were still tangled up in ropes. His legs were free, however, and as soon as he hit the ground he began to run with surprising speed across the lawn.

He raced past the still-disoriented Hathor (who was howling in rage and pain), the sluggish Khepre (who looked like he was having a hard time walking on his stumpy new legs), and the confused Ma'at (who, intent on getting away from the stinking shack had got quite far towards the chariot and, with Khepre's massive form blocking most of her view of the shack, couldn't see what was happening at first).

Montu was obviously heading for the track that served as the shack's driveway, which was also the track that Hathor, Barnabas, and Wilfred had used as they approached in the chariot. Since the chariot (and therefore Barnabas and Wilfred, who were guarding it along with their prisoner, Anti) stood directly on the path, it quickly became apparent that the fugitive falcon's trajectory would lead him directly into the two detectives.

"Oh!" yelped Wilfred, jumping out of the way.

"Eeeh!" yelled Barnabas, squinching up his face and leaping heroically *in* the way.

"Ack!" screeched Montu, as Barnabas' flying body

struck him directly in the knees. Knocked off balance, Montu tumbled and rolled. Before he could right himself, Ma'at grabbed him roughly by the scruff of his neck.

"Well done!" said Ma'at. Then, looking to where Barnabas lay rolled up in a tight little ball on the ground, added, "You're all right, really. You can stand up now."

Barnabas, who had closed his eyes in anticipation of a counterattack by Montu's sharp claws and jagged beak, squinted one eye open cautiously. Seeing that Montu had been contained by Ma'at (who was even now refastening the ropes about the recaptured prisoner), he opened both eyes fully and bounced to his feet. "*J'accuse* you too!" he cried happily, pointing at Montu. Montu rolled his eyes and shook his head.

Hathor, meanwhile, had recovered and was looking bemusedly from Barnabas to Montu and back again.

"Well," she said, picking a piece of glass out of her ear, "the little mouse has the heart of a lion, after all."

She nodded her approval before coming over to help Ma'at load the prisoners onto the chariot. Barnabas stood nearby, beaming with pride, whilst Wilfred, much impressed, regarded his employer with bright eyes.

Chapter Twenty-Seven

It took Hathor and Ma'at, working together, scarcely any time at all to put Anti and Montu onto the chariot. Soon, everyone else had boarded as well, and the now-crowded chariot carried them all to Anubis.

Luckily the ride was a short one, since Barnabas and Wilfred quickly discovered that the mood in the chariot was most disturbing. No one was happy. Indeed, everyone seemed extraordinarily hostile. The two detectives found the company of their companions most disturbing, and did the best they could to huddle together in a corner, as far from the others as was possible in the cramped cab of the chariot.

Khepre was sullen and withdrawn, for obvious reasons. Still, Barnabas thought that he ought to have tried to show at least a little polite gratitude, considering that they had risked their lives (and literally lost their heads, in a way, if one counted having one's head exchanged for that of a mouse as losing the head entirely) to free the thankless dung beetle.

Anti and Montu vacillated between surly anger wherein they mumbled snide and sometimes threatening remarks to each other ("Captured by a couple of mice! How ridiculous!" grumbled Anti. "If they were just an inch closer I'd reach out and peck them right on their stupid little foreheads," snarked Montu) and what appeared to be extreme depression punctuated by fits of loud sobbing. Barnabas suspected that their weeping was feigned (and indeed, poorly acted at that) and rolled his eyes at Wilfred whenever he heard their pitiful squawks.

But it was Hathor and Ma'at who spoiled the atmosphere the most. Ma'at was still extremely outraged at the treatment she had suffered at the hands of Anti and Montu, whilst

Hathor simply seemed to enjoy being angry. Together they talked of all those who had wronged or slighted them (in the most meager of ways, thought Barnabas; one fellow targeted by their outpouring of spite had done nothing worse than bring Hathor a bracelet in what she considered to be a slightly *off* shade of turquoise). The hostility of one fed the other, and soon they were aggressively planning all of the havoc they would wreak and the vengeance they would take once they had delivered the prisoners to Anubis.

"Oh my," whispered Barnabas to Wilfred after Hathor detailed her plans for the violent destruction of a village where apparently all of the residents had once "looked at her funny." "Didn't someone say something about it being difficult to stop her once she was riled up?"

"I believe so," said Wilfred. "Was it Thoth?"

"I have no idea," replied Barnabas. "I just seem to remember somebody saying the last time she got angry she rampaged all over Egypt."

"Which she seems ready to do again," observed Wilfred.

"Indeed," said Barnabas, flinching as Hathor mimed trampling some unfortunate sod or other so that the entire floor of the chariot shook.

Ma'at whooped with glee and cried, "Justice! Yes, justice for all!"

"But they managed to stop her with beer, remember?" supplied Wilfred helpfully.

"Ah, yes, of course," said Barnabas, although he had quite forgotten that part of the story. "So we shall give her beer."

"That should do it," agreed Wilfred. "Do you have any beer?"

"Of course I don't have any beer," snapped Barnabas, flapping his robes about to indicate that there was nowhere for him to hide beer (or indeed a beverage of any sort) in their pocket-less folds.

"Of course," said Wilfred, chastised.

Feeling guilty, Barnabas tried to smooth things over. "But I'm sure that Anubis must needs have some," he said.

Wilfred exhaled a great sigh of relief. "You must be right," he said. "I certainly hope so. If not, who knows what terrible things she'll get up to."

"And with Ma'at to encourage her..." Barnabas shuddered. "Her rampage would be most dreadful indeed. I would hate to be the cause of whatever destruction those two get up to."

"It wouldn't be our fault," pointed out Wilfred. "Just like we couldn't help what happened at Elephantine Isle."

"Ugh," said Barnabas. "Still. Let's just hope Anubis has some beer." Wilfred emphatically nodded his agreement.

So it was that when the chariot pulled up to Anubis' throne, Barnabas and Wilfred scarcely waited for the wheels to stop rolling before they hastily jumped over the side onto the strand. Anubis sat on his throne, and the two detectives rushed up to him.

"We have captured the perpetrators," said Barnabas needlessly, since Anubis could clearly see the two scowling falcons tied up in the chariot.

"And we need beer," said Wilfred. "The sooner the better," he added, looking anxiously back towards Hathor and Ma'at.

"Beer?" asked Anubis, confused. Then, seeing Hathor's angry face, understanding came over him. "Ahhh," he said. He gestured for a servant to approach, then whispered in his ear. The fellow took off at a run. He brusquely gestured for two other attendants to attend Hathor. With a meaningful wiggle of his eyebrows and a cock of his head, his orders were understood and the two attendants hurried over to distract the angry cow goddess.

One of the attendants, a fellow with a ram's head, was unknown to Barnabas and Wilfred, but they quickly recognized the one with the actual human head.

"What's his name again?" whispered Barnabas to Wilfred.

"Peter, I believe," responded Wilfred.

"Exactly what I was about to guess," whispered Barnabas. Then, louder, he called out, "Hullo, Peter!" and

261

waved.

Peter, however, had no time for niceties. He was frantically trying to prevent Hathor and Ma'at from embarking upon a murderous escapade together.

"May I ask you for advice on behalf of my wife?" he tried desperately. "She wrote a book, but some Russian fellow stole it and took all the credit. Tolstoy or something, I think his name was." Of course, Peter had no wife, and even if he had she certainly would have never met Mr. Tolstoy, since being Russian that curmudgeonly fellow obviously did not inhabit the Egyptian afterlife.

Hathor, however, took the bait, and pressed Peter for more details, which he quickly made up. As Hathor and Ma'at hissed and tsssk-ed and adjusted their plans to include the Cyrillic scrivener in their plans of mass destruction, Peter continued on, heedless of the trouble he might cause poor Mr. Tolstoy. "And then he kicked a cow for good measure!" he said, causing Hathor to nearly moo with fury.

"Ohhh," hissed Barnabas to Wilfred. "He may have gone too far, there."

"Indeed," agreed Wilfred, cringing at the force of Hathor's anger.

Even Anubis began to anxiously look over his shoulder in the direction the first servant had run off. "Where is he with that confounded beer?" he muttered.

Thankfully, the servant arrived with the beer in good time, before Hathor and Ma'at could work themselves fully into a proper rage. Everyone sighed with relief as the servant handed Hathor a giant pitcher (and one to Ma'at for good measure, as well). Both angry goddesses drank deeply, and soon enough their eyes began to droop sleepily.

"I told him to bring the strongest stuff we had," said Anubis by way of explanation.

"Good thinking," said Barnabas, nodding.

Ma'at stretched lazily and yawned. "Can we do the death and vengeance thing later?" she asked Hathor. "I feel awfully tired just now. I think I'll just go lie down awhile."

"Smashing idea," said Hathor. Her eyelashes fluttered as

her eyes began to close, and she even burped up a nice piece of cud. Her jaws worked slowly from side to side as she softly chewed it.

Barnabas and Wilfred crinkled their faces in disgust, but Anubis clapped happily. "There!" he exclaimed. "*That's* settled then." He glanced at Anti and Montu. "So, it is as I suspected," he said (somewhat infuriatingly, thought Barnabas, since the god had argued most vociferously *against* Anti's guilt). His eyes raked over to where Peter stood, exhausted from the stress of dealing with not just one but two angry goddesses. "Peter!" said Anubis. "I seem to remember you thought it was Set who was responsible?"

"Yes, sir, I suppose that I did, at that," said Peter.

"And," continued Anubis, cocking his head innocently to the side like a puppy, "I also seem to remember that you made a bet of sorts regarding the outcome of the investigation."

"A bet?" stammered Peter nervously.

"Yes, a bet," repeated Anubis. "Hmmm, what was it that you said, exactly?"

"I'm sure I don't remember making a bet at all," prevaricated Peter. "But if I did, it was probably a very small one. Maybe a pound or two."

"Oh!" cried Barnabas excitedly. "I remember! He said, 'If it's not Set then I'll be a bunny-head,' or something like that."

"Ah, yes! That was it!" cried Anubis. "Thank you for your keen powers of recollection, Mr. Tew."

"Yes, thank you," grumbled Peter sarcastically. Then, more humbly, he said to Anubis, "Although I'm sure we all know that it was a facetious comment, not a literal one, of course."

"I don't think I know that word, facetious," said Anubis, a mischievous glint in his eyes. Before Peter could even open his mouth to answer, Anubis snapped his fingers and just like that Peter's head turned into that of a bunny rabbit.

Barnabas and Wilfred looked on, eyes wide. One moment a man had stood before them; now, two great big round bunny eyes peeped out of a furry face while two big floppy bunny ears twitched above them.

"What?" said Peter. "What happened? Is something wrong?" He put his hands to his face and patted. Once he felt the fur, the length of his ears, and the two long front teeth sticking out of his mouth, he put his hands down again and hung his head sadly. "Oh," he said, whiskers twitching. "I'm a bunny rabbit, aren't I?"

"I'm afraid so," said Wilfred.

Barnabas, feeling guilty, looked away. He had been so excited to supply the answer to Anubis' question that he hadn't thought the repercussions through all the way."

"Ah, well." Peter sighed resignedly. "I suppose I asked for it." With that, he hopped away.

Wilfred, seeing Barnabas' chagrin, leaned in towards his employer. "It's not your fault, truly," he said. "Anubis was toying with him. He remembered all the while, you see."

"Really?" asked Barnabas hopefully. "I do hope that his having a bunny head doesn't all come down to what I said."

"I'm certain that Anubis was going to do it no matter what anyone said," replied Wilfred.

"He's a bit of a ratbag, isn't he?" whispered Barnabas.

"The worst sort, indeed," agreed Wilfred. "Not to be trusted in the slightest, I think."

"If you two are finished whispering," interjected Anubis, "I'd like to get on with your reward. Barnabas and Wilfred jumped and looked at each other with unease.

"I'm a bit afraid of what our reward might be," whispered Barnabas to Wilfred, trying not to move his lips so that Anubis wouldn't see or hear him speak.

"As am I," answered Wilfred in the same way. To Anubis, he said, "Serving the greater good is the only reward we require."

"Quite so," agreed Barnabas. "It has been our pleasure." He glanced down towards where he used to keep his pocket watch (when he was wearing proper clothing, that is; his pocket watch had in fact been lost at the same time as his nice British clothing). "Well, look at the time," he said anyway, even though he had no watch to consult. "We'd best be on our way. With your leave, of course." So saying, he made a polite bow and turned to leave, holding Wilfred's sleeve so as to pull him along as well. Wilfred, of course, needed no urging. "We could go back to the Grey Mouse," whispered Barnabas. "I'd love to see Bindi, um… Well, that is to say, I'd love to have the cheese platter, once more."

"Very well," agreed Wilfred, who would have gladly agreed to go anywhere that was away from the treacherous jackal god.

They were stopped in their tracks, however, by Anubis' booming voice. "I have *not* given my leave yet," he declared. "You will stay and take your reward."

"Oh dear," said Barnabas, turning around reluctantly. Then his innate politeness took over and he added, "Thank you very much, I'm sure."

"You don't even know what it is yet!" Anubis laughed.

"I'm certain it will be quite wonderful," said Barnabas, thinking that any reward from Anubis would almost certainly be the opposite of wonderful.

"First things first," said Anubis, snapping his fingers once more.

"Oh, Barnabas!" cried Wilfred at once. "Why, you're *you* again!"

"And you as well!" replied Barnabas. He reached up to touch the now unfamiliar contours of his very own human face. "Do I look quite the same? I mean, the way I used to?"

"Precisely," said Wilfred. "It is a perfect transformation. Do I?"

"Not a difference to be noticed," replied Barnabas. "No one would ever know you were ever a mouse at all." He furrowed his brow for a moment as he thought. "No one would even recognize *us*, who knew us from our mouse days," he said at last, his mood changed.

Wilfred knew immediately that he referred only to Bindi, the lovely hostess at the Grey Mouse. He patted Barnabas sympathetically on the shoulder, but diplomatically said nothing.

Anubis, however, was not quite finished with them yet.

"And another thing," he announced, making the two detectives groan with dread. "Since you have made such a smashing success of this, I have referred you for another job."

Barnabas' mood changed once more under the praise, and he straightened up and put a dignified expression on his face.

"We will be honored to take this new job," he said with excessively formal grandiosity. "Whatever it might be, Wilfred and I are up to the task."

Wilfred, for his part, thought it better to be careful before accepting any offers from Anubis, and elbowed Barnabas sharply in the ribs.

"Ow!" yelped Barnabas.

"I think what Barnabas was trying to say was that we could happily consider the new job after learning the facts of the case," asserted Wilfred to Anubis.

"Too late!" crowed Anubis gleefully. "Once I heard you had apprehended the criminals, I not only recommended you but accepted the job for you. You're completely committed now."

"Oh," said Wilfred. "That's, uh, great."

"See what confidence he has in us, Wilfred?" crowed Barnabas proudly.

"Yes, I do," said Wilfred, a bit sourly. "Who, may I ask, is the client?"

"Odin," answered Anubis.

"Odin?" cried Barnabas and Wilfred at the same time.

"You've heard of him?" asked Anubis blithely, pondering his fingernails.

"Why, isn't he a Norse god?" asked Barnabas.

"Indeed. I'm certain that he's not Egyptian at all," said Wilfred. "I thought that we would be living in the Egyptian afterlife, when all was said and done…"

"Well, plans change, you see," said Anubis. "So you'll be going to the Norse afterlife instead. Isn't that wonderful?"

"Sounds a bit, well, cold," pointed out Barnabas.

"Of course it is," said Anubis. "I do hope you'll find something more appropriate to wear." He looked in the direction of a chariot pulling up. "But no time now!" he cried, clapping his hands in delight. "Here's your ride. I'm sure you'll find something warm to wear before you get there. Otherwise, you'll probably freeze to death. But no matter. On your way now!"

With that, he waved them off, and paid them no more heed. Dismissed and knowing it was futile to argue, Barnabas and Wilfred walked gloomily over to the waiting chariot.

"And do be careful!" called Anubis as they boarded the chariot. "I hear they can be quite violent there! They are not as civilized as we are here, you see."

"That is a most concerning statement," whispered Wilfred. "I really don't want to see what Anubis considers uncivilised."

"Me either," agreed Barnabas. But there was nothing for it; the chariot was moving and they were on their way to Odin and the other wild gods of the North.

"Oh dear," said Wilfred.

"Oh dear, indeed," said Barnabas.

THE END

Fantastic Books
Great Authors

CROOKED
CAT

Meet our authors and discover
our exciting range:

- Gripping Thrillers
- Cosy Mysteries
- Romantic Chick-Lit
- Fascinating Historicals
- Exciting Fantasy
- Young Adult and Children's
  Adventures

Visit us at:
www.crookedcatbooks.com

Join us on facebook:
www.facebook.com/realcrookedcat